Robert Michael Ballantyne

Charlie to the Rescue

A Tale of the Sea and the Rockies

Robert Michael Ballantyne

Charlie to the Rescue
A Tale of the Sea and the Rockies

ISBN/EAN: 9783337072636

Printed in Europe, USA, Canada, Australia, Japan

Cover: Foto ©Andreas Hilbeck / pixelio.de

More available books at **www.hansebooks.com**

CHARLIE TO THE RESCUE

A TALE OF THE SEA AND THE ROCKIES

BY R. M. BALLANTYNE,

AUTHOR OF "BLOWN TO BITS;" "THE CORAL ISLAND;" "THE GARRET AND THE
GARDEN;" "BLUE LIGHTS, OR HOT WORK IN THE SOUDAN;" "THE FUGITIVES;"
"RED ROONEY;" "THE ROVER OF THE ANDES;" "THE WILD MAN OF THE
WEST;" "THE RED ERIC;" "FREAKS ON THE FELLS;" "THE YOUNG
TRAWLER;" "DUSTY DIAMONDS;" "THE BATTERY AND THE
BOILER;" "POST HASTE;" "BLACK IVORY;" "THE
IRON HORSE;" "FIGHTING THE FLAMES;"
"THE LIFEBOAT;" ETC. ETC.

With Illustrations by the Author.

NEW YORK:

THOMAS NELSON & SONS,

33 EAST 17TH STREET, UNION SQUARE,

1890.

PREFACE.

HAVING got nothing prefatorial to say, I avail myself of this blank page to say so.

R. M. B.

HARROW, 1890.

CONTENTS.

CONTENTS.

LIST OF ILLUSTRATIONS.

CHARLIE TO THE RESCUE

A TALE OF THE SEA AND THE ROCKIES

———————◆———————

CHAPTER I.

INTRODUCES THE HERO.

To be generally helpful was one of the chief points in the character of Charlie Brooke.

He was evidently born to aid mankind. He began by helping himself to everything in life that seemed at all desirable. This was natural, not selfish.

At first there were few things, apparently, that did seem to his infant mind desirable, for his earliest days were marked by a sort of chronic crossness that seemed quite unaccountable in one so healthy; but this was eventually traced to the influence of pins injudiciously disposed about the person by nurse. Possibly this experience may have tended to develop a spirit of brave endurance, and might perhaps account for the beautiful modifications of character that were subsequently observed in him. At all events, sweet, patient amiability was a prevailing feature in the boy long before the years of infancy were over, and this heavenly aspect of him was pleasantly diversified, in course of time, by occasional displays of resolute—we might almost say heroic — self-will, which proved a constant source of mingled pride and alarm to his widowed mother.

From a very early period of life little Charlie manifested an intense desire, purpose, and capacity for what may be called his life-work of rescuing human beings from trouble and danger. It became a passion with him as years rolled on, and was among the chief means that brought about the changes in his chequered career.

Appropriately enough he began—almost in baby-hood—by rescuing himself!

It happened thus. One day, when he had reached the immature age of five, he was left in the nursery for a few moments in company with a wash-tub, in which his mother had been cleansing the household linen.

Mrs. Brooke, it may be remarked, although in the middle ranks of life, was very much below the middle ranks in financial prosperity, and had there-fore to perform much household drudgery.

Charlie's earnest desire to please and obey his mother constantly came into collision with that self-will to which we have referred. Separately, these qualities may perhaps work quietly, at least as regards their possessor, but unitedly they form a mixture which is apt to become explosive in early youth.

"Don't touch the tub, Charlie; I'll be back directly," said Mrs. Brooke, as she was leaving the nursery. "Don't even go near it."

"No, muvver, I won't."

He spoke with much decision, for he adored water—not to drink but to play with—and seemed to realise the danger of his position, and the necessity for self-control.

The temptation to avail himself of the chance, however, was almost too much for him. Feeling that an internal conflict was pending, he toddled to the fire, turned his back to it *à la* paterfamilias, and glared at the tub, resolved, come what might, to be "dood." But fate was against him!

Suddenly he became aware that something more than radiated heat was operating in rear. He glanced behind. His cotton tunic was in flames! In the twinkling of an eye he was seated in the wash-tub, his hands clasped in horror as he thought of his guilt, and the flames thoroughly extinguished!

The solemn glare and pursed mouth with which he met his mother's look of blank amazement may be imagined but cannot be described—he looked so quiet, too, and so evidently contented, for the warm water was congenial!

"O Charlie! did I not say that——"

" Yes, muvver, but I'm bu'nt."

The fearsome and dripping black patch which presented itself to the agonised mother when she lifted him out of the tub sufficiently enlightened her and exonerated the child, but her anxiety was not relieved till she had stripped him naked and ascertained for certain that no scrap of his fair skin had been injured.

This may be said to have been the real commencement of Charlie Brook's career. We mention it chiefly to show that our hero was gifted with some power of ready resource even in childhood. He was also gifted with a fearless and daring disposition, a quietly enthusiastic spirit, a modest mien, and a strong muscular body.

Of course these admirable qualities were not fully developed in childhood, but the seeds were there. In due time the plants came up and the flowers bloomed.

We would here caution the reader—especially the youthful reader—against supposing that from this point our hero was engaged in rescue-work, and continued at it ever after without intermission. Like Samson, with his great strength, he exercised his powers only now and then—more than half unconscious of what was in him—and on many occasions without any definite purpose in view.

His first act of heroism was exercised, when

he had reached the age of nine, in behalf of a kitten.

It was on a magnificent summer day, soon after he had been sent to the village school, that the incident occurred. Charlie was walking at the time with one of his school-fellows named Shank Leather.

Shank was a little older than himself, and a good enough fellow in his way, but much given to boasting, and possessed of very few of the fine qualities that characterised our hero. The two were out for a holiday-ramble, a long way from home, and had reached a river on the banks of which they sat down to enjoy their mid-day meal. The meal was simple, and carried in their pockets. It consisted of two inch-and-a-half-thick slices of bread, with two lumps of cheese to match.

"I wish this river was nearer home," said Shank Leather, as they sat down under a spreading oak to dine.

"Why?" asked his companion, with a felicitous brevity and straightforwardness which occasionally marked his conversation.

"Because then I would have a swim in it every day."

"Can you swim?" asked Charlie, a slight elevation of the eyebrows indicating surprise not unmingled with admiration—for our hero was a hero-worshipper. He could not well have been a hero otherwise!

"Of course I can swim," returned Shank; "that is to say, a little; but I feel sure that I'll be a splendid swimmer some day."

His companion's look of admiration increased.

"What'll you take to drink?" asked Shank, drawing a large flask from the pocket in which he had concealed it up to that moment with the express purpose of giving his companion a pleasant surprise.

It may be well to add that the variety of drinks implied in his question was imaginary. Shank had only one flask, but in the exuberance of convivial generosity he quoted his own father—who was addicted to "the bottle."

"What is it?" asked Brooke, in curious expectancy.

"Taste and see," said his friend, uncorking the flask.

Charlie tasted, but did not "see," apparently, for he looked solemn, and tasted again.

"It's liquorice-water," said Shank, with the look of one who expects approval. "I made it myself!"

Nauseous in the extreme, it might have served the purpose of an emetic had not the digestion of the boys been ostrich-like, but, on hearing how it came into existence, Charlie put it a third time to his lips, took a good gulp, and then, nodding his head as he wiped his mouth with his cuff, declared that it was "wonderful."

"Yes, isn't it? There's not many fellows could make stuff like that."

"No, indeed," assented the other heartily, as he attacked the bread and cheese. "Does your father know you made it?"

"Oh yes, and he tasted it too—he'd taste anything in the shape of drink—but he spat it out, and then washed his mouth with brandy an' water. Mother took some too, and she said she had tasted worse drinks; and she only wished that father would take to it. That made father laugh heartily. Then I gave some to little May, and she said it was 'So nice.'"

"Ay. That was like little May," remarked Charlie, with a quiet laugh; "she'd say that a mess o' tar an' shoe-blacking was nice if *you* made it. But I say, Shank, let's see you swim. I'd give anything if I could swim. Do, like a brick as you are. There's a fine deep hole here under the bank."

He pointed to a pool in the river where the gurgling eddies certainly indicated considerable depth of water, but his friend shook his head.

"No, Charlie," he said, "you don't understand the danger as I do. Don't you see that the water runs into the hole at such a rate that there's a tree-mendous eddy that would sweep any man off his legs——"

"But you're goin' to swim, you know," interrupted his friend, "an' have got to be off your legs anyhow!"

"That's all *you* know," returned the other. "If a man's swept round by an eddy, don't you know, he'll be banged against things, and then the water rushes out of the hole with *such* a gush, an' goes thunderin' down below, over boulders and stones, and—an'—don't you see?"

"That's true, Shank; it does look dangerous, even for a man that can swim."

He put such emphasis on the "man" that his comrade glanced sharply at him, but the genuine innocence of our hero's face was too obvious to suggest irony. He simply saw that the use of the word *man* pleased his friend, therefore he used it.

Conversation was cut short at this point by the sudden appearance on the scene of two strangers— a kitten and a dog.

The assertion that "dogs delight to bark and bite" is, perhaps, too sweeping, but then it was made by a poet, and poets have an acknowledged licence—though not necessarily a dog-licence. Certain it is, however, that this dog—a mongrel cur —did bark with savage delight, and display all its teeth, with an evident desire to bite, as it chased a delirious tortoise-shell kitten towards the river.

It was a round, soft, lively kitten, with the hair on its little body sticking straight out, its heart in its mouth, and horror in its lovely eyes. It made straight for the tree under which the dinner was

going on.   Both boys started up.   Enemies in front
and rear !   Even a human general might have stood
appalled.   Two courses were still open—right and
left.   The kitten turned right and went wrong, for
that was the river-side.   No time for thought !
Barking cur and yelling boys !   It reached the
edge of the pool, spread out all its legs with a
catterwaul of despair, and went headlong into the
water.

Shank Leather gazed—something like glee mingled with his look of consternation.   Not so our
hero.   Pity was bursting his bosom.   With one
magnificent bound he went into the pool, caught the
kitten in his right hand, and carried it straight to
the bottom.   Next moment he re-appeared on the
surface, wildly beating the water with one hand
and holding the kitten aloft in the other.   Shank,
to do him justice, plunged into the river up to his
waist, but his courage carried him no further.
There he stuck, vainly holding out a hand and
shouting for help.

But no help was near, and it seemed as if the pair
of strugglers were doomed to perish when a pitiful
eddy swept them both out of the deep pool into the
foaming rapid below.   Shank followed them in
howling despair, for here things looked ten times
worse: his comrade being tossed from billow to
breaker, was turned heels over head, bumped against
boulders, stranded on shallows, overturned and

swept away again—but ever with the left arm beating wildly, and the right hand with the kitten, held high in air.

But the danger, except from being dashed against the boulders, was not really as great as it seemed, for every time that Brooke got a foothold for an instant, or was driven on a rock, or was surged, right-end-up, on a shoot of water, he managed to gasp a little air—including a deal of water. The kitten, of course, had the same chances, and, being passive, perhaps suffered less.

At the foot of the rapid they were whirled, as if contemptuously, into an eddy. Shank was there, as deep as he dared venture. He even pushed in up to the arm-pits, and, catching his comrade by the hair, dragged him to bank.

"O Charlie, I've saved ye!" he exclaimed, as his friend crawled out and sat down.

"Ay, an' you've saved the kitten too!" replied his friend, examining the poor animal.

"It's dead," said Shank; "dead as mutton."

"No, only stunned. No wonder, poor beast!"

With tender care the rescuer squeezed the water from the fur of the rescued. Then, pulling open his vest and shirt, he was about to place the kitten in his bosom to warm it.

"No use doin' that," said Leather. "You're as wet an' nigh as cold as itself."

"That's true. Sit down here," returned Brooke,

in a tone of command which surprised his comrade.
"Open your shirt."

Again Shank obeyed wonderingly. Next moment
he gave a gasp as the cold, wet creature was thrust
into his warm bosom.

"It makes me shiver all over," he said.

"Never mind," replied his friend coolly, as he
got up and wrung the water out of his own
garments.

"It's beginning to move, Charlie," said Shank,
after a few minutes.

"Give it here, then."

The creature was indeed showing feeble symptoms
of revival, so Brooke—whose bosom was not only
recovering its own heat, but was beginning to warm
the wet garments—thrust it into his own breast, and
the two friends set off homeward at a run.

At the nearest house they made inquiry as to the
owner of the kitten, but failed to find one. Our
hero therefore resolved to carry it home. Long
before that haven was reached, however, his clothes
were nearly dry, and the rescued one was purring
sweetly, in childlike innocence—all the horrors,
sufferings, and agonies of the past forgotten, apparently, in the enjoyment of the present.

CHAPTER II.

THE SHIPWRECK

WE have no intention of carrying our reader on step by step through all the adventures and deeds of Charlie Brooke. It is necessary to hasten over his boyhood, leaving untold the many battles fought, risks run, and dangers encountered.

He did not cut much of a figure at the village school—though he did his best, and was fairly successful — but in the playground he reigned supreme. At football, cricket, gymnastics, and, ultimately, at swimming, no one could come near him. This was partly owing to his great physical strength, for, as time passed by he shot upwards and outwards in a way that surprised his companions and amazed his mother, who was a distinctly little woman—a neat graceful little woman —with, like her stalwart son, a modest opinion of herself.

As a matter of course, Charlie's school-fellows almost worshipped him, and he was always so willing to help and lead them in all cases of danger or emergency, that "Charlie to the rescue!" became quite a familiar cry on the playground. Indeed it would have been equally appropriate in the school, for the lad never seemed to be so thoroughly happy as when he was assisting some boy less capable than himself to master his lessons.

About the time that Charlie left school, while yet a stripling, he had the shoulders of Samson, the chest of Hercules, and the limbs of Apollo. He was tall also—over six feet—but his unusual breadth deceived people as to this till they stood close to him. Fair hair, close and curly, with bright blue eyes and a permanent look of grave benignity, completes our description of him.

Rowing, shooting, fishing, boxing, and swimming seemed to come naturally to him, and all of them in a superlative degree. Swimming was, perhaps, his most loved amusement, and in this art he soon far outstripped his friend Leather. Some men are endowed with exceptional capacities in regard to water. We have seen men go into the sea warm and come out warmer, even in cold weather. Experience teaches that the reverse is usually true of mankind in northern regions, yet we once saw a man enter the sea to all appearance a white human being, after remaining in it upwards of an hour, and swimming away from shore, like a vessel outward bound, he came back at last the colour of a boiled lobster!

Such exceptional qualities did Charlie Brooke possess. A South Sea Islander might have envied but could not have excelled him.

It was these qualities that decided the course of his career just after he left school.

"Charlie," said his mother, as they sat eating their mid-day meal alone one day—the mother being, as we have said, a widow, and Charlie an only child—"what do you think of doing, now that you have left school? for you know my income renders it impossible that I should send you to college."

"I don't know what to think, mother. Of course I intend to do something. If you had only influence with some one in power who could enable a fellow to get his foot on the first round of any sort of ladder, something might be done, for you know I'm not exactly useless, though I can't boast of brilliant talents, but——"

"Your talents are brilliant enough, Charlie," said his mother, interrupting; "besides, you have been sent into this world for a purpose, and you may be sure that you will discover what that purpose is, and receive help to carry it out if you only ask God to guide you. Not otherwise," she added, after a pause.

"Do you *really* believe, mother, that *every* one who is born into the world is sent for a purpose, and with a specific work to do?"

"I do indeed, Charlie."

"What! all the cripples, invalids, imbeciles, even the very infants who are born to wail out their sad lives in a few weeks, or even days?"

"Yes—all of them, without exception. To suppose the opposite, and imagine that a wise, loving, and almighty Being would create anything for *no* purpose seems to me the very essence of absurdity. Our only difficulty is that we do not always see the purpose. All things are ours, but we must ask if we would have them."

"But I *have* asked, mother," said the youth, with an earnest flush on his brow. "You know I have done so often, yet a way has not been opened up. I believe in *your* faith, mother, but I don't quite believe in my own. There surely must be something wrong—a screw loose somewhere."

He laid down his knife and fork, and looked out at the window with a wistful, perplexed expression.

"How I wish," he continued, "that the lines had been laid down for the human race more distinctly, so that we could not err!"

"And yet," responded his mother, with a peculiar look, "such lines as *are* obviously laid down we don't always follow. For instance, it is written, 'Ask, and it shall be given you,' and we stop there, but the sentence does not stop: 'Seek, and ye shall find' implies care and trouble; 'Knock, and it shall be opened unto you' hints at perseverance, does it not?"

"There's something in that, mother," said Charlie, casting another wistful glance out of the window. "Come, I will go out and 'seek'! I see Shank Leather waiting for me. We agreed to go to the shore together, for we both like to watch the waves roaring in on a breezy day like this."

The youth rose and began to encase his bulky frame in a great pilot-cloth coat, each button of which might have done duty as an afternoon tea-saucer.

"I wish you would choose any companion to walk with but young Leather," said the widow, with a sigh. "He's far too like his father to do you any good."

"Mother, would you have me give up an old playmate and school-fellow because he is not perfect?" asked the youth in grave tones as he tied on a sou'wester.

"Well, no—not exactly, but——."

Not having a good reason ready, the worthy woman only smiled a remonstrance. The stalwart son stooped, kissed her and was soon outside, battling with the storm—for what he styled a breezy day was in reality a wild and stormy one.

Long before the period we have now reached Mrs. Brooke had changed her residence to the seacoast in the small town of Sealford. Her cottage stood in the centre of the village, about half-a-mile from the shore, and close to that of her bosom friend, Mrs. Leather, who had migrated along with her, partly to be near her and partly for the sake of her son Shank, who was anxious to retain the companionship of his friend Brooke. Partly, also, to get her tippling husband away from old comrades and scenes, in the faint hope that she might rescue him from the great curse of his life.

When Charlie went out, as we have said, he found that Shank had brought his sister May with him. This troubled our hero a good deal, for he had purposed having a confidential talk with his old comrade upon future plans and prospects, to the accompaniment of the roaring sea, and a third party was destructive of such intention. Besides, poor May, although exceedingly unselfish and sweet and good, was at that transition period of life when girl-hood is least attractive—at least to young men: when bones are obtrusive, and angles too conspicuous, and the form generally is too suggestive of flatness and longitude; while shyness marks the manners, and inexperience dwarfs the mind. We would not, however, suggest for a moment that May was ugly. By no means, but she had indeed reached what may be styled a plain period of life— a period in which some girls become silently sheepish, and others tomboyish; May was among the former, and therefore a drag upon conversation. But, after all, it mattered little, for the rapidly increasing gale rendered speech nearly impossible.

B

"It's too wild a day for you, May," said Brooke, as he shook hands with her; "I wonder you care to be out."

"She *doesn't* care to be out, but I wanted her to come, and she's a good obliging girl, so she came," said Shank, drawing her arm through his as they pressed forward against the blast in the direction of the shore.

Shank Leather had become a sturdy young fellow by that time, but was much shorter than his friend. There was about him, however, an unmistakable look of dissipation—or, rather, the beginning of it—which accounted for Mrs. Brooke's objection to him as a companion for her son.

We have said that the cottage lay about half-a-mile from the shore, which could be reached by a winding lane between high banks. These effectually shut out the view of the sea until one was close to it, though, at certain times, the roar of the waves could be heard even in Sealford itself.

Such a time was the present, for the gale had lashed the sea into wildest fury, and not only did the three friends hear it, as, with bent heads, they forced their way against the wind, but they felt the foam of ocean on their faces as it was carried inland sometimes in lumps and flakes. At last they came to the end of the lane, and the sea, lashed to its wildest condition, lay before them like a sheet of tortured foam.

"Grand! isn't it?" said Brooke, stopping and drawing himself up for a moment, as if with a desire to combat the opposing elements.

If May Leather could not speak, she could at all events gaze, for she had superb brown eyes, and they glittered, just then, like glowing coals, while a wealth of rippling brown hair was blown from its fastenings, and flew straight out behind her.

"Look! look there!" shouted her brother with a wild expression, as he pointed to a part of the rocky shore where a vessel was dimly seen through the drift.

"She's trying to weather the point," exclaimed Brooke, clearing the moisture from his eyes, and endeavouring to look steadily.

"She'll never weather it. See! the fishermen are following her alongshore," cried young Leather, dropping his sister's arm, and bounding away.

"Oh! don't leave me behind, Shank," pleaded May.

Shank was beyond recall, but our hero, who had also sprung forward, heard the pleading voice and turned back.

"Here, hook on to me," he cried quickly, for he was in no humour to delay.

The girl grasped his arm at once, and, to say truth, she was not much of a hindrance, for, although somewhat inelegant, as we have said, she was lithe as a lizard and fleet as a young colt.

A few minutes brought them to the level shore where Brooke left May to shelter herself with some fisher-women behind a low wall, while he ran along to a spot where a crowd of fishermen and old salts, enveloped in oil-skins, were discussing the situation as they leaned against the shrieking wind.

"Will she weather it, Grinder, think you?" he asked of an elderly man, whose rugged features resembled mahogany, the result of having bid defiance to wind and weather for nigh half a century.

"She may, Mr. Brooke, an' she mayn't," answered the matter-of-fact man of the sea, in the gruff monotone with which he would have summoned all hands to close reef in a hurricane. "If her tackle holds she'll do it. If it don't she won't."

"We've sent round for the rocket, anyhow," said a smart young fisherman, who seemed to rejoice in opposing his broad chest to the blast, and in listening to the thunder of the waves as they rolled into the exposed bay in great battalions, chasing each other in wild tumultuous fury, as if each were bent on being first in the mad assault upon the shore.

"Has the lifeboat coxswain been called?" asked Charlie, after a few minutes' silence, for the voice of contending elements was too great to render converse easy or agreeable.

"Yes, sir," answered the man nearest to him, "but she's bin called to a wreck in Mussel Bay, an' that brig will be all right or in Davy Jones's locker long afore th' lifeboat 'ud fetch round here."

Silence again fell on the group as they gazed out to sea, pushing eagerly down the beach until they were ankle-deep in the foam of each expended wave; for the brig was by that time close on the point of rocks, staggering under more sail than she could carry with safety.

"She'll do it!" exclaimed the smart young fisherman, ready to cheer with enthusiastic hope.

"Done for! Lost!" cried one, while something like a groan burst from the others as they saw the brig's topmasts go over the side, and one of her sails blown to ribbons. She fell away towards the rocks at once.

Like great black teeth these rocks seemed to leap in the midst of the foam, as if longing to grasp the ill-fated vessel, which had, indeed, all but weathered the dangerous point, and all might have been well if her gear had only held; but now, as if paralysed, she drifted into the bay where certain destruction awaited her.

Just at that moment a great cheer arose, for the rocket-cart, drawn by the men of the Coast-Guard, was seen rattling over the downs towards them.

Anxiety for the fate of the doomed brig was now

changed into eager hope for the rescue of her crew. The fishermen crowded round the Coast-Guard men as they ran the cart close down to the water's edge, and some of them—specially the smart young fellow already mentioned—made eager offer of their services. Charlie Brooke stood aloof, looking on with profound interest, for it was the first time he had ever seen the Manby rocket apparatus brought into action. He made no hasty offer to assist, for he was a cool youth—even while burning with impatient enthusiasm—and saw at a glance that the men of the Coast-Guard were well able to manage their own affairs and required no aid from him.

As the brig was coming straight in they could easily calculate where she would strike, so that the rocket men could set up their triangle and arrange their tackle without delay. This was fortunate, for the wreck was carried shoreward with great rapidity. She struck at last when within a short distance of the beach, and the faces of those on board could be distinctly seen, and their cries heard, as both masts snapped off and were swept over the side, where they tore at the shrouds like wild creatures, or charged the hulk like battering-rams. Instantly the billows that had borne the vessel on their crests burst upon her sides, and spurted high in air over her, falling back on her deck, and sweeping off everything that was moveable. It could be seen that only three or four men were on deck, and these kept well under the lee of the bulwarks near the stern where they were strongest.

"No passengers, I think," said one of the fishermen; "no women, anyhow."

"Not likely they'd be 'lowed on deck even if there was," growled Grinder, in his monotone.

"Now, then, out o' the way," cried the leader of the Coast-Guard men, as he laid a rocket in its place. "Line all clear, Fred?"

"All clear."

Next moment there was a burst of flame, a crash, and a vicious whizz as the powerful projectile leaped from its stand and sped out to sea, in grand defiance of the opposing gale, with its light line behind it.

A cheer marked its flight, but a groan told of its descent into the boiling sea, considerably to the left of the wreck.

"*What* a pity!" cried Shank Leather, who had come close to his friend when the rocket-cart arrived.

"No matter," said Brooke, whose compressed lips and flashing eyes told of deep but suppressed feelings. "There are more rockets."

He was right. While he was speaking, another rocket was placed and fired. It was well directed, but fell short. Another, and yet another, rose and fell, but failed to reach its mark, and the remainder of the rockets refused to go off from some unknown cause—either because they had been too long in stock or had become damp.

Meantime the brig was tossed farther and farther in, until she stuck quite fast. Then it became evident that she must soon break up, and her crew perish. Hasty plans and eager advice were proposed and given. Then the smart young fisherman suddenly sprang forward, and threw off his oil-coat and sou'wester.

"Here! hold on!" he cried, catching up the end of the rocket line, and fastening it round his waist, while he kicked off his heavy boots.

"You can't do it, Bill," cried some.

"Too far to swim," cried others.

"The sea's 'll knock the life out o' ye," said Grinder, "afore you 're clear o' the sand."

Despite these warnings the brave young fellow dashed into the foam, and plunged straight into the first mighty breaker that towered over his head. But he was too much excited to act effectively. He failed to time his plunge well. The wave fell upon him with a roar and crushed him down. In a few seconds he was dragged ashore almost insensible.

Example, whether good or bad, is infectious. Another strapping young fellow, stirred to emulation, ran forward, and, seizing the rope, tied it round his own waist, while they helped poor Bill up the beach and seated him on a sand-bank.

The second youth was more powerful than the first—and cooler. He made a better attempt, but only got past the first wave, when his comrades, seeing that he was exhausted, drew him back. Then a third—a broad burly youth—came forward.

At this point the soul of Shank Leather took fire, for he was by no means destitute of generous impulses, and he tried to get hold of the rope.

"Out o' the way," cried the burly youth, giving Leather a rough push that almost sent him on his back; "we don't want no land-lubbers for this kind o' work."

Up to this point Charlie Brooke, although burning with eager desire to take some active part in the rescue, had restrained himself and held back, believing, with characteristic modesty, that the fishermen knew far better than he did how to face the sea and use their appliances; but when he saw his friend stagger backward, he sprang to the front, caught hold of the line, and, seizing the burly fisherman by the arm, exclaimed, "You'll let *this* land-lubber try it, anyhow," and sent him spinning away like a capsized nine-pin.

There was a short laugh, as well as a cheer at this; but next moment all were gazing at the sea in breathless anxiety, for Brooke had rushed deep into the surf. He paused one moment, as the great wave curled over him, then went through it head-first with such force that he shot waist-high out of the sea on the other side. His exceptional swimming-powers now served him well, for his otter-like rapidity of action enabled him to avoid the crushing billows either by diving through them at the right moment, or holding back until they fell, and left him only the mad swirling foam to contend with. This last was bad enough, but here his great muscular strength and his inexhaustible caloric, with his cork-like power of flotation, enabled him to hold his own without exhaustion until another opportunity of piercing an unbroken wave offered. Thus he gradually forced his way through and beyond the worst breakers, which are always those nearest shore. Had any one been close to him, and able calmly to watch his movements, it would have been seen that, great as were the youth's powers, he did not waste them in useless battling with a force against which no man could effectively contend; that, with a cool head, he gave way to every irresistible force, swimming for a moment, as it were, with the current—or, rather, floating easily in the whirlpools—so as to conserve his strength; that, ever and anon, he struck out with all his might, rushing through foam and wave like a fish, and that, in the midst of it all, he saw and seized the brief moments in which he could take a gasping inhalation.

Those who watched him with breathless anxiety on shore saw little of all this as they payed out the line or perched themselves on tiptoe on the few boulders that here and there strewed the sand.

"Haul him back!" shouted the man who was farthest out on the line. "He's used up!"

"No, he's not, I know him well!" roared Shank Leather. "Pay out, men—pay out line!"

"Ay, ease away," said Grinder, in a thunderous growl. "He's a rigler walrus, he is. Niver see'd sich a feller since I left the southern seas. Ease away, boys."

A cheer followed his remark, for at that moment it was seen that our hero had reached the tail of the eddy which was caused by the hull of the wreck, and that one of her crew had darted from the cover of the vessel's bulwarks and taken shelter under the stump of the mainmast. His object was seen in a moment, for he unhooked a coil of rope from the belaying-pins, and stood ready to heave it to the approaching swimmer. In making even this preparation the man ran very great risk, for the stump was but a partial shelter—each wave that burst over the side sweeping wildly round it and leaping on the man higher than his waist, so that it was very difficult for him to avoid being torn from his position.

Charlie's progress was now comparatively easy. A few vigorous strokes brought him under the lea of the wreck, which, however, was by no means a quiet spot, for each divided wave, rushing round bow and stern, met there in a tumult of foam that almost choked the swimmer, while each billow that burst over the wreck poured a small Niagara on his head.

How to get on board in such circumstances was a subject that had troubled Charlie's mind as he drew near, but the action of the sailor unhooking the coil of rope at once relieved him. The moment he came within reach, the sailor, watching his opportunity between waves, threw out the coil. It was aimed by an accustomed hand and fell on the rescuer's head. Another minute and young Brooke stood on the deck. Without waiting an instant he leaped under the shelter of the stump of the main-mast beside the seaman. He was only just in time, for a wave burst in thunder on the weather side of the quivering brig, and, pouring over the bulwarks, almost dragged him from the belaying-pins to which he clung.

The instant the strain was off, he passed a rope round his waist and gave the end of it to the sailor.

"Here, make it fast," he said, beginning to haul with all his might on the line which he had brought from shore. "You're the skipper—eh?"

"Yes. Don't waste your breath in speech. I know what to do. All's ready."

These few words were an unspeakable relief to our hero, who was well aware that the working of the rocket apparatus required a slight amount of knowledge, and who felt from his manner and tone that the skipper was a thorough man. He glanced upwards as he hauled in the line, assisted by his companion, and saw that a stout rope with two loops on it had been fixed to the stump of the mast. Just as he noted this with satisfaction a large block with a thin line rove through it emerged from the boiling sea. It had been attached by the men on shore to the rocket line which Charlie had been hauling out with so much energy. Its name was indicated by the skipper.

"Here comes the *whip*," he cried, catching hold of the block when it reached him. "Hold me up, lad, while I make it fast to them loops."

While Charlie obeyed he saw that by fixing the tail-lines of the block quickly to the loops prepared for them, instead of winding them round the mast, —a difficult process in such a sea—much time was saved.

"There, *our* part o' the job is done now," said the skipper, pulling off his sou'wester as he spoke and holding it up as a signal to the men on shore.

Meanwhile those to whom he signalled had been watching every movement with intense eagerness, and with the expressions of men whose gaze has to penetrate with difficulty through a haze of blinding spray.

"They've got the block now," cried one man.

"Does that young feller know about fixin' of it?" asked another.

"Clap a stopper on your mugs; they're a-fixin' of it now," said old Grinder. "There's the signal! Haul away, lads!"

We must explain here that the "whip" above mentioned was a double or endless line, passing through the block which had been hauled out to the wreck by our hero.

By means of this whip one end of a stout cable was sent off to the wreck, and on this cable a sling-lifebuoy was hung to a pulley and also run out to the wreck. The working of the apparatus, though simple enough to seamen, would entail a complicated, perhaps incomprehensible, description to landsmen: we therefore pass it by with the remark that, connection with the shore having been established, and the sling-lifebuoy—or life-saving machine—run out, the crew received it with what was meant for a hearty cheer, but which exhaustion modified to a feeble shout.

"Now, lads," cried the skipper to his men, "look sharp! Let out the passengers."

"Passengers?" exclaimed Charlie Brooke in surprise.

"Ay—my wife an' little gurl, two women and an old gentleman. You don't suppose I'd keep 'em on deck to be washed overboard?"

As he spoke two of the men opened the doors of

the companion-hatch, and caught hold of a little girl of about five years of age, who was handed up by a woman.

"Stay! keep her under cover till I get hold of her," cried the skipper.

As he was passing from the mast to the companion a heavy sea burst over the bulwarks, and swept him into the scuppers. The same wave wrenched the child from the grasp of the man who held it and carried it right overboard. Like an eel, rather than a man, Charlie cleft the foam close behind her, caught her by the skirt and bore her to the surface, when a few strokes of his free arm brought him close under the lee of the wreck just in time to prevent the agonised father from leaping after his child. There was terrible suspense for a few minutes. At one moment our hero, with his burden held high aloft, was far down in the hollow of the watery turmoil, with the black hull like a great wall rising above him, while the skipper in the main-chains, pale as death but sternly silent, held on with his left hand and reached down with his right—every finger rigid and ready! Next moment a water-spout, so to speak, bore the rescuer upward on its crest, but not near enough—they went downward again. Once more the leaping water surged upwards; the skipper's strong hand closed like the grip of death on the dress, and the child was safe while its rescuer sank away from it.

"Help him!" shouted the skipper, as he staggered to the shelter of the companion.

But Charlie required no help. A loose rope hanging over the side caught his eye: he seized it and was on deck again in a few seconds. A minute later and he was down in the cabin.

There, terror-stricken, sat the skipper's wife, never venturing to move, because she had been told to remain there till called. Happily she knew nothing of the incident just described.

Beside her sat the other women, and, near to them, a stern old gentleman, who, with compressed lips, quietly awaited orders.

"Come, quick!" said Charlie, grasping by the arm one of the women.

It was the skipper's wife. She jumped up right willingly and went on deck. There she found her child already in the life-buoy, and was instantly lifted in beside it by her husband, who looked hastily round.

"Come here, Dick," he said to a little cabin-boy who clung to a stanchion near by. "Get in."

The boy looked surprised, and drew back.

"Get in, I say," repeated the skipper sternly.

"There's more women, sir," said the boy, still holding back.

"True—brave lad! but you're wanted to keep these from getting washed out. I am too heavy, you know."

The boy hesitated no longer. He squeezed himself into the machine beside the woman and child.

Then up at arm's-length went the skipper's sou'-wester as a signal that all was ready, and the fishermen began to haul the life-buoy to the shore.

It was an awful trip! Part of the distance, indeed, the trio were borne along well out of the sea, though the waves leaped hungrily up and sent spray over them, but as they drew near the shore they were dipped again and again into the foam, so that the little cabin boy needed all his energy and knowledge, as well as his bravery and strength, to prevent his charge being washed out. Amid ringing cheers from the fishermen—and a treble echo from the women behind the wall—they were at last safely landed.

"My lass, that friend o' your'n be a braave cheeld," said an old woman to May Leather, who crouched beside her.

" Ay, *that* he is!" exclaimed May, with a gush of enthusiasm in tone and eyes that made them all turn to look at her.

" Your brother?" asked a handsome, strapping young woman.

" No—I wish he was !"

" Hm! ha!" exclaimed the strapping young woman—whereat there was exchanged a significant laugh ; but May took no notice of it, being too

c

deeply engrossed with the proceedings on shore and sea.

Again the fishermen ran out the life-buoy and soon hauled it back with another woman; then a third. After that came the old gentleman, quite self-possessed and calm, though very pale and disheveled; and, following him, the crew, one by one, were rescued. Then came the hero of the hour, and last of all, as in duty bound, the skipper—not much too soon, for he had barely reached the land when the brig was overwhelmed and engulfed in the raging sea.

CHAPTER III.

"IT'S AN ILL WIND THAT BLAWS NAEBODY GUID."

THAT many if not most names have originated in the character or condition of individuals seems obvious, else why is it that so many people take after their names? We have no desire to argue the question, but hasten on to remark that old Jacob Crossley was said to be—observe, we do not say that he was—a notable illustration of what we refer to.

Jacob was "as cross as two sticks," if we are to believe Mrs. Bland, his housekeeper—and Mrs. Bland was worthy of belief, for she was an honest widow who held prevarication to be equivalent to lying, and who, besides having been in the old bachelor's service for many years, had on one occasion been plucked by him from under the feet of a pair of horses when attempting the more dangerous than nor'-west passage of a London crossing. Gratitude, therefore, rendered it probable that Mrs. Bland spake truly when she said that her master was as cross as two sticks. Of course we admit that her judgment may have been faulty.

Strange to say Mr. Crossley had no reason—
at least no very apparent reason—for being cross,
unless, indeed, the mere fact of his being an old
bachelor was a sufficient reason. Perhaps it was!
But in regard to everything else he had, as the
saying goes, nothing to complain of. He was a
prosperous East India merchant—not a miser,
though a cross old bachelor, and not a millionaire,
though comfortably rich. His business was prosperous, his friends were numerous, his digestion was
good, his nervous system was apparently all that
could be desired, and he slept well!

Standing one morning in the familiar British
position before his dining-room fire in London, he
frowningly contemplated his housekeeper as that indefatigable woman removed the breakfast equipage.

"Has the young man called this morning?"

"Not yet, sir."

"Well, when he comes tell him I had business in
the city and could wait no——"

A ring and a sharp knock interrupted him.
A few moments later Charlie Brooke was ushered
into the room. It was a smallish room, for
Mr. Crossley, although well off, did not see
the propriety of wasting money on unnecessary
space or rent, and the doorway was so low
that Charlie's hair brushed against the top as he
entered.

"I called, Mr. Crossley, in accordance with the

wish expressed in your letter. Although, being a stranger, I do not——"

The young man stopped at this point and looked steadily at the old gentleman with a peculiarly questioning expression.

"You recognise me, I see," said the old man, with a very slight smile.

"Well—I may be mistaken, but you do bear some resemblance to——"

"Just so, I'm the man that you hauled so violently out of the cabin of the wreck last week, and shoved so unceremoniously into the life-buoy, and I have sent for you, first, to thank you for saving my life, because they tell me that, but for your swimming off with a rope, we should certainly have all been lost; and, secondly, to offer you aid in any course of life you may wish to adopt, for I have been informed that you are not at present engaged in any special employment."

"You are very kind, sir, very kind," returned Charlie, somewhat embarrassed. "I can scarcely claim, however, to have saved your life, though I thankfully admit having had the opportunity to lend a hand. The rocket-men, in reality, did the work, for without their splendid working of apparatus my swimming off would have been useless."

Mr. Crossley frowned while the youth was speaking, and regarded him with some suspicion.

"You admit, I suppose," he rejoined sternly, "that if you had *not* swum off, the rocket apparatus would have been equally useless."

"By no means," returned Charlie, with that benignant smile that always accompanied his opposition in argument. "I do not admit that, because, if I had not done it, assuredly some one else would. In fact a friend of mine was on the point of making the attempt when I pulled him back and prevented him."

"And why did you prevent him?"

"Because he was not so well able to do it as I."

"Oh! I see. In other words, you have a pretty high opinion of your own powers."

"Possibly I have," returned the youth, somewhat sharply. "I lay claim to no exemption from the universal law of vanity which seems to affect the entire human race—especially the cynical part of it. At the same time, knowing from long experience that I am physically stronger, can swim better, and have greater power of endurance, though not greater courage, than my friend, it would be mere pretence were I to assume that in such matters I was his inferior. You asked me why I prevented him: I [told] you the reason exactly and straightforwardly. I repeat it."

"[Don't] be so ready to fire up, young man," said [the captain] with a deprecating smile. "I had no [intention of] hurting your feelings."

"I called,

"You have not hurt them, sir," returned Charlie, with almost provoking urbanity of manner and sweetness of voice, "you have only misunderstood me."

"Well, well, let it pass. Tell me, now, can I do anything for you?"

"Nothing, thank you."

"Eh?" exclaimed the old gentleman in surprise.

"Nothing, thank you," repeated his visitor. "I did not save you for the purpose of being rewarded, and I refuse to accept reward for saving you."

For a second or two Mr. Crossley regarded his visitor in silence, with a conflicting mixture of frown and smile—a sort of acidulated-drop expression on his rugged face. Then he asked—

"What is the name of this friend whom you prevented from swimming off to us?"

"Shank Leather."

"Is he a very great friend of yours?"

"Very. We have been playmates from childhood, and school-fellows till now."

"What is he?—his profession, I mean?"

"Nothing at present. That is to say, he has, like myself, been trained to no special profession, and the failure of the firm in the counting-house of which we have both served for some months has cast us adrift at the same time."

"Would it give you much satisfaction if I were to find good employment for your friend?"

"Indeed it would—the highest possible satisfaction," exclaimed Charlie, with the first symptom of enthusiasm in his tone and look.

"What can your friend Shank Leather do?" asked the old man brusquely.

"Oh! many things. He's capital at figures, thoroughly understands book-keeping, and—and is a hard-working fellow, whatever he puts his hand to."

"Is he steady?"

Charlie was silent for a few moments.

"Well, one cannot be sure," he answered, with some hesitation, "what meaning you attach to the word 'steady.' I——"

"Yes, yes, I see," interrupted Crossley, consulting his watch. "No time to discuss meanings of words just now. Will you tell your friend to call on me here the day after to-morrow at six o'clock? You live in Sealford, I have been told; does he live near you?"

"Yes, within a few minutes' walk."

"Well, tell him to be punctual. Punctuality is the soul of business. Hope I won't find your friend as independent as you seem to be! You are quite sure, are you, that I can do nothing for you? I have both money and influence."

The more determined that our hero became to decline all offers of assistance from the man who had misconstrued his motives, the more of urbanity marked his manner, and it was with a smile of ineffable good-nature on his masculine features that he repeated, " Nothing, thank you—quite sure. You will have done me the greatest possible service when you help my friend. Yet—stay. You mentioned money. There is an institution in which I am much interested, and which you might appropriately remember just now."

" What is that ? "

" The Lifeboat Institution."

" But it was not the Lifeboat Institution that saved *me*. It was the Rocket apparatus."

" True, but it *might* have been a lifeboat that saved you. The rockets are in charge of the Coast-Guard and need no assistance, whereas the Lifeboat Service depends on voluntary contributions, and the fact that it did not happen to save Mr. Crossley from a grave in the sea does not affect its claim to the nation's gratitude for the hundreds of lives saved by its boats every year."

" Admitted, my young friend, your reasoning is just," said the old gentleman, sitting down at a writing table and taking a cheque-book from a drawer ; " what shall I put down ? "

" You know your circumstances best," said Charlie, somewhat amused by the question.

" Most people in ordinary circumstances," returned the old man slowly as he wrote, " contribute a guinea to such charities."

"Many people," remarked Charlie, with a feeling of pity rather than contempt, "contribute five, or even fifteen."

"Ah, indeed—yes, well, Mr. Brooke, will you condescend to be the bearer of my contribution ? Fourteen St. John St., Adelphi, is not far from this, and it will save a penny of postage, you know !"

Mr. Crossley rose and handed the cheque to his visitor, who felt half disposed—on the strength of the postage remark—to refuse it and speak his mind somewhat freely on the subject, but, his eye happening to fall on the cheque at the moment, he paused.

"You have made a mistake, I think," he said. "This is for five *hundred* pounds."

"I make no mistakes, Mr. Brooke," returned the old man sternly. " You said something about five or fifteen. I could not well manage fifteen *hundred* just now, for it is bad times in the city at present. Indeed, according to some people, it is always bad times there, and, to say truth, some people are not far wrong—at least as regards their own experiences. Now, I must be off to business. Good-bye. Don't forget to impress on your friend the importance of punctuality."

Jacob Crossley held out his hand with an expression of affability which was for him quite marvellous.

" You 're a much better man than I thought you!"

exclaimed Charlie, grasping the proffered hand with a fervour that caused the other to wince.

"Young sir," returned Crossley, regarding the fingers of his right hand somewhat pitifully, " people whose physique is moulded on the pattern of Samson ought to bear in mind that rheumatism is not altogether unknown to elderly men. Your opinion of me was probably erroneous to begin with, and it is certainly false to end with. Let me advise you to remember that the gift of money does not necessarily prove anything except that a man has money to give—nay, it does not always prove even that, for many people are notoriously prone to give away money that belongs to somebody else. Five hundred pounds is to some men not of much more importance than five pence is to others. Everything is relative. Good-bye."

While he was speaking Mr. Crossley rang the bell and politely opened the dining-room door, so that our hero found himself in the street before he had quite recovered from his astonishment.

"Please, sir," said Mrs. Bland to her master after Charlie was gone, " Cap'en Stride is awaitin' in the library."

"Send him here," said Crossley, once more consulting his watch.

"Well, Captain Stride, I've had a talk with him," he said, as an exceedingly broad, heavy, short-legged man entered, with a bald head and a general air of salt water, tar, and whiskers about him. "Sit down. Have you made up your mind to take command of the *Walrus*?"

"Well, Mr. Crossley, since you're so *very* good," said the sea-captain with a modest look, "I had feared that the loss o'——"

"Never mind the loss of the brig, Captain. It was no fault of yours that she came to grief. Other ship-owners may do as they please. I shall take the liberty of doing as *I* please. So, if you are ready, the ship is ready. I have seen Captain Stuart, and I find that he is down with typhoid fever, poor fellow, and won't be fit for duty again for many weeks. The *Walrus* must sail not later than a week or ten days hence. She can't sail without a captain, and I know of no better man than yourself; so, if you agree to take command, there she is, if not I'll find another man."

"I'm agreeable, sir," said Captain Stride, with a gratified, meek look on his large bronzed face—a look so very different from the leonine glare with which he was wont to regard tempestuous weather or turbulent men. "Of course it'll come rather sudden on the missus, but w'en it blows hard what's a man got to do but make all snug and stand by?"

"Quite true, Stride. I have no doubt that you are nautically as well as morally correct, so I leave it to you to bring round the mistress, and consider that matter as settled. By the way, I hope that she and your little girl have not suffered from the wetting and rough handling experienced when being rescued."

"Not in the least, sir, thankee. In fact I incline to the belief that they are rather more frisky than usual in consekince. Leastwise *little* Maggie is."

"Glad to hear it. Now, about that young fellow."

"By which I s'pose you mean Mr. Brooke, sir?"

"The same. He has just left me, and upon my word, he's about the coolest young fellow I ever met with."

"That's just what I said to the missus, sir, the very night arter we was rescued. 'The way that young feller come off, Maggie,' says I, 'is most extraor'nar'. No fish that——' "

"Yes, yes, Stride, I know, but that's not exactly what I mean: it's his being so amazingly independent that——"

"'Zactly what I said, sir. 'Maggie,' says I, 'that young feller seemed to be quite independent of fin or tail, for he came right off in the teeth o' wind and tide——' "

"That's not what I mean either, Captain," interrupted the old gentleman, with slight impatience. "It's his independent spirit I refer to."

"Oh! I ax your pardon, sir."

"Well, now, listen, and don't interrupt me. But first let me ask, does he know that I am the owner of the brig that was lost?"

" Yes; he knows that."

" Does he know that I also own the *Walrus*."

" No, I'm pretty sure he don't. Leastwise I
didn't tell him, an' there's nobody else down there
as knows anything about you."

" So far, good. Now, Stride, I want you to help
me. The young goose is so proud, or I know not
what, that he won't accept any favours or rewards
from me, and I find that he is out of work just now,
so I'm determined to give him something to do in
spite of himself. The present supercargo of the
Walrus is a young man who will be pleased to fall
in with anything I propose to him. I mean, therefore, to put him in another ship and appoint young
Brooke to the *Walrus*. Fortunately the firm of
Withers and Co. does not reveal my name—I
having been Co. originally, though I'm the firm
now, so that he won't suspect anything, and what
I want is, that you should do the engaging of him
—being authorised by Withers and Co.—you understand ?"

" I follow you, sir. But what if he objects ?"

" He won't object. I have privately inquired
about him. He is anxious to get employment, and
has strong leanings to an adventurous life on the
sea. There's no accounting for taste, Captain !"

" Right you are, sir," replied the Captain, with an
approving nod. " That's what I said only this
mornin' to my missus. 'Maggie,' says I, 'salt water

hasn't a good taste, as even the stoopidest of mortals
knows, but w'en a man has had to lick it off his
lips at sea for the better part of half a century,
it's astonishin' how he not only gits used to it,
but even comes to like the taste of it.'   'Pooh!'
says she, 'don't tell me you likes it, for you don't!
It's all a d'lusion an' a snare.   I hates both the
taste an' the smell of it.'   'Maggie,' says I, quite
solemn-like, 'that may be so, but you're not me.'
'No, thank goodness!' says she—which you mustn't
suppose, sir, meant as she didn't like *me*, for she's
a true-hearted affectionate creetur—though I say it
as shouldn't—but she meant that she'd have had to
go to sea reg'lar if she had been me, an' that would
have done for her in about six weeks, more or less,
for the first time she ever went she was all but
turned inside——"

   "If you're going citywards," interrupted Mr.
Crossley, again pulling out his watch, "we may as
well finish our talk in the street."

   As Captain Stride was "quite agreeable" to
this proposal, the two left the house together, and,
hailing a hansom, drove off in the direction of the
city.

CHAPTER IV.

DRIFTING ON THE ROCKS.

On the sea-shore, not far from the spot where the brig had been wrecked, Charlie Brooke and Shank Leather walked up and down engaged in earnest conversation soon after the interviews just described.

Very different was the day from that on which the wreck had taken place. It seemed almost beyond possibility that the serene sky above, and the calm, glinting ocean which rippled so softly at their feet, could be connected with the same world in which inky clouds and snowy foam and roaring billows had but a short time before held high revelry.

"Well, Charlie," said his friend, after a pause, "it was very good of you, old boy, and I hope that I'll do credit to your recommendation. The old man seems a decent sort of chap, though somewhat cross-grained."

"He is kind-hearted, Shank; I feel quite sure of that, and hope sincerely that you will get on well with him."

"'With him'?" repeated Leather; "you don't seem to understand that the situation he is to get for me is *not* in connection with his own business, whatever that may be. It is in some other City firm, the name of which he has not yet mentioned. I can't myself understand why he is so close!"

"Perhaps because he has been born with a secretive nature," suggested Charlie.

"May be so. However, that's no business of mine, and it doesn't do to be too inquisitive when a man is offering you a situation of two hundred a year. It would be like looking a gift-horse in the mouth. All I care about is that I'm to go to London next week and begin work.—Why, you don't seem pleased to hear of my good fortune," continued Leather, turning a sharp look on his friend, who was gazing gravely at the sand, in which he was poking holes with his stick.

"I congratulate you, Shank, with all my heart, and you know it; but—I'm sorry to find that you are not to be in connection with Mr. Crossley himself, for there is more good in him than appears on the surface. Did he then make no mention of the nature of his own business?"

"None whatever. To say truth, that mysteriousness or secrecy is the only point about the old fellow's character that I don't like," said Leather, with a frown of virtuous disapproval. "'All fair and above-board,'

that's my motto. Speak out your mind and fear
nothing !"

At these noble sentiments a faint smile, if we may
say so, hovered somewhere in the recesses of Charlie
Brooke's interior, but not the quiver of a muscle
disturbed the solemnity of his face.

"The secrecy of his nature seems even to have
infected that skipper with—or rather by—whom he
was wrecked," continued Leather, "for when I asked
him yesterday about the old gentleman, he became
suddenly silent, and when I pressed him, he made
me a rigmarole speech something like this : 'Young
man, I make it a rule to know nothin' whatever
about my passengers. As I said only two days past
to my missus : "Maggie," says I, "it's of no use your
axin' me. My passengers' business is *their* business,
and my business is mine. All I've got to do is to
sail my ship, an' see to it that I land my passengers
in safety."'

"'You made a pretty mess of your business, then,
the last trip,' said I, for I was bothered with his
obvious determination not to give me any information."

"'Right you are, young man,' said he, 'and it
would have been a still prettier mess if your friend
Mr. Brooke hadn't come off wi' that there line!'"

"I laughed at this and recovered my temper, but
I could pump nothing more out of him. Perhaps
there was nothing to pump.—But now tell me, how

is it—for I cannot understand—that you refused all offers to yourself? You are as much 'out of work' just now as I am."

"That's true, Shank, and really I feel almost as incapable of giving you an answer as Captain Stride himself. You see, during our conversation Mr. Crossley attributed mean—at all events wrong—motives to me, and somehow I felt that I *could* not accept any favour at his hands just then. I suspect I was too hasty. I fear it was false pride——"

"Ha! ha!" laughed Leather; "'pride'! I wonder in what secret chamber of your big corpus your pride lies."

"Well, I don't know. It must be pretty deep. Perhaps it is engrained, and cannot be easily recognised."

"That last is true, Charlie. Assuredly it can't be recognised, for it's not there at all. Why, if you had been born with a scrap of false pride you and I could never have been friends—for I hate it!"

Shank Leather in saying this had hit the nail fairly on the head, although he had not intelligently probed the truth to the bottom. In fact a great deal of the friendship which drew these young men together was the result of their great dissimilarity of character. They acted on each other somewhat after the fashion of a well-adjusted piece of mechanism, the ratchets of selfishness and cog-wheels of vanity in Shank fitting easily into the pinions of good-will and modesty which characterised his friend, so that there was no jarring in their intercourse. This alone would not, perhaps, have induced the strong friendship that existed if it had not been coupled with their intimacy from childhood, and if Brooke had not been particularly fond of Shank's invalid mother, and recognised a few of her good characteristics faintly reproduced in her son, while Shank fully appreciated in Charlie that amiable temperament which inclines its happy possessor to sympathise much with others, to talk little of self, to believe all things and to hope all things, to the verge almost of infantine credulity.

"Well, well," resumed Charlie, with a laugh, "however that may be, I *did* decline Mr. Crossley's offers, but it does not matter much now, for that same worthy captain who bothered you so much has told me of a situation of which he has the gift, and has offered it to me."

"You don't say so! Is it a good one?"

"Yes, and well paid, I'm told, though I don't know the exact amount of the salary yet."

"And have you accepted?"

"I have. Mother agreed, after some demur, that it is better than nothing, so, like you, I begin work in a few days."

"Well now, how strangely things do happen sometimes!" said Leather, stopping and looking out seaward, where the remains of the brig could still be distinguished on the rocks that had fixed her doom. "But for that fortunate wreck and our saving the people in her, you and I might still have been whistling in the ranks of the Great Unemployed! —And what sort of a situation is it, Charlie?"

"You will smile, perhaps, when I tell you. It is to act as supercargo of the *Walrus*, which is commanded by Captain Stride himself."

Young Leather's countenance fell. "Why, Charlie," he said, "that means that you're going away to sea!"

"I fear it does."

"Soon?"

"In a week or two."

For some little time Leather did not speak. The news fell upon him with a shock of disagreeable surprise, for, apart from the fact that he really loved his friend, he was somehow aware that there were not many other young men who cared much for himself—in regard to which he was not a little surprised, for it never occurred to him that egotism and selfishness had anything to do with the coolness of his friends, or that none but men like our hero, with sweet tempers and self-forgetting dispositions, could by any possibility put up with him.

"Who are the owners of the *Walrus*, Charlie?" he asked, as they turned into the lane that led from the beach to the village.

"Withers and Co. of London."

"H'm—don't know them. They must be trustful fellows, however, to take a captain into their employ who has just lost his vessel."

"They have not *taken* him into their employ," said Charlie. "Captain Stride tells me he has been in their service for more than a quarter of a century, and they exonerate him from all blame in the loss of the brig. It does seem odd to me, however, that he should be appointed so immediately to a new ship, but, as you remarked, that's none of my business. Come, I'll go in with you and congratulate your mother and May on your appointment."

They had reached the door of Shank Leather's house by that time. It was a poor-looking house, in a poor side street or blind alley of the village, the haunt of riotous children during the day-time, and of maddening cats at night. Stray dogs now and then invaded the alley, but, for the most part, it was to children and cats that the region was given over. Here, for the purpose of enabling the proverbial "two ends" to "meet," dwelt a considerable population in houses of diminutive size and small accommodation. A few of these were persons who, having "seen better days," were anxious to hide their poverty and existence from the "friends" of those better days. There was likewise a sprinkling of individuals and families who, having grown callous to the sorrows of earth, had reached that condition wherein the meeting of the two ends is a matter of comparative indifference, because they never met, and were never more expected to meet—the blank, annually left gaping, being filled up, somehow, by a sort of compromise between bankruptcy, charity, and starvation.

To the second of these the Leather family belonged. They had been brought to their sad condition by that prolific source of human misery—the bottle.

To do the family justice, it was only the father who had succumbed. He had been a gentleman; he was now a sot. His wife—delicate owing to bad treatment, sorrow, and insufficient nourishment—was, ever had been, and ever would be, a lady and a Christian. Owing to the last priceless condition she was still alive. It is despair that kills, and despair had been banished from her vocabulary ever since she had laid down the arms of her rebellion and accepted the Saviour of mankind as her guide and consolation.

But sorrow, suffering, toil had not departed when the demon despair fled away. They had, however, been wonderfully lightened, and one of the brightest gleams of hope in her sad life was that she might possibly be used as the means of saving her husband. There were other gleams of light, however, one of the brightest of them being that May, her only daughter, was loving and sympathetic—or, as she sometimes expressed it, "as good as gold."

But there was also a very dark spot in her life: Shank, her only son, was beginning to show a tendency to tread in his father's steps.

Many golden texts were enshrined in the heart of poor Mrs. Leather, and not a few of these—painted by the hand of May—hung on the walls of their little sitting-room, but the word to which she turned her eyes in seasons of profoundest obscurity, and which served her as a sheet-anchor in the midst of the wildest storms, was, " Hope thou in God, for thou shalt *yet* praise Him." And alongside of that text, whenever she thought of it or chanced to look at it, there invariably flashed another: " Immanuel, God with us."

May and her mother were alone when the young men entered ; the former was at her lessons, the latter busy with knitting-needles.

Knitting was the means by which Mrs. Leather, with constant labour and inexhaustible perseverance, managed to fill up the gap between the before-mentioned "two ends," which her dissolute husband failed to draw together. She could read or assist May with her lessons, while her delicate fingers, working below the table, performed miraculous gyrations with steel and worsted. To most male minds, we presume, this is utterly incomprehensible. It is well not to attempt the description of that which one does not understand. The good lady knitted socks and stockings, and mittens and cuffs, and comforters, and other things, in absolutely over-whelming quantities, so that the accumulation in the press in which she stored them was at times quite marvellous. Yet that press never quite filled up, owing to the fact that there was an incurable leak in it—a sort of secret channel—through which the products of her toil flowed out nearly as fast as she poured them in.

This leak in the worsted press, strange to say, increased wonderfully just after the wreck described in a previous chapter, and the rivulet to which it gave rise flowed in the direction of the back-door of the house, emptying itself into a reservoir which always took the form of a little elderly lady, with a plain but intensely lovable countenance, who had been, perhaps still was, governess in a family in a neighbouring town where Mrs. Leather had spent some of her "better days." Her name was Molloy.

Like a burglar Miss Molloy came in a stealthy manner at irregular intervals to the back-door of the house, and swept the press of its contents, made them up into a bundle of enormous size, and carried them off on the shoulders of an appropriately dis-reputable blackguard boy—as Shank called him—whom she retained for the purpose. Unlike a bur-glar, however, Miss Molloy did not "bolt with the swag," but honestly paid for everything, from the hugest pair of gentlemen's fishing socks to the smallest pair of children's cuffs.

What Miss Molloy did with this perennial flow of woollen work, whom she came from, where she went to, who discovered her, and why she did it, were subjects of inquiry which baffled investigation, and always simmered in the minds of Shank and May, though the mind of Mrs. Leather herself seemed to be little if at all exercised by it. At all events she was uncommunicative on the point, and her children's curiosity was never gratified, for the mother was obdurate, and, torture being illegal at that time in England, they had no means of compelling disclosure. It was sometimes hinted by Shank that their little dog Scraggy—appropriately named !—knew more than he chose to tell about the subject, for he was generally present at the half-secret interviews, and always closed the scene with a sham but furious assault on the ever contemptuous blackguard boy. But Scraggy was faithful to his trust, and revealed nothing.

"I can't tell you how glad I am, Mrs. Leather, about Shank's good fortune," said Charlie, with a gentle shake of the hand, which Mr. Crossley would have appreciated. Like the Nasmyth steam-hammer, which flattens a ton of iron or gently cracks a hazel-nut, our Herculean hero could accommodate himself to circumstances ; "as your son says, it has been a lucky wreck for *us.*"

"Lucky indeed for *him,*" responded the lady, instantly resuming her knitting, which she generally kept down near her lap, well hidden by the table, while she looked at her visitor and talked, " but not very pleasant for those who have lost by it."

" Pooh ! mother, nobody has lost by it," said Shank in his free-and-easy style. " The owners don't lose, because of course it was insured ; and the Insurance Companies can't be said to lose, for the value of a small brig will be no more felt by them than the losing of a pin would be felt by yourself ; and the captain won't lose—except a few sea-garments and things o' that kind—for he has been appointed to another ship already. By the way, mother, that reminds me that Charlie has also got a situation through this lucky wreck, for Captain Stride feels so grateful that he has offered him the situation of supercargo in his new ship."

For once Mrs. Leather's knitting-needles came to a sudden stop, and she looked inquiringly at her young friend. So did May.

" Have you accepted it ?"

" Well, yes. I have."

" I 'm *so* sorry," said May ; " I don't know what Shank will do without you."

At that moment a loud knocking was heard at the door. May rose to open it, and Mrs. Leather looked anxiously at her son.

A savage undertoned growl and an unsteady step told all too plainly that the head of the house had returned home.

With sudden interest in worsted fabrics, which he was far from feeling, Charlie Brooke turned his back to the door, and, leaning forward, took up an end of the work with which the knitter was busy.

"That's an extremely pretty pattern, Mrs. Leather. Does it take you long to make things of the kind?"

"Not long; I—I make a good many of them."

She said this with hesitation, and with her eyes fixed on the doorway, through the opening of which her husband thrust a shaggy disheveled head, with dissipation stamped on a countenance which had evidently been handsome once.

But Charlie saw neither the husband's head nor the poor wife's gaze, for he was still bending over the worsted-work in mild admiration.

Under the impression that he had not been observed, Mr. Leather suddenly withdrew his head, and was heard to stumble up-stairs under the guidance of May. Then the bang of a door, followed by a shaking of the slimly-built house, suggested the idea that the poor man had flung himself on his bed.

"Shank Leather," said Charlie Brooke, that same night as they strolled on the sea-shore, "you gave expression to some sentiments to-day which I highly approved of. One of them was 'Speak out your mind, and fear nothing!' I mean to do so now, and expect that you will not be hurt by my following your advice."

"Well?" exclaimed Shank, with a dubious glance, for he disliked the seriousness of his friend's tone.

"Your father——" began Charlie.

"Please don't speak about *him*," interrupted the other. "I know all that you can say. His case is hopeless, and I can't bear to speak about it."

"Well, I won't speak about him, though I cannot agree with you that his case is hopeless. But it is yourself that I wish to speak about. You and I are soon to separate ; it must be for a good long while —it may be for ever. Now I must speak out my mind before I go. My old playmate, school-fellow, and chum, you have begun to walk in your poor father's footsteps, and you may be sure that if you don't turn round all your hopes will be blasted—at least for this life—perhaps also for that which is to come. Now don't be angry or hurt, Shank. Remember that you not only encouraged me, but advised me to speak out my mind."

"Yes, but I did not advise you to form a false, uncharitable judgment of your chum," returned Leather, with a dash of bitterness in his tone. "I admit that I'm fond of a social glass, and that I sometimes, though rarely, take a little—a very little —more than, perhaps, is necessary. But that is very different from being a drunkard, which you appear to assume that I am."

"Nay, Shank, I don't assume that. What I

said was that you are *beginning* to walk in your dear father's footsteps. No man ever yet became a drunkard without *beginning*. And I feel certain that no man ever, when beginning, had the most distant intention or expectation of becoming a drunkard. Your danger, dear old fellow, lies in your *not seeing* the danger. You admit that you like a social glass. Shank, I candidly make the same admission—I like it,—but after seeing your father, and hearing your defence, the danger has been so deeply impressed on *me*, that from this hour I resolve, God helping me, never more to taste a social glass."

"Well, Charlie, you know yourself best," returned his friend airily, "and if you think yourself in so great danger, of course your resolve is a very prudent one; but for myself, I admit that I see no danger, and I don't feel any particular weakness of will in regard to temptation."

"Ah, Shank, you remind me of an eccentric old lady I have heard of who was talking with a friend about the difficulties of life. 'My dear,' said the friend, 'I do find it such a *difficult* thing to resist temptation—don't you?' 'No,' replied the eccentric old lady, 'I don't, for I *never* resist temptation, I always give way to it!'"

"I can't quite make out how your anecdote applies to me, Charlie."

"Don't you see? You feel no weakness of will in

regard to temptation because you never give your will an opportunity of resisting it. You always give way to it. You see, I am speaking out my mind freely—as you have advised!"

"Yes, and you take the whole of my advice, and fear nothing, else you would not risk a quarrel by doing so. But really, my boy, it's of no use your troubling your head on that subject, for I feel quite safe, and I don't mean to give in, so there's an end on 't."

Our hero persevered notwithstanding, and for some time longer sought to convince or move his friend both by earnest appeal and light pleasantry, but to all appearance without success, although he reduced him to silence. He left him at last, and went home meditating on the truth of the proverb that "a man convinced against his will is of the same opinion still."

CHAPTER V.

ALL THINGS TO ALL MEN.

UNDER the influence of favouring breezes and bright skies the *Walrus* swept gaily over the ocean at the beginning of her voyage, with "stuns'ls alow and aloft, royals and sky-scrapers," according to Captain Stride. At least, if these were not the exact words he used, they express pretty well what he meant, namely, a "cloud of canvas."

But this felicitous state of things did not last. The tropics were reached, where calms prevailed with roasting heat. The Southern Atlantic was gained, and gales were met with. The celebrated Cape was doubled, and the gales, if we may say so, were trebled. The Indian Ocean was crossed, and the China Seas were entered, where typhoons blew some of the sails to ribbons, and snapped off the topmasts like pipe-stems. Then she sailed into the great Pacific, and for a time the *Walrus* sported pleasantly among the coral islands.

During all this time, and amid all these changes, Charlie Brooke, true to his character, was the

busiest and most active man on board. Not that
his own special duties gave him much to do, for,
until the vessel should reach port, these were rather
light; but our hero—as Stride expressed it—"must
always be doing." If he had not work to do he
made it—chiefly in the way of assisting other
people. Indeed there was scarcely a man or boy on
board who did not have the burden of his toil, whatever it was, lightened in consequence of young
Brooke's tendency to put his powerful shoulder
voluntarily to the wheel. He took the daily observations with the captain, and worked out the ship's
course during the previous twenty-four hours. He
handled the adze and saw with the carpenter,
learned to knot and splice, and to sew canvas with
the bo's'n's mate, commented learnedly and interest-
ingly on the preparation of food with the cook, and
spun yarns with the men on the forecastle, or listened
to the long-winded stories of the captain and
officers in the cabin. He was a splendid listener,
being much more anxious to ascertain exactly the
opinions of his friends and mates than to advance
his own. Of course it followed that Charlie was
a favourite.

With his insatiable desire to acquire information
of every kind, he had naturally, when at home,
learned a little rough-and-tumble surgery, with a
slight smattering of medicine. It was not much,
but it proved to be useful as far as it went, and his

E

"little knowledge" was not "dangerous," because he modestly refused to go a single step beyond it in the way of practice, unless, indeed, he was urgently pressed to do so by his patients. In virtue of his attainments, real and supposed, he came to be recognised as the doctor of the ship, for the *Walrus* carried no medical man.

"Look here, Brooke," said the only passenger on board—a youth of somewhat delicate constitution, who was making the voyage for the sake of his health,—"I've got horrible toothache. D'you think you can do anything for me?"

"Let's have a look at it," said Charlie, with kindly interest, though he felt half inclined to smile at the intensely lugubrious expression of the youth's face.

"Why, Raywood, that is indeed a bad tooth; nothing that I know of will improve it. There's a cavern in it big and black enough to call to remembrance the Black Hole of Calcutta! A red-hot wire might destroy the nerve, but I never saw one used, and should not like to try it."

"Horrible!" exclaimed Raywood. "I've been mad with pain all the morning, and can't afford to be driven madder. Perhaps, somewhere or other in the ship there may be a—a—thingumy."

"A whatumy?" inquired the other.

"A key, or—or—pincers," groaned Raywood, "for extracting—oh! man, couldn't you pull it out?"

"Easily," said Charlie, with a smile. "I've got a pair of forceps—always carry them in case of need, but never use them unless the patient is very bad, and *must* have it out."

Poor Raywood protested, with another groan, that his was a case in point, and it *must* come out; so Charlie sought for and found his forceps.

"It won't take long, I suppose?" said the patient rather nervously, as he opened his mouth.

"Oh no. Only a moment or——"

A fearful yell, followed by a gasp, announced to the whole ship's company that a crisis of some sort had been passed by some one, and the expert though amateur dentist congratulated his patient on his deliverance from the enemy.

Only three of the ship's company, however, had witnessed the operation. One was Dick Darvall, the seaman who chanced to be steering at the time, and who could see through the open skylight what was being enacted in the cabin. Another was the captain, who stood beside him. The third was the cabin-boy, Will Ward, who chanced to be cleaning some brasses about the skylight at the time, and was transfixed by what we may style delightfully-horrible sensations. These three watched the proceedings with profound interest, some sympathy, and not a little amusement.

"Mind your helm, Darvall," said the Captain, stifling a laugh as the yell referred to burst on his ears.

"Ay, ay, sir," responded the seaman, bringing his mind back to his duty, as he bestowed a wink on the brass-polishing cabin-boy.

"He's up to everything," said Darvall in a low voice, referring to our hero.

"From pitch-and-toss to manslaughter," responded the boy, with a broad grin.

"I do believe, Mr. Brooke, that you can turn your hand to anything," said Captain Stride, as Charlie came on deck a few minutes later. "Did you ever study doctoring or surgery ?"

"Not regularly," answered Charlie; "but occasionally I've had the chance of visiting hospitals and dissecting-rooms, besides hearing lectures on anatomy, and I have taken advantage of my opportunities. Besides, I'm fond of mechanics ; and tooth-drawing is somewhat mechanical. Of course I make no pretension to a knowledge of regular dentistry, which involves, I believe, a scientific and prolonged education."

"May be so, Mr. Brooke," returned the captain, "but your knowledge seems deep and extensive enough to me, for, except in the matter o' navigation, I haven't myself had much schoolin', but I do like to see a fellow that can use his hands. As I said to my missus, not two days before I left 'er : 'Maggie,' says I, 'a man that can't turn his hands to anything ain't worth his salt. For why? He's useless at sea, an', by consequence, can't be of much value on land.'"

"Your reasoning is unanswerable," returned Charlie, with a laugh.

"Not so sure o' that," rejoined the captain, with a modestly dubious shake of his head; "leastwise, however unanswerable it may be, my missus always manages to answer it—somehow."

At that moment one of the sailors came aft to relieve the man-at-the-wheel.

Dick Darvall was a grave, tall, dark, and handsome man of about five-and-twenty, with a huge black beard, as fine a seaman as one could wish to see standing at a ship's helm, but he limped when he left his post and went forward.

"How's the leg to-day, Darvall?" asked young Brooke, as the man passed.

"Better, sir, thankee."

"That's well. I'll change the dressing in half-an-hour. Don't disturb it till I come."

"Thankee, sir, I won't."

"Now then, Raywood," said Charlie, descending to the cabin, where his patient was already busy reading Maury's *Physical Geography of the Sea*, "let's have a look at the gum."

"Oh, it's all right," said Raywood. "D'you know, I think one of the uses of severe pain is to make one inexpressibly thankful for the mere absence of it. Of course there is a little sensation of pain left, which might make me growl at other times, but that positively feels comfortable now by contrast!"

"There is profound sagacity in your observations," returned Charlie, as he gave the gum a squeeze that for a moment or two removed the comfort; "there, now, don't suck it, else you'll renew the bleeding. Keep your mouth shut."

With this caution the amateur dentist left the cabin, and proceeded to the fore-part of the vessel. In passing the steward's pantry a youthful voice arrested him.

"Oh, please, sir," said Will Ward, the cabin-boy, advancing with a slate in his hand, "I *can't* make out the sum you set me yesterday, an' I'm quite sure I've tried and tried as hard as ever I could to understand it."

"Let me see," said his friend, taking the slate and sitting down on a locker. "Have you read over the rule carefully?"

"Yes, sir, I have, a dozen times at least, but it won't come right," answered the boy, with wrinkles enough on his young brow to indicate the very depths of puzzlement.

"Fetch the book, Will, and let's examine it."

The book was brought, and at his teacher's request the boy read:—

"Add the interest to the principal, and then multiply by——"

"Multiply?" said Charlie, interrupting. "Look!"

He pointed to the sum on the slate, and repeated "multiply."

"Oh!" exclaimed the cabin-boy, with a gasp of relief and wide-open eyes, "I've *divided!*"

"That's so, Will, and there's a considerable difference between division and multiplication, as you'll find all through life," remarked the teacher, with a peculiar lift of his eyebrows, as he handed back the slate and went on his way.

More than once in his progress "for'ard" he was arrested by men who wished him to give advice, or clear up difficulties in reference to subjects which his encouragement or example had induced them to take up, and to these claims on his attention or assistance he accorded such a ready and cheerful response that his pupils felt it to be a positive pleasure to appeal to him, though they each professed to regret giving him "trouble." The boatswain, who was an amiable though gruff man in his way, expressed pretty well the feelings of the ship's company towards our hero when he said: "I tell you, mates, I'd sooner be rubbed up the wrong way, an' kicked down the fore hatch by Mr. Brooke, than I'd be smoothed or buttered by anybody else."

At last the fo'c'sl was reached, and there our surgeon found his patient, Dick Darvall, awaiting him. The stout seaman's leg had been severely bruised by a block which had fallen from aloft and struck it during one of the recent gales.

"A good deal better to-day," said Charlie. "Does it pain you much?"

"Not nearly as much as it did yesterday, sir. It's my opinion that I'll be all right in a day or two. Seems to me outrageous to make so much ado about it."

"If we didn't take care of it, my man, it might cost you your limb, and we can't afford to bury such a well-made member before its time! You must give it perfect rest for a day or two. I'll speak to the captain about it."

"I'd rather you didn't, sir," objected the seaman. "I feel able enough to go about, and my mates'll think I'm shirkin' dooty."

"There's not a man a-board as'll think that o' Dick Darvall," growled the boatswain, who had just entered and heard the last remark.

"Right, bo's'n," said Brooke, "you have well expressed the thought that came into my own head."

"Have ye seen Samson yet, sir?" asked the boatswain, with an unusually grave look.

"No; I was just going to inquire about him. No worse, I hope?"

"I think he is, sir. Seems to me that he ain't long for this world. The life's bin too much for him: he never was cut out for a sailor, an' he takes things so much to heart that I do believe worry is doin' more than work to drive him on the rocks."

"I'll go and see him at once," said our hero.

Fred Samson, the sick man referred to, had been put into a swing-cot in a berth amidships to give him as much rest as possible. To all appearance he was slowly dying of consumption. When Brooke entered he was leaning on one elbow, gazing wistfully through the port-hole close to his head. His countenance, on which the stamp of death was evidently imprinted, was unusually refined for one in his station in life.

"I'm glad you have come, Mr. Brooke," he said slowly, as his visitor advanced and took his thin hand.

"My poor fellow," said Charlie, in a tone of low but tender sympathy, "I wish with all my heart I could do you any good."

"The sight of your kind face does me good," returned the sailor, with a pause for breath between almost every other word. "I don't want you to doctor me any more. I feel that I'm past that, but I want to give you a message and a packet for my mother. Of course you will be in London when you return to England. Will you find her out and deliver the packet? It contains only the Testament she gave me at parting and a letter."

"My dear fellow—you may depend on me," replied Brooke earnestly. "Where does she live?"

"In Whitechapel. The full address is with the packet. The letter enclosed tells all that I would say."

"But you spoke of a message," said— but here it was noticed that he paused and shut his eyes.

"Yes, yes," returned the dying man eagerly, "I forgot. Give her my dear love, and say that my last thoughts were of herself and God. She always feared that I was trusting too much in myself—in my own good resolutions and reformation; so I have been—but that's past. Tell her that God in His mercy has snapped that broken reed altogether, and enabled me to rest my soul on Jesus."

As the dying man was much exhausted by his efforts to speak, his visitor refrained from asking more questions. He merely whispered a comforting text of Scripture and left him apparently sinking into a state of repose.

Then, having bandaged the finger of a man who had carelessly cut himself while using his knife aloft, Charlie returned to the cabin to continue an interrupted discussion with the first mate on the subject of astronomy.

From all which it will be seen that our hero's tendencies inclined him to be as much as possible "all things to all men."

CHAPTER VI.

DISASTER, STARVATION, AND DEATH.

THE least observant of mortals must have frequently been impressed with the fact that events and incidents of an apparently trifling description often lead to momentous — sometimes tremendous —results.

Soon after the occurrence of the incidents referred to in the last chapter, a colony of busy workers in the Pacific Ocean were drawing towards the completion of a building on which they had been engaged for a long time. Like some lighthouses this building had its foundations on a rock at the bottom of the sea. Steadily, perseveringly, and with little cessation, the workers had toiled for years. They were small insignificant creatures, each being bent on simply performing the little bit of work which he, she, or it had been created to do probably without knowing or caring what the result might be, and then ending his, her, or its modest labours with life. It was when this marine building had risen to within eight or ten feet of the surface of the sea that the *Walrus* chanced to draw near to it, but no one on board was aware of the existence of that coral-reef, for up to the period we write of it had failed to attract the attention of chart-makers.

The vessel was bowling along at a moderate rate over a calm sea, for the light breeze overhead that failed to ruffle the water filled her topsails. Had the wind been stormy a line of breakers would have indicated the dangerous reef. As it was there was nothing to tell that the good ship was rushing on her doom till she struck with a violent shock and remained fast.

Of course Captain Stride was equal to the emergency. By the quiet decision with which he went about and gave his orders he calmed the fears of such of his crew as were apt to "lose their heads" in the midst of sudden catastrophe.

"Lower away the boats, lads. We'll get her off right away," he said, in a quick but quiet tone.

Charlie Brooke, being a strong believer in strict discipline, at once ran to obey the order, accompanied by the most active among the men, while others ran to slack off the sheets and lower the topsails.

In a few minutes nearly all the men were in the boats, with hawsers fixed to the stern of the vessel, doing their uttermost to pull her off.

Charlie had been ordered to remain on deck when the crew took to the boats.

"Come here, Mr. Brooke, I want you," said the Captain, leading his young friend to the taffrail. "It's pretty clear to me that the poor old *Walrus* is done for——"

"I sincerely hope not, sir," said Charlie, with anxious looks.

"A short time will settle the question," returned the Captain, with unwonted gravity. "If she don't move in a few minutes, I'll try what heaving out some o' the cargo will do. As supercargo, you know where it's all stowed, so, if you'll pint out to me which is the least valooable, an' at the same time heaviest part of it, I'll send the mate and four men to git it on deck. But to tell you the truth even if we do git her off I don't think she'll float. She's an oldish craft, not fit to have her bottom rasped on coral rocks. But we'll soon see."

Charlie could not help observing that there was something peculiarly sad in the tone of the old man's voice. Whether it was that the poor captain knew the case to be utterly hopeless, or that he was overwhelmed by this calamity coming upon him so soon after the wreck of his last ship, Charlie could not tell, but he had no time to think, for after he had pointed out to the mate the bales that could be most easily spared he was again summoned aft.

"She don't move," said the captain, gloomily. "We must git the boats ready, for if it comes on to blow only a little harder we'll have to take to 'em. So do you and the stooard putt your heads together an' git up as much provisions as you think the boats will safely carry. Only necessaries, of course, an' take plenty o' water. I'll see to it that charts, compasses, canvas, and other odds and ends are ready."

Again young Brooke went off, without saying a word, to carry out his instructions. Meanwhile one of the boats was recalled, and her crew set to lighten the ship by heaving part of the cargo overboard. Still the *Walrus* remained immovable on the reef, for the force with which she struck had sent her high upon it.

"If we have to take to the boats, sir," said Charlie, when he was disengaged, "it may be well to put some medicines on board, for poor Samson will——"

"Ay, ay, do so, lad," said the captain, interrupting; "I've been thinkin' o' that, an' you may as well rig up some sort o' couch for the poor fellow in the long-boat, for I mean to take him along wi' myself."

"Are you so sure, then, that there is no chance of our getting her off?"

"Quite sure. Look there." He pointed, as he spoke, to the horizon to windward, where a line of cloud rested on the sea. That'll not be long o' comin' here. It won't blow very hard, but it'll be hard enough to smash the old *Walrus* to bits. If you've got any valooables aboard that you'd rather not lose, you'd better stuff 'em in your pockets now. When things come to the wust mind your helm, an' look out, as I used to say to my missus——"

He stopped abruptly and turned away. Evidently the thought of the "missus" was too much for him just then.

Charlie Brooke hurried off to visit the sick man, and prepare him for the sad change in his position that had now become unavoidable. But another visitor had been to see the invalid before him. Entering the berth softly, and with a quiet look, so as not to agitate the patient needlessly, he found to his regret, though not surprise, that poor Fred Samson was dead. There was a smile on the pale face, which was turned towards the port window, as if the dying man had been taking a last look of the sea and sky when Death laid a hand gently on his brow and smoothed away the wrinkles of suffering and care. A letter from his mother, held tightly in one hand and pressed upon his breast told eloquently what was the subject of his last thoughts.

Charlie cut a lock of hair from the sailor's brow with his clasp-knife, and, taking the letter gently from the dead hand, wrapped it therein.

"There's no time to bury him now. His berth must be the poor fellow's coffin," said Captain Stride,

when the death was reported to him. "The swell
o' the coming squall has reached us already. Look
alive wi' the boats, men!"

By that time the rising swell was in truth lifting
the vessel every few seconds and letting her down
with a soft thud on the coral reef. It soon became
evident to every one on board that the *Walrus* had
not many hours to live—perhaps not many minutes
—for the squall to which the Captain had referred
was rapidly bearing down, and each successive thud
became more violent than the previous one. Knowing their danger full well, the men worked with a
will and in a few minutes three boats, well pro-
visioned, were floating on the sea.

The need for haste soon became apparent, for the
depth of water alongside was so insufficient that the
long-boat—drawing as she did considerably more
water than the others—touched twice when the
swells let her drop into their hollows.

It was arranged that Charlie should go in the
long-boat with the captain, Raywood the passenger,
and ten men of the crew. The remainder were to
be divided between the other two boats which were
to be in charge of the first and second officers
respectively.

"Jump in, Brooke," cried the Captain, as he sat
in the stern-sheets looking up at our hero, who
was busily engaged assisting the first mate to complete the arrangements of his boat, "we've struck

twice already. I must shove off. Is Raywood ready?"

"He's in the cabin looking for something, sir; I'll run and fetch him."

"Stay! We've touched again!" shouted the Captain. "You an' Raywood can come off with one o' the other boats. I'll take you on board when in deep water—shove off, lads."

"Jump in with me, sir," said the first mate, as he hastily descended the side.

"Come along, Raywood," shouted Charlie, as he followed. "No time to lose!"

The passenger rushed on deck, scrambled down the side, and took his seat beside Charlie, just as the long threatened squall burst upon them.

The painter was cut, and they drifted into deep water with the second mate's boat, which had already cast off.

Fortunate was it for the whole crew that Captain Stride had provided for every emergency, and that, among other safeguards, he had put several tarpaulins into each boat, for with these they were enabled to form a covering which turned off the waves and prevented their being swamped. The squall turned out to be a very severe one, and in the midst of it the three boats were so far separated that the prospect of their being able to draw together again until evening was very remote. Indeed the waves soon ran so high that it required

F

the utmost attention of each steersman to keep his craft afloat, and when at last the light began to fade the boats were almost out of sight of each other.

"No chance, I fear, of our ever meeting again," remarked the mate, as he cast a wistful look at the southern horizon where the sail of the long-boat could be barely seen like the wing of a sea-gull. "Your lot has been cast with us, Mr. Brooke, so you'll have to make the best of it."

"I always try to make the best of things," replied Charlie. "My chief regret at present is that Ray-wood and I, being two extra hands, will help to consume your provisions too fast."

"Luckily my appetite is a poor one," said Ray-wood, with a faint smile; "and it's not likely to improve in the circumstances."

"I'm not so sure o' that, sir," returned the mate, with an air that was meant to be reassuring; "fresh air and exposure have effected wonders before now in the matter of health—so they say. Another pull on the halyards, Dick; that looks like a fresh squall. Mind your sheets, Will Ward."

A prompt "Ay, ay, sir" from Dick Darvall and the cabin-boy showed that each was alive to the importance of the duty required of him, while the other men—of whom there were six—busied themselves in making the tarpaulin coverings more secure, or in baling out the water which, in spite of them, had found its way into the boat.

Charlie rose and seated himself on the thwart beside the fine-looking seaman Dick Darvall, so as to have a clearer view ahead under the sail.

"Long-boat nowhere to be seen now," he murmured half to himself after a long look.

"No, sir—nor the other boat either," said Darvall in a quiet voice. "We shall never see 'em no more."

"I hope you are wrong," returned Charlie; "indeed I feel sure that the weather will clear during the night, and that we shall find both boats becalmed not far off."

"Maybe so, sir," rejoined the sailor, in the tone of one willing to be, but not yet, convinced.

Our hero was right as to the first, but not as to the second, point. The weather did clear during the night, but when the sun arose next morning on a comparatively calm sea neither of the other boats was to be seen. In fact every object that could arrest the eye had vanished from the scene, leaving only a great circular shield of blue, of which their tiny craft formed the centre.

CHAPTER VII.

ADRIFT ON THE SEA.

"You are ill, Will Ward," was Dick Darvall's first remark when there was sufficient daylight to distinguish faces.

"You're another!" was the cabin-boy's quick, facetious retort, which caused Darvall to smile and had the effect of rousing the half-sleeping crew.

"But you *are* ill, my boy," repeated the seaman earnestly.

"No, Dick, not exactly ill," returned Will, with a faint smile, "but I'm queer."

Each man had spent that stormy night on the particular thwart on which he had chanced to sit down when he first entered the boat, so that all were looking more or less weary, but seamen are used to uncomfortable and interrupted slumbers. They soon roused themselves and began to look about and make a few comments on the weather. Some, recurring naturally to their beloved indulgence, pulled out their pipes and filled them.

"Have 'ee a light, Jim?" asked a rugged man, in a sleepy tone, of a comrade behind him.

"No, Jack, I haven't," answered Jim, in a less sleepy tone, slapping all his pockets and thrusting his hands into them. .

"Have *you*, Dick?" asked the rugged man in some anxiety.

"No, I haven't," replied Darvall, in a very serious voice, as he also took to slapping his pockets; "no —nor baccy!"

It was curious to note at this point how every seaman in that boat became suddenly sympathetic and wide awake, and took to hasty, anxious examination of all his pockets—vest, jacket, and trousers. The result was the discovery of a good many clay pipes, more or less blackened and shortened, with a few plugs of tobacco, but not a single match, either fusee or congreve. The men looked at each other with something akin to despair.

"Was no matches putt on board wi' the grub an' other things?" asked Jim in a solemn tone.

"And no tobacco?" inquired the mate.

No one could answer in the affirmative. A general sigh—like a miniature squall—burst from the sailors, and relieved them a little. Jim put his pipe between his lips, and meekly began, if we may say so, to smoke his tobacco dry. At an order from the mate the men got out the oars and began to pull, for there was barely enough wind to fill the sail.

"No rest for us, lads, 'cept when it blows," said

the mate. "The nearest land that I know of is five hundred miles off as the crow flies. We've got a compass by good luck, so we can make for it, but the grub on board won't hold out for quarter o' that distance, so, unless we fall in with a ship, or fish jump aboard of us, ye know what's before us."

"Have we any spirits aboard?" asked the rugged man, in a growling, somewhat sulky, voice.

"Hear—hear!" exclaimed Jim.

"No, Jack," returned the mate; "at least not for the purpose o' lettin' you have 'a short life an' a merry one.' Now, look here, men: it has pleased Providence to putt you an' me in something of a fix, and I shouldn't wonder if we was to have some stiffish experiences before we see the end of it. It has also pleased Providence to putt me here in command. You know I'm not given to boastin', but there are times when it is advisable to have plain speakin'. There *is* a small supply of spirits aboard, and I just want to tell 'ee—merely as a piece of useful information, and to prevent any chance o' future trouble—that as I've got charge o' them spirits I mean to *keep* charge of 'em."

The mate spoke in a low, soft voice, without the slightest appearance of threat or determination in his manner, but as he concluded he unbuttoned his pilot-cloth coat, and pointed to the butt of a revolver which protruded from one of his vest pockets.

The men made no reply, but instinctively glanced

at the two biggest and strongest men in the boat. These were Charlie Brooke and Dick Darvall. Obviously, before committing themselves further, they wished, if possible, to read in the faces of these two what they thought of the mate's speech. They failed to read much, if anything at all, for Charlie's eyes were fixed in dreamy expressionless abstraction on the horizon, and Dick was gazing up into the clouds, with a look of intense benignity—suggesting that he was holding pleasant intercourse with any celestial creatures who might be resident there.

Without a word the whole crew bent to their oars, and resigned themselves to the inevitable. Perhaps if each man had expressed his true feelings at that moment he would have said that he was glad to know there was a firm hand at the helm. For there are few things more uncomfortable in any community, large or small, than the absence of discipline, or the presence of a weak will in a position of power.

"But I say, Will," remarked Darvall, who pulled the stroke-oar, "you really do look ill. Is anything the matter with 'ee?"

"Nothin', Dick: 'cept that I'm tired," answered the cabin-boy.

"Breakfast will put that right," said our hero in an encouraging tone. "Let's feel your pulse. Hm! Well, might be slower. Come, Captain," he added, giving the mate his new title as he turned to

him, " will you allow me to prescribe breakfast
for this patient ?"

" Certainly, Doctor," returned the mate cheerily.
" Come, lads, we'll all have breakfast together."

In a few minutes the biscuit and salt junk
barrels were opened, and the mate measured out an
exactly equal proportion of food to each man. Then,
following the example of a celebrated commander,
and in order to prevent dissatisfaction on the part
of any with his portion, he caused one of the men
to turn his back on the food, and, pointing to one of
the portions said, " Who shall have this ?"

" The Doctor, sir," returned the man promptly.

The portion was immediately handed to Charlie
Brooke amid a general laugh.

Thus every portion was disposed of, and the men
sat down to eat in good-humour, in spite of the too
evident fact that they had been at once placed on
short allowance, for, when each had finished, he
assuredly wished for more, though no one ventured
to give expression to the wish.

The only exception was the little cabin-boy, who
made a brave attempt to eat, but utterly failed at
the second mouthful.

" Come, Will," said Charlie in a kindly tone, pre-
tending to misunderstand the state of matters,
" don't try to deceive yourself by prolonging your
breakfast. That won't make more of it. See, here,
I'm not up to eating much to-day, somehow, so I'll

be greatly obliged if you will dispose of half of mine as well as your own. Next time I am hungry, and you are not, I'll expect you to do the same."

But Will Ward could not be thus induced to eat. He was really ill, and before night was in a high fever. You may be sure that Dr. Brooke, as every one now called him, did his best to help the little sufferer, but, of course, he could do very little, for all the medicines which he had prepared had been put into the long-boat, and, in a small open boat, with no comforts, no medicines, and on short allowance of food, little could be done, except to give the boy a space of the floor on which to lie, to shield him from spray, and to cover him with blankets.

For a week the boat was carried over the sea by a fresh, steady breeze, during which time the sun shone out frequently, so that things seemed not so wretched as one might suppose to the shipwrecked mariners. Of course the poor cabin-boy was an exception. Although his feverish attack was a slight one he felt very weak and miserable after it. His appetite began to return, however, and it was evident that the short daily allowance would be insufficient for him. When this point was reached Dick Darvall one day, when rations were being served out, ventured to deliver an opinion.

"Captain and mates all," he said, while a sort of bashful smile played upon his sunburnt features, "it do seem to me that we should agree, each man, to give up a share of our rations to little Will Ward, so that he may be able to feed up a bit an' git the better o' this here sickness. We won't feel the want of such a little crumb each, an' he'll be ever so much the better for it."

"Agreed," chorused the men, apparently without exception.

"All right, lads," said the mate, while a rare smile lighted up for a moment his usually stern countenance; "when the need for such self-denial comes I'll call on ye to exercise it, but it ain't called for yet, because I've been lookin' after the interests o' Will Ward while he's been ill. Justice, you see, stands first o' the virtues in my mind, an' it's my opinion that it wouldn't be justice, but something very much the reverse, if we were to rob the poor boy of his victuals just because he couldn't eat them."

"Right you are, sir," interposed Dick Darvall.

"Well, then, holdin' these views," continued the mate, "I have put aside Will Ward's share every time the rations were served, so here's what belongs to him—in this keg for the meat, and this bag for the biscuit—ready for him to fall-to whenever his twist is strong enough."

There were marks of hearty approval, mingled with laughter, among the men on hearing this, but they stopped abruptly and listened for more on observing a perplexed look on their leader's face.

" But there's something that puzzles me about it, lads," resumed the mate, "and it is this, that the grub has somehow accumulated faster than I can account for, considering the smallness o' the addition to the lot each time."

On hearing this the men were a little surprised, but Charlie Brooke burst into a short laugh.

" What!" he exclaimed, "you don't mean to say that the victuals have taken root and begun to grow, do you ?"

"I don't mean to *say* anything," returned the mate quietly; "but I'm inclined to *think* a good deal if you've no objection, Doctor."

" How d'ee feel now, Will ?" said Charlie, stooping forward at the moment, for he observed that the boy—whose bed was on the floor at his feet—had moved, and was gazing up at him with eyes that seemed to have grown enormously since their owner fell sick.

"I feel queer—and—and—I'm inclined to *think*, too," returned Will in a faint voice.

Nothing more was said at that time, for a sudden shift in the wind necessitated a shift of the sail, but Dick Darvall nodded his head significantly, and it came to be understood that "Doctor" Brooke had regularly robbed himself of part of his meagre allowance in order to increase the store of the cabin-boy. Whether they were right in this conjecture has never been distinctly ascertained. But all attempts to benefit the boy were soon after frustrated, for, while life was little more than trembling in the balance with Will Ward, a gale burst upon them which sealed his fate.

It was not the rougher motion of the boat that did it, for the boy was used to that ; nor the flashing of the salt spray inboard, for his comrades guarded him to some extent from that. During the alarm caused by a wave which nearly swamped the boat, two of the crew in their panic seized the first things that came to hand and flung them overboard to prevent their sinking, while the rest baled with cans and sou'-westers for their lives. The portion of lading thus sacrificed turned out to be the staff of life—the casks of biscuit and pork !

It was a terrible shock to these unfortunates when the full extent of the calamity was understood, and the firmness of the mate, with a sight of the revolver, alone prevented summary vengeance being executed on the wretched men who had acted so hastily in their blind terror.

Only a small keg of biscuit remained to them. This was soon expended, and then the process of absolute starvation began. Every nook and cranny of the boat was searched again and again in the hope of something eatable being found, but only a small pot of lard—intended probably to grease the tackling—was discovered. With a dreadful expression in their eyes some of the men glared at it, and there would, no doubt, have been a deadly struggle for it if the mate had not said, " Fetch it here," in a voice which none dared to disobey.

It formed but a mouthful to each, yet the poor fellows devoured it with the greed of ravening wolves, and carefully licked their fingers when it was done. The little cabin-boy had three portions allotted to him, because Charlie Brooke and Dick Darvall added their allowance to his without allowing him to be aware of the fact.

But the extra allowance and kindness, although they added greatly to his comfort, could not stay the hand of Death. Slowly but surely the Destroyer came and claimed the young life. It was a sweet, calm evening when the summons came. The sea was like glass, with only that long, gentle swell which tells even in the profoundest calm of Ocean's instability. The sky was intensely blue, save on the western horizon, where the sun turned it into gold. It seemed as if all Nature were quietly indifferent to the sufferings of the shipwrecked men, some of whom had reached that terrible condition of starvation when all the softer feelings of humanity seem dead, for, although no whisper of their intention passed their lips, their looks told all too plainly that they awaited the death of the cabin-boy with impatience, that they might appease the intolerable pangs of hunger by resorting to cannibalism.

Charlie Brooke, who had been comforting the

dying lad all day, and whispering to him words of
consolation from God's book from time to time,
knew well what those looks meant.   So did the
mate, who sat grim, gaunt, and silent at his post,
taking no notice apparently of what went on around
him.   Fortunately the poor boy was too far gone to
observe the looks of his mates.

There was a can of paraffin oil, which had been
thrown into the boat under the impression that it
was something else.   This had been avoided hitherto
by the starving men, who deemed it to be poisonous.
That evening the man called Jim lost control of
himself, seized the can, and took a long draught of
the oil.   Whether it was the effect of that we cannot tell, but it seemed to drive him mad, for no
sooner had he swallowed it than he uttered a wild
shout, drew his knife, sprang up and leaped towards
the place where the cabin-boy lay.

The mate, who had foreseen something of the
kind, drew and levelled his revolver, but before he
could fire Charlie had caught the uplifted arm,
wrested the knife from the man, and thrust him
violently back.   Thus foiled Jim sprang up again,
and with a maniac's yell leaped into the sea, and
swam resolutely away.

Even in their dire extremity the sailors could
not see a comrade perish with indifference.   They
jumped up, hastily got out the oars, and pulled after
him, but their arms were very weak; before they

could overtake him the man had sunk to rise no more.

It was while this scene was being enacted that the spirit of the cabin-boy passed away. On ascertaining that he was dead Charlie covered him with a tarpaulin where he lay, but no word was uttered by any one, and the mate, with revolver still in hand, sat there—grim and silent—holding the tiller as if steering, and gazing sternly on the horizon. Yet it was not difficult to divine the thoughts of those unhappy and sorely tried men. Some by their savage glare at the cover that concealed the dead body showed plainly their dreadful desires. Brooke, Darvall, and the mate showed as clearly by their compressed lips and stern brows that they would resist any attempt to gratify these.

Suddenly the mate's brow cleared, and his eyes opened wide as he muttered, under his breath, " A sail!"

"A sail! a sail!" shrieked the man in the bow at the same moment, as he leaped up and tried to cheer, but he only gasped and fell back in a swoon into a comrade's arms.

It was indeed a sail, which soon grew larger, and ere long a ship was descried bearing straight towards them before a very light breeze. In less than an hour the castaways stood upon her deck —saved.

CHAPTER VIII.

INGRATITUDE.

A YEAR or more passed away, and then there came a cablegram from New York to Jacob Crossley, Esquire, from Captain Stride. The old gentleman was at breakfast when he received it, and his housekeeper, Mrs. Bland, was in the act of setting before him a dish of buttered toast when he opened the envelope. At the first glance he started up, overturned his cup of coffee, without paying the least attention to the fact, and exclaimed with emphasis—

" As I expected. It is lost !"

" 'Ow could you expect it, sir, to be anythink else, w'en you 've sent it all over the table-cloth ?" said Mrs. Bland, in some surprise.

" It is not that, Mrs. Bland," said Mr. Crossley, in a hurried manner; " it is my ship the *Walrus.* Of course I knew long ago that it must have been lost," continued the old gentleman, speaking his thoughts more to himself than to the housekeeper, who was carefully spooning up the spilt coffee·

"but the best of it is that the Captain has escaped."

"Well, I'm sure, sir," said Mrs. Bland, condescending to be interested, and to ignore, if not to forget, the coffee, "I'm very glad to 'ear it, sir, for Captain Stride is a pleasant, cheery sort of man, and would be agreeable company if 'e didn't use so much sea-languidge, and speak so much of 'is missis. An' I'm glad to 'ear it too, sir, on account o' that fine young man that sailed with 'im—Mr. Book, I think, was——"

"No, Mrs. Bland, it was Brooke; but that's the worst of the business," said the old gentleman; "I'm not quite sure whether young Brooke *is* among the saved. Here is what the telegram says :—

"'From Captain Stride to Jacob Crossley. Just arrived' (that's in New York, Mrs. Bland); '*Walrus* lost. All hands left her in three boats. Our boat made uninhabited island, and knocked to pieces. Eight months on the island. Rescued by American barque. Fate of other boats unknown. Will be home within a couple of weeks.'"

"Why, it sounds like *Robinson Crusoe*, sir, don't it? which I read when I was quite a gurl, but I don't believe it myself, though they do say it's all true. Young Mr. Leather will be glad to 'ear the good noos of 'is friend——"

"But this is *not* good news of his friend; it is only uncertain news," interrupted the old gentleman

G

quickly. "Now I think of it, Mrs. Bland, Mr. Leather is to call here by appointment this very morning, so you must be particularly careful not to say a word to him about this telegram, or Captain Stride, or anything I have told you about the lost ship—you understand, Mrs. Bland ?"

"Certainly, sir," said the housekeeper, somewhat hurt by the doubt thus implied as to the capacity of her understanding. "Shall I bring you some more toast, sir ?" she added, with the virtuous feeling that by this question she was returning good for evil.

"No, thank you. Now, Mrs. Bland, don't forget. Not a word about this to any one."

"'Ooks an' red-'ot pincers wouldn't draw a syllable out of *me*, sir," returned the good woman, departing with an offended air, and leaving her master to understand that, in her opinion, such instruments might have a very different effect upon *him*.

"Ass that I was to speak of it to her at all," muttered Mr. Crossley, walking up and down the room with spectacles on forehead, and with both hands in his trousers-pockets creating disturbance among the keys and coppers. "I might have known that she could not hold her tongue. It would never do to let Mrs. Brooke remain on the tenter-hooks till Stride comes home to clear the matter up. Poor Mrs. Brooke ! No wonder she is almost broken down. This hoping against hope is so wearing. And she's so lonely. To be sure, sweet May Leather runs out and in like a beam of sunshine; but it must be hard, very hard, to lose an only son in this way. It would be almost better to know that he was dead. H'm! and there's that good-for-nothing Shank. The rascal! and yet he's not absolutely good for nothing —if he would only give up drink. Well, while there's life there's hope, thank God! I'll give him another trial."

The old man's brow was severely wrinkled while he indulged in these mutterings, but it cleared, and a kindly look beamed on his countenance as he gave vent to the last expression.

Just then the door bell rang. Mr. Crossley resumed the grave look that was habitual to him, and next minute Shank Leather was ushered into the room.

The youth was considerably changed since we last met him. The year which had passed had developed him into a man, and clothed his upper lip with something visible to the naked eye. It had also lengthened his limbs, deepened his chest, and broadened his shoulders. But here the change for the better ended. In that space of time there had come over him a decided air of dissipation, and the freshness suitable to youth had disappeared.

With a look that was somewhat defiant he entered the room and looked boldly at his employer.

"Be seated, Mr. Leather," said the old gentleman

in a voice so soft that the young man evidently felt abashed, but he as evidently steeled himself against better feelings, for he replied—

"Thank you, Mr. Crossley, I'd rather stand."

"As you please," returned the other, restraining himself. "I sent for you, Mr. Leather, to tell you that I have heard with sincere regret of your last outbreak, and——"

"Yes, sir," said Shank, rudely interrupting, "and I came here not so much to hear what you have to say about my outbreak—as you are pleased to style a little jollification—as to tell you that you had better provide yourself with another clerk, for I don't intend to return to your office. I've got a better situation."

"Oh, indeed!" exclaimed Crossley in surprise.

"Yes, indeed," replied Shank insolently.

It was evident that the youth was, even at that moment, under the influence of his great enemy, else his better feelings would have prevented him from speaking so rudely to a man who had never shown him anything but kindness. But he was nettled by some of his bad companions having taunted him with his slavery to his besetting sin, and had responded to Mr. Crossley's summons under the impression that he was going to get what he styled a "wigging." He was therefore taken somewhat aback when the old gentleman replied to his last remark gently.

"I congratulate you, Mr. Leather, on getting a *better* situation (if it really should turn out to be better), and I sincerely hope it may—for your mother's sake as well as your own. This therefore disposes of part of my object in asking you to call— which was to say that I meant to pass over this offence and retain you in my employment. But it does not supersede the necessity of my urging you earnestly to give up drink, *not* so much on the ground that it will surely lead you to destruction as on the consideration that it grieves the loving Father who has bestowed on you the very powers of enjoyment which you are now prostituting, and who is at this moment holding out His hands to you and *waiting* to be gracious."

The old man stopped abruptly, and Shank stood with eyes fixed on the floor and frowning brow.

"Have you anything more to say to me?" asked Mr. Crossley.

"Nothing."

"Then good-morning. As I can do nothing else to serve you, I will pray for you."

Shank found himself in the street with feelings of surprise strong upon him.

"Pray for me!" he muttered, as he walked slowly along. "It never occurred to me before that he prayed at all! The old humbug has more need to pray for himself!"

CHAPTER IX.

TAKING his way to the railway station Shank Leather found himself ere long at his mother's door.

He entered without knocking.

"Shank!" exclaimed Mrs. Leather and May in the same breath.

"Ay, mother, it's me. A bad shilling, they say, always turns up. *I* always turn up, therefore *I* am a bad shilling! Sound logic that, eh, May?"

"I'm glad to see you, dear Shank," said careworn Mrs. Leather, laying her knitting-needles on the table; "you *know* I'm always glad to see you, but I'm naturally surprised, for this visit is out of your regular time."

"Has anything happened?" asked May anxiously. And May looked very sweet, almost pretty, when she was anxious. A year had refined her features, developed her mind and body, and almost converted her into a little woman. Indeed, mentally, she had become more of a woman than many girls in her neighbourhood who were much older. This was in all likelihood one of the good consequences of adversity.

"Ay, May, something has happened," answered the youth, flinging himself gaily into an arm-chair and stretching out his legs towards the fire ; "I have thrown up my situation. Struck work. That's all."

"Shank !"

"Just so. Don't look so horrified, mother; you've no occasion to, for I have the offer of a better situation. Besides—ha ! ha ! old Crossley—closefisted, crabbed, money-making, skin-flint old Crossley—is going to pray for me. Think o' that, mother—going to pray for *me* !"

"Shank, dear boy," returned his mother, "don't jest about religious things."

"You don't call old Crossley a religious thing, do you ? Why, mother, I thought you had more respect for him than that comes to ; you ought at least to consider his years !"

"Come, Shank," returned Mrs. Leather, with a deprecating smile, "be a good boy and tell me what you mean—and about this new situation."

"I just mean that my friend and chum and old schoolfellow Ralph Ritson—jovial, dashing, musical, handsome Ralph—you remember him—has got me a situation in California."

"Ralph Ritson ?" repeated Mrs. Leather, with a little sigh and an uneasy glance at her daughter, whose face had flushed at the mention of the youth's name.

"Yes," continued Shank, in a graver tone, for he had observed the flush on May's face. "Ralph's father, who is manager of a gold mine in California, has asked his son to go out and assist him at a good salary, and to take a clerk out with him—a stout vigorous fellow, well up in figures, book-keeping, carpenting, etc., and ready to turn his hand to anything, and Ralph has chosen me! What d'ee think o' that?"

From her silence and expression it was evident that the poor lady's thoughts were not quite what her son had hoped.

"Why don't you congratulate me, mother?" he asked, somewhat petulantly.

"Would it not be almost premature," she replied, with a forced smile, "to congratulate you before I know anything about the salary or the prospects held out to you? Besides, I cannot feel as enthusiastic about your friend Ralph as you do. I don't doubt that he is a well-meaning youth, but he is reckless. If he had only been a man like your former friend, poor Charlie Brooke, it would have been different, but——"

"Well, mother, it's of no use wishing somebody to be like somebody else. We must just take folk as we find them, and I find Ralph Ritson a remarkably fine, sensible fellow, who has a proper appreciation of his friends. And he's not a bad fellow. He and Charlie Brooke were fond of each other when we were all schoolboys together—at least he was fond of Charlie, like everybody else. But whether we like him or not does not matter now, for the thing is fixed. I have accepted his offer, and thrown old Jacob overboard."

"Dear Shank, don't be angry if I am slow to appreciate this offer," said the poor lady, laying aside her knitting and clasping her hands before her on the table, as she looked earnestly into her son's face, "but you must see that it has come on me very suddenly, and I'm so sorry to hear that you have parted with good old Mr. Crossley in anger——"

"We didn't part in anger," interrupted Shank. "We were only a little less sweet on each other than usual. There was no absolute quarrel. D' you think he'd have promised to pray for me if there was?"

"Have you spoken yet to your father?" asked the lady.

"How could I? I've not seen him since the thing was settled. Besides, what's the use? *He* can do nothing for me, an' don't care a button what I do or where I go."

"You are wrong, Shank, in thinking so. I *know* that he cares for you very much indeed. If he can do nothing for you *now*, he has at least given you your education, without which you could not do much for yourself."

" Well, of course I shall tell him whenever I see him," returned the youth, somewhat softened ; " and I'm aware he has a sort of sneaking fondness for me ; but I'm not going to ask his advice, because he knows nothing about the business. Besides, mother, I am old enough to judge for myself, and mean to take the advice of nobody."

"You are indeed old enough to judge for yourself," said Mrs. Leather, resuming her knitting, " and I don't wish to turn you from your plans. On the contrary, I will pray that God's blessing and protection may accompany you wherever you go, but you should not expect me to be instantaneously jubilant over an arrangement which will take you away from me for years perhaps."

This last consideration seemed to have some weight with the selfish youth.

" Well, well, mother," he said, rising, " don't take on about that. Travelling is not like what it used to be. A trip over the Atlantic and the Rocky Mountains is nothing to speak of now—a mere matter of a few weeks—so that a fellow can take a run home at any time to say ' How do' to his people. I'm going down now to see Smithers and tell him the news."

" Stay, I'll go with you—a bit of the way," cried May, jumping up and shaking back the curly brown hair which still hung in native freedom—and girlish fashion—on her shoulders.

May had a charming and rare capacity for getting ready to go out at a moment's notice. She merely threw on a coquettish straw hat, which had a knack of being always at hand, and which clung to her pretty head with a tenacity that rendered strings or elastic superfluous. One of her brother's companions—we don't know which—was once heard to say with fervour that no hat would be worth its ribbons that didn't cling powerfully to such a head without assistance! A shawl too, or cloak, was always at hand, somehow, and had this not been so May would have thrown over her shoulders an antimacassar or table-cloth rather than cause delay,—at least we think so, though we have no absolute authority for making the statement.

"Dear Shank," she said, clasping both hands over his arm as they walked slowly down the path that led to the shore, "is it really all true that you have been telling us? Have you fixed to go off with—with Mr. Ritson to California?"

"Quite true; I never was more in earnest in my life. By the way, sister mine, what made you colour up so when Ralph's name was mentioned? There, you're flushing again! Are you in love with him?"

"No, certainly not," answered the girl, with an air and tone of decision that made her brother laugh.

"Well, you needn't flare up so fiercely. You might be in love with a worse man. But why, then, do you blush?"

May was silent, and hung down her head.

"Come, May, you've never had any secrets from me. Surely you're not going to begin now—on the eve of my departure to a foreign land?"

"I would rather not talk about him at all," said the girl, looking up entreatingly.

But Shank looked down upon her sternly. He had assumed the parental *rôle*. "May, there is something in this that you ought not to conceal. I have a right to know it, as your brother—your protector."

Innocent though May was, she could not repress a faint smile at the idea of a protector who had been little else than a cause of anxiety in the past, and was now about to leave her to look after herself, probably for years to come. But she answered frankly, while another and a deeper blush overspread her face—

"I did not mean to speak of it, Shank, as you knew nothing, and I had hoped would never know anything about it, but since you insist, I must tell you that—that Mr. Ritson, I'm afraid, loves *me*— at least he——"

"Afraid! loves you! How do you know?" interrupted Shank quickly.

"Well, he said so—the last time we met."

"The rascal! Had he the audacity to ask you to marry him?—him—a beggar, without a sixpence except what his father gives him?"

"No, Shank, I would not let him get the length of that. I told him I was too young to—to think about such matters at all, and said that he must not speak to me again in such a way. But I was so surprised, flurried, and distressed, that I don't clearly remember what I said."

"And what did *he* say?" asked Shank, forgetting the parental *rôle* for a moment, and looking at May with a humorous smile.

"Indeed I can hardly tell. He made a great many absurd protestations, begged me to give him no decided answer just then, and said something about letting him write to me, but all I am quite sure of is that at last I had the courage to utter a very decided *NO*, and then ran away and left him."

"That was too sharp, May. Ralph is a first-rate fellow, with capital prospects. His father is rich and can give him a good start in life. He may come back in a few years with a fortune—not a bad kind of husband for a penniless lass."

"Shank!" exclaimed May, letting go her brother's arm and facing him with flashing eyes and heightened colour, "do you really think that a fortune would make me marry a man whom I did not love?"

"Certainly not, my dear sis," said the youth.

taking May's hand and drawing it again through his arm with an approving smile. "I never for a moment thought you capable of such meanness, but that is a very different thing from slamming the door in a poor fellow's face. You're not in love with anybody else. Ralph is a fine handsome young fellow. You might grow to like him in time—and if you did, a fortune, of course, would be no dis-advantage. Besides, he is to be my travelling companion, and might write to you about me if I were ill, or chanced to meet with an accident and were unable to write myself—don't you know?"

"He could in that case write to mother," said May, simply.

"So he could!" returned Shank, laughing. "I never thought o' that, my sharp sister."

They had reached the shore by that time. The tide was out; the sea was calm and the sun glinted brightly on the wavelets that sighed rather than broke upon the sands.

For some distance they sauntered in silence by the margin of the sea. The mind of each was busy with the same thought. Each was aware of that, and for some time neither seemed able to break the silence. The timid girl recovered her courage before the self-reliant man!

"Dear Shank," she said, pressing his arm, "you will probably be away for years."

"Yes, May—at least for a good long time."

"Oh forgive me, brother," continued the girl, with sudden earnestness, "but—but—you know your—your weakness——"

"Ay, May, I know it. Call it sin if you will—and my knowledge of it has something to do with my present determination, for, weak though I am, and bad though you think me——"

"But I *don't* think you *bad*, dear Shank," cried May, with tearful eyes; "I never said so, and never thought so, and——"

"Come, come, May," interrupted the youth, with something of banter in his manner, "you don't think me *good*, do you?"

"Well, no—not exactly," returned May, faintly smiling through her tears.

"Well, then, if I'm not good I must be bad, you know. There's no half-way house in this matter."

"Is there not, Shank? Is there not *very* good and *very* bad?"

"Oh, well, if you come to that, there's pretty-good, and rather-bad, and a host of other houses between these, such as goodish and baddish, but not one of them can be a *half-way* house."

"Oh yes, one of them can—*must* be."

"Which one, you little argumentative creature?" asked Shank.

"Why, middling-good of course."

"Wrong!" cried her brother, "doesn't middling-bad stand beside it, with quite as good a claim to be considered half-way? However, I won't press my victory too far. For the sake of peace we will agree that these are semi-detached houses in one block—and that will block the subject. But, to be serious again," he added, stopping and looking earnestly into his sister's face, "I wanted to speak to you on this weakness—this sin—and I thank you for breaking the ice. The truth is that I have felt for a good while past that conviviality——"

"Strong-drink, brother, call it by its right name," said May, gently pressing the arm on which she leaned.

"Well—have it so. Strong drink has been getting the better of me—mind I don't admit it *has* got the better of me yet—only *is getting*—and convivial comrades have had a great deal to do with it. Now, as you know, I'm a man of some decision of character, and I had long ago made up my mind to break with my companions. Of course I could not very well do this while—while I was—well, no matter why, but this offer just seemed to be a sort of godsend, for it will enable me to cut myself free at once, and the sea breezes and Rocky Mountain air and gold-hunting will, I expect, take away the desire for strong drink altogether."

"I hope it will—indeed I am *sure* it will if it is God's way of leading you," said May, with an air of confidence.

"Well, I don't know whether it is God who is leading me or——"

"Did you not call it a god-send just now?"

"Oh, but that's a mere form of speech, you know. However, I do know that it was on this very beach where we now stand that a friend led me for the first time to think seriously of this matter—more than a year ago."

"Indeed—who was it?" asked May eagerly.

"My chum and old school-fellow, poor Charlie Brooke," returned Shank, in a strangely altered voice.

Then he went on to tell of the conversation he and his friend had had on that beach, and it was not till he had finished that he became aware that his sister was weeping.

"Why, May, you're crying. What's the matter?"

"God bless him!" said May in fervent yet tremulous tones as she looked up in her brother's face. "Can you wonder at my feeling so strongly when you remember how kind Charlie always was to you—to all of us indeed—ever since he was a little boy at school with you; what a true-hearted and steady friend he has always been. And you called him poor Charlie just now, as if he were dead."

"True indeed, it is very, very sad, for we have great reason to fear the worst, and I have strong doubt that I shall never see my old chum again. But I won't give up hope, for it is no uncommon thing for men to be lost at sea, for years even, and to turn up at last, having been cast away on a desert island, like Robinson Crusoe, or something of that sort."

The thoughts which seemed to minister consolation to Shank Leather did not appear to afford much comfort to his sister, who hung her head and made no answer, while her companion went on—

"Yes, May, and poor Charlie was the first to make me feel as if I were a little selfish, though that, as you know, is not one of my conspicuous failings! His straightforwardness angered me a little at first, but his kindness made me think much of what he said, and—well, the upshot of it all is that I am going to California."

"I am glad—so glad and thankful he has had so much influence over you, dear Shank, and now, don't you think—that—that if Charlie were with you at this moment he would advise you not to go to Mr. Smithers to consult about your plans?"

For a few moments the brother's face betrayed a feeling of annoyance, but it quickly cleared away.

"You are right, May. Smithers is too much of a convivial harum-scarum fellow to be of much use in the way of giving sound advice. I'll go to see Jamieson instead. You can have no objection to him—surely. He's a quiet, sober sort of man, and never tries to tempt people or lead them into mischief—which is more than can be said of the other fellow.

"That is a very negative sort of goodness," returned May, smiling. "However, if you must go to see some one, Jamieson is better than Smithers; but why not come home and consult with mother and me?"

"Pooh! what can women know about such matters? No, no, May, when a fellow has to go into the pros and cons of Californian life it must be with *men.*"

"H'm! the men you associate with, having been at school and the desk all their lives up till now, must be eminently fitted to advise on Californian life! That did not occur to me at the first blush!" said May demurely.

"Go home, you cynical baggage, and help mother to knit," retorted Shank, with a laugh. "I intend to go and see Jamieson."

And he went. And the negatively good Jamieson, who never led people into temptation, had no objection to be led into that region himself, so they went together to make a passing call—a mere look in—on Smithers, who easily induced them to remain. The result was that the unselfish man with decision of character returned home in the early hours of morning—"screwed '!

CHAPTER X.

HOME-COMING AND UNEXPECTED SURPRISES.

UPWARDS of another year passed away, and at the end of that time a ship might have been seen approaching one of the harbours on the eastern seaboard of America. Her sails were worn and patched. Her spars were broken and spliced. Her rigging was ragged and slack, and the state of her hull can be best described by the word 'battered.' Everything in and about her bore evidence of a prolonged and hard struggle with the elements, and though she had at last come off victorious, her dilapidated appearance bore strong testimony to the deadly nature of the fight.

Her crew presented similar evidence. Not only were their garments ragged, threadbare, and patched, but the very persons of the men seemed to have been riven and battered by the tear and wear of the conflict. And no wonder; for the vessel was a South Sea whaler, returning home after a three years' cruise.

At first she had been blown far out of her course;

then she was very successful in the fishing, and then she was stranded on the reef of a coral island in such a position that, though protected from absolute destruction by the fury of the waves, she could not be got off for many months. At last the ingenuity and perseverance of one of her crew were rewarded by success. She was hauled once more into deep water and finally returned home.

The man who had been thus successful in saving the ship, and probably the lives of his mates—for it was a desolate isle, far out of the tracks of commerce —was standing in the bow of the vessel, watching the shore with his companions as they drew near. He was a splendid specimen of manhood, clad in a red shirt and canvas trousers, while a wide-awake took the place of the usual seafaring cap. He stood head and shoulders above his fellows.

Just as the ship rounded the end of the pier, which formed one side of the harbour, a small boat shot out from it. A little boy sculled the boat, and, apparently, had been ignorant of the ship's approach, for he gave a shout of alarm on seeing it and made frantic efforts to get out of its way. In his wild attempts to turn the boat he missed a stroke and went backwards into the sea.

At the same moment the lookout on the ship gave the order to put the helm hard a-starboard in a hurried shout.

Prompt obedience caused the ship to sheer off a

little, and her side just grazed the boat. All hands
on the forecastle gazed down anxiously for the boy's
reappearance.

Up he came next moment with a bubbling cry
and clutching fingers.

"He can't swim!" cried one.

"Out with a lifebelt!" shouted another.

Our tall seaman bent forward as they spoke, and,
just as the boy sank a second time, he shot like an
arrow into the water.

"He's all safe now," remarked a seaman quietly,
and with a nod of satisfaction, even before the
rescuer had reappeared.

And he was right. The red-shirted sailor rose
a moment later with the boy in his arms. Chuck-
ing the urchin into the boat he swam to the pier-
head with the smooth facility and speed of an otter
climbed the wooden piles with the ease of an
athlete; walked rapidly along the pier, and arrived
at the head of the harbour almost as soon as his
own ship.

"That's the tenth life he's saved since he came
aboard—to say nothin' o' savin' the ship herself,"
remarked the Captain to an inquirer, after the
vessel had reached her moorings. "An' none o' the
lives was as easy to manage as that one. Some o'
them much harder."

We will follow this magnificent seaman for a
time, good reader.

Having obtained permission to quit the South Sea whaler he walked straight to the office of a steam shipping company, and secured a fore-cabin passage to England. He went on board dressed as he had arrived, in the red shirt, ducks, and wide-awake—minus the salt water. The only piece of costume which he had added to his wardrobe was a huge double-breasted pilot-cloth coat, with buttons the size of an egg-cup. He was so unused, however, to such heavy clothing that he flung it off the moment he got on board the steamer, and went about thereafter in his red flannel shirt and ducks. Hence he came to be known by every one as Red Shirt.

This man, with his dark-blue eyes, deeply bronzed cheeks, fair hair, moustache, and beard, and tall herculean form, was nevertheless so soft and gentle in his manners, so ready with his smile and help and sympathy, that every man, woman, and child in the vessel adored him before the third day was over. Previous to that day many of the passengers, owing to internal derangements, were incapable of any affection, except self-love, and to do them justice they had not much even of that !

Arrived at Liverpool, Red Shirt, after seeing a poor invalid passenger safely to his abode in that city, and assisting one or two families with young children to find the stations, boats, or coaches that were more or less connected with their homes, got into a third-class carriage for London. On reaching the metropolis he at once took a ticket for *Scalford*.

Just as the train was on the point of starting two elderly gentlemen came on the platform, in that eager haste and confusion of mind characteristic of late passengers.

"This way, Captain," cried one, hailing the other, and pointing energetically with his brown silk umbrella to the Scalford carriages.

"No, no. It's at the next platform," returned the Captain frantically.

"I say it is *here*," shouted the first speaker sternly. "Come, sir, obey orders!"

They both made for an open carriage-door. It chanced to be a third class. A strong hand was held out to assist them in.

"Thank you," said the eldest elderly gentleman— he with the brown silk umbrella—turning to Red Shirt as he sat down and panted slightly.

"I feared that we'd be late, sir," remarked the other elderly gentleman on recovering breath.

"We are *not* late, Captain, but we should have been late for certain, if your obstinacy had held another half minute."

"Well, Mr. Crossley, I admit that I made a mistake about the place, but you must allow that I made no mistake about the hour. I was sure that my chronometer was right. If there's one thing on earth that I can trust to as reg'lar as the sun, it is this chronometer (pulling it out as he spoke), and it never fails. As I always said to my missis, 'Maggie,' I used to say, 'when you find this chronometer fail——' 'Oh! bother you an' your chronometer,' she would reply, takin' the wind out o' my sails—for my missus has a free-an'-easy way o' doin' that——"

"You 've just come off a voyage, young sir, if I mistake not," said Crossley, turning to Red Shirt, for he had quite as free-and-easy a way of taking the wind out of Captain Stride's sails as the "missus."

"Yes; I have just returned," answered Red Shirt, in a low soft voice, which scarcely seemed appropriate to his colossal frame. His red garment, by the way, was at the time all concealed by the pilot-coat, excepting the collar.

"Going home for a spell, I suppose?" said Crossley.

"Yes."

"May I ask where you last hailed from?" said Captain Stride, with some curiosity, for there was something in the appearance of this nautical stranger which interested him.

"From the southern seas. I have been away a long while in a South Sea whaler."

"Ah, indeed?—a rough service that."

"Rather rough; but I didn't enter it intentionally. I was picked up at sea, with some of my mates, in

an open boat, by the whaler. She was on the outward voyage, and couldn't land us anywhere, so we
were obliged to make up our minds to join as
hands."

"Strange!" murmured Captain Stride. "Then
you were wrecked somewhere—or your ship foun-
dered, mayhap—eh ?"

"Yes, we were wrecked—on a coral reef."

"Well now, young man, that is a strange coincidence. I was wrecked myself on a coral reef in
the very same seas, nigh three years ago. Isn't
that odd ?"

"Dear me, this is very interesting," put in Mr.
Crossley; "and, as Captain Stride says, a somewhat
strange coincidence."

"*Is* it so very strange, after all," returned Red
Shirt, "seeing that the Pacific is full of sunken
coral reefs, and vessels are wrecked there more or
less every year ?"

"Well, there's some truth in that," observed the
Captain. "Did you say it was a sunk reef your
ship struck on ?"

"Yes; quite sunk. No part visible. It was
calm weather at the time, and a clear night."

"Another coincidence!" exclaimed Stride, becoming still more interested. "Calm and clear, too,
when I was wrecked !"

"Curious," remarked Red Shirt in a cool indifferent tone, that began to exasperate the Captain.

"Yet, after all, there are a good many calm and clear nights in the Pacific, as well as coral reefs."

"Why, young man," cried Stride in a tone that made old Crossley smile, "you seem to think nothing at all of coincidences. It's very seldom— almost never—that one hears of so many coincidences happening on *this* side o' the line all at once —don't you see?"

"I see," returned Red Shirt; "and the same, exactly, may be said of the *other* side o' the line. I very seldom—almost never—heard of so many out there; which itself may be called a coincidence, d'ee see? a sort of negative similarity."

"Young man, I would suspect you were jesting with me," returned the Captain, "but for the fact that you told me of your experiences first, before you could know that mine would coincide with them so exactly."

"Your conclusions are very just, sir," rejoined Red Shirt, with a grave and respectful air; "but of course coincidences never go on in an unbroken chain. They *must* cease sooner or later. We left our wreck in *three* boats. No doubt you——"

"There again!" cried the Captain in blazing astonishment, as he removed his hat and wiped his heated brow, while Mr. Crossley's eyes opened to their widest extent. "*We* left our wreck in *three* boats! My ship's name was——"

" The *Walrus*," said Red Shirt quietly, "and her Captain's name was Stride !"

Old Crossley had reached the stage that is known as petrified with astonishment. The Captain being unable to open his eyes wider dropped his lower jaw instead.

"Surely," continued Red Shirt, removing his wide-awake, and looking steadily at his companions, " I must have changed very much indeed when two of my——"

" Brooke !" exclaimed Crossley, grasping one of the sailor's hands.

" Charlie !" gasped the Captain, seizing the other hand.

What they all said after reaching this point it is neither easy nor necessary to record. Perhaps it may be as well to leave it to the reader's vivid imagination. Suffice it to say, that our hero irritated the Captain no longer by his callous indifference to coincidences. In the midst of the confusion of hurried question and short reply, he pulled them up with the sudden query anxiously put—

" But now, what of my mother ? "

" Well—excellently well in health, my boy," said Crossley, "but wofully low in spirits about your-self—Charlie. Yet nothing will induce her to entertain the idea that you have been drowned. Of course we have been rather glad of this—though most of our friends, Charlie, have given you up for lost long ago. May Leather, too, has been much the same way of thinking, so she has naturally been a great comfort to your mother."

"God bless her for that. She's a good little girl," said Charlie.

"Little girl," repeated both elderly gentlemen in a breath, and bursting into a laugh. "You forget, lad," said the Captain, "that three years or so makes a considerable change in girls of her age. She's a tall, handsome young woman now; ay, and a good-looking one too. Almost as good-lookin' as what my missus was about her age—an' not unlike my little Mag in the face—the one you rescued, you remember—who is also a strappin' lass now."

"I'm very glad to hear they are well, Captain," said Charlie; "and, Shank, what of——"

He stopped, for the grave looks of his friends told him that something was wrong.

"Gone to the dogs," said the Captain.

"Nay, not quite gone—but going fast."

"And the father?"

"Much as he was, Charlie, only somewhat more deeply sunk. The fact is," continued Crossley, "it is this very matter that takes us down to Sealford to-day. We have just had fresh news of Shank—who is in America—and I want to consult with Mrs. Leather about him. You see I have agents out there who may be able to help us to save him."

"From drink, I suppose?" interposed our hero.

"From himself, Charlie, and that includes drink and a great deal more. I dare say you are aware—at least if you are not I now tell you—that I have long taken great interest in Mrs. Leather and her family, and would go a long way, and give a great deal, to save Shank. You know—no, of course you don't, I forgot—that he threw up his situation in my office—Withers & Co. (ay, you may smile, my lad, but we humbugged you and got the better of you that time. Didn't we, Captain?) Well, Shank was induced by that fellow Ralph Ritson to go away to some gold-mine or other worked by his father in California, but when they reached America they got news of the failure of the Company and the death of old Ritson. Of course the poor fellows were at once thrown on their own resources, but instead of facing life like men they took to gambling. The usual results followed. They lost all they had and went off to Texas or some such wild place, and for a long time were no more heard of. At last, just the other day, a letter came from Ritson to Mrs. Leather, telling her that her son is very ill—perhaps dying—in some out o' the way place. Ritson was nursing him, but, being ill himself, unable to work, and without means, it would help them greatly if some money could be sent—even though only a small sum."

Charlie Brooke listened to this narrative with

compressed brows, and remained silent a few seconds. "My poor chum!" he exclaimed at length. Then a flash of fire seemed to gleam in his blue eyes as he added, "If I had that fellow Ritson by the——"

He stopped abruptly, and the fire in the eyes died out, for it was no part of our hero's character to boast—much less to speak harshly of men behind their backs.

"Has money been sent?" he asked.

"Not yet. It is about that business that I'm going to call on poor Mrs. Leather now. We must be careful, you see. I have no reason, it is true, to believe that Ritson is deceiving us, but when a youth of no principle writes to make a sudden demand for money, it behoves people to think twice before they send it."

" Ay, to think three times—perhaps even four or five," broke in the Captain, with stern emphasis. "I know Ralph Ritson well, the scoundrel, an' if I had aught to do wi' it I'd not send him a penny. As I said to my——"

"Does your mother know of your arrival?" asked Mr. Crossley abruptly.

"No; I meant to take her by surprise."

"Humph! Just like you young fellows. In some things you have no more brains than geese. Being made of cast-iron and shoe-leather you assume that everybody else is, or ought to be, made of the same raw material. Don't you know that surprises of this sort are apt to kill delicate people?"

Charlie smiled by way of reply.

"No, sir," continued the old gentleman firmly, "I won't let you take her by surprise. While I go round to the Leathers my good friend Captain Stride will go in advance of you to Mrs. Brooke's and break the news to her. He is accustomed to deal with ladies."

"Right you are, sir," said the gratified Captain, removing his hat and wiping his brow. "As I said, no later than yesterday to——"

A terrific shriek from the steam-whistle, and a plunge into the darkness of a tunnel stopped—and thus lost to the world for ever—what the Captain said upon that occasion.

CHAPTER XI.

TELLS OF HAPPY MEETINGS AND SERIOUS CONSULTATIONS.

WHETHER Captain Stride executed his commission well or not we cannot tell, and whether the meeting of Mrs. Brooke with her long-lost son came to near killing or not we will not tell. Enough to know that they met, and that the Captain—with that delicacy of feeling so noticeable in seafaring men—went outside the cottage door and smoked his pipe while the meeting was in progress. After having given sufficient time, as he said, "for the first o' the squall to blow over," he summarily snubbed his pipe, put it into his vest pocket, and re-entered.

"Now, missus, you'll excuse me, ma'am, for cuttin' in atween you, but this business o' the Leathers is pressin', an' if we are to hold a confabulation wi' the family about it, why——"

"Ah, to be sure, Captain Stride is right," said Mrs. Brooke, turning to her stalwart son, who was seated on the sofa beside her. "This is a very, *very* sad business about poor Shank. You

I

had better go to them, Charlie. I will follow you in a short time.

"Mr. Crossley is with them at this moment. I forgot to say so, mother."

"Is he? I'm *very* glad of that," returned the widow. "He has been a true friend to us all. Go, Charlie. But stay. I see May coming. The dear child always comes to me when there is anything good or sorrowful to tell. But she comes from the wrong direction. Perhaps she does not yet know of Mr. Crossley's arrival."

"May! Can it be?" exclaimed Charlie in an undertone of surprise as he observed, through the window, the girl who approached.

And well might he be surprised, for this, although the same May, was very different from the girl he left behind him. The angles of girlhood had given place to the rounded lines of young womanhood. The rich curly brown hair, which used to whirl wildly in the sea-breezes, was gathered up in a luxuriant mass behind her graceful head, and from the forehead it was drawn back in two wavy bands, in defiance of fashion, which at that time was beginning to introduce the detestable modern fringe. Perhaps we are not quite unbiassed in our judgment of the said fringe, for it is intimately associated in our mind with the savages of North America, whose dirty red faces, in years past, were wont to glower at us from beneath just such a fringe, long before it was adopted by the fair dames of England !

In other respects, however, May was little changed, except that the slightest curl of sadness about her eyebrows made her face more attractive than ever, as she nodded pleasantly to the Captain, who had hastened to the door to meet her.

"So glad to see you, Captain Stride," she said, shaking hands with unfeminine heartiness. "Have you been to see mother? I have just been having a walk before——"

She stopped as if transfixed, for at that moment she caught sight of Charlie and his mother through the open door.

Poor May flushed to the roots of her hair; then she turned deadly pale, and would have fallen had not the gallant Captain caught her in his arms. But by a powerful effort of will she recovered herself in time to avoid a scene.

"The sight of you reminded me so strongly of our dear Shank!" she stammered, when Charlie, hastening forward, grasped both her hands and shook them warmly. "Besides—some of us thought you were dead."

"No wonder you thought of Shank," returned Charlie, "for he and I used to be so constantly together. But don't be cast down, May. We'll get Shank out of his troubles yet."

"Yes, and you know he has Ralph Ritson with

him," said Mrs. Brooke; "and he, although not quite as steady as we could wish, will be sure to care for such an old friend in his sickness. But you'd better go, Charlie, and see Mrs. Leather. They will be sure to want you and Captain Stride. May will remain here with me. Sit down beside me, dear, I want to have a chat with you."

"Perhaps, ma'am, if I make so bold," interposed the Captain, "Mr. Crossley may want to have Miss May also at the council of war."

"Mr. Crossley! is *he* with my mother?" asked the girl eagerly.

"Yes, Miss May, he is."

"Then I *must* be there. Excuse me, dear Mrs. Brooke."

And without more ado May ran out of the house. She was followed soon after by Charlie and the Captain, and Mrs. Brooke was left alone, expressing her thankfulness and joy of heart in a few silent tears over her knitting.

There was a wonderful similarity in many respects between Mrs. Brooke and her friend Mrs. Leather. They both knitted—continuously and persistently. This was a convenient if not a powerful bond, for it enabled them to sit for hours together—busy, yet free to talk. They were both invalids—a sympathetic bond of considerable strength. They held the same religious views—an indispensable bond where two people have to be much together, and are in earnest. They were both poor—a natural bond which draws people of a certain kind very close together, physically as well as spiritually—and both, up to this time at least, had long-absent and semi-lost sons. Even in the matter of daughters they might be said, in a sense, to be almost equal, for May, loving each, was a daughter to both Lastly, in this matter of similarity, the two ladies were good—good as gold, according to Captain Stride, and he ought to have been an authority, for he frequently visited them and knew all their affairs. Fortunately for both ladies, Mrs. Brooke was by far the stronger-minded—hence they never quarrelled!

In Mrs. Leather's parlour a solemn conclave was seated round the parlour table. They were very earnest, for the case under consideration was urgent, as well as very pitiful. Poor Mrs. Leather's face was wet with tears, and the pretty brown eyes of May were not dry. They had had a long talk over the letter from Ritson, which was brief and to the point, but meagre as to details.

"I rather like the letter, considering who wrote it," observed Mr. Crossley, laying it down after a fourth perusal. "You see he makes no whining or discontented reference to the hardness of their luck, which young scapegraces are so fond of doing; nor does he make effusive professions of regret or repentance, which hypocrites are so prone to do. I think it bears the stamp of being genuine on the face of it. At least it appears to be straightforward."

"I 'm so glad you think so, Mr. Crossley," said Mrs. Leather; "for Mr. Ritson is such a pleasant young man—and so good-looking, too!"

The old gentleman and the Captain both burst into a laugh at this.

"I 'm afraid," said the former, "that good looks are no guarantee for good behaviour. However, I have made up my mind to send him a small sum of money—not to Shank, Mrs. Leather, so you need not begin to thank me. I shall send it to Ritson."

"Well, thank you all the same," interposed the lady, taking up her knitting and resuming operations below the table, gazing placidly all the while at her friends like some consummate conjuror, "for Ralph will be sure to look after Shank."

"The only thing that puzzles me is, how are we to get it sent to such an out-o'-the-way place— Traitor's Trap! It 's a bad name, and the stupid fellow makes no mention of any known town near to it, though he gives the post-office. If I only knew its exact whereabouts I might get some one to take the money to him, for I have agents in many parts of America."

After prolonged discussion of the subject, Mr. Crossley returned to town to make inquiries, and the Captain went to take his favourite walk by the

sea-shore, where he was wont, when paying a visit
to Sealford, to drive the Leathers' little dog half-
mad with delight by throwing stones into the sea
for Scraggy to go in for—which he always did,
though he never fetched them out.

In the course of that day Charlie Brooke left his
mother to take a stroll, and naturally turned in the
direction of the sea. When half-way through the
lane with the high banks on either side he encountered May.

"What a pleasant pretty girl she has become!"
was his thought as she drew near.

"Nobler and handsomer than ever!" was hers as
he approached.

The thoughts of both sent a flush to the face of
each, but the colour scarcely showed through the
bronzed skin of the man.

"Why, what a woman you have grown, May!"
said Charlie, grasping her hand, and attempting to
resume the old familiar terms—with, however,
imperfect success.

"Isn't that natural?" asked May, with a glance
and a little laugh.

That glance and that little laugh, insignificant in
themselves, tore a veil from the eyes of Charlie
Brooke. He had always been fond of May Leather,
after a fashion. *Now* it suddenly rushed upon him
that he was fond of her after another fashion! He
was a quick thinker and just reasoner. A poor

man without a profession and no prospects has no right to try to gain the affections of a girl. He became grave instantly.

"May," he said, "will you turn back to the shore with me for a little? I want to have a talk about Shank. I want you to tell me all you know about him. Don't conceal anything. I feel as if I had a right to claim your confidence, for, as you know well, he and I have been like brothers since we were little boys."

May had turned at once, and the tears filled her eyes as she told the sad story. It was long, and the poor girl was graphic in detail. We can give but the outline here.

Shank had gone off with Ritson not long after the sailing of the *Walrus*. On reaching America, and hearing of the failure of the company that worked the gold mine, and of old Ritson's death, they knew not which way to turn. It was a tremendous blow, and seemed to have rendered them reckless, for they soon took to gambling. At first they remained in New York, and letters came home pretty regularly, in which Shank always expressed hopes of getting more respectable work. He did not conceal their mode of gaining a livelihood, but defended it on the ground that "a man must live!"

For a time the letters were cheerful. The young men were "lucky." Then came a change of luck, and a consequent change in the letters, which came less frequently. At last there arrived one from Shank, both the style and penmanship of which told that he had not forsaken the great curse of his life —strong drink. It told of disaster, and of going off to the "Rockies" with a party of "discoverers," though what they were to discover was not mentioned.

"From that date till now," said May in conclusion, "we have heard nothing about them till this letter came from Mr. Ritson, telling of dear Shank being so ill, and asking for money."

"I wish any one were with Shank rather than that man," said Charlie sternly; "I have no confidence in him whatever, and I knew him well as a boy."

"Nevertheless, I think we may trust him. Indeed I feel sure he won't desert his wounded comrade," returned May, with a blush.

The youth did not observe the blush. His thoughts were otherwise engaged, and his eyes were at the moment fixed on a far-off part of the shore, where Captain Stride could be seen urging on the joyful Scraggy to his fruitless labours.

"I wish I could feel as confident of him as you do, May. However, misfortune as well as experience may have made him a wiser, perhaps a better, man. But what troubles me most is the uncertainty of the money that Mr. Crossley is going to send ever reaching its destination."

"Oh! if we only knew some one in New York who would take it to them," said May, looking piteously at the horizon, as if she were apostrophising some one on the other side of the Atlantic.

"Why, you talk as if New York and Traitor's Trap were within a few miles of each other," said Charlie, smiling gently. "They are hundreds of miles apart."

"Well, I suppose they are. But I feel so anxious about Shank when I think of the dear boy lying ill, perhaps dying, in a lonely place far far away from us all, and no one but Mr. Ritson to care for him! If I were only a man I would go to him myself."

She broke down at this point, and put her handkerchief to her face.

"Don't cry, May," began the youth in sore perplexity, for he knew not how to comfort the poor girl in the circumstances, but fortunately Captain Stride caught sight of them at the moment, and gave them a stentorian hail.

"Hi! halloo! back your to-o-o-ps'ls. I'll overhaul ye in a jiffy."

How long a nautical jiffy may be we know not, but, in a remarkably brief space of time, considering the shortness and thickness of his sea-legs, the Captain was alongside, blowing, as he said, "like a grampus."

That night Charlie Brooke sat with his mother in

her parlour. They were alone—their friends having considerately left them to themselves on this their first night.

They had been talking earnestly about past and present, for the son had much to learn about old friends and comrades, and the mother had much to tell.

"And now, mother," said Charlie, at the end of a brief pause, "what about the future?"

"Surely, my boy, it is time enough to talk about that to-morrow, or next day. You are not obliged to think of the future before you have spent even one night in your old room."

"Not absolutely obliged, mother. Nevertheless, I should like to speak about it. Poor Shank is heavy on my mind, and when I heard all about him to-day from May, I—— She's wonderfully improved that girl, mother. Grown quite pretty?"

"Indeed she is—and as good as she's pretty," returned Mrs. Brooke, with a furtive glance at her son.

"She broke down when talking about Shank to-day, and I declare she looked quite beautiful! Evidently Shank's condition weighs heavily on her mind."

"Can you wonder, Charlie?"

"Of course not. It's natural, and I quite sympathised with her when she exclaimed, 'If I were only a man I would go to him myself.'"

"That's natural too, my son. I have no doubt she would, poor dear girl, if she were only a man."

"Do you know, mother, I've not been able to get that speech out of my head all this afternoon. 'If I were a man—if I were a man,' keeps ringing in my ears like the chorus of an old song, and then——"

"Well, Charlie, what then?" asked Mrs. Brooke, with a puzzled glance.

"Why, then, somehow the chorus has changed in my brain and it runs—'I *am* a man! I *am* a man!'"

"Well?" asked the mother, with an anxious look.

"Well—that being so, I have made up my mind that *I* will go out to Traitor's Trap and carry the money to Shank, and look after him myself. That is, if you will let me."

"O Charlie! how can you talk of it?" said Mrs. Brooke, with a distressed look. "I have scarcely had time to realise the fact that you have come home, and to thank God for it, when you begin to talk of leaving me again—perhaps for years, as before."

"Nay, mother mine, you jump to conclusions too hastily. What I propose is not to go off again on a long voyage, but to take a run of a few days in a first-class steamer across what the Americans call the big fish-pond; then go across country comfortably by rail; after that hire a horse and have a gallop somewhere or other; find out Shank and bring him home. The whole thing might be done in a few weeks, and no chance, almost, of being wrecked."

"I don't know, Charlie," returned Mrs. Brooke, in a sad tone, as she laid her hand on her son's arm and stroked it. "As you put it, the thing sounds all very easy, and no doubt it would be a grand, a noble thing to rescue Shank—but—but, why talk of it to-night, my dear boy? It is late. Go to bed, Charlie, and we will talk it over in the morning."

"How pleasantly familiar that 'Go to bed, Charlie,' sounds," said the son, laughing, as he rose up.

"You did not always think it pleasant," returned the good lady, with a sad smile.

"That's true, but I think it uncommonly pleasant *now*. Good-night, mother."

"Good-night, my son, and God bless you."

CHAPTER XII.

CHANGES THE SCENE CONSIDERABLY !

WE must transport our reader now to a locality somewhere in the region lying between New Mexico and Colorado. Here, in a mean-looking out-of-the-way tavern, a number of rough-looking men were congregated, drinking, gambling, and spinning yarns. Some of them belonged to the class known as cow-boys—men of rugged exterior, iron constitutions, powerful frames, and apparently reckless dispositions, though underneath the surface there was considerable variety of character to be found.

The landlord of the inn—if we may so call it, for it was little better than a big shanty—was known by the name of David. He was a man of cool courage. His customers knew this latter fact well, and were also aware that, although he carried no weapon on his person, he had several revolvers in handy places under his counter, with the use of which he was extremely familiar and expert.

In the midst of a group of rather noisy characters

who smoked and drank in one corner of this inn or shanty, there was seated on the end of a packing-case, a man in the prime of life, who, even in such rough company, was conspicuously rugged. His leathern costume betokened him a hunter, or trapper, and the sheepskin leggings, with the wool outside, showed that he was at least at that time a horseman. Unlike most of his comrades, he wore Indian moccasins, with spurs strapped to them. Also a cap of the broad-brimmed order. The point about him that was most striking at first sight was his immense breadth of shoulder and depth of chest, though in height he did not equal many of the men around him. As one became acquainted with the man, however, his massive proportions had not so powerful an effect on the mind of an observer as the quiet simplicity of his expression and manner. Good-nature seemed to lurk in the lines about his eyes and the corners of his mouth, which latter had the peculiarity of turning down instead of up when he smiled; yet withal there was a stern gravity about him that forbade familiarity.

The name of the man was Hunky Ben, and the strangest thing about him—that which puzzled these wild men most—was that he neither drank nor smoked nor gambled! He made no pretence of abstaining on principle. One of the younger men, who was blowing a stiff cloud, ventured to ask him whether he really thought these things wrong.

"Well, now," he replied quietly, with a twinkle in his eye, "I'm no parson, boys, that I should set up to diskiver what's right an' what's wrong. I've got my own notions on them points, you bet, but I'm not goin' to preach 'em. As to smokin', I won't make a smoked herrin' o' my tongue to please anybody. Besides, I don't want to smoke, an' why should I do a thing I don't want to just because other people does it? Why should I make a new want when I've got no end o' wants a'ready that's hard enough to purvide for? Drinkin's all very well if a man wants Dutch courage, but I don't want it—no, nor French courage, nor German, nor Chinee, havin' got enough o' the article home-growed to sarve my purpus. When that's used up I may take to drinkin'—who knows? Same wi' gamblin'. I've no desire to bust up any man, an' I don't want to be busted up myself, you bet. No doubt drinkin', smokin', an' gamblin' makes men jolly—them at least that's tough an' that wins!— but I'm jolly without 'em, boys,—jolly as a cotton-tail rabbit just come of age."

"An' ye look it, old man," returned the young fellow, puffing cloudlets with the utmost vigour; "but come, Ben, won't ye spin us a yarn about your frontier life?"

"Yes, do, Hunky," cried another in an entreating voice, for it was well known all over that region that the bold hunter was a good story-teller, and as he had served a good deal on the frontier as guide to the United States troops, it was understood that he had much to tell of a thrilling and adventurous kind; but although the men about him ceased to talk and looked at him with expectancy, he shook his head, and would not consent to be drawn out.

"No, boys, it can't be done to-day," he said; "I've no time, for I'm bound for Quester Creek in hot haste, an' am only waitin' here for my pony to freshen up a bit. The Redskins are goin' to give us trouble there by all accounts."

"The red devils!" exclaimed one of the men, with a savage oath; "they're always givin' us trouble."

"That," returned Hunky Ben, in a soft voice, as he glanced mildly at the speaker,—"that is a sentiment I heer'd expressed almost exactly in the same words, though in Capatchee lingo, some time ago by a Redskin chief—only he said it was pale-faced devils who troubled *him*. I wonder which is worst. They can't both be worst, you know!"

This remark was greeted with a laugh, and a noisy discussion thereupon began as to the comparative demerits of the two races, which was ere long checked by the sound of a galloping horse outside. Next moment the door opened, and a very tall man of commanding presence and bearing entered the room, took off his hat, and looked round with a slight bow to the company

K

There was nothing commanding, however, in the quiet voice with which he asked the landlord if he and his horse could be put up there for the night.

The company knew at once, from the cut of the stranger's tweed suit, as well as his tongue, that he was an Englishman, not much used to the ways of the country—though, from the revolver and knife in his belt, and the repeating rifle in his hand, he seemed to be ready to meet the country on its own terms by doing in Rome as Rome does.

On being told that he could have a space on the floor to lie on, which he might convert into a bed if he had a blanket with him, he seemed to make up his mind to remain, asked for food, and while it was preparing went out to attend to his horse. Then, returning, he went to a retired corner of the room, and flung himself down at full length on a vacant bench, as if he were pretty well exhausted with fatigue.

The simple fare of the hostelry was soon ready; and when the stranger was engaged in eating it, he asked a cow-boy beside him how far it was to Traitor's Trap.

At the question there was a perceptible lull in the conversation, and the cow-boy, who was a very coarse forbidding specimen of his class, said that he guessed Traitor's Trap was distant about twenty mile or so.

"Are you goin' thar, stranger?" he asked, eyeing his questioner curiously.

"Yes, I'm going there," answered the Englishman; "but from what I've heard of the road, at the place where I stayed last night, I don't like to go on without a guide and daylight—though I would much prefer to push on to-night if it were possible."

"Wall, stranger, whether possible or not," returned the cow-boy, "it's an ugly place to go past, for there's a gang o' cut-throats there that's kep' the country fizzin' like ginger-beer for some time past. A man that's got to go past Traitor's Trap should go by like a greased thunderbolt, an' he should never go alone."

"Is it, then, such a dangerous place?" asked the Englishman, with a smile that seemed to say he thought his informant was exaggerating.

"Dangerous!" exclaimed the cow-boy. "Ay, an' will be as long as Buck Tom an' his boys are unhung. Why, stranger, I'd get my life insured, you bet, before I'd go thar again—except with a big crowd o' men. It was along in June last year I went up that way; there was nobody to go with me, an' I was forced to do it by myself—for I *had* to go—so I spunked up, saddled Bluefire, an' sloped. I got on lovely till I came to a pass just on t'other side o' Traitor's Trap, when I began to cheer up, thinkin' I'd got off square; but I hadn't gone another hundred yards when up starts Buck

Tom an' his men with 'hands up.' I went head down flat on my saddle instead, I was so riled. Bang went a six-shooter, an' the ball just combed my back hair. I suppose Buck was so took by surprise at a single man darin' to disobey his orders that he missed. Anyhow I socked spurs into Blue-fire, an' made a break for the open country ahead. They made after me like locomotives wi' the safety-valves blocked, but Bluefire was more 'n a match for 'em. They kep' blazin' away all the time too, but never touched me, though I heard the balls whistlin' past for a good while. Bluefire an' me went, you bet, like a nor'easter in a passion, an' at last they gave it up. No, stranger, take my advice an' don't go past Traitor's Trap alone. I wouldn't go there at all if I could help it."

"I don't intend to go past it. I mean to go *into* it," said the Englishman, with a short laugh, as he laid down his knife and fork, having finished his slight meal; "and, as I cannot get a guide, I shall be forced to go alone."

"Stranger," said the cow-boy in surprise, "d'ye want to meet wi' Buck Tom?"

"Not particularly."

"An' are ye aware that Buck Tom is one o' the most hardened, sanguinacious blackguards in all Colorado?"

"I did not know it before, but I suppose I may believe it now."

As he spoke the Englishman rose and went out to fetch the blanket which was strapped to his saddle. In going out he brushed close past a man who chanced to enter at the same moment.

The new comer was also a tall and strikingly handsome man, clothed in the picturesque garments of the cow-boy, and fully armed. He strode up to the counter, with an air of proud defiance, and demanded drink. It was supplied him. He tossed it off quickly, without deigning a glance at the assembled company. Then in a deep-toned voice he asked—

"Has the Rankin Creek Company sent that account and the money?"

Profound silence had fallen on the whole party in the room the moment this man entered. They evidently looked at him with profound interest if not respect.

"Yes, Buck Tom," answered the landlord, in his grave off-hand manner. "They have sent it, and authorised me to pay you the balance."

He turned over some papers for a few minutes, during which Buck Tom did not condescend to glance to one side or the other, but kept his eye fixed sternly on the landlord.

At that moment the Englishman re-entered, went to his corner, spread his blanket on the floor, lay down, put his wide-awake over his eyes, and resigned himself to repose, apparently unaware that anything special was going on, and obtusely blind to the quiet but eager signals wherewith the cow-boy was seeking to direct his attention to Buck Tom.

In a few minutes the landlord found the paper he wanted, and began to look over it.

" The company owes you," he said, " three hundred dollars ten cents for the work done," said the landlord slowly.

Buck nodded his head as if satisfied with this.

" Your account has run on a long while," continued the landlord, " and they bid me explain that there is a debit of two hundred and ninety-nine dollars against you. Balance in your favour one dollar ten cents."

A dark frown settled on Buck Tom's countenance, as the landlord laid the balance due on the counter, and for a few moments he seemed in uncertainty as to what he should do, while the landlord stood conveniently near to a spot where one of his revolvers lay. Then Buck turned on his heel, and was striding towards the door, when the landlord called him back.

" Excuse my stopping you, Buck Tom," he said, " but there's a gentleman here who wants a guide to Traitor's Trap. Mayhap you wouldn't object to——"

" Where is he ?" demanded Buck, wheeling round, with a look of slight surprise.

"There," said the landlord, pointing to the dark corner where the big Englishman lay, apparently fast asleep, with his hat pulled well down over his eyes.

Buck Tom looked at the sleeping figure for a few moments.

"H'm! well, I might guide him," he said, with something of a grim smile, "but I'm travelling too fast for comfort. He might hamper me. By the way," he added, looking back as he laid his hand on the door, "you may tell the Rankin Creek Company, with my compliments, to buy a new lock to their office door, for I intend to call on them some day soon and balance up that little account on a new system of 'rithmetic! Tell them I give 'em leave to clap the one dollar ten cents to the credit of their charity account."

Another moment and Buck Tom was gone. Before the company in the tavern had quite recovered the use of their tongues, the hoofs of his horse were heard rattling along the road which led in the direction of Traitor's Trap.

"Was that really Buck Tom?" asked Hunky Ben, in some surprise.

"Ay—or his ghost," answered the landlord.

"I can swear to him, for I saw him as clear as I see you the night he split after me," said the cowboy, who had warned the Englishman.

"Why didn't you put a bullet into him to-night, Crux?" asked a comrade.

"Just so—you had a rare chance," remarked another of the cow-boys, with something of a sneer in his tone.

"Because I'm not yet tired o' my life," replied Crux, indignantly. "Buck Tom has got eyes in the back o' his head, I do believe, and shoots dead like a flash——"

"Not that time he missed you at Traitor's Trap, I think," said the other.

"Of course not—'cause we was both mounted that time, and scurryin' over rough ground like wild-cats. The best o' shots would miss thar an' thus. Besides, Buck Tom took nothin' from me, an' ye wouldn't have me shoot a man for missin' me —surely. If you're so fond o' killin', why didn't you shoot him yourself?—*you* had a rare chance!"

Crux grinned—for his ugly mouth could not compass a smile—as he thought thus to turn the tables on his comrade.

"Well, he's got clear off, anyhow, returned the comrade, an' it's a pity, for——"

He was interrupted by the Englishman raising himself and asking in a sleepy tone if there was likely to be moonlight soon.

The company seemed to think him moonstruck to ask such a question, but one of them replied that the moon was due in half an hour.

"You've lost a good chance, sir," said Crux, who had a knack of making all his communications as disagreeably as possible, unless they chanced to be unavoidably agreeable, in which case he made the worst of them. "Buck Tom hisself has just bin here, an' might have agreed to guide you to Traitor's Trap if you'd made him a good offer."

"Why did you not awake me?" asked the Englishman in a reproachful tone, as he sprang up, grasped his blanket hastily, threw down a piece of money on the counter, and asked if the road wasn't straight and easy for a considerable distance.

"Straight as an arrow for ten mile," said the landlord, as he laid down the change which the Englishman put into an apparently well-filled purse.

"I'll guide you, stranger, for five dollars," said Crux.

"I want no guide," returned the other, somewhat brusquely as he left the room.

A minute or two later he was heard to pass the door on horseback at a sharp trot.

"Poor lad, he'll run straight into the wolf's den; but why he wants to do it puzzles me," remarked the landlord, as he carefully cleaned a tankard. "But he would take no warning."

"The wolf doesn't seem half as bad as he's bin painted," said Hunky Ben, rising and offering to pay his score.

"Hallo, Hunky—not goin' to skip, are ye?" asked Crux.

"I told ye I was in a hurry. Only waitin' to

rest my pony. My road is the same as the stranger's, at least part o' the way. I'll overhaul an' warn him."

A few minutes more and the broad-shouldered scout was also galloping along the road or track which led towards the Rocky mountains in the direction of Traitor's Trap.

CHAPTER XIII.

HUNKY BEN IS SORELY PERPLEXED.

IT was one of Hunky Ben's few weaknesses to take pride in being well mounted. When he left the tavern he bestrode one of his best steeds—a black charger of unusual size, which he had purchased while on a trading trip in Texas—and many a time had he ridden it while guiding the United States troops in their frequent expeditions against ill-disposed Indians. Taken both together it would have been hard to equal, and impossible to match, Hunky Ben and his coal-black mare.

From the way that Ben rode, on quitting the tavern, it might have been supposed that legions of wild Indians were at his heels. But after going about a few miles at racing speed he reined in, and finally pulled up at a spot where a very slight pathway diverged. Here he sat quite still for a few minutes in meditation. Then he muttered softly to himself—for Ben was often and for long periods alone in the woods and on the plains, and found it somewhat "sociable-like" to mutter his thoughts audibly:

"You've not cotched him up after all, Ben," he said. "Black Polly a'most equals a streak o' lightnin', but the Britisher got too long a start o' ye, an' he's clearly in a hurry. Now, if I follow on he'll hear your foot-falls, Polly, an' p'raps be scared into goin' faster to his doom. Whereas, if I go off the track here an' drive ahead so as to git to the Blue Fork before him, I'll be able to stop the Buck's little game, an' save the poor fellow's life. Buck is sure to stop him at the Blue Fork, for it's a handy spot for a road-agent,[1] and there's no other near."

Hunky Ben was pre-eminently a man of action. As he uttered or thought the last word he gave a little chirp which sent Black Polly along the diverging track at a speed which almost justified the comparison of her to lightning.

The Blue Fork was a narrow pass or gorge in the hills, the footpath through which was rendered rugged and dangerous for cattle because of the rocks that had fallen during the course of ages from the cliffs on either side. Seen from a short distance off on the main track the mountains beyond had a brilliantly blue appearance, and a few hundred yards on the other side of the pass the track forked—hence the name. One fork led up to Traitor's Trap, the other to the fort of Quester Creek, an out-post of United States troops for which

_____
[1] A highwayman.

Hunky Ben was bound with the warning that the Redskins were contemplating mischief. As Ben had conjectured, this was the spot selected by Buck Tom as the most suitable place for way-laying his intended victim. Doubtless he supposed that no Englishman would travel in such a country without a good deal of money about him, and he resolved to relieve him of it.

It was through a thick belt of wood that the scout had to gallop at first, and he soon outstripped the traveller who kept to the main and, at that part, more circuitous road, and who was besides obliged to advance cautiously in several places. On nearing his destination, however, Ben pulled up, dismounted, fastened his mare to a tree, and proceeded the rest of the way on foot at a run, carrying his repeating rifle with him. He had not gone far when he came upon a horse. It was fastened, like his own, to a tree in a hollow.

"Ho! ho!" thought Ben, "you prefer to do yer dirty work on foot, Mr. Buck! Well, you're not far wrong in such a place."

Advancing now with great caution, the scout left the track and moved through the woods more like a visible ghost than a man, for he was well versed in all the arts and wiles of the Indian, and his mocca-sined feet made no sound whatever. Climbing up the pass at some height above the level of the road, so that he might be able to see all that took place below, he at last lay down at full length, and drew himself in snake fashion to the edge of the thicket that concealed him. Pushing aside the bushes gently he looked down, and there, to his satisfaction, beheld the man he was in search of, not thirty yards off.

Buck Tom was crouching behind a large mass of rock close to the track, and so lost in the dark shadow of it that no ordinary man could have seen him; but nothing could escape the keen and practised eye of Hunky Ben. He could not indeed make out the highwayman's form, but he knew that he was there and that was enough. Laying his rifle on a rock before him in a handy position he silently watched the watcher.

During all this time the Englishman—whom the reader has doubtless recognised as Charlie Brooke—was pushing on as fast as he could in the hope of overtaking the man who could guide him to Traitor's Trap.

At last he came to the Blue Forks, and rode into the pass with the confidence of one who suspects no evil. He drew rein, however, as he advanced, and picked his way carefully along the encumbered path.

He had barely reached the middle of it, where a clear space permitted the moonbeams to fall brightly on the ground, when a stern voice suddenly broke the stillness of the night with the words—

"Hands up!"

Charlie Brooke seemed either to be ignorant of the ways of the country and of the fact that disobedience to the command involved sudden death, or he had grown unaccountably reckless, for instead of raising his arms and submitting to be searched by the robber who covered him with a revolver, he merely reined up and took off his hat, allowing the moon to shine full on his countenance.

The effect on Buck Tom was singular. Standing with his back to the moon, his expression could not be seen, but his arm dropped to his side as if it had been paralysed, and the revolver fell to the ground.

Never had Buck Tom been nearer to his end than at that moment, for Hunky Ben, seeing clearly what would be the consequence of the Englishman's noncompliance with the command, was already pressing the trigger that would have sent a bullet into Buck Tom's brain, but the Englishman's strange conduct induced him to pause, and the effect on the robber caused him to raise his head and open wide his eyes —also his ears!

"Ah! Ralph Ritson, has it come to this?" said Charlie, in a voice that told only of pity and surprise.

For some moments Ralph did not speak. He was evidently stunned. Presently he recovered, and, passing his hand over his brow, but never taking his eyes off the handsome face of his former friend, he said in a low tone—

"I—I—don't feel very sure whether you're flesh and blood, Brooke, or a spirit—but—but——"

"I'm real enough to be able to shake hands, Ritson," returned our hero, dismounting, and going up to his former friend, who suffered him to grasp the hand that had been on the point of taking his life. "But can it be true, that I really find you a——"

"It is true, Charlie Brooke; quite true—but while you see the result, you do not see, and cannot easily understand, the hard grinding injustice that has brought me to this. The last and worst blow I received this very night. I have urgent need of money—not for myself, believe me—and I came down to David's store, at some personal risk, I may add, to receive payment of a sum due me for acting as a cow-boy for many months. The company, instead of paying me——"

"Yes, I know; I heard it all," said Charlie.

"You were only shamming sleep, then?"

"Yes; I knew you at once."

"Well, then," continued Buck Tom (as we shall still continue to style him), "the disappointment made me so desperate that I determined to rob you —little thinking who you were—in order to help poor Shank Leather——"

"Does Shank stand in urgent need of help?" asked Charlie, interrupting.

"He does indeed. He has been very ill. We

have run out of funds, and he needs food and physic of a kind that the mountains don't furnish."

"Does he belong to your band, Ritson?"

"Well—nearly; not quite!"

"That is a strange answer. How far is it to where he lies just now?"

"Six miles, about."

"Come, then, I will go to him if you will show me the way," returned Charlie, preparing to remount. I have plenty of that which poor Shank stands so much in need of. In fact I have come here for the express purpose of hunting him and you up. Would it not be well, by the way, to ride back to the store for some supplies?"

"No need," answered Buck Tom, stooping to pick up his revolver. "There's another store not far from this, to which we can send to-morrow. We can get what we want there."

"But what have you done with your horse?" asked Charlie; "I heard you start on one."

"It is not far off. I'll go fetch it."

So saying the robber entered the bushes and disappeared. A few minutes later the clattering of hoofs was heard, and in another moment he rode up to the spot where our hero awaited him.

"Follow me," he said; "the road becomes better half a mile further on."

During all this time Hunky Ben had stood with his rifle ready, listening with the feelings of a man in a dream. He watched the robber and his victim ride quietly away until they were out of sight. Then he stood up, tilted his cap on one side, and scratched his head in great perplexity.

"Well, now," he said at length, "this is about the queerest affair I've comed across since I was raised. It's a marcy I was born with a quiet spirit, for another chip off the small end of a moment an' Buck Tom would have bin with his fathers in their happy, or otherwise, huntin' grounds! It's quite clear that them two have bin friends, mayhap pards, in the old country. An' Buck Tom (that's Ritson, I think he called him) has bin driven to it by injustice, has he? Ah! Buck, if all the world that suffers injustice was to take to robbery it's not many respectable folk would be left to rob. Well, well, my comin' off in such a splittin' hurry to take care o' this Britisher is a wild-goose chase arter all! It's not the first one you've bin led into anyhow, an' it's time you was lookin' arter yer own business, Hunky Ben."

While giving vent to these remarks in low muttering tones, the scout was quickly retracing his steps to the place where he had tied up Black Polly. Mounting her he returned to the main track, proceeded along it until he reached the place beyond the pass where the roads forked; then, selecting that which diverged to the left, he set off at a hard gallop in the direction of Quester Creek.

CHAPTER XIV.

THE HAUNT OF THE OUTLAWS.

AFTER riding through the Blue Fork Charlie and Buck Tom came to a stretch of open ground of considerable extent, where they could ride abreast, and here the latter gave the former some account of the condition of Shank Leather.

"Tell me, Ritson," said Charlie, "what you mean by Shank 'nearly' and 'not quite' belonging to your band."

The outlaw was silent for some time. Then he seemed to make up his mind to speak out.

"Brooke," he said, "it did, till this night, seem to me that all the better feelings of my nature—whatever they were—had been blotted out of existence, for since I came to this part of the world the cruelty and injustice that I have witnessed and suffered have driven me to desperation, and I candidly confess to you that I have come to hate pretty nigh the whole human race. The grip of your hand and tone of your voice, however, have told me that I have not yet sunk to the lowest possible depths.

But that is not what I mean to enlarge on. What I wish you to understand is, that after Shank and I had gone to the dogs, and were reduced to beggary, I made up my mind to join a band of men who lived chiefly by their wits, and sometimes by their personal courage. Of course I won't say who they are, because we still hang together, and there is no need to say what we are. The profession is variously named, and not highly respected.

"Shank refused to join me, so we parted. He remained for some time in New York doing odd jobs for a living. Then he joined a small party of emigrants, and journeyed west. Strange to say, although the country is wide, he and I again met accidentally. My fellows wanted to overhaul the goods of the emigrants with whom he travelled. They objected. A fight followed in which there was no bloodshed, for the emigrants fled at the first war-whoop. A shot from one of them, however, wounded one of our men, and one of theirs was so drunk at the time of the flight that he fell off his horse and was captured. That man was Shank. I recognised him when I rode up to see what some of my boys were quarrelling over, and found that it was the wounded man wanting to shove his knife into Shank.

"The moment I saw his face I claimed him as an old chum, and had him carried up to our head-quarters in Traitor's Trap. There he has remained ever since, in a very shaky condition, for the fall seems to have injured him internally, besides almost breaking his neck. Indeed I think his spine is damaged,—he recovers so slowly. We have tried to persuade him to say that he will become one of us when he gets well, but up to this time he has steadily refused. I am not sorry; for, to say truth, I don't want to force any one into such a line of life —and he does not look as if he'd be fit for it, or anything else, for many a day to come."

"But how does it happen that you are in such straits just now?" asked Charlie, seeing that Buck paused, and seemed unwilling to make further explanations.

"Well, the fact is, we have not been successful of late; no chances have come in our way, and two of our best men have taken their departure—one to gold-digging in California, the other to the happy hunting grounds of the Redskin, or elsewhere. Luck, in short, seems to have forsaken us. Pious folk," he added, with something of a sneer, "would say, no doubt, that God had forsaken us."

"I think pious people would not say so, and they would be wrong if they did," returned Charlie. "In my opinion God never forsakes any one; but when His creatures forsake him He thwarts them. It cannot be otherwise if His laws are to be vindicated."

"It may be so. But what have I done," said Buck Tom fiercely, "to merit the bad treatment and insufferable injustice which I have received since I came to this accursed land? I cannot stand injustice. It makes my blood boil, and so, since it is rampant here, and everybody has been unjust to me, I have made up my mind to pay them back in their own coin. There seems to me even a spice of justice in that."

"I wonder that you cannot see the fallacy of your reasoning, Ritson," replied Charlie. "You ask, 'What have I done?' The more appropriate question would be, 'What have I *not* done?' Have you not, according to your own confession, rebelled against your Maker and cast Him off; yet you expect Him to continue His supplies of food to you; to keep up your physical strength and powers of enjoying life, and, under the name of Luck, to furnish you with the opportunity of breaking His own commands by throwing people in your way to be robbed! Besides which, have you not yourself been guilty of gross injustice in leading poor weak Shank Leather into vicious courses—to his great, if not irreparable, damage? I don't profess to teach theology, Ralph Ritson, my old friend, but I do think that even an average cow-boy could understand that a rebel has no claim to forgiveness—much less to favour—until he lays down his arms and gives in."

"Had any other man but you, Charlie Brooke, said half as much as you have just said to me, I would have blown his brains out," returned the outlaw sternly.

"I'm very glad no other man did say it, then," returned Charlie, "for your hands must be sufficiently stained already. But don't let anger blind you to the fact, Ralph, that you and I were once old friends; that I am your friend still, and that, what is of far greater importance, the Almighty is still your friend, and is proving His friendship by thwarting you."

"You preach a strange doctrine," said Buck Tom, laughing softly, "but you must end your sermon here in the meantime, for we have reached the entrance to Traitor's Trap, and have not room to ride further abreast. I will lead, and do you follow with care, for the path is none o' the safest. My asking you to follow me is a stronger proof than you may think that I believe in your friendship. Most strangers whom I escort up this gorge are usually requested to lead the way, and I keep my revolver handy lest they should stray from the track!"

The defile or gorge which they had reached was not inappropriately named, for, although the origin of the name was unknown, the appearance of the place was eminently suggestive of blackness and treachery. Two spurs of the mountain range formed a precipitous and rugged valley which, even in daylight, wore a forbidding aspect, and at night seemed the very portal to Erebus.

"Keep close to my horse's tail," said Buck Tom,

as they commenced the ascent. "If you stray here, ever so little, your horse will break his neck or legs."

Thus admonished, our hero kept a firm hand on the bridle, and closed up as much as possible on his guide. The moon was by this time clouded over, so that, with the precipitous cliffs on either side, and the great mass of the mountains further up, there was only that faint sombre appearance of things which is sometimes described as darkness visible. The travellers proceeded slowly, for, besides the danger of straying off the path, the steepness of the ascent rendered rapid motion impossible. After riding for about three miles thus in absolute silence, they came to a spot where the track became somewhat serpentine, and Charlie could perceive dimly that they were winding amongst great fragments of rock which were here and there over-canopied by foliage, but whether of trees or bushes he could not distinguish. At last they came to a halt in front of what appeared to be a cliff.

"Dismount here," said Buck in a low voice, setting the example.

"Is this the end of our ride?"

"It is. Give me the bridle. I will put up your horse. Stand where you are till I return."

The outlaw led the horses away, leaving his former friend and schoolfellow in a curious position, and a not very comfortable frame of mind.

When a man is engaged in action—especially if it be exciting and slightly dangerous—he has not time to think much about his surroundings, at least about their details, but now, while standing there in the intense darkness, in the very heart—as he had reason to believe—of a robber's stronghold, young Brooke could not help questioning his wisdom in having thus thrown himself into the power of one who had obviously deteriorated and fallen very low since the time when in England they had studied and romped together. It was too late, however, to question the wisdom of his conduct. There he was, and so he must make the best of it. He did not indeed fear treachery in his former friend, but he could not help reflecting that the reckless and perhaps desperate men with whom that friend was now associated might not be easy to restrain, especially if they should become acquainted with the fact that he carried a considerable sum of money about him.

He was yet pondering his position when Buck Tom returned.

"Ralph Ritson," he said, laying his hand on the arm of the outlaw, "you'll forgive my speaking plainly to you, I know. With regard to yourself I have not a shadow of doubt that you will act the part of an honourable host, though you follow a dishonourable calling. But I have no guarantee that those who associate with you will respect my

property.   Now, I have a considerable sum of
money about me in gold and silver, which I brought
here expressly for the benefit of our poor friend
Shank Leather.   What would you advise me to do
in regard to it ? "

"Intrust it to my care," said Buck promptly.

Charlie could not see the outlaw's face very
clearly, but he could easily detect the half-amused
half-mocking tone in which the suggestion was made.

"My good fellow," said Charlie, in a hearty voice,
"you evidently think I am afraid to trust you.
That is a mistake.   I do not indeed trust to any
remnant of good that is in your poor human nature,
but I have confidence in the good feeling which God
is arousing in you just now.   I will freely hand
over the money if you can assure me that you can
guard it from your comrades."

"*This* will make it secure from *them*," returned
Buck, with a short defiant laugh.

"Humph!" exclaimed Charlie with a shrug.
"I've not much confidence in *that* safeguard.   No
doubt, in certain circumstances, and on certain occasions, the revolver is a most important and useful instrument, but taking it all round I would not
put much store by it.   When you met me at the
Blue Fork to-night, for instance, of what use was
my revolver to me ?   And, for the matter of that,
after you had dropped it on the road of what use
was yours to you ?   It only wants one of your

fellows to have more pluck and a quicker eye and hand than yourself to dethrone you at once."

"Well, none of my fellows," returned Buck Tom good-humouredly, "happen to have the advantage of me at present, so you may trust me and count this one o' the 'certain occasions' in which the revolver is 'a most important instrument.'"

"I dare say you are right," responded Charlie, smiling, as he drew from the breast of his coat a small bag and handed it to his companion.

"You know exactly, of course, how much is here?" asked Buck Tom.

"Yes, exactly."

"That's all right," continued Buck, thrusting the bag into the bosom of his hunting coat; "now I'll see if any o' the boys are at home. Doubtless they are out—else they'd have heard us by this time. Just wait a minute."

He seemed to melt into the darkness as he spoke. Another minute and he re-appeared.

"Here, give me your hand," he said; "the passage is darkish at first."

Charlie Brooke felt rather than saw that they had passed under a portal of some sort, and were advancing along a narrow passage. Soon they turned to the left, and a faint red light—as of fire—became visible in the distance. Buck Tom stopped.

"There's no one in the cave but *him*, and he's asleep. Follow me."

The passage in which they stood led to a third and shorter one, where the light at its extremity was intense, lighting up the whole of the place so as to reveal its character. It was a corridor about seven feet high and four feet wide cut out of the solid earth; arched in the roof and supported here and there by rough posts to make it still more secure. Charlie at once concluded that it led to one of those concealed caverns, of which he had heard more than once while crossing the country, the entrances of which are made in zig-zag form in order to prevent the possibility of a ray of light issuing from the outside opening.

On reaching the end of the third passage he found that his conjecture was right, for the door-way or opening on his left hand conducted into a spacious cave, also hollowed out of the earth, but apparently against a perpendicular cliff, for the inner end of it was of unhewn rock. The roof of the cave was supported by pillars which were merely sections of pine-trees with the bark left on. These pillars and the earthen walls were adorned with antlers, skulls, and horns of the Rocky mountain sheep, necklaces of grizzly-bear's claws, Indian bows and arrows, rifles, short swords, and various other weapons and trophies of the chase, besides sundry articles of clothing. At the inner end of the cave a large fireplace and chimney had been rudely built, and in this was roaring the pine-wood fire which had lighted them in, and which caused the whole interior to glow with a vivid glare that seemed to surpass that of noon-day.

A number of couches of pine-brush were spread round the walls, and on one of these lay a sleeping figure. The face was turned towards the visitor, who saw at a glance that it was that of his former friend and playmate—but it was terribly changed. Hard toil, suffering, sickness, dissipation, had set indelible marks on it, and there was a slight curve about the eyebrows which gave the idea of habitual pain. Yet, strange to say, worn and lined though it was, the face seemed far more attractive and refined than it had ever been in the days of robust health.

Buck Tom went to the fire and began to stir the contents of a big pot that hung over it, while Charlie advanced and stood for some minutes gazing at the countenance of his friend, unwilling to disturb his slumbers, yet longing to cheer him with the glad news that he had come to succour him. He chanced, however, to touch a twig of the pine branches on which the sleeper lay, and Shank awoke instantly, raised himself on one elbow, and returned his friend's gaze earnestly, but without the slightest symptom of surprise.

"O Charlie," he said at last, in a quiet voice, "I wish you hadn't come to me to-night."

He stopped, and Charlie felt quite unable to

speak, owing to intense pity mingled with astonishment, at such a reception.

"It's too bad of you," Shank went on, "worrying me so in my dreams. I' weary of it; and if you only knew what a *terri* disappointment it is to me when I awake and don't find you there, you wouldn't tantalise me so. You always look so terribly real too! Man, I could almost pledge my life that you are no dece on this time, but—but I'm so used to it now tha——"

"Shank, my dear boy," said Charlie, finding words at last, "it *is* no deception——"

He stopped abruptly, for the intense look of eager anxiety, doubt and hope in the thin expressive face alarmed him.

"Charlie!" gasped, rather than said, the invalid, "you—you never *spoke* to me before in my dreams, and—you never *touched*—the grip of your strong h—— O God, *can* it be true?"

At this point Buck Tom suddenly left off his occupation at the fire and went out of the cave.

"O GOD! CAN IT BE TRUE?"—Page 174.

CHAPTER XV.

LOST AND FOUND.

"Try to be calm, Shank," said Charlie, in a soothing tone, as he kneeled beside the shadow that had once been his sturdy chum, and put an arm on his shoulder. "It is indeed myself *this* time. I have come all the way from England to seek you, for we heard, through Ritson, that you were ill and lost in these wilds, and now, through God's mercy, I have found you."

While Charlie Brooke was speaking, the poor invalid was breathing hard and gazing at him, as if to make quite sure it was all true.

"Yes," he said at last, unable to raise his voice above a hoarse whisper, "lost—and—and—found! O Charlie, my friend—my chum—my——"

He could say no more, but, laying his head like a little child on the broad bosom of his rescuer, he burst into a passionate flood of tears.

Albeit strong of will, and not by any means given to the melting mood, our hero was unable for a minute or two to make free use of his voice.

"Come, now, Shank, old man, you mustn't give way like that. You wouldn't, you know, if you had not been terribly reduced by illness——"

"Yes, I would! yes, I would!" interrupted the sick man, almost passionately; "I'd howl, I'd roar, I'd blubber like a very idiot, I'd do any mortal thing, if the doing of it would only make you understand how I appreciate your great kindness in coming out here to save me."

"Oh no, you wouldn't," said Charlie, affecting an easy off-hand tone, which he was far from feeling; "you wouldn't do anything to please me."

"What d' ye mean?" asked Shank, with a look of surprise.

"Well, I mean," returned the other, gently, "that you won't even do such a trifle as to lie down and keep quiet to please me."

A smile lighted up the emaciated features of the sick man, as he promptly lay back at full length and shut his eyes.

"There, Charlie," he said, "I'll behave, and let you do all the talking; but don't let go my hand, old man. Keep a tight grip of it. I'm terrified lest you drift off again, and—and melt away."

"No fear, Shank. I'll not let go my hold of you, please God, till I carry you back to old England."

"Ah! old England! I'll never see it again. I feel that. But tell me"— he started up again, with a return of the excited look—"is father any better?"

"N—no, not exactly—but he is no worse. I'll tell you all about everything if you will only lie down again and keep silent."

The invalid once more lay back, closed his eyes and listened, while his friend related to him all that he knew about his family affairs, and the kindness of old Jacob Crossley, who had not only befriended them when in great distress, but had furnished the money to enable him (Charlie) to visit these outlandish regions for the express purpose of rescuing Shank from all his troubles and dangers.

At this point the invalid interrupted him with an anxious look.

"Have you the money with you?"

"Yes."

"All of it?"

"Yes. Why do you ask?"

"Because," returned Shank, with something of a groan, "you are in a den of thieves!"

"I know it, my boy," returned Charlie, with a smile, "and so, for better security, I have given it in charge to our old chum, Ralph Ritson."

"What!" exclaimed Shank, starting up again with wide open eyes; "you have met Ralph, then?"

"I have. He conducted me here."

"And you have intrusted your money to *him*?"

"Yes—all of it; every cent!"

"Are you aware," continued Shank, in a solemn

M

tone, "that Ralph Ritson is Buck Tom—the noted chief of the outlaws ?"

"I know it."

"And you trust him ?"

"I do. I have perfect confidence that he is quite incapable of betraying an old friend."

For some time Shank looked at his companion in surprise ; then an absent look came into his eyes, and a variety of expressions passed over his wan visage.   At last he spoke.

"I don't know how it is, Charlie, but somehow I think you are right.   It's an old complaint of mine, you know, to come round to your way of thinking, whether I admit it or not.   In days of old I usually refused to admit it, but believed in you all the same ! If any man had told me this morning—ay, even half an hour since—that he had placed money in the hands of Buck Tom for safe keeping, know-ing who and what he is, I would have counted him an incurable fool ; but now, somehow, I do believe that you were quite right to do it, and that your money is as safe as if it were in the Bank of England."

"But I did not intrust it to Buck Tom, knowing who and what he *is*," returned Charlie, with a signi-ficant smile, "I put it into the hands of Ralph Ritson, knowing who and what he *was*."

"You're a good fellow, Charlie," said Shank, squeezing the hand that held his, "and I believe it is that very trustfulness of yours which gives you so great power and influence with people. I know it has influenced me for good many a time in the past, and would continue to do so still if I were not past redemption."

"No man is past redemption," said the other quietly; "but I'm glad you agree with me about Ralph, for——"

He stopped abruptly, and both men turned their eyes towards the entrance to the cave.

"Did you hear anything?" asked Shank, in a low voice.

"I thought so—but it must have been the shifting of a log on the fire," said the other, in a similarly low tone.

"Come, now, Charlie," said Shank, in his ordinary tones, "let me hear something about yourself. You have not said a word yet about what you have been doing these three years past."

As he spoke a slight noise was again heard in the passage, and, next moment, Buck Tom re-entered carrying a lump of meat. Whether he had been listening or not they had no means of knowing, for his countenance was quite grave and natural in appearance.

"I suppose you have had long enough, you two, to renew your old acquaintance," he said. "It behoves me now to get ready some supper for the boys against their return, for they would be ill-pleased to come home to an empty kettle, and their appetites are surprisingly strong. But you needn't interrupt your conversation. I can do my work without disturbing you."

"We have no secrets to communicate, Buck," returned Shank, "and I have no doubt that the account of himself, which our old chum was just going to give, will be as interesting to you as to me."

"Quite as interesting," rejoined Buck; "so pray go on, Brooke. I can listen while I look after the cookery."

Thus urged, our hero proceeded to relate his own adventures at sea—the wreck of the *Walrus*, the rescue by the whaler, and his various experiences both afloat and ashore.

"The man, Dick Darvall, whom I have mentioned several times," said Charlie, in conclusion, "I met with again in New York, when I was about to start to come here, and as I wanted a companion, and he was a most suitable man, besides being willing to come, I engaged him. He is a rough and ready, but a handy and faithful, man, who had some experience in woodcraft before he went to sea, but I have been forced to leave him behind me at a ranch a good many miles to the south of David's store, owing to the foolish fellow having tried to jump a creek in the dark and broken his horse's leg. We could not get another horse at the time, and as I was very anxious to push on—being so near my journey's end—and the ranch was a comfortable enough berth, I left him behind, as I have said, with directions to stay till I should return, or to push on if he could find a safe guide."

While Charlie Brooke was relating the last part of his experience, it might have been observed that the countenance of Buck Tom underwent a variety of curious changes, like the sky of an April day. A somewhat stern frown settled on it at last, but neither of his companions observed the fact, being too much interested in each other.

"What was the name o' the ranch where your mate was left?" asked Buck Tom, when his guest ceased speaking.

"The ranch of Roaring Bull," answered Charlie. "I should not wonder," he added, "if its name were derived from its owner's voice, for it sounded like the blast of a trombone when he shouted to his people."

"Not only his ranch but himself is named after his voice," returned Buck. "His real name is Jackson, but it is seldom used now. Every one knows him as Roaring Bull. He's not a bad fellow at bottom, but something overbearing, and has made a good many enemies since he came to this part of the country six years ago."

"That may be so," remarked Brooke, "but he was very kind to us the day we put up at his place, and

Dick Darvall, at all events, is not one of his enemies.
Indeed he and Roaring Bull took quite a fancy to
each other. It seemed like love at first sight.
Whether Jackson's pretty daughter had anything
to do with the fancy on Dick's part of course I can't
say. Now, I think of it, his readiness to remain
behind inclines me to believe it had!"

"Well, come outside with me, and have a chat
about old times. It is too hot for comfort here. I
dare say our friend Shank will spare you for quarter
of an hour, and the pot can look after itself. By
the way, it would be as well to call me Buck Tom—
or Buck. My fellows would not understand Ralph
Ritson. They never heard it before. Have a
cigar?"

"No, thank you, I have ceased to see the advantage of poisoning one's-self merely because it is the
fashion to do so."

"The poison is wonderfully slow," said Buck.

"But not less wonderfully sure," returned Charlie,
with a smile.

"As you will," rejoined Buck, rising and going
outside with his visitor.

The night was very still and beautiful, and,
the clouds having cleared away, the moonbeams
struggled through the foliage and revealed the
extreme wildness and seclusion of the spot which
had been chosen by the outlaws as their fortress.

Charlie now saw that the approach to the entrance

of the cave was a narrow neck of rock resembling a natural bridge, with a deep gully on either side, and that the cliff which formed the inner end of the cavern overhung its base, so that if an enemy were to attempt to hurl rocks down from above these would drop beyond the cave altogether. This much he saw at a glance. The minute details and intricacies of the place of course could not be properly seen or understood in the flickering and uncertain light which penetrated the leafy canopy, and, as it were, played with the shadows of the fallen rocks that strewed the ground everywhere, and hung in apparently perilous positions on the mountain slopes.

The manner of the outlaw changed to that of intense earnestness the moment he got out to the open air.

"Charlie Brooke," he said, with more of the tone and air of old familiar friendship than he had yet allowed himself to assume, "it's of no use exciting poor Shank unnecessarily, so I brought you out here to tell you that your man Dick Darvall is in deadly peril, and nothing but immediate action on my part can save him; I must ride without delay to his rescue. You cannot help me in this. I know what you are going to propose, but you must trust and obey me if you would save your friend's life. To accompany me would only delay and finally mar my plans. Now, will you——"

A peculiar whistle far down the gorge caused the outlaw to cease abruptly and listen.

The whistle was repeated, and Buck answered it at once with a look of great surprise.

"These are my fellows back already!" he said.

"You seem surprised. Did you, then, not expect them so soon?"

"I certainly did not; something must have gone wrong," replied Buck, with a perplexed look. Then, as if some new idea had flashed upon him, "Now, look here, Brooke, I must ask you to trust me implicitly and to act a part. Your life may depend on your doing this."

"The first I can do with ease, but as to the latter, my agreeing to do so depends on whether the action you require of me is honourable. You must forgive me, Rits——"

"Hush! Don't forget that there is no such man as Ralph Ritson in these mountains. *My* life may depend on your remembering that. Of course I don't expect you to act a dishonourable part,—all I want you to do just now is to lie down and pretend to go to sleep."

"Truly, if that is all I am ready," said Charlie; "at all events I will shut my eyes and hold my tongue."

"A useful virtue at times, and somewhat rare," said Buck, leading his guest back into the cavern. "Now, then, Brooke, lie down there," pointing to a couch of pine-brush in a corner, "and try to sleep if you can."

Our hero at once complied, stretched himself at full length with his face to the light, and apparently went to sleep, but with his left arm thrown over his forehead as if to protect his eyes from the glare of the fire. Thus he was in a position to see as well as hear all that went on. Buck Tom went to the sick man and whispered something to him. Then, returning to the fire, he continued to stir the big pot, and sniff its savoury contents with much interest.

CHAPTER XVI.

FRIENDS AND FOES—PLOTS AND COUNTERPLOTS –
THE RANCH IN DANGER.

IN a few minutes the sound of heavy feet and gruff voices was heard in the outside passage, and next moment ten men filed into the room and saluted their chief heartily.

Charlie felt an almost irresistible tendency to open his eyes, but knew that the risk was too great, and contented himself with his ears. These told him pretty eloquently what was going on, for suddenly, the noise of voices and clattering of footsteps ceased, a dead silence ensued, and Charlie knew that the whole band were gazing at him with wide open eyes and, probably, open mouths. Their attention had been directed to the stranger by the chief. The silence was only momentary, however.

"Now, don't begin to whisper, pards," said Buck Tom, in a slightly sarcastic tone. "When will ye learn that there is nothing so likely to waken a sleeper as whisperin'? Be natural—be natural, and tell me, as softly as ye can in your natural tones, what has brought you back so soon. Come, Jake, you have got the quietest voice. The poor man is pretty well knocked up and needs rest. I brought him here."

"Has he got much——?" the sentence was completed by Jake significantly slapping his pocket.

"A goodish lot. But come, sit down and out wi' the news. Something must be wrong."

"Wall, I guess that somethin' *is* wrong. Everything's wrong, as far as I can see. The Redskins are up, an' the troops are out, an' so it seemed o' no use our goin' to bust up the ranch of Roarin' Bull, seein' that the red devils are likely to be there before us. So we came back here, an' I'm glad you've got suthin' in the pot, for we're about as empty as kettledrums."

"Humph!" ejaculated Buck, "didn't I tell you not to trouble Roarin' Bull—that he and his boys could lick you if you had been twenty instead of ten. But how came ye to hear o' this cock-and-bull story about the Redskins?"

"We got it from Hunky Ben, an' he's not the boy to go spreadin' false reports."

Charlie Brooke ventured at this point to open his eye-lids the smallest possible bit, so that any one looking at him would have failed to observe any motion in them. The little slit, however, admitted the whole scene to the retina, and he perceived that ten of the most cut-throat-looking men conceivable were seated in a semicircle in the act of receiving portions from the big pot into tin plates. Most of them were clothed in hunters' leathern costume, wore long boots with spurs, and were more or less bronzed and bearded.

Buck Tom, *alias* Ralph Ritson, although as tall and strong as any of them, seemed a being of quite angelic gentleness beside them. Yet Buck was their acknowledged chief. No doubt it was due to the superiority of mind over matter, for those out-laws were grossly material and matter-of-fact!

"There must be some truth in the report if Hunky Ben carried it," said Buck, looking up quickly, "but I left Ben sitting quietly in David's store not many hours ago."

"No doubt that's true, Captain," said Jake, as he ladled the soup into his capacious mouth; "never-theless we met Hunky Ben on the pine-river prairie scourin' over the turf like all possessed on Black Polly. We stopped him of course an' asked the news."

"'News!' cried he, 'why, the Redskins have dug up the hatchet an' riz like one man. They've clar'd out Yellow Bluff, an' are pourin' like Niagara down upon Rasper's Creek. It's said that they'll visit Roarin' Bull's ranch to-morrow. No time for more talk, boys. Oratin' ain't in my line. I'm off to Quester Creek to rouse up the troops.' Wi' that Hunky wheeled round an' went off like a runaway streak o' lightnin'. I sent a couple o' shots after him, for I 'd took a fancy to Black Polly—but them bullets didn't seem to hit somehow."

"Boys," cried Buck Tom, jumping up when he heard this, "if Hunky Ben said all that, you may depend on 't it's true, an' we won't have to waste time this night if we 're to save the ranch of Roarin' Bull."

"But we don't want to save the ranch of Roarin' Bull, as far as I 'm consarned," said Jake rather sulkily.

Buck wheeled round on the man with a fierce glare, but, as if suddenly changing his mind, he said in a tone of well-feigned surprise—"What! *you*, Jake, of all men—such a noted lady-killer—indifferent about the fate of the ranch of Roaring Bull, and pretty Miss Mary Jackson in it, at the mercy of the Redskins!"

"Well, if it comes to that, Captain, I 'll ride as far and as fast as any man to rescue a girl, pretty or plain, from the Redskins," said Jake, recovering his good-humour.

"Well, then, cram as much grub as you can into you in five minutes, for we must be off by that time. Rise, sir," said Buck, shaking Charlie with some violence. "We ride on a matter of life an' death—to save women. Will you join us?"

"Of course I will!" cried Charlie, starting up with a degree of alacrity and vigour that favourably impressed the outlaws, and shaking off his simulated sleep with wonderful facility.

"Follow me, then," cried Buck, hastening out of the cave.

"But what of Shank?" asked Charlie, in some anxiety, when they got outside. "He cannot accompany us ; may we safely leave him behind ?"

"Quite safely. This place is not known to the savages who are on the warpath, and there is nothing to tempt them this way even if it were. Besides, Shank is well enough to get up and gather firewood, kindle his fire, and boil the kettle for himself. He is used to being left alone. See, here is our stable under the cliff, and yonder stands your horse. Saddle him. The boys will be at our heels in a moment. Some of them are only too glad to have a brush wi' the Redskins, for they killed two of our band lately."

This last remark raised an uncomfortable feeling in the mind of Charlie, for was he not virtually allying himself with a band of outlaws, with intent to attack a band of Indians of whom he knew little or nothing, and with whom he had no quarrel ? There was no time, however, to weigh the case critically. The fact that savages were about to attack the ranch in which his comrade Dick Darvall was staying, and that there were females in the place, was enough to settle the question. In a minute or two he had saddled his horse, which he led out and fastened to a tree, and while the outlaws were busy making preparations for a start he ran back to the cave.

"Shank," said he, sitting down beside his friend and taking his hand, "you have heard the news. My comrade Darvall is in great danger. I must away to his rescue. But be sure, old fellow, that I will return to you soon."

"Yes, yes—I know," returned Shank, with a look of great anxiety; "but, Charlie, you don't know half the danger you run. Don't fight with Buck Tom— do you hear?"

"Of course I won't," said Charlie, in some surprise.

"No, no, that's not what I mean," said Shank, with increasing anxiety. "Don't fight *in company with him.*"

At that moment the voice of the outlaw was heard at the entrance shouting, "Come along, Brooke, we're all ready."

"Don't be anxious about me, Shank; I'll take good care," said Charlie, as he hastily pressed the hand of the invalid and hurried away.

The ten men with Buck at their head were already mounted when he ran out.

"Pardon me," he said, vaulting into the saddle, "I was having a word with the sick man."

"Keep next to me, and close up," said Buck, as he wheeled to the right and trotted away.

Down the Traitor's Trap they went at what was to Charlie a break-neck but satisfactory pace, for now that he was fairly on the road a desperate anxiety lest they should be too late took possession of him. Across an open space they went, at the bottom of which ran a brawling rivulet. There was no bridge, but over or through it went the whole band without the slightest check, and onward at full gallop, for the country became more level and open just beyond.

The moon was still shining although sinking towards the horizon, and now for the first time Charlie began to note with what a stern and reckless band of men he was riding, and a feeling of something like exultation arose within him as he thought on the one hand of the irresistible sweep of an onslaught from such men, and, on the other, of the cruelties that savages were known to practise. In short, rushing to the rescue was naturally congenial to our hero.

About the same time that the outlaws were thus hastening for once on an honourable mission—though some of them went from anything but honourable motives—two other bands of men were converging to the same point as fast as they could go. These were a company of United States troops, guided by Hunky Ben, and a large band of Indians under their warlike chief Bigfoot.

Jackson, *alias* Roaring Bull, had once inadvertently

given offence to Bigfoot, and as that chief was both by nature and profession an unforgiving man he had vowed to have his revenge. Jackson treated the threat lightly, but his pretty daughter Mary was not quite as indifferent about it as her father. The stories of Indian raids and frontier wars and barbarous cruelties had made a deep impression on her sensitive mind, and when her mother died, leaving her the only woman at her father's ranch— with the exception of one or two half-breed women, who could not be much to her as companions—her life had been very lonely, and her spirit had been subjected to frequent, though hitherto groundless, alarms.

But pretty Moll, as she was generally called, was well protected, for her father, besides having been a noted pugilist in his youth, was a big, powerful man, and an expert with rifle and revolver. Moreover, there was not a cow-boy within a hundred miles of her who would not (at least thought he would not) have attacked single-handed the whole race of Redskins if Moll had ordered him to do so as a proof of affection.

Now, when strapping, good-looking Dick Darvall came to the ranch in the course of his travels and beheld Mary Jackson, and received the first broadside from her bright blue eyes, he hauled down his colours and surrendered with a celerity which would have mightily amused the many comrades to whom he had said in days of yore that his heart was as hard as rock, and he had never yet seen the woman as could soften it!

But Dick, more than most of his calling, was a modest, almost a bashful, man. He behaved to Mary with the politeness that was natural to him, and with which he would have approached any woman. He did not make the slightest attempt to show his admiration of her, though it is quite within the bounds of possibility that his "speaking" brown eyes may have said something without his permission! Mary Jackson, being also modest in a degree, of course did not reveal the state of her feelings, and made no visible attempt to ascertain his, but her bluff sagacious old father was not obtuse—neither was he reticent. He was a man of the world—at least of the back-woods world—and his knowledge of life, as there exhibited, was founded on somewhat acute experience. He knew that his daughter was young and remarkably pretty. He saw that Dick Darvall was also young—a dashing and unusually handsome sailor—something like what Tom Bowling may have been. Putting these things together, he came to the very natural conclusion that a wedding would be desirable; believing, as he did, that human nature in the Rockies is very much the same as to its foundation elements as it is elsewhere. Moreover, Roaring Bull was very much in want of a stout son-in-law at that time, so he fanned the flame which he fondly hoped was beginning to arise. This he did in a somewhat blundering and obvious manner, but Dick was too much engrossed with Mary to notice it, and Mary was too ignorant of the civilised world's ways to care much for the proprieties of life.

Of course this state of things created an awful commotion in the breasts of the cow-boys who were in the employment of Mary's father and herded his cattle. Their mutual jealousies were sunk in the supreme danger that threatened them all, and they were only restrained from picking a quarrel with Dick and shooting him by the calmly resolute look in his brown eyes, coupled with his great physical power and his irresistible good-nature. Urbanity seemed to have been the mould in which the spirit of this man-of-the-sea had been cast, and gentleness was one of his chief characteristics. Moreover, he could tell a good story, and sing a good song in a fine bass voice. Still further, although these gallant cow-boys felt intensely jealous of this new-comer, they could not but admit that they had nothing tangible to go upon, for the sailor did not apparently pay any pointed attention to Mary, and she certainly gave no special encouragement to him.

There was one cow-boy, however, of Irish descent, who could not or would not make up his mind to take things quietly, but resolved, as far as he was concerned, to bring matters to a head. His name was Pat Reilly.

He entered the kitchen on the day after Dick's arrival and found Mary alone and busily engaged with the dinner.

"Miss Jackson," said Pat, "there's a question I've bin wantin' to ax ye for a long time past, an' with your lave I'll putt it now."

"What is it, Mr. Reilly?" asked the girl somewhat stiffly, for she had a suspicion of what was coming. A little negro girl in the back kitchen named Buttercup also had a suspicion of what was coming, and stationed herself with intense delight behind the door, through a crack in which she could both hear and see.

"Mary, my dear," said Pat insinuatingly, "how would you like to jump into double harness with me an' jog along the path o' life together?"

Poor Mary, being agitated by the proposal, and much amused by the manner of it, bent over a pot of something and tried to hide her blushes and amusement in the steam. Buttercup glared, grinned, hugged herself, and waited for more.

Pat, erroneously supposing that silence meant consent, slipped an arm round Mary's waist. No man had ever yet dared to do such a thing to her. The indignant girl suddenly wheeled round and brought her pretty little palm down on the cowboy's cheek with all her might—and that was considerable!

"Who's a-firin' off pistles in de kitchen?"

demanded Buttercup in a serious tone, as she popped her woolly head through the doorway.

"Nobody, me black darlin'," said Pat; "it's only Miss Mary expressin' her failin's in a cheeky manner. That's all!"

So saying the rejected cow-boy left the scene of his discomfiture, mounted his mustang, took his departure from the ranch of Roarin' Bull without saying farewell, and when next heard of had crossed the lonely Guadalupe mountains into Lincoln County, New Mexico.

But to return. While the troops and the outlaws were hastening thus to the rescue of the dwellers in Bull's ranch, and the blood-thirsty Redskins were making for the same point, bent on the destruction of all its inhabitants, Roaring Bull himself, his pretty daughter, and Dick Darvall, were seated in the ranch enjoying their supper, all ignorant alike of the movements of friend and foe, with Buttercup waiting on them.

One messenger, however, was speeding on his way to warn them of danger. This was the cow-boy Crux, who had been despatched on Bluefire by Hunky Ben just before that sturdy scout had started to call out the cavalry at Quester Creek.

CHAPTER XVII.

THE ALARM AND PREPARATIONS FOR DEFENCE.

"FROM what you say I should think that my friend Brooke won't have much trouble in findin' Traitor's Trap," remarked Dick Darvall, pausing in the disposal of a venison steak which had been cooked by the fair hands of Mary Jackson herself, "but I'm sorely afraid o' the reception he'll meet with when he gets there, if the men are such awful blackguards as you describe."

"They're the biggest hounds unhung," growled Roaring Bull, bringing one hand down on the board by way of emphasis, while with the other he held out his plate for another steak.

"You're too hard on some of them, father," said Mary, in a voice the softness of which seemed appropriate to the beauty of her face.

"Always the way wi' you wenches," observed the father. "Some o' the villains are good-lookin', others are ugly; so, the first are not so bad as the second—eh, lass ?"

Mary laughed. She was accustomed to her father's somewhat rough but not ill-natured rebuffs.

"Perhaps I may be prejudiced, father," she returned; "but, apart from that, surely you would never compare Buck Tom with Jake the Flint, though they do belong to the same band."

"You are right, my lass," rejoined her father. "They do say that Buck Tom is a gentleman, and often keeps back his boys from devilry—though he can't always manage that, an' no wonder, for Jake the Flint is the cruellest monster 'tween this an' Texas if all that's said of him be true."

"I wish my comrade was well out o' their clutches," said Dick, with a look of anxiety; "an' it makes me feel very small to be sittin' here enjoyin' myself when I might be ridin' on to help him if he should need help."

"Don't worry yourself on that score," said the host. "You couldn't find your way without a guide though I was to give ye the best horse in my stable—which I'd do slick off if it was of any use. There's not one o' my boys on the ranch just now, but there'll be four or five of 'em in to-morrow by daylight, an' I promise you the first that comes in. They all know the country for three hundred miles around—every inch—an' you may ride my best horse till you drop him if ye can. There, now, wash down your victuals an' give us a yarn, or a song."

"I'm quite sure," added Mary, by way of encouragement, "that with one of the outlaws for an old friend, Mr. Brooke will be quite safe among them——"

"But he's *not* an outlaw, Miss Mary," broke in Darvall. "Leastwise we have the best reason for believin' that he's detained among them against his will. Hows'ever, it's of no use cryin' over spilt milk. I'm bound to lay at anchor in this port till mornin', so, as I can't get up steam for a song in the circumstances, here goes for a yarn."

The yarn to which our handsome seaman treated his audience was nothing more than an account of one of his numerous experiences on the ocean, but he had such a pleasant, earnest, truth-like, and confidential way of relating it, and, withal interlarded his speech with so many little touches of humour, that the audience became fascinated and sat in open-eyed forgetfulness of all else. Buttercup, in particular, became so engrossed as to forget herself as well as her duties, and stood behind her master in an expectant attitude, glaring at the story-teller, with bated breath, profound sympathy, and extreme readiness to appreciate every joke whether good or bad.

In the midst of one of the most telling of his anecdotes the speaker was suddenly arrested by the quick tramp of a galloping horse, the rider of which, judging from the sound, seemed to be in hot haste.

All eyes were turned inquiringly on the master of the ranch. That cool individual, rising with quiet yet rapid action, reached down a magazine repeating rifle that hung ready loaded above the door of the room.

Observing this, Dick Darvall drew a revolver from his coat-pocket and followed his host to the outer door of the house. Mary accompanied them, and Buttercup retired to the back kitchen as being her appropriate stronghold.

They had hardly reached and flung open the door when Bluefire came foaming and smoking into the yard with Crux the cow-boy on his back.

"Wall, Roaring Bull," cried Crux, leaping off his horse and coming forward as quietly as if there were nothing the matter. "I'm glad to see you O. K., for the Cheyenne Reds are on the war-path, an' makin' tracks for your ranch. But as they've not got here yet, they won't likely attack till the moon goes down. Is there any chuck goin'? I'm half starved."

"Ay, Crux, lots o' chuck here. Come in an' let's hear all about. Where got ye the news?"

"Hunky Ben sent me. He wasn't thinkin' o' you at first, but when a boy came in wi' the news that a crowd o' the Reds had gone round by Pine Hollow —just as he was fixin' to pull out for Quester Creek to rouse up the cavalry—he asked me to come on here an' warn you."

While he was speaking the cow-boy sat down to supper with the air of a man who meant business, while the host and his sailor guest went to look after the defences of the place.

"I'm glad you are here, Dick Darvall," said the former, "for it's a bad job to be obliged to fight without help agin a crowd o' yellin' Reds. My boys won't be back till sun-up, an' by that time the game may be played out."

"D'ee think the Redskins'll attack us to-night then?" asked the sailor as he assisted to close th gates of the yard.

"Ay, that they will, lad. They know the value o' time better than most men, and, when they see their chance, are not slow to take advantage of it. As Crux said, they won't attack while the moon shines, so we have plenty of time to git ready for them. I wish I hadn't sent off my boys, but as bad luck would have it a bunch o' my steers have drifted down south, an' I can't afford to lose them—so, you see, there's not a man left in the place but you an' me an' Crux to defend poor Mary."

For the first time in his life Dick Darvall felt a distinct tendency to rejoice over the fact that he was a young and powerful man! To live and, if need be, die for Mary was worth living for!

"Are you well supplied with arms an' ammunition?" he asked.

"That am I, and we'll need it all," answered the host, as he led Dick round to the back of the yard where another gate required fastening.

"I don't see that it matters much," said Dick in a questioning tone, "whether you shut the gates or not. With so few to defend the place the house will be our only chance."

"When you've fought as much wi' Reds as I have, Dick, you'll larn that delay, even for five minutes, counts for a good deal."

"Well, there's somethin' in that. It minds me what one o' my shipmates who had bin in the London fire brigade once said. 'Dick,' said he, 'never putt off what you've got to do. Sometimes I've bin at a fire where the loss of only two minutes caused the destruction of a store worth ten thousand pound, more or less. We all but saved it as it was—so near were we, that if we had bin *one* minute sooner I do believe we'd have saved it. But when we was makin' for that fire full sail, a deaf old applewoman came athwart our bows an' got such a fright that she went flop down right in front of us. To steer clear of her we'd got to sheer off so that we all but ran into a big van, and, what wi' our lights an' the yellin', the horses o' the van took fright and backed into us as we flew past, so that we a'most went down by the starn. One way or another we lost two minutes, as I've said, an' the owners o' that store lost about ten thousand pounds —more or less.'"

"That was a big pile, Dick," observed the ranchman, as they turned from the gate towards the house, "not easy to replace."

"True—my shipmate never seemed to be quite

sure whether it was more or less that was lost, but he thought the Insurance offices must have found it out by that time. It's a pity there's only three of us, for that will leave one side o' the house undefended."

"All right, Dick; you don't trouble your head about that, for Buttercup fights like a black tiger. She's a'most as good as a man—only she can't manage to aim, so it's no use givin' her a rifle. She's game enough to fire it, but the more she tries to hit the more she's sure to miss. However, she's got a way of her own that sarves well enough to defend her side o' the house. She always takes charge o' the front. My Mary can't fight, but she's a heroine at loadin'—an' that's somethin' when you're hard pressed ! Come, now, I'll show ye the shootin' irons an' our plan of campaign."

Roaring Bull led the way back to the room, or central hall, where they had supped, and here they found that the débris of their feast had already been cleared away, and that arms of various kinds, with ammunition, covered the board.

"Hospitable alike to friend and foe," said Jackson gaily. "Here, you see, Mary has spread supper for the Reds !"

Darvall made no response to this pleasantry, for he observed that poor Mary's pretty face was very pale, and that it wore an expression of mingled sadness and anxiety.

"You won't be exposed to danger, I hope," said Dick, in a low earnest tone, while Jackson was loudly discussing with Crux the merits of one of the repeating rifles—of which there were half-a-dozen on the table.

"Oh no! It is not that," returned the girl sadly. "I am troubled to think that, however the fight goes, some souls, perhaps many, will be sent to their account unprepared. For myself, I shall be safe enough as long as we are able to hold the house, and it may be that God will send us help before long."

"You may be quite sure," returned Dick, with suppressed emotion, "that no Redskin shall cross this threshold as long as we three men have a spark o' life left."

A sweet though pitiful smile lighted up Mary's pale face for a moment, as she replied that she was quite sure of that, in a tone which caused Darvall's heart to expand, so that his ribs seemed unable to contain it, while he experienced a sensation of being stronger than Samson and bigger than Goliath!

"And I suppose," continued Dick, "that the troops won't be long of coming. Is the man—what's his name, Humpy Ben—trustworthy?"

"Trustworthy!" exclaimed the maiden, with a flush of enthusiasm; "there is not a more trust-worthy man on this side of the Rocky mountains, or the other side either, I am quite sure."

Poor Darvall's heart seemed suddenly to find
plenty of room within the ribs at that moment, and
his truthful visage must have become something of
an index to his state of mind, for, to his surprise,
Mary laughed.

"It seems to me so funny," she continued, "to
hear any one ask if Hunky—not Humpy—Ben is
to be trusted."

"Is he, then, such a splendid young fellow?"
asked the seaman, with just the slightest touch of
bitterness in his tone, for he felt as if a rock something like Gibraltar had been laid on his heart.

"Well, he's not exactly young," answered Mary,
with a peculiar expression that made her questioner
feel still more uncomfortable, "yet he is scarcely
middle-aged, but he certainly *is* the most splendid
fellow on the frontier; and he saved my life once."

"Indeed! how was that?"

"Well, it was this way. I had been paying a
short visit to his wife, who lives on the other side
of the——"

"Come along, Darvall," cried Roaring Bull at
that moment. "The moon's about down, an' we'll
have to take our stations. We shall defend the
outworks first, to check them a bit and put off some
time, then scurry into the house and be ready for
them when they try to clear the fence. Follow me.
Out wi' the lights, girls, and away to your posts."

"I'll hear the end of your story another time,

Miss Mary," said Dick, looking over his shoulder and following his host and Crux to the outer door.

The seaman was conscious of a faint suspicion that Mary was wrestling with another laugh as he went off to defend the outworks, but he also, happily, felt that the Rock of Gibraltar had been removed from his heart!

CHAPTER XVIII.

DEFENCE OF THE RANCH OF ROARING BULL.

EVERY light and every spark of fire had been extinguished in the ranch of Roaring Bull when its defenders issued from its doorway. They were armed to the teeth, and glided across the yard to the fence or stockade that enclosed the buildings, leaving the door slightly open so as to be ready for speedy retreat.

It had been arranged that, as there was a large open field without bush or tree in the rear of the ranch, they should leave that side undefended at first.

"They'll never come into the open as long as they can crawl up through the bush," Jackson had said, while making his final dispositions. "They're a'most sure to come up in front, thinkin' we're all a-bed. Now, mind—don't stand still, boys, but walk along as ye fire, to give 'em the notion there's more of us. An' don't fire at nothin'. They'd think we was in a funk. An' when you hear me whistle get into the house as quick as a cotton-tail rabbit an' as sly as a snake."

After the moon went down, everything in and

around the ranch was as silent as the grave, save now and then the stamp of a hoof on the floor of a shed, where a number of horses stood saddled and bridled ready to mount at a moment's notice; for Jackson had made up his mind, if it came to the worst, to mount and make a bold dash with all his household through the midst of his foes, trusting to taking them by surprise and to his knowledge of the country for success.

For a long time, probably two hours, the three men stood at their posts motionless and silent; still there was no sign, either by sight or sound, of an enemy. The outline of the dark woods was barely visible against the black sky in front of each solitary watcher, and no moving thing could be distinguished in the open field behind either by Crux or Darvall, to each of whom the field was visible. Jackson guarded the front.

To Dick, unaccustomed as he was to such warfare, the situation was very trying, and might have told on his nerves severely if he had not been a man of iron mould; as it was, he had no nerves to speak of! But he was a man of lively imagination. More than fifty times within those two hours did he see a black form moving in the darkness that lay between him and the wood, and more than fifty times was his Winchester rifle raised to his shoulder; but as often did the caution "don't fire at nothin'" rise to his memory.

The stockade was of peculiar construction, because its owner and maker was eccentric and a mechanical genius. Not only were the pickets of which it was composed very strong and planted with just space between to permit of firing, but there was a planking of strong boards, waist high, all round the bottom inside, which afforded some protection to defenders by concealing them when they stooped and changed position.

While matters were in this state outside, Mary Jackson and Buttercup were standing at an upper window just opposite the front gate, the latter with a huge bell-mouthed blunderbuss of the last century, loaded with buckshot in her hands. Mary stood beside her sable domestic ready to direct her not as to how, but where and when, to use the ancient weapon.

"You must be *very* careful, Buttercup," said Mary in a low voice, "*not* to fire till I tell you, and to point only *where* I tell you, else you'll shoot father. And *do* keep your finger off the trigger! By-the-way, have you cocked it?"

"O missy, I forgit dat," answered the damsel with a self-condemned look, as she corrected the error. "But, don' you fear, Missy Mary. I's use' to dis yar blunn'erbus. Last time I fire 'im was at a raven. Down goed de raven, blow'd to atims, an' down goed me too—cause de drefful t'ing kicks like a Texas mule. But bress you, I don' mind dat. I's used to it!"

Buttercup gave a little sniff of grave scorn with her flat nose, as though to intimate that the ordinary ills of life were beneath her notice.

We have said that all fires had been extinguished, but this is not strictly correct, for in the room where the two maidens watched there was an iron stove so enclosed that the fire inside did not show, and as it was fed with charcoal there were neither flames nor sparks to betray its presence. On this there stood a large cast-iron pot full of water, the bubbling of which was the only sound that broke the profound stillness of the night, while the watchers scarcely breathed, so intently did they listen.

At last the patient and self-restraining Dick saw a dark object moving towards his side of the stockade, which he felt was much too real to be classed with the creatures of his imagination which had previously given him so much trouble. Without a moment's hesitation the rifle flew to his shoulder, and the prolonged silence was broken by the sharp report, while an involuntary half-suppressed cry proved that he had not missed his mark. The dark object hastily retreated. A neighbouring cliff echoed the sounds, and two shots from his comrades told the sailor that they also were on the alert.

Instantly the night was rendered hideous by a series of wild yells and whoops, while, for a moment, the darkness gave place to a glare of light as a hundred rifles vomited their deadly contents, and the sound of many rushing feet was heard upon the open sward in front of the ranch.

The three male defenders had ducked their heads below the protecting breast-work when the volley was fired, and then, discarding all idea of further care, they skipped along their respective lines, yelling and firing the repeaters so rapidly, that, to any one ignorant of the true state of things, it must have seemed as if the place were defended by a legion of demons. To add to the hullabaloo Buttercup's blunderbuss poured forth its contents upon a group of red warriors who were rushing towards the front gate, with such a cannon-like sound and such wonderful effect, that the rush was turned into a sudden and limping retreat. The effect, indeed, was more severe even than Buttercup had intended, for a stray buckshot had actually taken a direction which had been feared, and grazed her master's left arm! Happily the wound was very slight, and, to do the poor damsel justice, she could not see that her master was jumping from one place to another like a caged lion. Like the same animal, however, he gave her to understand what she had done, by shouting in a thunderous bass roar that fully justified his sobriquet—

"Mind your eye, Buttercup! Not so low next time!"

The immediate result of this vigorous defence was to make the Indians draw off and retire to the woods—presumably for consultation. By previous arrangement the negro girl issued from the house with three fresh repeaters in her arms, ran round to the combatants with them and returned with their almost empty rifles. These she and Mary proceeded to reload in the hall, and then returned to their post at the upper front window.

The morning was by this time pretty well advanced, and Jackson felt a little uncertain as to what he should now do. It was still rather dark; but in a very short time, he knew, dawn would spread over the east, when it would, of course, be quite impossible to defend the walls of the little fort without revealing the small number of its defenders. On the other hand, if they should retire at once the enemy might find a lodgement within, among the outbuildings, before there was light enough to prevent them by picking off the leaders; in which case the assailants would be able to apply fire to the wooden walls of the house without much risk.

"If they manage to pile up enough o' brush to clap a light to," he grumbled to himself in an under tone, "it's all up wi' us."

The thought had barely passed through his brain, when a leaden messenger, intended to pass through it, carried his cap off his head, and the fire that had discharged it almost blinded him. Bigfoot, the chief of the savages, had wriggled himself, snake-

fashion, up to the stockade unseen, and while
Roaring Bull was meditating what was best to be
done, he had nearly succeeded in rendering him
unable to do anything at all.

The shot was the signal for another onslaught.
Once more the woods rang with fiendish yells and
rattling volleys. Bigfoot, with the agility and
strength of a gorilla, leaped up and over the stockade
and sprung down into Jackson's arms, while Darvall
and Crux resumed their almost ubiquitous process
of defence, and Buttercup's weapon again thundered
forth its defiance.

This time the fight was more protracted. Bigfoot's career was indeed stopped for the time being,
for Jackson not only crushed the life almost out
of him by an unloving embrace, but dealt him a
prize-fighter's blow which effectually stretched him
on the ground. Not a moment too soon, however,
for the white man had barely got rid of the red
one, when another savage managed to scale the wall.
A blow from the butt of Jackson's rifle dropped him,
and then the victor fired so rapidly, and with such
effect, that a second time the Reds were repulsed.

Jackson did not again indulge in meditation,
but blew a shrill blast on a dog-whistle—a precon-
certed signal—on hearing which his two comrades
made for the house door at full speed.

Only one other of the Indians, besides the two
already mentioned, had succeeded in getting over the

stockade. This man was creeping up to the open door of the house, and, tomahawk in hand, had almost reached it when Dick Darvall came tearing round the corner.

"Hallo! Crux," cried Dick, "that you?"

The fact that he received no reply was sufficient for Dick, who was too close to do more than drive the point of his rifle against the chest of the Indian, who went down as if he had been shot, while Dick sprang in and held open the door. A word from Jackson and Crux as they ran forward sufficed. They passed in and the massive door was shut and barred, while an instant later at least half-a-dozen savages ran up against it and began to thunder on it with their rifle-butts and tomahawks.

"To your windows!" shouted Jackson, as he sprang up the wooden stair-case, three steps at a time. "Fresh rifles here, Mary!"

"Yes, father," came in a silvery and most unwarlike voice from the hall below.

Another moment and three shots rang from the three sides of the house, and of the three Indians who were at the moment in the act of clambering over the stockade, one fell inside and two out. Happily, daylight soon began to make objects distinctly visible, and the Indians were well aware that it would now be almost certain death to any one who should attempt to climb over.

It is well known that, as a rule, savages do not

throw away their lives recklessly. The moment it became evident that darkness would no longer serve them, those who were in the open retired to the woods, and potted at the windows of the ranch, but, as the openings from which the besieged fired were mere loop-holes made for the purpose of defence, they had little hope of hitting them at long range except by chance. Those of the besiegers who happened to be near the stockade took shelter behind the breast-work, and awaited further orders from their chief —ignorant of the fact that he had already fallen.

From the loop-holes of the room which Jackson had selected to defend, the shed with the saddled horses was visible, so that no one could reach it without coming under the fire of his deadly weapon. There was also a window in this room opening upon the back of the house and commanding the field which we have before mentioned as being unde-fended while the battle was waged outside. By casting a glance now and then through this window he could see any foe who might show himself in that direction. The only part of the fort that seemed exposed to great danger now was the front door, where the half-dozen savages, with a few others who had joined them, were still battering away at the impregnable door.

Dick, who held the garret above, could not see the door, of course, nor could he by any manœuvre manage to bring his rifle to bear on it from his

"NOW, BUTTERCUP. GIVE IT 'EM HOT." Page 217.

loop-hole, and he dared not leave his post lest more Indians should manage to scale the front stockade.

Buttercup, in the room below, had indeed a better chance at her window, but she was too inexpert in warfare to point the blunderbuss straight down and fire with effect, especially knowing, as she did, that the sight of her arm in the act would be the signal for a prompt fusillade. But the girl was not apparently much concerned about that or anything else. The truth is that she possessed in an eminent and enviable degree the spirit of entire trust in a leader. She was under orders, and awaited the word of command with perfect equanimity! She even smiled slightly—if such a mouth could be said to do anything slightly—when Mary left her to take fresh rifles to the defenders overhead.

At last the command came from the upper regions, in tones that caused the very savages to pause a moment and look at each other in surprise. They did not pause long, however!

"Now, Buttercup," thundered Roaring Bull, "give it 'em—hot!"

At the word the girl calmly laid aside her weapon, lifted the big iron pot with familiar and business-like facility, and emptied it over the window.

The result is more easily imagined than described. A yell that must have been heard miles off was the prelude to a stampede of the most lively nature. It was intensified, if possible, by the further action

of the negress, who, seizing the blunderbuss, pointed
it at the flying crowd, and, shutting both eyes, fired !
Not a buckshot took effect on the savages, for Buttercup, if we may say so, aimed too low, but the
effect was more stupendous than if the aim had
been good, for the heavy charge drove up an inde-
scribable amount of peppery dust and small stones
into the rear of the flying foe, causing another yell
which was not an echo but a magnified reverberation
of the first.   Thus Buttercup had the satisfaction of
utterly routing her foes without killing a single man !

Daylight had fairly set in by that time, and the
few savages who had not succeeded in vaulting the
stockade had concealed themselves behind the
various outhouses.

The proprietor of the ranch began now to have
some hope of keeping the Indians at bay until the
troops should succour him.   He even left his post
and called his friends to a council of war, when a
wild cheer was heard in the woods.   It was followed
by the sound of firing.   No sooner was this heard
than the savages concealed outside of the breastwork
rose as one man and ran for the woods.

"It's the troops !" exclaimed Dick hopefully.

"Troopers never cheer like that," returned Jackson
with an anxious look.   "It's more like my poor
cow-boys, and, if so, they will have no chance wi'
such a crowd o' Reds.   We must ride to help them,
an' you'll have to ride with us, Mary.   We

daren't leave you behind, lass, wi' them varmints skulkin' around."

"I'm ready, father," said Mary with a decided look, though it was evident, from the pallor of her cheek, that she was ill at ease.

"Now, look here, Dick," said Jackson, quickly, "you will go down and open the front gate. I'll go with 'ee wi' my repeater to keep an eye on the hidden reptiles, so that if one of them shows so much as the tip of his ugly nose he'll have cause to remember it. You will go to my loophole, Crux, an' keep your eyes open all round—specially on the horses. When the gate is open I'll shout, and you'll run down to the shed wi' the women.—You understand?" Crux nodded.

Acting on this plan Dick ran to the gate; Jackson followed, rifle in hand, and, having reached the middle of the fort, he faced round; only just in time to see a gun barrel raised from behind a shed. Before he could raise his own weapon a shot was heard and the gun-barrel disappeared, while the Indian who raised it fell wounded on the ground.

"Well done, Crux!" he exclaimed, at the same moment firing his own rifle at a head which was peeping round a corner. The head vanished instantly and Darvall rejoined him, having thrown the gate wide open.

"Come round wi' me an' drive the reptiles out," cried Jackson. At the same time he uttered a roar that a bull might have envied, and they both rushed round to the back of the outhouses where three Indians were found skulking.

At the sudden and unexpected onslaught, they fired an ineffectual volley and fled wildly through the now open gate, followed by several shots from both pursuers, whose aim, however, was no better than their own had been.

Meanwhile Crux and the girls, having reached the shed according to orders, mounted their respective steeds and awaited their comrades. They had not long to wait. Jackson and Dick came round the corner of the shed at full speed, and, without a word, leaped simultaneously into their saddles.

"Keep close to me, girls,—close up!" was all that Jackson said as he dashed spurs into his horse, and, sweeping across the yard and through the gate, made straight for that part of the woods where yells, shouts, and firing told that a battle was raging furiously.

CHAPTER XIX.

THE RESCUE AND ITS CONSEQUENCES.

THE ground in the neighbourhood of the ranch favoured the operations of an attacking party, for it was so irregular and so cumbered with knolls and clumps of trees that the defenders of the post scarce dared to make a sally, lest their retreat should be cut off by a detached party of assailants.

Hence Jackson would never have dreamed of quitting his house, or ceasing to act on the defensive, had he not been under the natural impression that it was his own returning cow-boys who had been attacked and out-numbered by the Indians. Great, therefore, was his surprise when, on rounding a bluff and coming into view of the battle-field, the party engaged with the Indians, though evidently white men, were neither his own men nor those of the U. S. troops.

He had just made the discovery, when a band of about fifty warriors burst from the woods and rushed upon him.

" Back to back, boys ! girls, keep close ! " shouted Jackson, as he fired two shots and dropped two

Indians. He pulled at a third, but there was no answering report, for the magazine of his repeater was empty.

Crux and Darvall turned their backs towards him and thus formed a sort of triangle, in the midst of which were the two girls. But this arrangement, which might have enabled them to hold out for some time, was rendered almost abortive by the ammunition having been exhausted.

"So much for bein' in too great a hurry!" growled Jackson between his clenched teeth, as he clubbed his rifle and made a savage blow at the Indian who first came close to him. It was evident that the Indians were afraid to fire lest they should wound or kill the women; or, perhaps, understanding how matters stood, they wished to capture the white men alive, for, instead of firing at them, they circled swiftly round, endeavouring to distract their attention so as to rush in on them.

Bigfoot, who had recovered from his blow and escaped from the ranch, made a sudden dash at Dick when he thought him off his guard, but Dick was not easily caught off his guard in a fight. While in the act of making a furious demonstration at an Indian in front, which kept that savage off, he gave Bigfoot a "back-handed wipe," as he called it, which tumbled the chief completely off his horse.

Just then a turn of affairs in favour of the whites was taking place on the battle-field beyond. The party there had attacked the savages with such fury as to scatter them right and left, and they were now riding down at racing speed on the combatants, whose fortunes we have followed thus far.

Two men rode well in advance of the party with a revolver in each hand.

"Why, it's Charlie Brooke! Hurrah!" yelled Darvall with delight.

"An' Buck Tom!" roared Jackson in amazement.

So sudden was the onset that the Indians were for a moment paralysed, and the two horsemen, firing right and left as they rode up, dashed straight into the very midst of the savages. In a moment they were alongside of their friends, while the rest of the outlaw band were already engaged on the outskirts of the crowd.

The very danger of the white men constituted to some extent their safety; for they were so outnumbered and surrounded that the Indians seemed afraid to fire lest they should shoot each other. To add to the confusion, another party of whites suddenly appeared on the scene and attacked the "Reds" with a wild cheer. This was Jackson's little band of cow-boys. They numbered only eight; but the suddenness of their appearance tended further to distract the savages.

While the noise was at its height a sound, or rather sensation, of many feet beating the earth was felt. Next moment a compact line was seen to wheel round the bluff where the fight was going on, and a stentorian "Charge!" was uttered, as the United States cavalry, preceded by Hunky Ben, bore down with irresistible impetuosity on the foe.

But the Indians did not await this onset. They turned and fled, scattering as they went, and the fight was quickly turned into a total rout and hot pursuit, in which troopers, outlaws, travellers, ranchmen, scouts, and cow-boys joined. The cavalry, however, had ridden far and fast, so that the wiry little mustangs of the plains soon left them behind, and the bugle ere long recalled them all.

It was found on the assembling of the forces that not one of the outlaws had returned. Whether they were bent on wreaking their vengeance still more fully on their foes, or had good reason for wishing to avoid a meeting with the troops, was uncertain; but it was shrewdly suspected that the latter was the true reason.

"But you led the charge with Buck Tom, sir," said Jackson to Charlie, in considerable surprise, "though how you came to be in *his* company is more than I can understand."

"Here's somebody that can explain, may-be," said one of the cow-boys, leading forward a wounded man whose face was covered with blood, while he limped as if hurt in the legs. "I found him tryin' to crawl into the brush. D'ye know him, boys?"

"Why, it's Jake the Flint!" exclaimed several voices simultaneously; while more than one hand was laid on a revolver, as if to inflict summary punishment.

"I claim this man as my prisoner," said the commander of the troops, with a stern look that prevented any attempt at violence.

"Ay, you've got me at last," said the outlaw, with a look of scorn. "You've bin a precious long time about it too."

"Secure him," said the officer, deigning no reply to these remarks.

Two troopers dismounted, and with a piece of rope began to tie the outlaw's hands behind him.

"I arrest you also," said the commander to Charlie, who suddenly found a trooper on each side of him. These took him lightly by each arm, while a third seized his bridle.

"Sir!" exclaimed our hero, while the blood rushed to his forehead, "I am *not* an outlaw!"

"Excuse me," returned the officer politely, "but my duty is plain. There are a good many gentlemanly outlaws about at present. You are found joining in fight with a notorious band. Until you can clear yourself you must consider yourself my prisoner.—Disarm and bind him."

For one moment Charlie felt an almost irresistible impulse to fell the men who held him, but fortunately the absurdity of his position forced itself on him, and he submitted, well knowing that his innocence would be established immediately.

"Is not this man one of your band, Jake?" asked the officer quietly.

"Yes, he is," replied the man with a malevolent grin. "He's not long joined. This is his first scrimmage with us."

Charlie was so thunderstruck at this speech that he was led back to the ranch in a sort of dazed condition. As for Dick Darvall, he was rendered speechless, and felt disposed to regard the whole thing as a sort of dream, for his attempted explanations were totally disregarded.

Arrived at the house, Charlie and Jake were locked up in separate rooms, and sentries placed beneath their windows—this in addition to the security of hand-cuffs and roped arms. Then breakfast was prepared for the entire company, and those who had been wounded in the fight were attended to by Hunky Ben—a self-taught surgeon—with Mary and Buttercup to act as dressers.

"I say, Jackson," observed Darvall, when the worthy ranch-man found leisure to attend to him, "of course *you* know that this is all nonsense—an abominable lie about my friend Brooke being an outlaw?"

"Of course I do, Dick," said Jackson, in a tone of sympathy; "an' you may be cock-sure I'll do what I can to help 'im. But he'll have to prove himself a true man, an' there *are* some mysteries about him that it puzzles me to think how he 'll clear 'em up."

"Mysteries?" echoed Dick.

"Ay, mysteries. I 've had some talk wi' Hunky Ben, an' he 's as much puzzled as myself, if not more."

"Well, then, I 'm puzzled more than either of ye," returned Dick, "for my friend and mate is as true a man—all straight an' aboveboard—as ever I met with on sea or land."

"That may be, boy, but there 's some mystery about him, somehow."

"Can ye explain what the mystery is, Jackson?"

"Well, this is what Hunky Ben says. He saw your friend go off the other night alone to Traitor's Trap, following in the footsteps o' that notorious outlaw Buck Tom. Feelin' sure that Buck meant to waylay your friend, Hunky followed him up and overshot him to a place where he thought it likely the outlaw would lay in wait. Sure enough, when he got there he found Buck squattin' behind a big rock. So he waited to see what would turn up and be ready to rescue your friend. An' what d' ye think did turn up?"

"Don' know," said Dick, with a look of solemn wonder.

"Why, when Buck stepped out an' bid him throw up his hands, your friend merely looked at Buck and said somethin' that Hunky couldn't hear, an' then Buck dropped his pistol, an' your friend got off his horse and they shook hands and went off as thick as thieves together. An' now, as you've seen an' heard, your friend turns up headin' a charge of the outlaws—an' a most notable charge it was—alongside o' Buck Tom. Jake the Flint too claims him for a comrade. Pretty mysterious all that, ain't it?"

"May I ask," said Dick, with some scorn in his tone, "who is this Hunky Ben, that his word should be considered as good as a bank-note?"

"He's the greatest scout an' the best an' truest man on the frontier," replied Jackson.

"H'm! so Miss Mary seems to think too."

"An' Mary thinks right."

"An' who may this Jake the Flint be?" asked the sailor.

"The greatest scoundrel, cattle and horse stealer, and cut-throat on the frontier."

"So then," rejoined Dick, with some bitterness, "it would seem that my friend and mate is taken up for an outlaw on the word o' the two greatest men on the frontier!"

"It looks like it, Dick, coupled, of course, wi' your friend's own actions. But never you fear, man. There must be a mistake o' some sort, somewhere, an' it's sure to come out, for I'd as soon believe my Mary to be an outlaw as your friend— though I never set eyes on him before the other day.

The fact is, Dick, that I've learned physiognomy since —— "

" Fizzi-what-umy ? " interrupted Dick.

" Physiognomy—the study o' faces—since I came to live on the frontier, an' I'm pretty sure to know an honest man from a rogue as soon as I see him an' hear him speak—though I can't always prove myself right."

While Dick and his host were thus conversing, and the soldiers were regaling themselves in the hall, the commander of the troops and Hunky Ben were engaged in earnest conversation with Charlie Brooke, who gave an account of himself that quite cleared up the mystery of his meeting, and afterwards being found associated with, the outlaws.

" It's a queer story," said Hunky Ben, who, besides being what his friends called a philosopher, was prone at times to moralise. " It's a queer story, an' shows that a man shouldn't bounce at a conclusion till he's larned all the ins an' outs of a matter."

" Of course, Mr. Brooke," said the officer, when Dick had finished his narration, "your companion knows all this and can corroborate what you have said ? "

" Not all," replied Charlie. " He is an old shipmate whom I picked up on arriving at New York, and only knows that I am in search of an old school-fellow who has given way to dissipation and

got into trouble here. Of my private and family
affairs he knows nothing."

"Well, you have cleared yourself, Mr. Brooke,"
continued the Captain, whose name was Wilmot,
"but I'm sorry to have to add that you have not
cleared the character of your friend Leather, whose
name has for a considerable time been associated
with the notorious band led by your old school-
fellow Ritson, who is known in this part of the
country as Buck Tom. One of the worst of this
gang of highwaymen, Jake the Flint, has, as you
know, fallen into my hands, and will soon receive
his deserts as a black-hearted murderer. I have
recently obtained trustworthy information as to the
whereabouts of the gang, and I am sorry to say
that I shall have to ask you to guide me to their
den in Traitor's Trap."

"Is it my duty to do this?" asked Charlie, with
a troubled look at the officer.

"It is the duty of every honest man to facilitate
the bringing of criminals to justice."

"But I have strong reason for believing that my
friend Leather, although reckless and dissipated,
joined these men unwillingly—was forced to do it
in fact—and has been suffering from the result of a
severe injury ever since joining, so that he has not
assisted them at all in their nefarious work. Then,
as to Ritson, I am convinced that he repents of his
course of conduct. Indeed, I know that his men

have been rebellious of late, and this very Jake has been aspiring to the leadership of the gang."

"Your feelings regarding these men may be natural," returned the captain, "but my duty is to use you in this matter. Believing what you say of yourself I will treat you as a gentleman, but if you decline to guide me to the nest of this gang I must treat you still as a prisoner."

"May I have a little time to think over the matter before answering?"

"So that you may have a chance of escaping me?" replied the Captain.

"Nothing was further from my thoughts," said Charlie, with a flush of indignation.

"I believe you, Mr. Brooke," rejoined the Captain with gravity. "Let me know any time before twelve to-day what course you deem it right to take. By noon I shall sound boot and saddle, when you will be ready to start. Your nautical friend here may join us if he chooses."

Now, while this investigation into the affairs of one prisoner was going on, the other prisoner, Jake, was busily employed investigating his own affairs with a view to escape.

How he fared in this investigation we reserve for another chapter.

CHAPTER XX.

JAKE THE FLINT IN DIFFICULTIES.

THE man who, at the time we write of, was
known by the name of Jake the Flint had acquired
the character of the most daring and cruel scoundrel
in a region where villains were by no means rare.
His exploits indicated a spirit that was utterly
reckless of life, whether his own or that of his fellow-
men, and many were the trappers, hunters, and
Redskins who would have given a good deal and
gone far to have the chance of putting a bullet in
his carcass.

But, as is not unfrequently the case with such
men, Jake seemed to bear a charmed life, and when
knife, bullet, and rope, cut short the career of many
less guilty men, Jake had hitherto managed to elude
his captors—at one time by strategy, at another by
a bold dash for life, and sometimes by "luck." No
one had a kind word for Jake, no one loved, though
many feared, admired, and hated him. This may
seem strange, for it is usually found that even in the
case of the most noted outlaws there is a woman or
a man, or both—who cling to them with affection.

Perhaps the fact that Jake was exceptionally harsh and cruel at all times, may account for this, as it accounted for his sobriquet of Flint. He was called by some of those who knew him a "God-forsaken man." We merely state the fact, but are very far from adopting the expression, for it ill becomes any man of mortal mould to pronounce his fellow-man God-forsaken.

In the meantime we feel it to be no breach of charity to say that Jake had forsaken God, for his foul language and bloody deeds proved the fact beyond all question. He was deceitful as well as cruel, and those who knew him best felt sure that his acting under Buck Tom was a mere ruse. There is little doubt that he had done so for the purpose of obtaining an influence over a gang of desperadoes, ready to hand, as it were, and that the moment he saw his opportunity he would kill Buck Tom and take command. The only thing that had kept him from doing so sooner, it was thought, was the fact that Buck had the power to gain the affection of his men, as well as to cause them to fear him, so that Jake had not yet found the time ripe for action.

After the outlaw had been put into the room by himself, as already stated, the door locked, and a sentry posted below the window, he immediately turned with all his energy to examine into his circumstances and prospects. First of all his wrists were manacled. That, however, gave him little concern, for his hands were unusually small and delicate, and he knew from experience that he could slip them out of any handcuffs that would close easily on his wrists—a fact that he had carefully concealed, and of which men were not yet aware, as he had not yet been under the necessity of availing himself of the circumstance.

The rope with which he had been bound on the way to the ranch had been removed, the handcuffs being deemed sufficient. As the window of his prison was over thirty feet from the ground, and a sentinel with a carbine and revolver stood below, it was thought that the bird who had so frequently escaped his cage before was safe at last, and fairly on his way to the gallows.

Not so thought Jake the Flint. Despair did not seem to be a possibility to him. Accordingly, he examined his prison carefully, and with a hopeful smile. The examination was soon completed, for the room presented no facilities whatever for escape. There was no bed from which to take the sheets and blankets to extemporise a rope. No mattress to throw over the window so as to break a heavy man's fall. No chimney by which to ascend to the roof, no furniture, indeed, of any kind beyond a deal chair and table. The door was of solid oak and bolted outside.

Obviously the window was his only chance. He went to it and looked out. The depth was too much, he knew, for even his strong bones to stand the shock; and the sentinel paced to and fro underneath with loaded carbine.

"If any one would only lay a feather-bed down there," thought Jake, "I'd jump an' take my chance."

While he was gazing meditatively on the fair prospect of land and water that lay before him, one of the bolts of the door was withdrawn, then another, and the door slowly opened.

For an instant the outlaw gathered himself up for a rush, with a view to sell his life dearly, and he had even begun to draw one of his hands out of the manacles, when the folly and hopelessness of the attempt struck him. He quickly checked himself, and met his jailor (one of the troopers) with a smiling countenance as he entered and laid a loaf and a jug of water on the table.

The rattle of a musket outside told Jake that his jailor had not come alone.

Without a word the man turned, and was leaving the room, when Jake, in a voice of great humility, asked him to stop.

"You couldn't remove these things, could you?" he said, holding out his fettered hands.

"No," answered the trooper, sharply.

"Ah!" sighed Jake, "I feared it was agin the rules. You couldn't let me have the use of a file, could you, for a few minutes? What! agin' rules too? It's a pity, for I'm used to brush my teeth with a file of a mornin', an' I like to do it before breakfast."

Jake interlarded his speech with a variety of oaths, with which we will not defile the paper, but he could extract no further reply from the trooper than a glance of scorn.

Left to himself, Jake again went to the window, which was a small cottage one, opening inwards like a door. He opened it and looked out. The sentinel instantly raised his carbine and ordered him to shut it.

"Hullo! Silas, is that you?" cried Jake in surprise, but paying no attention to the threat, "I thought you had quit for Heaven durin' the last skrimidge wi' the Reds down in Kansas? Glad to see you lookin' so well. How's your wife an' the child'n, Silas?"

"Come now, Jake," said the trooper sternly, "you know it's all up with you, so you needn't go talkin' bosh like that—more need to say your prayers. Stand back and shut the window, I say, else I'll put a bullet through your gizzard."

"Well now, Silas," said Jake, remonstratively, and opening the breast of his red shirt as he spoke, "I didn't expect that of an old friend like you—indeed I didn't. But, see here, if you raaly are goin' to fire take good aim an' keep clear o' the heart and liver. The gizzard lies hereabout (pointing to his breast)

and easy to hit if you've a steady hand. I know
the exact spot, for I 've had the cuttin' up of a good
bunch o' men in my day, an' I can't bear to see a
thing muddled. But hold on, Silas, I won't put ye
to the pain o' shootin' me. I'll shut the window if
you'll make me a promise."

"What's that?" demanded the trooper, still
covering the outlaw, however, with his carbine.

"You know I'm goin' to my doom—that's what
poetical folk call it, Silas—an' I want you to help
me wind up my affairs, as the lawyers say. Well,
this here (holding up a coin) is my last dollar, the
remains o' my fortin', Silas, an' this here bit o' paper
that I'm rappin' round it is my last will an' testi-
monial. You'll not refuse to give it to my only
friend on arth, Hunky Ben, for I've no wife or
chick to weep o'er my grave, even though they
knew where it was. You'll do this for me, Silas,
won't you?"

"All right—pitch it down."

Jake threw the coin, which fell on the ground a
few feet in front of the trooper, who stooped to pick
it up.

With one agile bound the outlaw leaped from the
window and descended on the trooper's back, which
was broken by the crashing blow, and Jake rolled
over him with considerable violence, but the poor
man's body had proved a sufficient buffer, and Jake
rose unhurt. Deliberately taking the carbine from

the dead man's hand, and plucking the revolver from his belt, he sauntered off in the direction of the stables. These being too small to contain all the troop-horses, some of the animals were picketed in an open shed, and several troopers were rubbing them down. The men took Jake for one of the cow-boys of the ranch, for he passed them whistling.

Entering the stable he glanced quickly round, selected the finest horse, and, loosing its halter from the stall, turned the animal's head to the door.

"What are ye doin' wi' the captain's horse?" demanded a trooper, who chanced to be in the neighbouring stall.

"The captain wants it. Hold his head till I get on him. He's frisky," said Jake, in a voice of authority.

The man was taken aback and obeyed; but as Jake mounted he turned suddenly pale.

The outlaw, observing the change, drew the revolver, and, pointing it at the trooper's head, said, in a low savage voice, "A word, a sound, and your brains are on the floor!"

The man stood open-mouthed, as if petrified. Jake shook the reins of the fiery horse and bounded through the door-way, stooping to the saddle-bow as he went. He could see, even at that moment, that the trooper, recovering himself, was on the point of uttering a shout. Wheeling round in the saddle he fired, and the man fell with a bullet in his brain.

The shot of course aroused the whole ranch. Men rushed into the yard with and without arms in wild confusion, but only in time to see a flying horseman cross the square and make for the gate. A rattling irregular volley was sent after him, but the only effect it had was to cause the outlaw to turn round in the saddle and wave his hat, while he gave vent to a yell of triumph. Another moment and he was beyond the bluff and had disappeared.

"Boot and saddle!" instantly rang out at the ranch, and every preparation was made for pursuit, though, mounted as Jake was on the best horse of the troop, they could not hope to overtake him.

Hunky Ben, at his own particular request, was permitted to go on in advance.

"You see, sir," he said to the captain, "my Black Polly an't quite as good as your charger, but she's more used to this sort o' country, an' I can take the short cuts where your horse could hardly follow."

"Go, Ben, and good luck go with you! Besides, we can do without you, now that we have Mr. Brooke to guide us."

"Come wi' me, sir," said Hunky Ben, as he passed Charlie on his way to the stables. "Don't you hesitate, Mr. Brooke, to guide the captain to the cave of Buck Tom. I'm goin' on before you to hunt up the reptiles—to try an' catch Jake the Flint!"

The scout chuckled inwardly as he said this.

"But why go in advance? You can never overtake the scoundrel with such a start and on such a horse."

"Never you mind what I can or can't do," said Ben, entering the stable where the dead trooper still lay, and unfastening Black Polly. "I've no time to explain. All I know is that your friend Leather is sure to be hanged if he's cotched, an' I'm sure he's an innocent man—therefore, I'm goin' to save him. It's best for you to know nothin' more than that, for I see you're not used to tellin' lies. Can you trust me?"

"Certainly I can. The look of your face, Ben, even more than the character you bear, would induce me to trust you."

"Well then, Mr. Brooke, the first sign o' trust is to obey orders without askin' questions."

"True, when the orders are given by one who has a right to command," returned Charlie.

"Just so, an' my right to command lies in the fact that the life o' your friend Leather depends on your obedience."

"I'm your humble servant, then. But what am I to do?"

"Do whatever Captain Wilmot orders without objectin', an' speak nothing but the truth. You don't need to speak the *whole* truth, hows'ever," added the scout thoughtfully, as he led out his coal-black steed. " Your friend Leather has got a Christian name of course. Don't mention it. I don't want to hear it. Say nothin' about it to anybody. The time may come when it may be useful to drop the name of Leather and call your friend Mister —— whatever the tother name may be. Now mind what I 've said to ye."

As he spoke the last words the scout touched the neck of his beautiful mare, and in another minute was seen racing at full speed over the rolling plain.

CHAPTER XXI.

WHEN Jake escaped from the ranch of Roaring Bull he tried the mettle of Captain Wilmot's charger to the uttermost, for well he knew that the pursuit would be instant and vigorous; that his late comrade Charlie Brooke could guide the troops to the cavern in Traitor's Trap, and that if his companions, who would doubtless ride straight back, were to escape, they must be warned in time. He also knew that the captain's charger was a splendid one. In order to accomplish his purpose, therefore, he would ride it to death.

The distance between the ranch and the outlaws' cave was not so great but that any mustang in the plains could have traversed it in a day, but the cruel man had made up his mind that the captain's charger should do it in a few hours. It is not so much distance as pace that kills. Had any consideration whatever been extended to the noble creature by the ignoble brute who rode it, the good horse would have galloped to the head of the Trap

almost without turning a hair. At first he strode
out over the rolling prairie with the untiring vigour
of a well-made frame and a splendid constitution,
leaping the little cracks and inequalities of the
ground in the exuberance of his strength; though
there was no need to bound, and coursing over the
knolls as easily as he cantered down the hollows,
while his flashing eye betokened at once a courage-
ous and a gentle spirit. But when the lower slopes
of the hills were reached, and steepish gradients
were met with here and there, the horse began to
put back first one ear and then the other, and sometimes both, as if in expectation of the familiar
"well done," or pat on the neck, or check of the
rein with which the captain had been wont to sanc-
tion a slackening of the pace, but no such grace was
allowed him. On the contrary, when the first symptom appeared of a desire to reduce speed Jake
drove his cruel spurs into the charger's glossy side.
With a wild snort and bound the horse stretched
out again and spurned the ground as if in indignant
surprise.

Then the breath began to labour slightly; the
sweat to darken his rich brown coat, and the white
foam to fleck his broad chest. Still Jake pressed
him on with relentless fury. It could not be
expected that a man who cared not for his fellows
would have much consideration for his beast.
Murder of a deeper dye than that of a horse was

seething in the outlaw's brain. This to him useless
expedition, which had so nearly cost him his life,
would be the last that Buck Tom should command.
After blowing out *his* brains he would warn the
others of the impending danger and lead them away
to other and more favourable fields of enterprise.

At this point the good horse stumbled and almost
threw his rider, who, with horrible curses, plied the
spurs and tugged at the bit until blood was mingled
with the flying foam. Never, save once—when
Captain Wilmot was caught alone in the plains by
Cheyenne Indians and had to fly for his life—had
the good charger been urged to anything like such
an effort as he was now called on to make, and *then*
there was no cruelty mingled with the urging. The
very tone of his master's voice, as he patted the
neck and shook the rein and gently touched him
with the spur, must have convinced the intelligent
creature that it was a matter of life or death—
that there was a stern need-be for such haste.

Turning at last into the gorge of the Trap, the
charger gasped and sobbed with distress as he faced
the steep ascent and tried, with the unabated
courage of a willing heart, to pull himself together
while the unmerciful monster still drove in the
spurs and galled his tender mouth. But the brave
effort was unavailing. Stumbling over a root that
crossed the path, the horse plunged forward, and
fell with a crash, sending his rider over his head.

Jake, alighting on his face and right shoulder, lay stunned for a few seconds. Then he jumped up, displaying torn garments and a face covered with blood.

Running to the horse's head he seized the rein and shook it savagely, kicking the animal's face with his heavy boots in his anxiety to make it rise, but the poor charger was beyond his cruelty by that time, for its neck had been broken by the fall.

Oh! it was one of those sights which are fitted to make even thoughtless men recognise the need of a Saviour for the human race, and to reject with something like scorn the doctrine—founded on wholly insufficient evidence—that there is no future of compensation for the lower animals!.

The outlaw did not waste time in vain regrets. Bestowing a meaningless curse on the dead charger, he turned and went up the narrow glen at a smart pace, but did not overstrain himself, for he knew well that none of the troop-horses could have kept up with him. He counted on having plenty of time to warn his comrades and get away without hurry. But he reckoned without his host—being quite ignorant of the powers of Black Polly, and but slightly acquainted with those of her master Hunky Ben.

Indeed so agile were the movements of Polly, and so thoroughly was the scout acquainted with the by-paths and short cuts of that region, that he actually passed the fugitive and reached the head of Traitor's Trap before him. This he managed by forsaking the roads, keeping a straighter line for the outlaws' cave, and passing on foot over the shoulder of a hill where a horseman could not go. Thus he came down on the cavern, about half-an-hour before Jake's arrival. Clambering to the crevice in the cliff against which the cave abutted, and sliding down into a hollow on its earthen roof, he cautiously removed a small stone from its position, and disclosed a hole through which he could both hear and see most of what took place inside.

Lest any one should wonder at the facility with which the ground lent itself to this manœuvre, we may as well explain that the bold scout possessed one of those far-reaching minds which are not satisfied without looking into *everything*,—seeing to the bottom of, and peering round to the rear of, all things, as far as possible. He always acted on the principle of making himself acquainted with every road and track and by-path, every stream, pond, river, and spring in the land. Hence he was well aware of this haunt of outlaws, and, happening to be near it one day when its owners were absent, he had turned aside to make the little arrangement of a peep-hole, in the belief that it might possibly turn out to be of advantage in course of time!

The clump of shrubs and grass on the rugged bank, which formed the top of the cave, effectually concealed the natural hollow which he had deepened, and the overhanging mass of the rugged cliff protected it from rain and dew.

What Hunky Ben saw on looking through his peep-hole filled him with surprise and pity, and compelled him to modify his plans.

Almost below him on a brush couch, lay the tall form of Buck Tom, with the unmistakable hue of approaching death upon his countenance. Beside him, holding his head, kneeled the much-wasted figure of Leather—the reputed outlaw. Seated or standing around in solemn silence were six of the outlaws, most of whom bore tokens of the recent fight, in the form of bandage on head or limb.

"I brought you to this, Leather; God forgive me," said the dying man faintly.

"No, you didn't, Ralph," replied the other, calling him by his old familiar name, "I brought myself to it. Don't blame yourself, Ralph; you weren't half so bad as me. You'd never have been here but for me. Come, Ralph, try to cheer up a bit; you're not dying. It's only faint you are, from loss of blood and the long gallop. When you've had a sleep and some food, you'll feel stronger. We'll fetch a doctor soon, an' he'll get hold o' the bullet. Dear Ralph, don't shake your head like that an' look so solemn. Cheer up, old boy!"

Leather spoke with a sort of desperate fervour, but Ralph could not cheer up.

"No," he said sadly, "there is no cheer for me. I've thrown my life away. There's no hope—no mercy for me. I've been trying to recall the past, an' what mother used to teach me, but it won't come. There's only one text in all the Bible that comes to me now. It's this—'Be sure your sin will find you out!' That's true, boys," he said, turning a look on his comrades. "Whatever else may be false, *that's* true, for I *know* it."

"That's so, dear Ralph," said Leather earnestly, "but it's no less true that ——"

Just then a noise was heard in the outer passage; then hurrying footsteps. Instinctively every man drew his revolver and faced the door. Next moment Jake entered.

"Here, one of you; a drink—I'm fit to —— ha!"

His eyes fell on the figure of Buck and he shrank back for a moment in silent surprise.

"Yes, Jake," said the dying man, with a glance of pity not unmingled with scorn, "it has come sooner than you or I expected, and it will save you some trouble—maybe some regret. I've seen through your little game, Jake, and am glad I've been spared the necessity of thwarting you."

He stopped owing to weakness, and Jake, recovering himself, hastily explained the reason of his sudden appearance.

"Fetch me a rag an' some water, boys," he continued. "It looks worse than it is—only skin deep.

And we've not a moment to lose. Those who have
a mind may follow *me*. Them that wants to swing
may stop."

"But how about Buck Tom?" asked one who
was not quite so depraved as the others.

"What's the use o' askin'?" said Jake. "It's
all up with him, don't you see? Besides, he's safe
enough. They'd never have the heart to hang a
dying man."

"An' Leather!" cried another. "We mustn't
quit Leather. He's game for many a fight yet.
Come, Leather; we'll help you along, for they're
sure to string you up on the nearest tree."

"Don't trouble yourself about me," said Leather,
looking round, for he still kneeled beside his old
friend, "I don't intend to escape. Look to your-
selves, boys, an' leave us alone."

"Unless you're all tired o' life you'll quit here
an' skip for the woods," said Jake, as, turning round,
he hurriedly left the place.

The others did not hesitate, but followed him
at once, leaving Buck Tom, and his friend to shift
for themselves.

During all this scene Hunky Ben had been intently gazing and listening—chiefly the latter.
When the outlaws filed past him he found it extremely difficult to avoid putting a bullet into the
Flint, but he restrained himself because of what yet
remained to be done.

As soon as the outlaws were well out of sight
Ben arose and prepared for action. First of all he
tightened his belt.   Then he pulled the hood of his
coat well over his head, so that it effectually concealed his face, and, still further to accomplish
the end in view, he fastened the hood in front with
a wooden pin.   Proceeding to the stable he found,
as he had hoped and expected, that the outlaws had
left one or two horse-cloths behind in their flight.
In one of these he enveloped his person in such a
way as to render it unrecognisable.   Then he walked
straight into the cave, and, without a word of warning, threw his strong arms around Shank Leather
and lifted him off the ground.

Of course Leather shouted and struggled at first,
but as well might a kitten have struggled in the
grip of a grizzly bear.   In his worn condition he
felt himself to be utterly powerless.   Buck Tom
made a feeble effort to rise and help him, but the
mere effort caused him to fall back with a groan
of helpless despair.

Swiftly his captor bore Leather up the side of
the hill till he got behind a clump of trees, into the
heart of which he plunged, and then set his burden
down on his feet.   At the same time, throwing back
his hood and flinging away the horse-cloth, he stood
up and smiled.

"Hunky Ben, or his ghost !" exclaimed Shank,
forgetting his indignation in his amazement.

"You're right, young man, though you've only see'd me once that I know of. But most men that see me once are apt to remember me."

"Well, Hunky," said Leather, while the indignation began to return, "you may think this very amusing, but it's mean of a big strong man like you to take advantage of a fellow that's as weak as a child from wounds an' fever. Lend me one o' your six-shooters, now, so as we may stand on somewhat more equal terms and——but a truce to boasting! I'm sure that you wouldn't keep smiling at me like a Cheshire cat if there wasn't something behind this."

"You're right, Mr. Leather," said Ben, becoming at once grave and earnest. There *is* somethin' behind it—ay, an' somethin' before it too. So much, that I have barely time to tell 'ee. So, listen wi' both ears. There's a bunch o' men an' troops close to the Trap even now, on their way to visit your cave. If they find you—you know what that means?"

"Death," said Leather quietly.

"Ay, death; though ye don't desarve it," said Ben.

"But I *do* deserve it," returned Shank in the same quiet voice.

"Well, may-hap you do," rejoined the scout coolly, "but not, so far as I know, in connection wi' your present company. Now, there's Buck Tom——"

"Ay, what of him?" asked Shank, anxiously.

"Well, in the nat'ral course o' things, death is

comin' to him too, an' that 'll save him from bein' strung up—for they 're apt to do that sort o' thing hereaway in a loose free-an-easy style that 's awkward sometime.   I was within an inch of it myself once, all through a mistake—I 'll tell 'ee about that when I 've got more time, maybe.   Well, now, I 'm keen to save you an' Buck Tom if I can, and what I want you to understand is, that if you expect me to help you at a time when you stand considerable in need o' help, you 'll have to do what I tell 'ee."

"And what would you have me do?" asked Shank, with a troubled look.

"Remain here till I come for 'ee, and when you meet me in company say nothin' about havin' met me before."

"Can I trust you, Hunky Ben?" said Shank, looking at him earnestly.

"If you *can't* trust me, what d' ye propose to do ?" asked the scout with a grin.

"You 're right, Ben.   I *must* trust you, and, to say truth, from the little I know of you, I believe I 've nothing to fear.   But my anxiety is for Ralph—Buck Tom, I mean.   You 're sure, I suppose, that Mr. Brooke will do his best to shield him ?"

"Ay, sartin sure, an', by the way, don't mention your Christian name just now—whatever it is—nor for some time yet.   Good-day, an' keep quiet till I come.   We 've wasted overmuch time a'ready."

So saying, the scout left the coppice, and, flinging

open his coat, re-entered the cave a very different-looking man from what he was when he left it.

"Hunky Ben!" exclaimed Buck, who had recovered by that time. "I wish you had turned up half-an-hour since, boy. You might have saved my poor friend Leather from a monster who came here and carried him away bodily."

"Ay? That's strange, now. Hows'ever, worse luck might have befel him, for the troops are at my heels, an' ye know what would be in store for him if he was here."

"Yes, indeed, I know it, Ben, and what is in store for me too; but Death will have his laugh at them if they don't look sharp."

"No, surely," said the scout, in a tone of real commiseration, "you're not so bad as that, are you?"

"Truly am I," answered Buck, with a pitiful look, "shot in the chest. But I saw you in the fight, Ben; did you guide them here?"

"That's what I did—at least I told 'em which way to go, an' came on in advance to warn you in time, so 's you might escape. To tell you the plain truth, Ralph Ritson, I've bin told all about you by your old friend Mr. Brooke, an' about Leather too, who, you say, has bin carried off by a monster?"

"Yes—at least by a monstrous big man."

"You're quite sure o' that?"

"Quite sure."

"An' you would know the monster if you saw him again ?"

"I think I would know his figure, but not his face, for I did not see it."

"Strange!" remarked the scout, with a simple look; " an' you 're sartin sure you don't know where Leather is now ?"

"Not got the most distant idea."

"That 's well now; stick to that, an' there 's no fear o' Leather. As to yourself—they 'll never think o' hangin' you till ye can walk to the gallows—so cheer up, Buck Tom. It may be that ye desarve hangin', for all I know; but not just at present. I 'm a bit of a surgeon, too—bein' a sort o' Jack-of-all-trades, and know how to extract bullets. What between Mr. Brooke an' me an' time, wonders may be worked, if you 're wise enough to keep a tight rein on your tongue."

While the scout was speaking, the tramp of cavalry was heard outside, and a few minutes later Captain Wilmot entered the cave, closely followed by Charlie Brooke.

CHAPTER XXII.

THE CAVE OF THE OUTLAWS INVADED BY GHOSTS AND U.S. TROOPS.

WE need scarcely say that Buck Tom was wise enough to put a bridle on his tongue after the warning hint he had received from the scout. He found this all the easier that he had nothing to conceal save the Christian name of his friend Leather, and, as it turned out, this was never asked for by the commander of the troops. All that the dying outlaw could reveal was that Jake the Flint had suddenly made his appearance in the cave only a short time previously, had warned his comrades, and, knowing that he (Buck) was mortally wounded, and that Leather was helplessly weak from a wound which had nearly killed him, had left them both to their fate. That, just after they had gone, an unusually broad powerful man, with his face concealed, had suddenly entered the cave and carried Leather off, in spite of his struggles, and that, about half-an-hour later, Hunky Ben had arrived to find the cave deserted by all but himself. Where the other outlaws had gone to he could not tell—of course they would not reveal that to a comrade who was sure to fall into the hands of their enemies.

"And you have no idea," continued the captain, "who the man is that carried your friend Leather so hurriedly away?"

"Not the slightest," returned Buck. "Had my revolver been handy and an ounce of strength left in me, you wouldn't have had to ask the question."

"Passing strange!" murmured Captain Wilmot, glancing at the scout, who was at the moment seated on a keg before the fire lighting his pipe, and with a look of simple benignant stolidity on his grave countenance. "Have *you* no idea, Ben, where these outlaws have taken themselves off to?"

"No more 'n a lop-eared rabbit, Captain Wilmot," answered the scout. "You see there's a good many paths by which men who knows the place could git out o' the Trap, an' once out o' it there's the whole o' the Rockie range where to pick an' choose."

"But how comes it, Ben, that you missed Jake? Surely the road is not so broad that you could pass him unseen! Yet you arrived here before him?"

"That's true, sir, but sly coons like the Flint can retire into the brush when they don't want to be overhauled. That wasn't the way of it, however. With such a splendid animal as your poor horse, Captain, an' ridden to death as it was—an' as I 'spected it would be—I knowed I had no chance o' comin' up wi' the Flint, so I took advantage o' my knowledge o' the lay o' the land, an' pushed ahead by a straighter line—finishin' the last bit on futt over the ridge of a hill. That sent me well ahead o' the Flint, an' so I got here before him. Havin' ways of eaves-droppin' that other people don't know on, I peeped into the cave here and saw and heard how matters stood. Then I thought o' harkin' back on my tracks an' stoppin' the Flint wi' a bullet, but I reflected 'what good'll that do? The shot would wake up the outlaws an' putt them on the scent all the same.' Then I tried to listen what their talk was about, so as I might be up to their dodges; but I hadn't bin listenin' long when in tramps the Flint an' sounds the alarm. Of course I might have sent him an' p'r'aps one o' the others to their long home from where I stood; but I've always had an objection to shoot a man behind his back. It has such a sneakin' sort o' feel about it! An' then, the others—I couldn't see how many there was—would have swarmed out on me, an' I'd have had to make tracks for the scrub, an' larn nothin' more. So I fixed to keep quiet an' hear and see all that I could —p'r'aps find out where they fixed to pull out to. But I heard nothin' more worth tellin'. They only made some hurried, an' by no means kindly, observa-tions about poor Buck an' Leather an' went off over the hills. I went into the woods a bit myself arter that, just to be well out o' the way, so to speak, an' when I got back here Leather was gone!"

R

"And you didn't see the man that carried him off?"

"No, I didn't see him."

"You'd have shot him, of course, if you had seen him?"

"No, indeed, captain, I wouldn't."

"No! why not?" asked the captain with a peculiar smile.

"Well, because," answered the scout, with a look of great solemnity, "I wouldn't shoot such a man on any account—no matter what he was doin'!"

"Indeed!" returned the other with a broadening smile. "I had no idea you were superstitious, Ben. I thought you feared neither man nor devil."

"What I fear an' what I don't fear," returned the scout with quiet dignity, "is a matter which has never given me much consarn."

"Well, don't be hurt, Hunky Ben, I don't for one moment question your courage, only I fancied that if you saw any one rescuing an outlaw you would have tried to put a bullet into him whether he happened to be a man or a ghost."

"But I have told you," broke in Buck Tom with something of his old fire, "that Leather is *not* an outlaw."

"I have only *your* word for that, and you know what that is worth," returned the captain. "I don't want to be hard on one apparently so near his end, and to say truth, I'm inclined to believe you, but we know that this man Leather has been for a long time in your company—whether a member of your band or not must be settled before another tribunal. If caught, he stands a good chance of being hanged. And now," added the captain, turning to a sergeant who had entered the cave with him, "tell the men to put up their horses as best they may. We camp here for the night. We can do nothing while it is dark, but with the first gleam of day we will make a thorough search of the neighbourhood."

While the troopers and their commander were busy making themselves as comfortable as possible in and around the cave, the scout went quietly up to the clump of wood where Leather was in hiding, and related to that unfortunate all that had taken place since he left him.

"It is very good of you, Hunky, to take so much interest in me and incur so much risk and trouble; but do you know," said Leather, with a look of surprise, not unmingled with amusement, "you are a puzzle to me, for I can't understand how you could tell Captain Wilmot such a heap o' lies —you that has got the name of bein' the truest-hearted scout on the frontier!"

"You puzzle me more than I puzzle you, Leather," returned the scout, with a simple look. "What lies have I told?"

"Why, all you said about what you saw and heard when you said you were eavesdroppin' must have been nonsense, you know, for how could you

hear and see what took place in the cave through
tons of rock and earth?"

"How I saw and heard, my son Leather, is a private affair of my own, but it was no lie.

Leather looked incredulous.

"Then you said," he continued, "that you didn't
see the man that carried me away."

"No more I did, boy. I *never* saw him!"

"What! not even in a looking-glass?"

"Not even in a lookin'-glass," returned Hunky.
"I've seed his *reflection* there many a time,—an' a
pretty good-lookin' reflection it was—but I've never
see'd himself—that I knows on! No, Leather, if
Captain Wilmot had axed me if I saw *you* carried
off, I might ha' been putt in a fix, but he didn't ax me
that. He axed if I'd seen the man that carried you
off an' I told the truth when I said I had *not*. Moreover I wasn't bound to show him that he wasn't fit to
be a lawyer—specially when he was arter an innocent man, an' might p'r'aps hang him without a
trial. It was my duty to guide the captain in pursuit of outlaws, an' it is my duty to shield an innocent man. Between the two perplexin' duties I
tried to steer as straight a course as I could, but I
confess I had to steer pretty close to the wind."

"Well, Hunky, it is my duty to thank you instead
of criticising you as I have done, but how do you
come to be so sure that I'm innocent?"

"P'r'aps because ye putt such an innocent

question," replied Ben, with a little smile. "D'ye raily think, Leather, that an old scout like me is goin' to let you see through all the outs and ins by which I comes at my larnin'! It's enough for you to know, boy, that I know a good deal more about you than ye think—more p'r'aps than ye know about yerself. I don't go for to say that you're a born angel, wantin' nothin' but a pair o' wings to carry ye off to the better land—by no means, but I do know that as regards jinin' Buck Tom's boys, or takin' a willin' part in their devilish work, ye are innocent, an' that's enough for me."

"I'm glad you know it and believe it, Ben," said Leather, earnestly, "for it is true. I followed Buck, because he's an old, old chum, and I did it at the risk of my life, an' then, as perhaps you are aware, we were chased and I got injured. So far I am innocent of acting with these men, but O Ben, I don't admit my innocence in anything else! My whole life—well, well—it's of no use talkin'. Tell me, d'ye think there's any chance o' Buck getting over this?"

"He may. Nobody can tell. I'll do my best for him. I never lose hope of a man, after what I've see'd in my experience, till the breath is fairly out of him."

"Thank God for these words, Ben."

"Yes," continued the scout, "and your friend Brooke is at this moment sunk in the blue dumps because you have been carried off by a great mysterious monster!"

"Then he doesn't know it was you?" exclaimed Leather.

"In course not. An' he doesn't know you are within five hundred yards of him. An' what's more, you mustn't let him know it was me, for that must be kept a dead secret, else it'll ruin my character on the frontier. We must surround it wi' mystery, my boy, till all is safe. But I didn't come up here to enjoy an evenin's conversation. You're not safe where you are, Leather. They'll be scourin' all round for you long before sun-up, so I must putt you where you'll be able to look on an' grin at them."

"Where will that be?" asked Leather, with some curiosity.

"You know the cliff about five hundred feet high that rises just over on the other side o' the valley— where the water-shoot comes down?"

"Ay, it's likely I do, for I've seen it every mornin' for months past."

"An' you remember the hole near the top o' the cliff?"

"Yes—that looks about the size of a crow?"

"Whatever it looks like it's three times the size of a man, an' it's the mouth of a cave," returned the scout. "Now, I'll lead you to the track that'll let you up to that cave. It's a splendid place, full of all sorts o' holes an' places where a man couldn't find you even if he know'd you was there. Once up, you may sit down, smoke your pipe in the mouth o' the cave, an' enjoy yourself, lookin' on at the hunt arter yourself. Here's a bit o' chuck I've brought to keep you from wearyin', for they may keep it up all day. When all danger is past I'll come up for ye. You needn't show more o' yourself, however, than the top o' your head. A man can never be over-cautious when he's bein' hunted down. An' mind, don't leave the place till I come for you."

Handing a cold roast fowl and a loaf to his companion, the scout got up and led him away to the spot which he had just described. It was by that time quite dark, but as Hunky Ben knew every inch of the ground he glided along almost as quickly as if it had been broad day, followed, with some difficulty, by poor Leather, who was still in a state of great prostration, partly because of his injury and partly in consequence of his previous dissipation. As the place, however, was not much more than half-a-mile distant his powers of endurance were not much tried. The scout led him across the narrow valley just above the outlaws' cave, and then, entering a steep rocky defile, he began to ascend a place that was more suitable for goats than men. After half-an-hour of upward toil they reached a plateau where the track—if it may be so styled—seemed

to run in a zig-zag manner until it reached a
small hole in the solid rock. Through this they
entered and found themselves within a cavern
and in total darkness.

"We may rest a bit now," said the scout. "There's
a ledge hereabouts. There you are. Sit down.
I'll have to take your hand here lest you fall off
the bridge into the holes on each side o' the track."

"Are the holes dangerous ?" asked Leather.

"They're dangerous enough to be worth takin'
care of, anyhow, for if ye was to tumble into one
you'd never come out again. There, now, let's go
on, for if I don't git back soon, they'll be wonderin'
if the monster hasn't run away wi' me too, as well
as you !"

After advancing a short distance in total darkness—Ben feeling his way carefully step by step—
they came suddenly to the hole in the front of the
cave to which reference has been already made.
The place had evidently been used before as a place
of refuge and temporary abode, for, near this front-
mouth of the cave was found a litter of pine branches
which had plainly been used as a bed.

"Sit ye down there, Leather," said the scout,
"see, or, rather, hear—for the eyes aren't of much
use just now—I've set down the grub an' a flask
o' water beside ye. Don't strike a light unless you
want to have your neck stretched. Daylight won't
be long o' lettin' ye see what's goin' on. You won't

weary, for it'll be as good as a play, yourself bein' chief actor an' audience all at the same time!"

Saying this the scout melted, as it were, into the darkness of the cavern, and, with noiseless moccasined feet, retraced his steps to the rear entrance.

Left to himself the poor wanderer found both time and food for reflection, for he did not dare in the darkness to move from the spot where he had seated himself. At first an eerie feeling of indefinable fear oppressed him, but this passed away as the busy thoughts went rambling back to home and the days of comparative innocence gone by. Forgetting the dark surroundings and the threatening dangers, he was playing again on the river banks, drinking liquorice-water, swimming, and rescuing kittens with Charlie Brooke. Anon, he was wandering on the sea-beach with his sister, brown-eyed Mary, or watching the manly form of his old friend and chum buffeting the waves towards the wreck on the Sealford Rocks. Memory may not be always faithful, but she is often surprisingly prompt. In the twinkling of an eye Shank Leather had crossed the Atlantic again and was once more in the drinking and gambling saloons —the "Hells" of New York—with his profoundly admired "friend" and tempter Ralph Ritson. It was a wild whirl and plunge from bad to worse through which Memory led him now—scenes at which he shuddered and on which he would fain have closed his eyes if possible, but Memory knows not the meaning of mercy. She tore open his eyes and, becoming unusually strict at this point, bade him look particularly at all the minute details of his reckless life—especially at the wrecks of other lives that had been caused by the wreck of his own. Then the deepest deep of all seemed to be reached when he rose—or rather fell—from the condition of tempted to that of tempter, and, some-how, managed for a time to lead even the far stronger-minded Ralph Ritson on the road to ruin. But he did not lead him long. The stronger nature soon re-asserted itself; seized the reins; led the yielding Leather to the cities of the far west; from gambling took to robbing, till at last the gay and handsome Ritson became transformed into the notorious Buck Tom, and left his weaker chum to care for himself.

It was at this point—so Memory recalled to him —that he, Leather, was stopped, in mid and mad, career, by a man of God with the love of Jesus in his heart and on his lips. And at this point Memory seemed to change her action and proved herself, although unmerciful, pre-eminently faithful. She reminded him of the deep contrition that God wrought in his heart; of the horror that over whelmed him when he thought of what he was, and what he had done; of the sudden resolve he had formed to follow Ritson, and try to stop him in the fearful career on which he had entered. Then came the memory of failure; of desperate anxieties; of futile entreaties; of unaccountably resolute perseverance; of joining the outlaw band to be near his friend; of being laughed to scorn by them all; of being chased by U.S. troops at the very commencement of his enterprise; of being severely wounded, rescued, and carried off during the flight by Buck Tom, and then—a long blank, mingled with awful dreams and scenes, and ribald songs, and curses—some of all which was real, and some the working of a fevered brain.

So terribly vivid were these pictures of memory, that one of the shouts of dreamland absolutely awoke him to the fact that he had extended his wearied limbs on his couch of pine brush and fallen asleep. He also awoke to the perception that it was broad daylight, and that a real shout had mingled with that of dreamland, for after he had sat up and listened intently for a few moments, the shout was repeated as if at no great distance.

CHAPTER XXIII.

THE TROOPS OUTWITTED BY THE SCOUT AND HIS FRIENDS.

CREEPING quickly to the mouth of the cave Leather peeped cautiously out, and the scene that met his startled gaze was not calculated to restore that equanimity which his recent dreams had disturbed.

The narrow and rugged valley which lay spread out below him was alive with horsemen, trotting hither and thither as if searching for some one, and several parties on foot were scaling gorges and slopes, up which a horseman could not scramble.

The shout which had awakened the fugitive was uttered by a dismounted trooper who had climbed higher on the face of the cliff than his fellows, and wished to attract the attention of those below.

" Hi! hallo!" he cried, "send Hunky Ben up here. " I've found a track that seems to lead to somewhere, but it'll need the scout's nose to ferret it out."

Leather's heart beat wildly, for, from the position of the man, he could not doubt that he had discovered the track leading up to the cave. Before he could think how he should act, a response came to the call from Hunky Ben.

"Ay, ay," he shouted, in a voice so bold and resonant, that Leather felt it was meant to warn him of his danger, "Ay, ay. Hold on! Don't be in a hurry. The tracks branch out further on, an' some o' them are dangerous. Wait till I come up. There's a cave up there, I'll lead ye to it."

This was more than enough for Leather. He turned hastily to survey his place of refuge. It was a huge dismal cavern with branching tunnels around that disappeared in thick obscurity, and heights above that lost themselves in gloom; holes in the sides and floor that were of invisible depth, and curious irregular ledges, that formed a sort of arabesque fringe to the general confusion.

One of these ornamental ledges, stretching along the roof with many others, lost itself in the gloom and seemed to be a hopeful living-place—all the more hopeful that it was in the full blaze of light that gushed in through the front opening of the cave. This opening, it will be remembered, was on the face of the cliff and inaccessible. But Leather found that he could not reach the ledge. Hastening to the dark side of the cave, however, he saw that by means of some projections and crevices in the rocky wall he could reach the end of the ledge. Creeping along it he soon found himself close to

the opening, surrounded by strong light, but effectually concealed from view by the ledge.   It was as
if he were on a natural rafter, peeping down on the
floor below!   As there was a multitude of such
ledges around, which it would take several men
many hours to examine, he began to breathe more
freely, for, would the searchers not naturally think
that a fugitive would fly to the darkest recesses of
his place of refuge, rather than to the brightest
and most accessible spot ?

He gave vent to a sigh of relief, and was congratulating himself upon his wisdom, when his eyes
chanced to fall on the flask of water and cold roast
fowl and loaf lying conspicuous in the full glare of
light that flooded the front part of the cave!

If the fowl had been thrust whole into his
throat it could scarcely have added to the gush of
alarm that choked him.   He slipped incontinently
from his arabesque ledge and dropped upon the
floor.   Securing the tell-tale viands with eager haste
he dashed back into the obscurity and clambered
with them back to his perch.   And not much too
soon, for he had barely settled down when the voice
of the scout was heard talking pretty loudly.

"Come along, Captain Wilmot," he said, "give
.me your hand, sir.   It's not safe to walk alone here,
even wi' a light."

"Here, where are you ?   Oh !   All right.   Haven't
you got a match ? " asked the captain.

"Nothin' that would burn more 'n a few seconds. We're better without a light, for a gust o' wind might blow it out an' leave us worse than we was. Mind this step. There."

"Well, I'm glad I didn't bring any of my men in here," said the Captain, as he kicked one of his heavy boots violently against a projection of rock.

"Ay—'tis as well you didn't," returned the scout, in a tone suggestive of the idea that he was smiling. "For there's holes on both sides, an' if one o' your men went down, ye might read the funeral sarvice over him at once, an' be done with it. There's a glimmer o' daylight at last. We'll soon be at the other end now."

"A horrible place, truly," said the Captain, "and one that it would be hard to find a fellow in even if we knew he was here."

"Didn't I say so, Captain? but ye wouldn't be convinced," said Hunky Ben, leading his companion into the full light of the opening and coming to a halt close to the ledge above which the fugitive lay. "Besides, Leather could never have found his way here alone."

"You forget," returned Wilmot, with a peculiar smile, "the monster might have shown him the way or even have carried him hither."

"Ah, true," answered the scout, with solemn gravity. "There's somethin' in that."

Wilmot laughed.

"What a splendid view," he said, going forward to the opening—"and see, here is a bed of pine brush. No doubt the cave must have been used as a place of refuge by the Redskins in days gone by."

"Ay, an' by the pale-faces too," said the scout. "Why, I 've had occasion to use it myself more than once. And, as you truly observe, sir, there's small chance of findin' a man once he's in here. As well run after a rabbit in his hole."

"Or search for a needle in a haystack," observed the Captain, as he gazed with curious interest around and above him. "Well, Ben, I give in. You were right when you said there was no probability of my finding any of the outlaws here."

"I'm ginerally right when I speak about what I understand," returned the scout calmly. "So now, Captain, if you're satisfied, we may as well go an' have a look at the other places I spoke of."

Assenting to this the two men left the place, but Leather continued to lie perfectly still for a considerable time after their footsteps had died away. Then, gliding from his perch, he dropped on the floor and ran to the opening where he saw the troopers still riding about, but gradually going farther and farther away from him. The scene was not perhaps, as the scout had prophesied, quite "as good as a play," but it certainly did become more and more entertaining as the searchers receded and distance lent enchantment to the view.

When at last the troops had disappeared, Shank bethought him of the food which Hunky Ben had so thoughtfully provided, and, sitting down on the brush couch, devoted himself to breakfast with a hearty appetite and a thankful spirit.

Meanwhile Captain Wilmot, having satisfied himself that the outlaws had fairly escaped him, and that Buck Tom was too ill to be moved, retired to a cool glade in the forest and held a council of war with the scout and Charlie Brooke.

"Now, Ben," he said, dismounting and seating himself on a mossy bank, while a trooper took charge of the horses and retired with them to a neighbouring knoll, "it is quite certain that in the present unsettled state of the district I must not remain here idle. It is equally certain that it would be sudden death to Buck Tom to move him in his present condition, therefore some men must be left behind to take care of him. Now, though I can ill afford to spare any of mine, I feel that out of mere humanity some sacrifice must be made, for we cannot leave the poor fellow to starve."

"I can relieve you on that point," said the scout, "for if you choose I am quite ready to remain."

"And of course," interposed Charlie, "I feel it my duty to remain with my old friend to the end."

"Well, I expected you to say something of this sort. Now," said the captain, "how many men will you require?"

" None at all, Captain," answered Ben decisively.

" But what if these scoundrels should return to their old haunt ? " said Wilmot.

" Let them come," returned the scout. " Wi' Mr. Brooke, an' Dick Darvall, an' three Winchesters, an' half-a-dozen six-shooters, I 'd engage to hold the cave against a score o' such varmin. If Mr. Brooke an' Dick are willin' to ——"

" I am quite willing, Ben, and I can answer for my friend Dick, so don't let that trouble you."

" Well, then, that is settled. I 'll go off at once," said the captain, rising and signing to the trooper to bring up the horses. " But bear in remembrance, Hunky Ben, that I hold you responsible for Buck Tom. If he recovers you must produce him."

The scout accepted the responsibility; the arrangements were soon made; " boots and saddles " was sounded, and the troopers rode away leaving Charlie Brooke, Dick Darvall, Buck Tom, and the scout in possession of the outlaws' cave.

CHAPTER XXIV.

THE MEETING OF OLD FRIENDS IN CURIOUS CIRCUMSTANCES.

WHEN the soldiers were safely away Hunky Ben returned to the cave and brought Leather down.

Charlie Brooke's love for his old school-fellow and playmate seemed to become a new passion, now that the wreck of life and limb presented by Shank had awakened within him the sensation of profound pity. And Shank's admiration for and devotion to Charlie increased tenfold now that the terrible barrier of self had been so greatly eliminated from his own nature, and a new spirit put within him.

By slow degrees, and bit by bit, each came to know and understand the other under the influence of new lights and feelings. But their thoughts about themselves, and their joy at meeting in such peculiar circumstances, had to be repressed to some extent in the presence of their common friend Ralph Ritson——*alias* Buck Tom—for Charlie knew him only as an old school-fellow, though to Leather he had been a friend and chum ever since they had landed in the New World.

The scout, during the first interval of leisure on the previous day, had extracted the ball without much difficulty from Buck's chest, through which it had passed, and was found lying close under the skin at his back. The relief thus afforded and rest obtained under the influence of some medicine administered by Captain Wilmot had brightened the poor fellow up to some extent; and Leather, seeing him look so much better on his return, began to entertain some hopes of his recovery.

Buck himself had no such hope; but, being a man of strong will, he refused to let it be seen in his demeanour that he thought his case to be hopeless. Yet he did not act from bravado, or the slightest tincture of that spirit which resolves to "die game." The approach of death had indeed torn away the veil and permitted him to see himself in his true colours, but he did not at that time see Jesus to be the Saviour of even "the chief of sinners." Therefore his hopelessness took the form of silent submission to the inevitable.

Of course Charlie Brooke spoke to him more than once of the love of God in Christ, and of the dying thief who had looked to Jesus on the cross and was saved, but Buck only shook his head. One afternoon in particular Charlie tried hard to remove the poor man's perplexities.

"It's all very well, Brooke," said Buck Tom, "and very kind of you to interest yourself in me, but the love of God and the salvation of Christ are not for me. You don't know what a sinner I have been, a rebel all my life—*all* my life, mark you. I would count it mean to come whining for pardon now that the game is up. I *deserve* hell—or whatever sort o' punishment is due—an' I'm willing to take it."

"Ralph Ritson," said Brooke impressively, "you are a far greater sinner than you think or admit."

"Perhaps I am," returned the outlaw sadly, and with a slight expression of surprise. "Perhaps I am," he repeated. "Indeed I admit that you are right, but—but your saying so is a somewhat strange way to comfort a dying man. Is it not?"

"I am *not* trying to comfort you. I am trying, by God's grace, to convince you. You tell me that you have been a rebel all your days?"

"Yes; I admit it."

"There are still, it may be, a few days yet to run, and you are determined, it seems, to spend these in rebellion too—up to the very end!"

"Nay, I do not say that. Have I not said that I *submit* to whatever punishment is due? Surely that is not rebellion. I can do nothing *now* to make up for a misspent life, so I am willing to accept the consequences. Is not that submission to God— at least as far as lies in my power?"

"No; it is *not* submission. Bear with me when I say it is rebellion, still deeper rebellion than ever.

God says to you, ' You have destroyed yourself but in *me* is your help.'   He says, ' Though your sins be as scarlet they shall be white as snow.'   He says, ' Believe on the Lord Jesus Christ and you shall be saved,' and assures you that ' whoever will ' may come to Him, and that no one who comes shall be cast out—yet in the face of all that you tell me that the love of God and the salvation of Christ are not for you !   Ralph, my friend, you think that if you had a chance of living your life over again you would do better and so deserve salvation.   That is exactly what God tells us we cannot do, and then He tells us that Himself, in Jesus Christ, has . provided salvation from sin *for* us, offers it as a free unmerited gift; and immediately we dive to the deepest depth of sin by deliberately refusing this deliverance from sin unless we can somehow manage to deserve it."

" I cannot see it," said the wounded man thoughtfully.

" Only God Himself, by His Holy Spirit, can enable you to see it," said his companion ; and then, in a low earnest voice, with eyes closed and his hand on his friend's arm, he prayed that the outlaw might be " born again."

Charlie Brooke was not one of those who make long prayers, either " for a pretence " or otherwise. Buck Tom smiled slightly when his friend stopped at the end of this one sentence.

"Your prayer is not long-winded, anyhow!" he said.

"True, Ralph, but it is comprehensive. It requires a good deal of expounding and explaining to make man understand what we say or think. The Almighty needs none of that. Indeed He does not need even the asking, but He *bids* us ask, and that is enough for me. I have seen enough of life to understand the value of unquestioning obedience whether one comprehends the reason of an order or not."

"Ay," returned Buck quickly, "when he who gives the order has a right to command."

"That is so much a matter of course," rejoined Charlie, "that I would not think of referring to it while conversing with an intelligent man. By the way—which name would you like to be called, by Ralph or Buck?"

"It matters little to me," returned the outlaw languidly, "and it won't matter to anybody long. I should prefer 'Ralph,' for it is not associated with so much evil as the other, but you know our circumstances are peculiar just now, so, all things considered, I had better remain Buck Tom to the end of the chapter. I'll answer to whichever name comes first when the roll is called in the next world."

The conversation was interrupted at this point by the entrance of Hunky Ben bearing a deer on his lusty shoulders. He was followed by Dick Darvall.

"There," said the former, throwing the carcass on

the floor, " I told ye I wouldn't be long o' bringin'
in somethin' for the pot."

"Ay, an' the way he shot it too," said the
seaman, laying aside his rifle, " would have made
even a monkey stare with astonishment. Has
Leather come back, by the way? I see'd him
goin' full sail through the woods when I went out
this mornin'."

" He has not yet returned," said Charlie. " When
I relieved him and sat down to watch by our friend
here, he said he felt so much better and stronger
that he would take his gun and see if he couldn't
find something for the pot. I advised him not to
trust his feelings too much, and not to go far, but—
ah, here he comes to answer for himself."

As he spoke a step was heard outside, and next
moment Shank entered, carrying a brace of rabbits
which he flung down, and then threw himself on a
couch in a state of considerable exhaustion.

" There," said he, wiping the perspiration from
his forehead. " They've cost me more trouble than
they're worth, for I'm quite done up. I had no
idea I had become so weak in the legs. Ralph, my
dear fellow," he added, forgetting himself for the
moment as he rose and went to his friend's side,
" I have more sympathy with you, now that I have
found out the extent of my own weakness. Do you
feel better?"

" Yes, old boy—much—much better."

"That's all right. I'm convinced that—hallo! why, who shot the deer?"

"Hunky Ben has beat you," said Charlie.

"Beat Leather!" exclaimed Darvall, "why, he beats all creation. I never see'd anything like it since I went to sea."

"Since you came ashore, you should say. But come, Dick," said Charlie, "let's hear about this wonderful shooting. I'm sure it will amuse Buck —unless he's too wearied to listen."

"Let him talk," said the invalid. "I like to hear him."

Thus exhorted and encouraged the seaman recounted his day's experience.

"Well, you must know, messmates," said he, "that I set sail alone this mornin', havin' in my pocket the small compass I always carry about me—also my bearin's before startin', so as I shouldn't go lost in the woods—though that wouldn't be likely in such an narrow inlet as this Traitor's Trap, to say nothin' o' the landmarks alow and aloft of all sorts. I carried a Winchester with me, because, not bein' what you may call a crack shot, I thought it would give me a better chance to have a lot o' resarve shots in the locker, d'ye see? I carried also a six-shooter, as it might come handy, you know, if I fell in wi' a Redskin or a bear, an' got to close quarters. Also my cutlass, for I've bin used to that aboard ship when I was in the navy.

" Well, away I went—makin' sail down the valley to begin with, an' then a long tack into the mountains right in the wind's eye, that bein' the way to get on the blind side o' game. I hadn't gone far when up starts a bird o' some sort——"

" What like was it ? " asked the scout.

" No more notion than the man in the moon," returned the sailor. " What wi' the flutter an' scurry an' leaves, branches an' feathers—an' the start—I see'd nothin' clear, an' I was so anxious to git somethin' for the pot, that six shots went arter it out o' the Winchester, before I was quite sure I'd begun to fire—for you must know I've larned to fire uncommon fast since I come to these parts. Hows'ever, I hit nothin'——"

" Not quite so bad as that, Dick," interrupted the scout gravely.

" Well, that's true, but you better tell that part of it yourself, Hunky, as you know more about it than me."

" It wasn't of much consequence," said the scout, betraying the slightest possible twinkle in his grey eyes, " but Dick has a knack o' lettin' drive without much regard to what's in front of him. I happened to be more in front of him than that bird when he began to fire, an' the first shot hit my right leggin', but by good luck only grazed the bark. Of course I dropped behind a rock when the storm began and lay quiet there, and when a lull came I halloo'd."

"Yes, he did halloo," said Dick, resuming the narrative, "an' that halloo was more like the yell of a bull of Bashan than the cry of a mortal man. It made my heart jump into my throat an' stick there, for I thought I must have killed a whole Redskin tribe at one shot——"

"Six shots, Dick. Tell the exact truth an' don't contradic' yourself," said Hunky.

"No, it wasn't," retorted the seaman stoutly. "It was arter the *first* shot that you gave the yell. Hows'ever, I allow that the echoes kep' it goin' till the six shots was off—an' I can tell you, messmates, that the hallooin' an' flutterin' an' scurryin' an' echoin' an' thought of Redskins in my brain all mixed up wi' the blatterin' shots, caused such a rumpus that I experienced considerable relief when the smoke cleared away an' I see'd Hunky Ben in front o' me laughin' fit to bu'st his sides."

"Well, to make a long yarn short, I joined Hunky and allowed him to lead, seein' that he understands the navigation hereaway better than me."

"'Come along,' says he, 'an' I'll let you have a chance at a deer.'

"'All right,' says I, an' away we went up one hill an' down another—for all the world as if we was walkin' over a heavy Atlantic swell—till we come to a sort o' pass among the rocks.

"'I'm goin' to leave you here to watch,' says he, 'an' I'll go round by the futt o' the gully an' drive the deer up. They'll pass quite close, so you've only to——'

"Hunky stopped short as he was speakin' and flopped down as if he'd bin shot—haulin' me along wi' him.

"'Keep quiet,' says he, in a low voice. 'We're in luck, an' don't need to drive. There's a deer comin' up at this very minute—a young one. You'll take it. I won't fire unless you miss.'

"You may be sure I kep' quiet, messmates, arter that. I took just one peep, an' there, sure enough, I saw a brown beast comin' up the pass. So we kep' close as mice. There was a lot o' small bushes not ten yards in front of us, which ended in a cut —a sort o' crack—in the hill-side, a hundred yards or more from the place where we was crouchin'.

"'Now,' whispers Hunky to——"

"I never whisper!" remarked the scout.

"Well, well; he said, in a low v'ice to me, says he, 'd'ye see that openin' in the bushes?' 'I do,' says I. 'Well then,' says he, 'it's about ten yards off; be ready to commence firin' when it comes to that openin'.' 'I will,' says I. An', sure enough, when the brown critter came for'id at a walk an' stopped sudden wi' a look o' surprise as if it hadn't expected to see me, bang went my Winchester four times, like winkin', an' up went the deer four times in the air, but niver a bit the worse was he. Snap I went a fifth time; but there was no shot, an' I

gave a yell, for I knew the cartridges was done. By
that time the critter had reached the crack in the
hill I told ye of, an' up in the air he went to clear
it, like an Indy-rubber ball. I felt a'most like to
fling my rifle at it in my rage, when bang! went a
shot at my ear that all but deaf'ned me, an' I wish
I may niver fire another shot or furl another
t'gallant-s'l if that deer didn't crumple up in the
air an' drop down stone dead—as dead as it now
lays there on the floor."

By the time Dick Darvall had ended his narrative
—which was much more extensive than our report
of it—steaks of the deer were sputtering in a fry-
ing-pan, and other preparations were being made
for a hearty meal, to which all the healthy men
did ample justice. Shank Leather did what he
could, and even Buck Tom made a feeble attempt
to join.

That night a strict watch was kept outside the
cave—each taking it by turns, for it was just
possible, though not probable, that the outlaws
might return to their old haunt. No one appeared,
however, and for the succeeding eight weeks the
party remained there undisturbed, Shank Leather
slowly but surely regaining strength; his friend,
Buck Tom, as slowly and surely losing it; while
Charlie, Dick, and Hunky Ben ranged the neighbouring forest in order to procure food. Leather usually
remained in the cave to cook for and nurse his

friend.   It was pleasant work to Shank, for love
and pity were at the foundation of the service.
Buck Tom perceived this and fully appreciated it.
Perchance he obtained some valuable light on
spiritual subjects from Shank's changed tone and
manner, which the logic of his friend Brooke had
failed to convey.   Who can tell ?

CHAPTER XXV.

SHOWS HOW THE SEAMAN WAS SENT ON A DELICATE MISSION
AND HOW HE FARED.

"SHANK," said Charlie one day as they were sitting in the sunshine near the outlaws' cave. waiting for Dick and the scout to return to their mid-day meal, "it seems to me that we may be detained a good while here, for we cannot leave Ralph, and it is evident that the poor fellow won't be able to travel for many a day——"

"If ever," interposed Shank sorrowfully.

"Well, then, I think we must send down to Bull's Ranch, to see if there are any letters for us. I feel sure that there must be some, and the question arises—who are we to send?"

"*You* must not go, Charlie, whoever goes. You are the only link in this mighty wilderness, that connects Ralph and me with home—and hope. Weak and helpless as we are, we cannot afford to let you out of our sight."

"Well, but if I don't go I can't see my way to asking the scout to go, for he alone thoroughly understands the ways of the country and of the

Indians—if any should chance to come this way. Besides, considering the pledge he is under to be accountable for Buck Tom, I doubt if he would consent to go."

"The question is answered, then," said Shank, "for the only other man is Dick Darvall."

"True; and it strikes me that Dick will be very glad to go," returned Charlie with a smile of peculiar meaning.

"D' ye think he's getting tired of us, Charlie?"

"By no means. But you know he has a roving disposition, and I think he has a sort of fondness for Jackson—the boss of the ranch."

It was found when the question was put to him, that Dick was quite ready to set out on the mission required of him. He also admitted his fondness for Roaring Bull!

"But what if you should lose your way?" asked the scout.

"Find it again," was Dick's prompt reply.

"And what if you should be attacked by Indians?"

"Fight 'em, of course."

"But if they should be too many to fight?"

"Why, clap on all sail an' give 'em a starn chase, which is always a long one. For this purpose, however, I would have to command a good craft, so I 'd expect you to lend me yours, Hunky Ben."

"What! my Polly?"

"Even so.   Black Polly."

The scout received this proposal gravely, and shook his head at first, for he was naturally fond of his beautiful mare, and, besides, doubted the sailor's horsemanship, though he had perfect faith in his courage and discretion. Finally, however, he gave in; and accordingly, one fine morning at day-break, Dick Darvall, mounted on Black Polly, and armed with his favourite Winchester, revolvers, and cutlass, "set sail" down Traitor's Trap to visit his lady-love!

Of course he knew that his business was to obtain letters and gather news. But honest Dick Darvall could not conceal from himself that his main object was—Mary Jackson!

Somehow it has come to be supposed or assumed that a jack-tar cannot ride. Possibly this may be true of the class as a whole to which Jack belongs, but it is not necessarily true of all, and it certainly is not true of some. Dick Darvall was an expert horseman—though a sailor. He had learned to ride when a boy, before going to sea, and his after-habit of riding the "white horses" of the Norseman, did not cause him to forget the art of managing the "buckers" of the American plains. To use his own words, he felt as much at home on the hurricane deck of a Spanish pony, as on the fo'c'sl of a man-of-war, so that the scout's doubt of his capacity as a rider was not well founded.

Tremendous was the bound of exultation which

T

our seaman felt, then, when he found himself
on the magnificent black mare, with the fresh
morning air fanning his temples, and the bright
morning sun glinting through a cut in the
eastern range.

Soon he reached the lower end of the valley,
which being steep he had descended with tightened
rein.   On reaching the open prairie he gave the
mare her head and went off with a wild whoop like
an arrow from a bow.

Black Polly required neither spur nor whip.
She possessed that charmingly sensitive spirit which
seems to receive an electric shock from its rider's
lightest chirp.   She was what you may call an anxiously willing steed, yet possessed such a tender
mouth that she could be pulled up as easily as she
could be made to go.   A mere child could have
ridden her, and Dick found in a few minutes that
a slight check was necessary to prevent her scour-
ing over the plains at racing speed.   He restrained
her, therefore, to a grand canter, with many a stride
and bound interspersed, when such a thing as a rut
or a little bush came in her way.

With arched neck, glistening eyes, voluminous
mane, and flowing tail she flew onward, hour after
hour, with many a playful shake of the head, and
an occasional snort, as though to say "This is mere
child's play; *do* let me put on a spurt!"

It may not be fair to credit such a noble creature

with talking, or even thinking, slang, but Dick Darvall clearly understood her to say something of the sort, for after a while he reduced speed to a kind of india-rubber walk and patted her neck, saying—

"No, no, lass, you mustn't use up your strength at the beginning. We've got a longish trip before us, Polly, an' it won't do to clap on all sail at the beginnin' of the voyage."

At David's store Dick stopped for a short time to obtain a little refreshment for himself and Polly. There he found a group of cow-boys discussing the affairs of their neighbours, and enlarging noisily on things in general under the brain-clearing and reason-inspiring influence of strong drink! To these he recounted briefly the incidents of the recent raid of the troops into Traitor's Trap, and learned that Jake the Flint had "drifted south into Mexico where he was plying the trade of cattle and horse stealer, with the usual accompaniments of that profession—fighting, murdering, drinking, etc." Some of the deeds of this notorious outlaw, as narrated by the cow-boy Crux, who happened to be there, made the blood of Dick run cold—and Dick's blood was not easily made to run otherwise than naturally by any one—except, of course, by Mary Jackson, who could at all events make it run hot, also fast or slow, very much according to her own sweet will!

But the seaman had no time to lose. He had

still a long way to go, and the day was advancing. Remounting Black Polly he was soon out again on the prairie, sweeping over the grassy waves and down into the hollows with a feeling of hilarious jollity, that was born of high health, good-nature, pleasant circumstances, and a free-and-easy mind.

Nothing worthy of particular notice occurred after this to mar the pleasure of our sailor's "voyage" over the prairie until he reached a belt of woodland, through which for half a mile he had to travel. Here he drew rein and began to traverse the bit of forest at a quiet amble, partly to rest Polly, and partly that he might more thoroughly enjoy the woodland scenery through the umbrageous canopy of which the sun was sending his slanting rays and covering the sward with a confused chequer-work of green and gold.

And here Dick Darvall became communicative; entered into conversation, so to speak, with himself. After a few minutes, however, this did not prove a sufficient outlet to his exuberant spirits.

"Come, Dick," he exclaimed, "give us a song. Your voice ain't, perhaps, much to speak of as to quality, but there's no end of quantity. Strike up, now; what shall it be?"

Without replying to the question he struck up "Rule Britannia" in tones that did not justify his disparaging remark as to quality. He reached the other end of the wood and the end of the song at

the same time. "Britons," shouted he with un-
alterable determination—

"Never, never, ne—ver, shall be—Redskins!"

This unnatural termination was not an intentional
variation. It was the result of a scene that suddenly burst upon his view.

Far away on the prairie two riders were seen
racing at what he would have styled a slant away
from him. They were going at a pace that suggested
fleeing for life.

"Redskins—arter somethin'," murmured Dick, pulling up, and shading his eyes from the sun with his
right hand, as he gazed earnestly at the two riders.

"No—n—no. They're whites," he continued,
"one o' them a man; t'other a woman. I can make
that out, anyhow."

As he spoke, the racing riders topped a far-off
knoll; halted, and turned round as if to gaze back
towards the north—the direction from which they
had come. Then, wheeling round as if in greater
haste than ever, they continued their headlong gallop
and disappeared on the other side of the knoll.

Dick naturally turned towards the north to see,
if possible, what the two riders were flying from.
He was not kept long in doubt, for just then a band
of horsemen was seen topping the farthest ridge in
that direction, and bearing down on the belt of
woodland, along the edge of which they galloped
towards him.

There was no mistaking who they were. The war-whoop, sounding faint and shrill in the distance, and the wild gesticulations of the riders, told the story at once to our seaman—two pale-faces, pursued by a band of bloodthirsty savages!

Unskilled though he was in backwoods warfare, Dick was not unfamiliar with war's alarms, nor was he wanting in common sense. To side with the weaker party was a natural tendency in our seaman. That the pursuers were red, and the pursued white, strengthened the tendency, and the fact that one of the latter was a woman settled the question. Instantly Dick shook the reins, drove his unarmed heels against the sides of Polly, and away they went after the fugitives like a black thunderbolt, if there be such artillery in nature!

A wild yell told him that he was seen.

"Howl away, ye land lubbers!" growled Dick. "You'll have to fill your sails wi' a stiffer breeze than howlin' before ye overhaul this here craft."

Just then he reached the crest of a prairie billow, whence he could see the fugitives still far ahead of him. Suddenly a suspicion entered the seaman's mind, which made his heart almost choke him. What if this should be Mary Jackson and her father? Their relative size countenanced the idea, for the woman seemed small and the man unusually large.

In desperate haste Dick now urged on his gallant

steed to her best pace, and well did she justify the praises that had been often bestowed on her by Hunky Ben. In a very brief space of time she was close behind the fugitives, and Dick was now convinced that his suspicions as to who they were was right. He rode after them with divided feelings—tremblingly anxious lest Mary should fall into the hands of their ruthless foes—exultantly glad that he had come there in time to fight, or die if need be, in her defence.

Suddenly the male fugitive, who had only glanced over his shoulder from time to time, pulled up, wheeled round, and quickly raised his rifle.

"Hallo! get on, man; don't stop!" Dick yelled, in a voice worthy of Bull himself. Taking off his hat he waved it violently above his head. As he spoke he saw the woman's arm flash upwards; a puff of smoke followed, and a bullet whistled close over his head.

Next moment the fugitives had turned and resumed their headlong flight. A few more minutes sufficed to bring Dick and the black mare alongside, for the latter was still vigorous in wind and limb, while the poor jaded animals which Mary and her father rode were almost worn out by a prolonged flight.

"Dick Darvall," exclaimed Jackson, as the former rode up, "I never was gladder to see any man than I am to see you this hour, though but for my Mary

I'd surely have sent you to kingdom come. Her
ears are better than mine, you see. She recognised
the voice an' knocked up my rifle just as I pulled
the trigger. But I'm afeared it's too late, lad."

The way in which the man said this, and the look
of his pale haggard face, sent a thrill to the heart
of Dick.

"What d'ye mean?" he said, looking anxiously
at Mary, who with a set rigid expression on her pale
face was looking straight before her, and urging her
tired pony with switch and rein.

"I mean, lad, that we've but a poor chance to
reach the ranch wi' such knocked-up brutes as
these. Of course we can turn at bay an' kill as
many o' the red-devils as possible before it's all
over wi' us, but what good would that do to Mary?
If we could only check the varmins, there might be
some hope, but——"

"Jackson!" exclaimed the seaman, in a firm tone,
"I'll do my best to check them. God bless you,
Mary—good-bye. Heave ahead, now, full swing!"

As he spoke, Dick pulled up, while the others continued their headlong flight straight for the ranch,
which was by that time only a few miles distant.

Wheeling round, Dick cantered back to the knoll
over which they had just passed and halted on the
top of it. From this position he could see the band,
of about fifty Indians, careering towards him and
yelling with satisfaction, for they could also see

him—a solitary horseman—clear cut against the bright sky.

Dick got ready his repeating rifle. We have already mentioned the fact that he had learned to load and fire this formidable weapon with great rapidity, though he had signally failed in his attempts to aim with it. Being well aware of his weakness, he made up his mind in his present desperate extremity not to aim at all! He had always felt that the difficulty of getting the back and front sights of the rifle to correspond with the object aimed at was a slow, and, in his case, an impossible process. He therefore resolved to simply point his weapon and fire!

"Surely," he muttered to himself, even in that trying moment, "surely I can't altogether miss a whole bunch o' fifty men an' horses!"

He waited until he thought the savages were within long range, and then, elevating his piece a little, fired.

The result justified his hopes. A horse fell dead upon the plain, and its owner, although evidently unwounded, was for the time *hors de combat*.

True to his plan, Dick kept up such a quick continuous fire, and made so much noise and smoke, that it seemed as if a whole company of riflemen were at work instead of one man, and several horses on the plain testified to the success of the pointing as compared with the aiming principle!

Of course the fire was partly returned, and for a time the stout seaman was under a pretty heavy rain of bullets, but as the savages fired while galloping their aim was necessarily bad.

This fusillade had naturally the effect of checking the advance of the Indians—especially when they drew near to the reckless man, who, when the snap of his rifle told that his last cartridge was off, wheeled about and fled as fast as Black Polly could lay hoofs to the plain.

And now he found the value of the trustworthy qualities of his steed, for, instead of guiding her out of the way of obstacles, he gave her her head, held tight with his legs, and merely kept an eye on the ground in front to be ready for any swerve, bound, or leap, that might be impending. Thus his hands were set free to re-charge the magazine of his rifle, which he did with deliberate rapidity.

The truth is, that recklessness has a distinct tendency to produce coolness. And there is no one who can afford to be so deliberate, and of whom other men are so much afraid, as the man who has obviously made up his mind to die fighting.

While Dick was loading-up, Black Polly was encouraged by voice and heel to do her best, and her best was something to see and remember! When the charging was finished, Dick drew rein and trotted to the next knoll he encountered, from which point he observed with some satisfaction that the fugitives were still pressing on, and that the distance between them and their foe had slightly increased.

But the seaman had not much time to look or think, for the band of Redskins was drawing near. When they came within range he again opened fire. But this time the savages divided, evidently with the intention of getting on both sides of him, and so distracting his attention. He perceived their object at once, and reserved his fire until they turned and with frantic yells made a simultaneous dash on him right and left. Again he waited till his enemies were close enough, and then opened fire right and left alternately, while the Indians found that they had outwitted themselves and scarcely dared to fire lest the opposite bands should hit each other.

Having expended the second supply of ammunition, Dick wheeled round and took to flight as before. Of course the mare soon carried him out of range, and again he had the satisfaction of observing that the fugitives had increased their distance from the foe.

"One more check o' this kind," thought Dick, "and they 'll be safe—I think."

While thus thinking he was diligently re-charging, and soon cantered to the top of a third knoll, where he resolved to make his final stand. The ranch was by that time dimly visible on the horizon, and the weary fugitives were seen struggling towards it. But Dick found, on halting and looking back, that the Indians had changed their tactics. Instead of directing their attention to himself, as on the previous occasions, they had spread out to the right and left and had scattered, besides keeping well out of range.

"What are the sinners up to now?" muttered the seaman in some perplexity.

He soon perceived that they meant to go past him altogether, if possible, and head towards the fugitives in separate groups.

"Ay, but it's *not* possible!" exclaimed Dick, answering his own thoughts as he turned swiftly, and stretched out after his friends. Seeing this, the savages tried to close in on him from both sides, but their already winded ponies had no chance against the grand Mexican mare, which having been considerately handled during the day's journey was comparatively fresh and in full vigour.

Shooting ahead he now resolved to join his friends, and a feeling of triumph began to rise within his breast as he saw them pushing steadily onward. The ranch, however, was still at a considerable distance, while the Indians were rapidly gaining ground.

At that moment, to Dick's horror, the pony which Mary Jackson rode stumbled and fell, sending its rider over its head. But the fair Mary, besides being a splendid horsewoman, was singularly agile and quick in perception. For some time she had anticipated the catastrophe, and, at the first indication of a stumble, leaped from the saddle and actually alighted on her feet some yards ahead. Of course she fell with some violence, but the leap broke her fall, and probably saved her neck. She sprang up instantly, and grasping the reins, tried to raise her pony. It was too late. The faithful creature was dead.

Jackson, pulling up, wheeled round and was back at her side instantly. Almost at the same moment Dick Darvall came up, threw the mare almost on her haunches, leaped from the saddle, and ran to Mary. As he did so, the crash of a pistol shot at his ear almost deafened him, and a glance showed him that Jackson had shot his horse, which fell dead close to his daughter's pony.

"Kill your horse, Dick," he growled sharply, as he exerted his great strength to the utmost, and dragged the haunches of his own steed close to the head of the other. "It's our only chance."

Dick drew his revolver, and aimed at the heart of Black Polly, but for the soul of him he could not pull the trigger.

"No—I won't!" he cried, grasping the lasso which always hung at the saddle-bow. "Hobble the fore-legs!"

There was such determination in the sailor's com-

mand, that Jackson felt bound to obey. At the
same moment Dick bound the horse's hind-legs. He
fully understood what Jackson intended, and the
latter was as quick to perceive the seaman's drift.
Seizing the reins, while his friend caught hold of
the lasso, Dick cried, "Out o' the way, Mary!" and
with a mighty effort the two men threw the mare
on her side.

"First-rate!" cried Jackson, while his companion
held down the animal's head. "It couldn't have
dropped better. Jump inside, Mary, an' lie down
flat behind your pony. Let Mary have the reins,
Dick. She knows how to hold its head down without showin' herself."

Even while he was speaking, Jackson and Dick
leaped into the triangle of horses thus formed, and,
crouching low, disappeared from the sight of the
savages, who now came on yelling with triumph, for
they evidently thought themselves sure of their
victims by that time,

"Are ye a good shot, Dick?" asked Jackson, as
he gazed sternly at the approaching foe.

"No—abominably bad."

"Fire low then. You may catch the horses if ye
miss the Redskins. Anyhow you'll hit the ground
if you aim low, an' it's wonderful what execution a
bullet may do arter hittin' mother Earth."

"I never aim," replied the sailor. "Only a waste
o' time. I just point straight an' fire away."

"Do it, then," growled Roaring Bull, with something that sounded like a short laugh.

At the same moment he himself took quick aim at the foe and fired; the leading horse and man immediately rolled upon the plain.

As both men were armed with repeating rifles the fusillade was rapid, and most of the savages, who seldom fight well in the open, were repulsed. But several of them, headed apparently by their chief, rode on fearlessly until within pistol-shot.

Then the two defenders of this peculiar fortress sprang up with revolvers in each hand.

"Lie close, Mary," cried Jackson as he fired, and the chief's horse rolled over, almost reaching their position with the impetus of the charge. The chief himself lay beside his horse, for another shot had ended his career. As two other horses had fallen, the rest of the band wheeled aside and galloped away, followed by a brisk fire from the white men, who had again crouched behind their breast-work and resumed their rifles.

Bullets were by that time flying over them in considerable numbers, for those Indians who had not charged with their chief had, after retiring to a safe distance, taken to firing at long range. At this work Dick's rifle and straight pointing were of little use, so he reserved his fire for close quarters, while Jackson, who was almost a certain shot at average ranges, kept the savages from drawing nearer.

"Lie closer to the pony, Miss Mary," said Dick, as a shot passed close over the girl and whistled between him and his comrade. "Were you hurt in the fall?"

"No, not in the least. Don't you think they'll hear the firing at the ranch, father?"

"Ay, lass, if there's anybody to hear it, but I sent the boys out this mornin' to hunt up a bunch o' steers that have drifted south among Wilson's cattle, an' I fear they've not come back yet. See, the reptiles are goin' to try it again!"

As he spoke, the remnant of the Redskins who pressed home the first charge, having held a palaver, induced the whole band to make another attempt, but they were met with the same vigour as before —a continuous volley at long range, which emptied several saddles, and then, when the plucky men of the tribe charged close, the white men stood up, as before, and plied them with revolvers so rapidly that they were fain to wheel aside and retire.

"Ammunition's gettin' low," said Dick, in an anxious tone.

"Then I'll waste no more," growled Jackson, "but only fire when I'm safe to hit."

As he spoke a distant cheer was heard, and, looking back, they saw, with a rebound of hope, that a band of five or six cow-boys were coming from the ranch and galloping full swing to the rescue. Behind them, a few seconds later, appeared a line of men who came on at a swinging trot.

"AMMUNITION'S GETTIN' LOW," SAID DICK.—Page 304.

"Troopers, I do believe!" exclaimed Jackson.

"Thank God!" said Mary, with a deep sigh of relief as she sat up to look at them. The troopers gave a cheer of encouragement as they thundered past to the attack, but the Indians did not await the onset. At the first sight of the troops they fled, and in a few minutes pursued and pursuers alike were out of sight—hidden behind the prairie waves.

"I can't tell you how thankful I am that I didn't shoot the mare," said Dick, as they unfastened the feet of Black Polly and let her rise. "I'd never have been able to look Hunky Ben in the face again arter it."

"Well, I'm not sorry you spared her," said Jackson; "as for the two that are dead, they're no great loss—yet I've a kind o' regret too, for the poor things served us well."

"Faithfully—even to death," added Mary, in a sorrowful tone as she stooped to pat the neck of her dead pony.

"Will you mount, Miss Mary, and ride home?" asked the sailor.

"Thank you—no, I'd rather walk with father. We have not far to go now."

"Then we'll all walk together," said Jackson.

Dick threw Black Polly's bridle over his arm, and they all set off at a smart walk for the ranch of Roaring Bull, while the troops and cow-boys chased the Redskins back into the mountains whence they had come.

U

CHAPTER XXVI.

TREATS OF VARIOUS INTERESTING MATTERS, AND TELLS OF NEWS
FROM HOME.

DICK DARVALL now learned that, owing to the disturbed state of the country, Captain Wilmot had left a small body of men to occupy Bull's ranch for a time; hence their presence at the critical moment when Jackson and his daughter stood so much in need of their assistance. He also found that there were two letters awaiting the party at Traitor's Trap—one for Charles Brooke, Esq., and one for Mr. S. Leather. They bore the postmarks of the old country.

"You'd better not start back wi' them for three or four days, Dick," said Jackson, when they were seated that evening in the hall of the ranch, enjoying a cup of coffee made by the fair hands of Mary.

Dick shook his head. "I'm acting post-boy just now," said he, "an' it would ill become me to hang off an' on here waitin' for a fair wind when I can beat into port with a foul one."

"But if the Redskins is up all round, as some o'

the boys have reported, it's not merely a foul wind but a regular gale that's blowin', an' it would puzzle you to beat into port in the teeth o' that."

"I think," remarked Mary, with an arch smile, "that Mr. Darvall had better 'lay to' until the troops return to-night and report on the state of the weather."

To this the gallant seaman declared that he would be only too happy to cast anchor altogether where he was for the rest of his life, but that duty was duty, and that, blow high or blow low, fair weather or foul, duty had to be attended to.

"That's true, O high-principled seaman!" returned Jackson; "and what d'ye consider your duty at the present time?"

"To deliver my letters, O Roarin' Bull!" replied Dick.

"Just so, but if you go slick off when Redskins are rampagin' around, you'll be sure to get nabbed an' roasted alive, an' so you'll *never* deliver your letters."

"It's my duty to try," said Dick. "Hows'ever," he added, turning to Mary with a benignant smile, "I'll take your advice, Miss Mary, an' wait for the report o' the soldiers."

When the troopers returned, their report was, that the Redskins, after being pretty severely handled, had managed to reach the woods, where it would have been useless to follow them so close upon

night; but it was their opinion that the band, which
had so nearly captured the boss of the ranch and
his daughter, was merely a marauding band, from
the south, of the same Indians who had previously
attacked the ranch, and that, as for the Indians of
the district, they believed them to be quite peace-
ably disposed.

"Which says a good deal for them," remarked
the officer in command of the troops, "when we
consider the provocation they receive from Buck
Tom, Jake the Flint, and such-like ruffians."

"The moon rises at ten to-night, Dick," said
Jackson, as they went together to the stables to
see that the horses were all right.

"That's so," said the sailor, who noticed something
peculiar in the man's tone; "what may be the reason
o' your reference to that bit of astronomy?"

"Why, you see," returned the other, "post-boys in
these diggin's are used to travellin' night an' day.
An' the troopers' report o' the weather might be worse.
You was sayin' somethin' about duty, wasn't you?"

"Right, Jackson," returned Dick, "but Black
Polly is not used to travellin' night an' day. If she
was, I'd take her back to-night, for moonlight is
good enough for a man that has twice taken soundin's
along the road, an' who's well up in all the buoys,
beacons, an' landmarks, but it would be cruelty to
the good mare."

"Duty first, Dick, the mare second. You don't

need to trouble about her. I'll lend ye one o' my
best horses an' take good care 'o' Black Polly till
Hunky Ben claims her."

"Thank 'ee, Jackson, but I'll not part wi' Black
Polly till I've delivered her to her owner. I won't
accept your invite to stop here three or four days,
but neither will I start off to-night. I've too much
regard for the good mare to do that."

"Ho! ho!" thought his host, with an inward
chuckle, "it's not so much the mare as Mary that
you've a regard for, my young sailor!"

But in spite of his name the man was much
too polite to express this opinion aloud. He merely
said, "Well, Dick, you know that you're welcome
to squat here as long or as short a time as you like,
an' use the best o' my horses, if so disposed, or do
the postboy business on Black Polly. Do as ye like
wi' me an' mine, boy, for it's only fair to say that
but for your help this day my Mary an' me would
have bin done for."

They reached the stable as he was speaking,
and Jackson at once turned the conversation on the
horses, thus preventing a reply from Dick—in regard
to which the latter was not sorry.

In the stall the form of Black Polly looked
grander than ever, for her head nearly touched the
roof as she raised it and turned a gleaming eye on
the visitors, at the same time uttering a slight
whinny of expectation.

"Why, I do believe she has transferred her affections to you, Dick," said Jackson. "I never heard her do that before except to Hunky Ben, and she's bin many a time in that stall."

"More likely that she expected Ben had come to bid her good-night," returned the sailor.

But the way in which the beautiful creature received Dick's caresses induced Jackson to hold to his opinion. It is more probable, however, that some similarity of disposition between Dick Darvall and Hunky Ben had commended itself to the mare, which was, as much as many a human being, of an amiable, loving disposition. She thoroughly appreciated the tenderness and forbearance of her master, and, more recently, of Dick. No doubt the somewhat rough way in which she had been thrown to the ground that day may have astonished her, but it evidently had not soured her temper.

That night Dick did not see much of Mary. She was far too busy attending to, and providing for, the numerous guests at the ranch to be able to give individual attention to any one in particular—even had she been so disposed.

Buttercup of course lent able assistance to her mistress in these domestic duties, and, despite her own juvenility—we might perhaps say, in consequence of it—gave Mary much valuable advice.

"Dat man's in a bad way," said she, as, with her huge lips pouting earnestly, she examined the contents of a big pot on the fire. The black maiden's lips were so pronounced and expressive that they might almost be said to constitute her face!

"What man?" asked Mary, who, with her sleeves tucked up to the elbows, was manipulating certain proportions of flour, water, and butter.

"Why, Dick, ob course. He's de only man wuth speakin' about."

Mary blushed a little in spite of herself, and laughed hilariously as she replied—

"Dear me, Butter, I didn't think he had made such a deep impression on you."

"'Snot on'y on me he's made a 'mpress'n," returned the maid, carelessly. "He makes de same 'mpress'n on eberybody."

"How d'you know?" asked Mary.

"'Cause I see," answered the maid.

She turned her eyes on her mistress as she spoke, and immediately a transformation scene was presented. The eyes dwindled into slits as the cheeks rose, and the serious pout became a smile so magnificent that ivory teeth and scarlet gums set in ebony alone met the gaze of the beholder.

"Buttercup," exclaimed Mary, stamping her little foot firmly, "it's boiling over!"

She was right. Teeth and gums vanished. The eyes returned, so did the pout, and the pot was whipped off the fire in a twinkling, but not before a mighty hiss was heard and the head of the black maiden was involved in a cloud of steam and ashes!

"I told you so!" cried Mary, quoting from an ancient MS.

"No, you di'n't," retorted her servitor, speaking from the depths of her own consciousness.

We refrain from following the conversation beyond this point, as it became culinary and flat.

Next day Dick Darvall, refreshed—and, owing to some quite inexplicable influences, enlivened—mounted Black Polly and started off alone for Traitor's Trap, leaving his heart and a reputation for cool pluck behind him.

Of course he was particularly watchful and circumspect on the way up, but saw nothing to call for a further display of either pluck or coolness. On arriving at the cave he found his friends there much as he had left them. Buck Tom, owing to the skilled attentions which he had received from that amateur surgeon, Hunky Ben, and a long refreshing sleep—the result of partial relief from pain—was a good deal better; and poor Leather, cheered by the hope thus raised of his friend's recovery, was himself considerably improved in health and spirits.

Fortunately for his own peace of mind, it never seemed to occur to Shank that a return to health meant, for Buck Tom, death on the gallows. Perhaps his own illness had weakened Shank's powers of thought. It may be, his naturally thoughtless disposition helped to render him oblivious of the solemn fact, and no one was cruel enough to remind him of it. But Buck himself never forgot it; yet he betrayed no symptom of despondency, neither did he indicate any degree of hope. He was a man of resolute purpose, and had the power of subduing —at least of absolutely concealing—his feelings. To those who nursed him he seemed to be in a state of gentle, colourless resignation.

Charlie Brooke and Hunky Ben, having been out together, had returned well laden with game; and Leather was busy at the fire preparing a savoury mess of the same for his sick friend when Dick arrived.

"News from the old country!" he exclaimed, holding up the letters on entering the cave. "Two for Charles Brooke, Esq., and one for Mister Leather!"

"They might have been more polite to me. Hand it here," said the latter, endeavouring to conceal under a jest his excitement at the sight of a letter from home; for his wild life had cut him off from communication for a very long time.

"One of mine is from old Jacob Crossley," said Charlie, tearing the letter open with eager interest.

"An' mine is from sister May," exclaimed Shank.

If any one had observed Buck Tom at that moment, he would have seen that the outlaw started and rose almost up on one elbow, while a deep flush suffused his bronzed countenance. The action and the flush were only momentary, however. He sank down again and turned his face to the wall.

Charlie also started and looked at Shank when the name of May was mentioned, and the eye of Hunky Ben was on him at the moment. But Hunky of course could not interpret the start. He knew little of our hero's past history—nothing whatever about May. Being a western scout, no line of his mahogany-looking face indicated that the start aroused a thought of any kind.

While the recipients of the letters were busily perusing their missives, Dick Darvall gave the scout a brief outline of his expedition to the ranch, reserving the graphic narration of incidents to a more fitting occasion, when all the party could listen.

"Dick, you're a trump," said the scout.

"I'm a lucky fellow, anyhow," returned Dick.

"In very truth ye are, lad, to escape from such a big bunch o' Redskins without a scratch; why——"

"Pooh!" interrupted the sailor, "that's not the luck I'm thinkin' of. Havin' overhauled Roarin' Bull an' his little girl in time to help rescue them, that's what I call luck—d'ee see?"

"Yes, I see," was Hunky Ben's laconic reply.

Perhaps the scout saw more than was intended, for he probably observed the glad enthusiasm with which the bold seaman mentioned Roaring Bull's

little girl. We cannot tell. His wooden countenance betrayed no sign, and he may have seen nothing; but he was a western scout, and accustomed
to take particular note of the smallest signs of the
wilderness.

"Capital—first-rate!" exclaimed Charlie, looking
up from his letter when he had finished it.

"Just what I was going to say, or something of
the same sort," said Leather, as he folded his epistle.

"Then there's nothing but good news?" said
Charlie.

"Nothing. I suppose it's the same with you, to
judge from your looks," returned Shank.

"Exactly. Perhaps," said Charlie, "it may interest
you all to hear my letter. There are no secrets in
it, and the gentleman who writes it is a jolly old
fellow, Jacob Crossley by name. You know him,
Dick, as the owner of the *Walrus*, though you've
never seen him."

"All right. I remember; fire away," said Dick.

"It is dated from his office in London," continued
our hero, "and runs thus:—

"My dear Brooke,—We were all very glad to
hear of your safe arrival in New York, and hope
that long before this reaches your hand you will
have found poor Leather and got him to some place
of comfort, where he may recover the health that
we have been given to understand he has lost.

"I chanced to be down at Sealford visiting your

mother when your letter arrived; hence my knowledge of its contents.   Mrs. Leather and her daughter
May were then as *usual*.   By the way, what a
pretty girl May has become!   I remember her such
a rumpled up, dress-anyhow, harum-scarum sort of
a girl, that I find it hard to believe the tall, graceful, modest creature I meet with now is the same
person!   Captain Stride says she is the finest craft
he ever saw, except that wonderful 'Maggie,' about
whose opinions and sayings he tells us so much.

"But this is a double digression.   To return:
your letter of course gave us all great pleasure.   It
also gave your mother and May some anxiety, where
it tells of the necessity of your going up to that
wild-west place, Traitor's Trap, where poor Leather
is laid up.   Take care of yourself, my dear boy, for
I'm told that the red savages are still given to those
roasting, scalping, and other torturing that one has
read of in the pages of Fenimore Cooper.

"By the way, before I forget it, let me say, in
reference to the enclosed bill, it is a loan which I
have obtained for Leather, at very moderate interest,
and when more is required more can be obtained on
the same terms.   Let him understand this, for I
don't wish that he should think, on the one hand,
that he is drawing on his mother's slender resources,
or, on the other hand, that he is under obligation to
any one.   I send the bill because I feel quite sure
that you started on this expedition with too little.

It is drawn in your name, and I think you will be able to cash it at any civilised town—even in the far west!

"Talking of Captain Stride—*was* I talking of him? Well, no matter. As he is past work now, but thinks himself very far indeed from that condition, I have prevailed on him to accept a new and peculiar post arising out of the curious evolutions of the firm of Withers and Co. which satisfies the firm completely and suits the captain to a T. As the work can be done anywhere, a residence has been taken for him in Sealford, mid-way between that of your mother and Mrs. Leather, so that he and his wife and little girl can run into either port when so disposed. As Mrs. L., however (to use his own phraseology), is almost always to be found at anchor in the Brooke harbour, he usually kills both with the same visit. I have not been to see him yet in the new abode, and do not know what the celebrated Maggie thinks of it.

"When you find Leather, poor fellow, tell him that his mother and sister are very well. The former is indefatigable in knitting those hundreds of socks and stockings for poor people, about which there has been, and still is, and I think ever will be, so much mystery. The person who buys them from her must be very deep as well as honest, for no inquiries ever throw any fresh light on the subject, and he—or she, whichever it is—pays regularly as the worsted work is delivered—so I'm told! It is a little old lady who pays—but I've reason to believe that she's only a go-between—some agent of a society for providing cheap clothing for the poor, I fancy, which the poor stand very much in need of, poor things! Your good mother helps in this work —at least so I am told, but I'm not much up in in the details of it yet. I mean to run down to see them in a few days and hear all about it.

"Stride, I forgot to say, is allowed to smoke a pipe in your mother's parlour when he pays her a visit. This is so like her amiability, for she hates tobacco as much as I do. I ventured on a similarly amiable experiment one day when the worthy Captain dined with me, but the result was so serious that I have not ventured to repeat it. You remember my worthy housekeeper, Mrs. Bland? Well, she kicked over the traces and became quite unmanageable. I had given Stride leave to smoke after dessert, because I had a sort of idea that he could not digest his food without a pipe. You know my feelings with regard to *young* fellows who try to emulate chimneys, so you can understand that my allowing the Captain to indulge was no relaxation of my principles, but was the result of a strong objection I had to spoil the dinner of a man who was somewhat older than myself by cramming my principles down his throat

"But the moment that Mrs. Bland entered I knew

by the glance of her eye, as well as by the sniff of her nose, that a storm was brewing up—as Stride puts it—and I was not wrong. The storm burst upon me that evening. It's impossible, and might be tedious, to give you all the conversation that we had after Stride had gone, but the upshot was that she gave me warning.

"'But, my good woman,' I began——

"'It's of no use good-womaning me, Mr. Crossley,' said she, 'I couldn't exist in a 'ouse w'ere smokin' is allowed. My dear father died of smokin'—at least, if he didn't, smokin' must 'ave 'ad somethink to do with it, for after the dear man was gone a pipe an' a plug of the nasty stuff was found under 'is piller, so I can't stand it; an' what's more, Mr. Crossley, I *won't* stand it! Just think, sir, 'ow silly it is to put a bit of clay in your mouth an' draw smoke through it, an' then to spit it out again as if you didn't like it; as no more no one *does* on beginnin' it, for boys only smoke to look like men, an' men only smoke because they've got up the 'abit an' can't 'elp it. W'y, sir, you may git up *any* 'abit. You may git the 'abit of walkin' on your 'ands an' shakin' your legs in the hair if you was to persevere long enough, but that would only prove you a fool fit for a circus or a lunatic asylum. You never see the hanimals smokin'. They knows better. Just fancy! what would you think if you saw the cab 'osses all a-settin' on their tails in the rank

smokin' pipes an' cigars! What would you think
of a 'oss w'en 'is cabby cried, "Gee-up, there's a fare
a 'owlin' for us," an' that 'oss would say, "Hall right,
cabby, just 'old on, hold man, till I finish my pipe"?
No, Mr. Crossley, no, I ——'

"'But, my good soul!' I burst in here, 'do
listen ——'

"'No use good-soulin' me, Mr. Crossley. I tell
you I won't stand it. My dear father died of it, an'
I *can't* stand it ——'

"'I *hate* it, Mrs. Bland, myself!'

" I shouted this interruption in such a loud fierce
tone that the good woman stopped and looked at
me in surprise.

"'Yes, Mrs. Bland,' I continued, in the same tone,
'I detest smoking. You know I always did, but
now more than ever, for your reasoning has convinced me that there are *some* evil consequences of
smoking which are almost worse than smoking itself!
Rest assured that never again shall the smell of the
noxious weed defile the walls of this house.'

"'Lauk, sir!' said Mrs. Bland.

" I had subdued her, Charlie, by giving in with
dignity. I shall try the same rôle next breeze that
threatens.

" I almost feel that I owe you an apology for the
length of this epistle. Let me conclude by urging
you to bring poor Leather home, strong and well.
Tell him from me that there is a vacant situation in

the firm of Withers and Co. which will just suit him. He shall have it when he returns—if God spares me to see him again. But I'm getting old, Charlie, and we know not what a day may bring forth."

"A kind—a very kind letter," said Leather earnestly, when his friend had finished reading.

"Why, he writes as if he were your own father, Brooke," remarked Buck Tom, who had been listening intently. "Have you known him long?"

"Not long. Only since the time that he gave me the appointment of supercargo to the *Walrus*, but the little I have seen of him has aroused in me a feeling of strong regard."

"My sister May refers to him here," said Leather, with a peculiar smile, as he re-opened his letter. "The greater part of this tells chiefly of private affairs which would not interest any of you, but here is a passage which forms a sort of commentary on what you have just heard:—

"'You will be amused to hear,' she writes, 'that good Captain Stride has come to live in Sealford. Kind old Mr. Crossley has given him some sort of work connected with Withers and Co.'s house which I can neither understand nor describe. Indeed, I am convinced it is merely work got up on purpose by Mr. Crossley as an excuse for giving his old friend a salary, for he knows that Captain Stride would be terribly cast down if offered a *pension*, as that would be equivalent to pronouncing him unfit

X

for further duty, and the Captain will never admit
himself to be in that condition till he is dying.
Old Jacob Crossley—as you used to call him—
thinks himself a very sagacious and "deep" man, but
in truth there never was a simpler or more trans-
parent one.   He thinks that we know nothing
about who it is that sends the old lady to buy up
all the worsted-work that mother makes, but we
know perfectly well that it is himself, and dear
mother could never have gone on working with
satisfaction and receiving the money for it all if we
had not found out that he buys it for our fishermen, who are said really to be very much in need
of the things she makes.

"'The dear old man is always doing something
kind and considerate in a sly way, under the
impression that nobody notices.   He little knows
the power of woman's observation!   By the way,
that reminds me that he is not ignorant of woman's
powers in other ways.   We heard yesterday that
his old and faithful—though rather trying—housekeeper had quarrelled with him about smoking!   We
were greatly surprised, for we knew that the old
gentleman is not, and never was, a smoker.   She
threatened to leave, but we have since heard, I am
glad to say, that they have made it up!'"

"H'm! there's food for meditation in all that,"
said Dick Darvall, as he knocked the ashes out of
his pipe and put it in his vest pocket.

CHAPTER XXVII.

HUNKY BEN AND CHARLIE GET BEYOND THEIR DEPTH, AND BUCK TOM GETS BEYOND RECALL.

WHILE hunting together in the woods near Traitor's Trap one day Charlie Brooke and Hunky Ben came to a halt on the summit of an eminence that commanded a wide view over the surrounding country.

" 'Tis a glorious place, Ben," said Brooke, leaning his rifle against a tree and mounting on a piece of rock, the better to take in the beautiful prospect of woodland, river, and lake. "When I think of the swarms of poor folk in the old country who don't own a foot of land, have little to eat, and only rags to cover them, I long to bring them out here and plant them down where God has spread His blessings so bountifully, where there is never lack of work, and where Nature pays high wages to those who obey her laws."

"No doubt there 's room enough here," returned the scout, sitting down and laying his rifle across his knees. " I 've often thowt on them subjects, but my thowts only lead to puzzlement; for, out here in the wilderness, a man can't git all the information needful to larn him about things in the old world. Dear, dear, it do seem strange to me that any man should choose to starve in the cities when there's the free wilderness to roam about in. I mind havin' a palaver once wi' a stove-up man when I was ranchin' down in Kansas on the Indian Territory Line. Screw was his name, an' a real kind-hearted fellow he was too—only he couldn't keep his hand off that curse o' mankind, the bottle. I mentioned to him my puzzlements about this matter, an' he up fist an' come down on the table wi' a crack that made the glasses bounce as if they 'd all come alive, an' caused a plate o' mush in front of him to spread itself all over the place—but he cared nothin' for that, he was so riled up by the thowts my obsarvation had shook up.

"'Hunky Ben,' says he, glowerin' at me like a bull wi' the measles, 'the reason we stay there an' don't come out here or go to the other parts o' God's green arth is 'cause we can't help ourselves an' don't know how—or what—don't know nothin' in fact!'

"'That's a busted-up state o' ignorance, no doubt,' said I, in a soothin' sort o' way, for I see'd the man was riled pretty bad by ancient memories, an' looked gittin' waxier. He wore a black eye, too, caught in a free fight the night before, which didn't improve his looks. 'You said we just now,' says I. 'Was you one o' them?'

"'Of course I was,' says he, tamin' down a little, 'an' I 'd bin one o' them yet—if not food for worms by this time—if it hadn't bin for a dook as took pity on me.'

"'What 's a dook?' says I.

"'A dook?' says he. 'Why, he 's a *dook*, you know; a sort o' markis—somewheres between a lord an' a king. I don't know zackly where, an' hang me if I care; but they 're a bad lot, are some o' them dooks—rich as Pharaoh, king o' J'rus'lem, an' hard as nails—though I 'm bound for to say they ain't all alike. Some on 'em 's no better nor costermongers, others are *men*; men what keeps in mind that the same God made us all an' will call us all to the same account, an' that the same kind o' worms 'll finish us all off at last. But this dook as took pity on me was a true blue. He wasn't one o' the hard sort as didn't care a rush for us so long as his own stummick was full. Neether was he one o' the butter-mouths as dursen't say bo to a goose. He spoke out to me like a man, an' he knew well enough that I 'd bin born in the London slums, an' that my daddy had bin born there before me, an' that my mother had caught her death o' cold through havin' to pawn her only pair o' boots to pay my school fees an' then walk barefutt to the court in a winter day to answer for not sendin' her boy to the board school—*her* send me to school!— she might as well have tried to send daddy himself;

an' him out o' work, too, an' all on us starvin'. My dook, when he hear about it a'most bust wi' passion. I hear 'im arterwards talkin' to a overseer, or somebody, "confound it," says he—no, not quite that, for my dook he *never* swore, only he said somethin' pretty stiff—"these people are starvin'," says he, "an' pawnin' their things for food to keep 'em alive, an' they can't git work nohow," says he, "an' yet you worry them out o' body an' soul for school fees!" 'I didn't hear no more, for the overseer smoothed 'im down somehows. But that dook—that good *man*, Hunky Ben, paid my passage to Ameriky, an' sent me off wi' his blessin' an' a Bible. Unfortnitly I took a bottle wi' me, an when I got to the other side I got hold of another bottle, an' another—an' there stands the last of 'em.'

"An' wi' that, Mr. Brooke, he fetched the bottle in front of him such a crack wi' his fist as sent it all to smash against the opposite wall.

"'Well done, Screw!' cried the boy at the bar, laughin'; 'have another bottle?'

"Poor Screw smiled in a sheepish way, for the rile was out of him by that time, an', says he, 'Well, I don't mind if I do. A shot like that deserves another!'

"Ah me!" continued the scout, "it do take the manhood out of a fellow, that drink. Even when his indignation's roused and he tries to shake it off, he can't do it."

"Well do I know that, Ben. It is only God who can help a man in such a case."

The scout gravely shook his head. "Seems to me, Mr. Brooke, that there's a screw loose somewheres in our theology, for I've heard parsons as well as you say that—as if the Almighty condescended to help us only when we're in bad straits. Now, though I'm but a scout and pretend to no book larnin', it comes in strong upon me that if God made us an' measures our movements, an' gives us every beat o' the pulse, an' counts the very hairs of our heads, we stand in need of His help in *every* case and at *all* times; that we can't save ourselves from mischief under any circumstances, great or small, without Him."

"I have thought of that too, sometimes," said Charlie, sitting down on the rock beside his companion, and looking at him in some perplexity, "but does not the view you take savour somewhat of fatalism, and seek to free us from responsibility in regard to what we do?"

"It don't seem so to me," replied the scout, "I'm not speakin', you see, so much of doin' as of escapin'. No doubt we are *perfectly* free to *will*, but it don't follow that we are free to *act*. I'm quite free to *will* to cut my leg off or to let it stay on; an' if I carry out my will an' *do* it, why, I'm quite free there too—an' also responsible. But I ain't free to sew it on again however much I may will to do so

—leastwise if I do it won't stick. The consekinces
o' my deed I must bear, but who will deny that
the Almighty could grow on another leg if He
chose? Why, some creeters he *does* allow to get
rid of a limb or two, an' grow new ones! So, you
see, I'm responsible for my deeds, but, at the same
time, I must look to God for escape from the consekinces, if He sees fit to let me escape. A man,
bein' free, may drink himself into a drunkard, but
he's *not* free to cure *himself*. He can't do it. The
demon Crave has got him by the throat, forces him
to open his mouth, and pours the fiery poison down.
The thing that he is free to do is to will. He may,
if he chooses, call upon God the Saviour to help
him; an' my own belief is that no man ever made
such a call in vain."

"How, if that be so, are we to account for the
failure of those who try, honestly strive, struggle,
and agonise, yet obviously fail?"

"It's not for the like o' me, Mr. Brooke, to ex-
pound the outs an' ins o' all mysteries. Yet I will
p'int out that you, what they call, beg the question
when you say that such people 'honestly' strive.
If a man tries to unlock a door with all his might
and main, heart and soul, honestly tries, by turnin'
the key the wrong way, he'll strive till doomsday
without openin' the door! It's my opinion that a
man may get into difficulties of his own free-will. He
can get out of them only by applyin' to his Maker."

During the latter part of this conversation the hunters had risen and were making their way through the trackless woods, when the scout stopped suddenly and gazed for a few seconds intently at the ground. Then he kneeled and began to examine the spot with great care. "A footprint here," he said, "that tells of recent visitors."

"Friends, Ben, or foes?" asked our hero, also going on his knees to examine the marks. "Well, now, I see only a pressed blade or two of grass, but nothing the least like a footprint. It puzzles me more than I can tell how you scouts seem so sure about invisible marks."

"Truly, if they was invisible you would have reason for surprise, but my wonder is that you don't see them. Any child in wood-craft might read them. See, here is the edge o' the right futt making a faint impression where the ground is soft—an' the heel; surely ye see the heel!"

"A small hollow I do see, but as to its being a heel-print I could not pronounce on that. Has it been made lately, think you?"

"Ay, last night or this morning at latest; and it was made by the futt of Jake the Flint. I know it well, for I've had to track him more than once an' would spot it among a thousand."

"If Jake is in the neighbourhood, wouldn't it be well to return to the cave? He and some of his gang might attack it in our absence."

"No fear o' that," replied the scout, rising from his inspection, the "futt p'ints away from the cave. I should say that the Flint has bin there durin' the night, an' found that we kep' too sharp a look-out to be caught sleepin'. Where he went to arter that no one can tell, but we can hoof it an' see. Like enough he went to spy us out alone, an' then returned to his comrades."

So saying, the scout "hoofed it" through the woods at a pace that tested Charlie Brooke's powers of endurance, exceptionally good though they were. After a march of about four miles in comparative silence they were conducted by the footprints to an open space in the midst of dense thicket, where the fresh ashes of a camp fire indicated that a party had spent some time.

"Just so. They came to see what was up and what could be done, found that nothin' partiklar was up an' nothin' at all could be done, so off they go, mounted, to fish in other waters. Just as well for us."

"But not so well for the fish in the other waters," remarked Charlie.

"True, but we can't help that. Come, we may as well return now."

While Charlie and the scout were thus following the trail, Buck Tom, lying in the cave, became suddenly much worse. It seemed as if some string in his system had suddenly snapped and let the poor human wreck run down.

"Come here, Leather," he gasped faintly.

Poor Shank, who never left him, and who was preparing food for him at the time, was at his side in a moment, and bent anxiously over him.

"D'you want anything?" he asked.

"Nothing, Shank. Where's Dick?"

"Outside; cutting some firewood."

"Don't call him. I'm glad we are alone," said the outlaw, seizing his friend's hand with a feeble, tremulous grasp. "I'm dying, Shank, dear boy. You forgive me?"

"Forgive you, Ralph! Ay—long, long ago I——" He could not finish the sentence.

"I know you did, Shank," returned the dying man, with a faint smile. "How it will fare with me hereafter I know not. I've but one word to say when I get there, and that is—*guilty*! I—I loved your sister, Shank. Ay—you never guessed it. I only tell you now that I may send her a message. Tell her that the words she once said to me about a Saviour have never left me. They are like a light in the darkness now. God bless you—Shank—and —May."

With a throbbing heart and listening ear Shank waited for more; but no more came. The hand he still held was lifeless, and the spirit of the outlaw had entered within the veil of that mysterious Hereafter.

CHAPTER XXVIII.

CHASE, CAPTURE, AND END OF JAKE THE FLINT.

IT was growing dark when Brooke and the scout reached the cave that evening and found that Buck Tom was dead; but they had barely time to realise the fact when their attention was diverted by the sudden arrival of a large band of horsemen—cowboys and others—the leader of whom seemed to be the cow-boy Crux.

Hunky Ben and his friends had, of course, made rapid preparations to receive them as foes, if need were; but, on recognising who composed the cavalcade, they went out to meet them.

"Hallo! Hunky," shouted Crux, as he rode up and leaped off his steed, "have they been here?"

"Who d' ye mean?" demanded the scout.

"Why, Jake the Flint, to be sure, an' his murderin' gang.   Haven't ye heard the news?"

"Not I.   Who d' ye think would take the trouble to come up here with noos?"

"They 've got clear off, boys," said Crux, in a voice of great disappointment.   "So we must off saddle, an' camp where we are for the night."

While the rest of the party dismounted and dispersed to look for a suitable camping-ground, Crux explained the reason of their unexpected appearance.

After the Flint and his companions had left their mountain fastness, as before described, they had appeared in different parts of the country and committed various depredations; some of their robberies having been accompanied with bloodshed and violence of a nature which so exasperated the people that an organised band had at length been gathered to go in pursuit of the daring outlaw. But Jake was somewhat Napoleonic in his character, swift in his movements, and sudden in his attacks; so that, while his exasperated foes were searching for him in one direction, news would be brought of his having committed some daring and bloody deed far off in some other quarter. His latest acts had been to kill and rob a post-runner, who happened to be a great favourite in his locality, and to attack and murder, in mere wanton cruelty, a family of friendly Indians, belonging to a tribe which had never given the whites any trouble. The fury of the people, therefore, was somewhat commensurate with the wickedness of the man. They resolved to capture him, and, as there was a number of resolute cow-boys on the frontier, to whom life seemed to be a bauble to be played with, kept, or cast lightly away, according to circumstances, it seemed as if the effort made at this time would be successful.

The latest reports that seemed reliable were to the effect that, after slaying the Indians, Jake and his men had made off in the direction of his old stronghold at the head of Traitor's Trap. Hence the invasion by Crux and his band.

"You'll be glad to hear—or sorry, I'm not sure which—" said the scout, "that Buck Tom has paid his last debt."

"What! defunct?" exclaimed Crux.

"Ay. Whatever may have bin his true character an' deeds, he's gone to his account at last."

"Are ye sure, Hunky?"

"If ye don't believe me, go in there an' you'll see what's left of him. The corp ain't cold yet."

The rugged cow-boy entered at once, to convince himself by ocular demonstration.

"Well," said he, on coming out of the cave, "I wish it had been the Flint instead. He'll give us some trouble, you bet, afore we bring him to lie as flat as Buck Tom. Poor Buck! They say he wasn't a bad chap in his way, an' I never heard of his bein' cruel, like his comrades. His main fault was castin' in his lot wi' the Flint. They say that Jake has bin carousin' around, throwin' the town-folk everywhere into fits."

That night the avengers in search of Jake the Flint slept in and around the outlaws' cave, while the chief of the outlaws lay in the sleep of death in a shed outside. During the night the scout went out to see that the body was undisturbed, and was startled to observe a creature of some sort moving near it. Ben was troubled by no superstitious fears, so he approached with the stealthy, cat-like tread which he had learned to perfection in his frontier life. Soon he was near enough to perceive, through the bushes, that the form was that of Shank Leather, silent and motionless, seated by the side of Buck Tom, with his face buried in his hands upon his knees. A deep sob broke from him as he sat, and again he was silent and motionless. The scout withdrew as silently as he had approached, leaving the poor youth to watch and mourn over the friend who had shared his hopes and fears, sins and sorrows, so long—long at least in experience, if not in numbered years.

Next morning at daybreak they laid the outlaw in his last resting-place, and then the avengers prepared to set off in pursuit of his comrades.

"You'll join us, I fancy," said Crux to Charlie Brooke.

"No; I remain with my sick friend Leather. But perhaps some of my comrades may wish to go with you."

It was soon arranged that Hunky Ben and Dick Darvall should join the party.

"We won't be long o' catchin' him up," said Crux, "for the Flint has become desperate of late, an' we're pretty sure of a man when he gets into that fix."

The desperado to whom Crux referred was one of those terrible human monsters who may be termed a growth of American frontier life, men who, having apparently lost all fear of God, or man, or death ; carry their lives about with hilarious indifference, ready to risk them at a moment's notice on the slightest provocation, and to take the lives of others without a shadow of compunction. As a natural consequence, such maniacs, for they are little else, are feared by all, and even brave men feel the necessity of being unusually careful while in their company.

Among the various wild deeds committed by Jake and his men was one which led them into serious trouble and proved fatal to their chief. Coming to a village, or small town, one night, they resolved to have a regular spree, and for this purpose encamped a short way outside the town till it should be quite dark. About midnight the outlaws, to the number of eight, entered the town, each armed with a Winchester and a brace of revolvers. Scattering themselves, they began a tremendous fusillade, as fast as they could fire, so that nearly the whole population, supposing the place was attacked by Indians, turned out and fled to the mountains behind the town. The Flint and his men made straight for the chief billiard-room, which they found deserted, and there, after helping themselves to all the loose cash available, they began to drink. Of course they soon became wild under the influence of the liquor, but retained sense enough to mount their horses and gallop away before the people of the place mustered courage to return and attack the foe.

It was while galloping madly away after this raid that the murderous event took place which ended in the dispersal of the gang.

Daylight was creeping over the land when the outlaws left the town. Jake was wild with excite-ment at what had occurred, as well as with drink, and began to boast and swear in a horrible manner. When they had ridden a good many miles, one of the party said he saw some Redskins in a clump of wood they were approaching.

" Did ye ?" cried Jake, flourishing his rifle over his head and uttering a terrible oath, "then I'll shoot the first Redskin I come across."

" Better not, Jake," said one of his men. " They're all friendly Injins about here."

"What's the odds to me !" yelled the drunken wretch. " I'll shoot the first I see as I would a rabbit."

At that moment they were passing a bluff covered with timber, and, unfortunately, a poor old Indian woman came out of the wood to look at the horse-men as they flew past.

Without an instant's hesitation Jake swerved aside, rode straight up to the old creature, and blew out her brains.

Accustomed as they were to deeds of violence

and bloodshed, his comrades were overwhelmed with horror at this, and, fearing the consequences of the dastardly murder, rode for life away over the plains.

But the deed had been witnessed by the relatives of the poor woman. Without sound or cry, fifty Red men leaped on their horses and swept with the speed of light along the other side of the bluff, which concealed them from the white men's sight. Thus they managed to head them, and when Jake and his gang came to the end of the strip of wood, the Red men, armed with rifle and revolver, were in front of them.

There was something deadly and unusual in the silence of the Indians on this occasion. Concentrated rage seemed to have stopped their power to yell. Swift as eagles they swooped down and surrounded the little band of white men, who, seeing that opposition would be useless, and, perhaps, cowed by the sight of such a cold-blooded act, offered no resistance at all, while their arms were taken from them.

With lips white from passion, the Indian chief in command demanded who did the deed. The outlaws pointed to Jake, who sat on his horse with glaring eyes and half-open mouth like one stupefied. At a word from the chief, he was seized, dragged off his horse, and held fast by two powerful men while a third bound his arms. A spear was driven deep

into the ground to serve as a stake, and to this Jake
was tied. He made no resistance. He seemed to
have been paralysed, and remained quite passive
while they stripped him naked to the waist. His
comrades, still seated on their horses, seemed incapable of action. They had, no doubt, a presentiment
of what was coming.

The chief then drew his scalping knife, and
passed it swiftly round the neck of the doomed man
so as to make a slight incision. Grasping the flap
raised at the back of the neck, he tore a broad band
of skin from Jake's body, right down his back to
his waist. A fearful yell burst from the lips of the
wretched man, but no touch of pity moved the hearts
of the Red men, whose chief prepared to tear off
another strip of skin from the quivering flesh.

At the same moment the companions of the Flint
wheeled their horses round, and, filled with horror,
fled at full speed from the scene.

The Red men did not attempt to hinder them.
There was no feud at that time between the white
men and that particular tribe. It was only the
murderer of their old kinswoman on whom they
were bent on wreaking their vengeance, and with
terrible cruelty was their diabolical deed accom-
plished. The comrades of the murderer, left free to
do as they pleased, scattered as they fled, as if each
man were unable to endure the sight of the other,
and they never again drew together.

On the very next day Crux and his band of avengers were galloping over the same region, making
straight for the town which the outlaws had thrown
into such consternation, and where Crux had been
given to understand that trustworthy news of the
Flint's movements would probably be obtained.

The sun was setting, and a flood of golden light
was streaming over the plains, when one of the band
suggested that it would be better to encamp where
they were than to proceed any further that night.

"So we will, boy," said Crux, looking about for a
suitable spot, until his eye fell on a distant object
that riveted his attention.

"A strange-looking thing that," remarked the
scout, who had observed the object at the same
moment. "Somethin' like a man, but standin'
crooked-like in a fashion I never saw a man stand
before, though I've seen many a queer sight in my
day."

"We'll soon clear up the mystery," said Crux,
putting spurs to his horse and riding straight for
the object in question, followed by the whole cavalcade.

"Ay, ay, bloody work bin goin' on here, I see,"
muttered the scout as they drew near.

"The accursed Redskins!" growled Crux.

We need scarcely say that it was the dead body
of Jake they had thus discovered. Tied to the spear
which was nearly broken by the weight of the muti-

lated carcass. Besides tearing most of the skin off the wretched man's body, the savages had scalped Jake; but a deep wound over the region of the heart showed that they had, at all events, ended his sufferings before they left him.

While the avengers—whose vengeance was thus forestalled—were busy scraping a shallow grave for the remains of the outlaw, a shout was raised by several of the party who dashed after something into a neighbouring copse. An Indian had been discovered there, and the cruelties which had been practised on the white man had, to a great extent, transferred their wrath from the outlaw to his murderers. But they found that the rush was needless, for the Indian who had been observed was seated on the ground beside what appeared to be a newly formed grave, and he made no attempt to escape.

He was a very old and feeble man, yet something of the fire of the warrior gleamed from his sunken eyes as he stood up and tried to raise his bent form into an attitude of proud defiance.

" Do you belong to the tribe that killed this white man ? " said Hunky Ben, whose knowledge of most of the Indian dialects rendered him the fitting spokesman of the party.

" I do," answered the Indian in a stern yet quavering voice that seemed very pitiful, for it was evident that the old man thought his last hour had

come, and that he had made up his mind to die as
became a dauntless Indian brave.

At that moment a little Indian girl, who had
hitherto lain quite concealed in the tangled grass,
started up like a rabbit from its lair and dashed
into the thicket.   Swiftly though the child ran,
however, one of the young men of the party was
swifter.   He sprang off in pursuit, and in a few
moments brought her back.

"Your tribe is not at war with the pale-faces,"
continued the scout, taking no notice of this episode.
" They have been needlessly cruel."

For some moments the old man gazed sternly at
his questioner as if he heard him not.   Then the
frown darkened, and, pointing to the grave at his
feet, he said—

" The white man was *more* cruel."

" What had he done ? " asked the scout.

But the old man would not reply.   There came
over his withered features that stony stare of resolute
contempt which he evidently intended to maintain
to the last in spite of torture and death.

" Better question the child," suggested Dick
Darvall, who up to that moment had been too much
horrified by what he had witnessed to be able to
speak.

The scout looked at the child.   She stood trembling beside her captor, with evidences of intense
terror on her dusky countenance, for she was only

too well accustomed to the cruelties practised by white men and red on each other to have any hope either for the old man or herself.

"Poor thing!" said Hunky Ben, laying his strong hand tenderly on the girl's head. Then, taking her hand, he led her gently aside, and spoke to her in her own tongue.

There was something so unexpectedly soft in the scout's voice, and so tender in his touch, that the little brown maid was irresistibly comforted. When one falls into the grasp of Goodness and Strength, relief of mind, more or less, is an inevitable result. David thought so when he said, "Let me fall now into the hand of the Lord." The Indian child evidently thought so when she felt that Hunky Ben was strong and perceived that he was good.

"We will not hurt you, my little one," said the scout, when he had reached a retired part of the copse, and, sitting down, placed the child on his knee. "The white man who was killed by your people was a very bad man. We were looking for him to kill him. Was it the old man that killed him?"

"No," replied the child, "it was the chief."

"Why was he so cruel in his killing?" asked the scout.

"Because the white man was a coward. He feared to face our warriors, but he shot an old woman!" answered the little maid; and then, in-

spired with confidence by the scout's kind and
pitiful expression, she related the whole story of
the savage and wanton murder perpetrated by the
Flint, the subsequent vengeance of her people, and
the unchecked flight and dispersion of Jake's comrades. The old woman who had been slain, she
said, was her grandmother, and the old man who
had been captured was her grandfather.

"Friends, our business has been done for us,"
said the scout on rejoining his comrades, "so we've
nothing to do but return home."

He then told them in detail what the Indian
girl had related.

"Of course," he added, "we've no right to find
fault wi' the Redskins for punishin' the murderer
arter their own fashion, though we might wish they
had bin somewhat more merciful ——"

"No, we mightn't," interrupted Crux stoutly.
"The Flint got off easy in *my* opinion. If I had
had the doin' o't, I'd have roasted him alive."

"No, you wouldn't, Crux," returned Ben, with a
benignant smile. "Young chaps like you are always,
accordin' to your own showin', worse than the devil
himself when your blood's roused by indignation at
cruelty or injustice, but you sing a good deal softer
when you come to the scratch with your enemy in
your power."

"You're wrong, Hunky Ben," retorted Crux firmly.
"Any man as would blow the brains out of a poor

old woman in cold blood, as the Flint did, desarves the worst that can be done to him."

"I didn't say nowt about what *he* desarves," returned the scout; "I was speakin' about what *you* would do if you 'd got the killin' of him."

"Well, well, mates," said Dick Darvall, a little impatiently, "seems to me that we 're wastin' our wind, for the miserable wretch, bein' defunct, is beyond the malice o' red man or white. I therefore vote that we stop palaverin', 'bout ship, clap on all sail an' lay our course for home."

This suggestion met with general approval, and the curious mixture of men and races, which had thus for a brief period been banded together under the influence of a united purpose, prepared to break up.

"I suppose you an' Darvall will make tracks for Traitor's Trap," said Crux to Hunky Ben.

"That 's my trail to be," answered the scout. "What say you, Black Polly? Are ye game for such a spin to-night?"

The mare arched her glossy neck, put back both ears, and gave other indications that she would have fully appreciated the remarks of her master if she had only understood them.

"Ah! Bluefire and I don't talk in that style," said Crux, with a laugh. "I give him his orders an' he knows that he 's got to obey. He and I will make a bee-line for David's Store an' have a drink. Who 'll keep me company?"

Several of the more reckless among the men intimated their willingness to join the toper. The rest said they had other business on hand than to go carousin' around.

"Why, Crux," said one who had been a very lively member of the party during the ride out, "d'ye know, boy, that it's writ in the book o' Fate that you an' I an' all of us, have just got so many beats o' the pulse allowed us—no more an' no less —an' we're free to run the beats out fast or slow, just as we like? There's nothin' like drink for makin' em go fast!

"I don't believe that, Robin Stout," returned Crux ; "an' even if I did believe it I'd go on just the same, for I prefer a short life and a merry one to a long life an' a wishywashy miserable one."

"Hear ! hear !" exclaimed several of the topers.

"Don't ye think, Crux," interposed Darvall, "that a long life an' a happy one might be better than either ?"

"Hear! *hear*!" remarked Hunky Ben, with a quiet laugh.

"Well, boys," said one fine bright-looking young fellow, patting the neck of his pony, "whether my life is to be long or short, merry, wishywashy or happy, I shall be off cow-punching for the next six months or so, somewhere about the African bend, on the Colorado River, in South Texas, an' I mean to try an' keep my pulse a-goin' *without* drink.

I've seen more than enough o' the curse that comes to us all on account of it, and I won't be caught in *that* trap again."

"Then you 've bin caught in it once already, Jo Pinto?" said a comrade.

"Ay, I just have, but, you bet, it's the last time. I don't see the fun of makin' my veins a channel for firewater, and then finishin' off with D. T., if bullet or knife should leave me to go that length."

"I suppose, Pinto," said Crux, with a smile of contempt, "that you 've bin to hear that mad fellow Gough, who's bin howlin' around in these parts of late?"

"That's so," retorted Pinto, flushing with sudden anger. "I 've been to hear J. B. Gough, an' what's more I mean to take his advice in spite of all the flap-jack soakers 'tween the Atlantic and the Rockies. He's a true man, is Gough, every inch of him, and men and women that's bin used chiefly to cursin' in time past have heaped more blessin's on that man's head than would sink you, Crux,—if put by mistake on *your* head—right through the lowest end o' the bottomless pit."

"Pretty deep that, anyhow!" exclaimed Crux, with a careless laugh, for he had no mind to quarrel with the stout young cow-boy whose black eyes he had made to flash so keenly.

"It seems to me," said another of the band, as he hung the coils of his lasso round the horn of his

Mexican saddle, "that we must quit talkin' unless we make up our minds to stop here till sun-up. Who's goin' north ? My old boss is financially busted, so I've hired to P. T. Granger, who has started a new ranch at the head o' Pugit's Creek. He wants one or two good hands I know, an' I've reason to believe he's an honest man. I go up trail at thirty dollars per month. The outfit's to consist of thirty hundred head of Texas steers, a chuck wagon and cook, with thirty riders includin' the boss himself an' six horses to the man."

A couple of stout-looking cow-boys offered to join the last speaker on the strength of his representations, and then, as the night bid fair to be bright and calm, the whole band scattered and galloped away in separate groups over the moon-lit plains.

CHAPTER XXIX.

THEY RETURN TO THE RANCH OF ROARING BULL, WHERE SOMETHING SERIOUS HAPPENS TO DICK DARVALL.

WHEN Dick Darvall and Hunky Ben returned from the expedition which we have just described, they found all right at the cave, except that a letter to Leather had been sent up from Bull's ranch which had caused him much grief and anxiety.

"I have been eagerly awaiting your return, Ben," said Charlie Brooke, when he and the scout went outside the cave to talk the matter over, "for the news in this letter has thrown poor Leather back considerably, and, as he will continue to fret about it and get worse, something must be done."

He paused for a few moments, and the scout gravely waited for him to resume.

"The fact is," continued Charlie, "that poor Leather's father has been given far too much to the bottle during a great part of his life, and the letter just received tells us that he has suddenly left home and gone no one knows where. Now, my friend Leather and his father were always very fond of each other, and the son cannot forgive himself for having at various times rather encouraged his father in drinking, so that his conscience is reproaching him terribly, as you may well believe, and he insists on it that he is now quite able to undertake the voyage home. You and I know, Ben, that in his present state it would be madness for him to attempt it; yet to lie and fret here would be almost as bad. Now, what is your advice?"

For some moments the scout stood silent with his eyes on the ground and his right hand grasping his chin—his usual attitude when engaged in meditation.

"Is there enough o' dollars," he asked, "to let you do as ye like?"

"No lack of dollars, I dare say, when needed," replied Charlie.

"Then my advice," returned the scout promptly, "is to take Leather straight off to-morrow mornin' to Bull's ranch; make him comfortable there, call him Mister Shank,—so as nobody 'll think he 's been the man called Leather, who 's bin so long ill along wi' poor Buck Tom's gang,—and then you go off to old England to follow his father's trail till you find him. Leather has great belief in you, sir, and the feelin' that you are away doin' your best for him will do more to relieve his mind and strengthen his body than tons o' doctor's stuff. Dick Darvall could remain to take care of him if he has no objection."

"I rather think he would be well pleased to do so," replied Charlie, with a laugh of significance, which the scout quietly subjected to analysis in what he styled his brain-pan, and made a note of the result in his mental memorandum book!

"But I doubt if Leather ——"

"Shank," interrupted the scout. "Call him Shank from now, so's we may all git used to it; tho' p'r'aps it ain't o' much importance, for most o' the men that saw him here saw him in uncommon bad condition an' would hardly know him again, besides, they won't likely be at Bull's ranch, an' the captain an' troops that were here have been ordered down south. Still one can never be too careful when life and death may be i' the balance. Your friend niver was one o' the outlaws, but it mightn't be easy to prove that."

"Well, then," resumed our hero, "I was going to say that I fear Shank won't be able to stand the journey even to the ranch."

"No fear of that, sir. We'll carry him down to the foot o' the Trap, an' when we git out on the plain mount him on one o' the horses left by poor Buck—the one that goes along so quiet that they've given it the name o' the Wheelbarrow."

"Should I speak to him to-night about our plan, Ben?"

"No. If I was you I'd only say we're goin' to take him down to Bull's ranch i' the mornin'.

That 'll take his mind a bit off the letter, an' then it 'll give him an extra lift when you tell him the rest o' the plan."

In accordance with this arrangement, on the following morning a litter was made with two stout poles and a blanket between. On this the invalid was laid after an early breakfast; another blanket was spread over him, and the scout and Dick, taking it up between them, carried him out of Traitor's Trap, while Charlie Brooke, riding Jackson's horse, led the Wheelbarrow by the bridle. As for Black Polly, she was left to follow at her own convenience, a whistle from Hunky Ben being at any moment sufficient to bring her promptly to her master's side.

On reaching the plain the litter was laid aside, the blankets were fastened to the horses, and Shank prepared, as Dick said, to board Wheelbarrow.

"Now then, Shank," said the seaman, while helping his friend, "don't be in a hurry. Nothin' was ever done well in a hurry either afloat or ashore. Git your futt well into the stirrup an' don't take too much of a spring, else you 'll be apt to go right over on the starboard side. Hup you go!"

The worthy sailor lent such willing aid that there is little doubt he would have precipitated the catastrophe against which he warned, had not Hunky Ben placed himself on the "starboard side" of the steed and counteracted the heave. After that all went well; the amble of the Wheelbarrow fully justified the title, and in due course the party arrived at the ranch of Roaring Bull, where the poor invalid was confined to his room for a considerable time thereafter, and became known at the ranch as Mr. Shank.

One evening Charlie Brooke entered the kitchen of the ranch in search of his friend Dick Darvall, who had a strange fondness for Buttercup, and frequently held converse with her in the regions of the back-kitchen.

"I dun know whar he is, massa Book," answered the sable beauty when appealed to, "he's mostly somewhar' around when he's not nowhar else."

"I shouldn't wonder if he was," returned Charlie with a hopeful smile. "I suppose Miss Mary's not around anywhere, is she?"

"I shouldn't wonder if she wasn't; but she ain't here, massa," said the black maid earnestly.

"You are a truthful girl, Butter—stick to that, and you'll get on in life."

With this piece of advice Charlie left the kitchen abruptly, and thereby missed the eruption of teeth and gums that immediately followed his remark.

Making his way to the chamber of his sick friend, Charlie sat down at the open window beside him.

"How d'you feel this evening, my boy?" he asked.

"A little better, but—oh dear me!—I begin to despair of getting well enough to go home, and it's

z

impossible to avoid being worried, for unless father is sought for and found soon he will probably sink altogether. You have no idea, Charlie, what a fearful temptation drink becomes to those who have once given way to it and passed a certain point."

"I don't know it personally—though I take no credit for that—but I have some idea of it, I think, from what I have seen and heard. But I came to relieve your mind on the subject, Shank. I wanted to speak with Dick Darvall first to see if he would fall in with my plan, but as I can't find him just now I thought it best to come straight to you about it. Hallo! There is Dick."

"Where?" said Shank, bending forward so as to see the place on which his friend's eyes were fixed.

"There, don't you see? Look across that bit of green sward, about fifty yards into the bush, close to that lopped pine where a thick shrub overhangs a fallen tree——"

"I see—I see!" exclaimed Shank, a gleeful expression banishing for a time the look of suffering and anxiety that had become habitual to him. "Why, the fellow is seated beside Mary Jackson!"

"Ay, and holding a very earnest conversation with her, to judge from his attitude," said Charlie. "Probably inquiring into the market-price of steers —or some absorbing topic of that sort."

"He's grasping her hand now!" exclaimed Shank, with an expanding mouth.

"And she lets him hold it. Really this becomes interesting," observed Charlie, with gravity. "But, my friend, is not this a species of eavesdropping? Are we not taking mean advantage of a pair who fondly think themselves alone? Come, Shank, let us turn our backs on the view and try to fix our minds on matters of personal interest."

But the young men had not to subject themselves to such a delicate test of friendship, for before they could make any attempt to carry out the suggestion, Dick and Mary were seen to rise abruptly and hasten from the spot in different directions. A few minutes later Buttercup was observed to glide upon the scene and sit down upon the self-same fallen tree. The distance from the bedroom window was too great to permit of sounds reaching the observers' ears, or of facial contortions meeting their eyes very distinctly, but there could be no doubt as to the feelings of the damsel, or the meaning of those swayings to and fro of her body, the throwing back of her head, and the pressing of her hands on her sides. Suddenly she held out a black hand as if inviting some one in the bush to draw near. The invitation was promptly accepted by a large brown dog—a well-known favourite in the ranch household.

Rover—for such was his name—leaped on the fallen tree and sat down on the spot which had previously been occupied by the fair Mary. The position was evidently suggestive, for Buttercup immediately began to gesticulate and clasp her hands as if talking very earnestly to the dog.

"I verily believe," said Shank, "that the blacking-ball is re-enacting the scene with Rover! See! she grasps his paw, and ——"

"My friend," said Charlie, "we are taking mean advantage again! And, behold! like the other pair, they are flitting from the scene, though not quite in the same fashion."

This was true, for Buttercup, reflecting, probably, that she might be missed in the kitchen, had suddenly tumbled Rover off the tree and darted swiftly from the spot.

"Come now, Shank," said Charlie, resuming the thread of discourse which had been interrupted, "it is quite plain to Dick and to myself that you are unfit to travel home in your present state of health, so I have made up my mind to leave you here in the care of honest Jackson and Darvall, and to go home myself to make inquiries and search for your father. Will this make your mind easy? For that is essential to your recovery at the present time."

"You were always kind and self-sacrificing, Charlie. Assuredly, your going will take an enormous weight off my mind, for you are much better fitted by nature for such a search than I am—to say nothing of health. Thank you, my dear old boy, a thousand times. As for Dick Darvall," added Shank, with a laugh, "before this evening I would have doubted whether he would be willing to remain with me after your departure, but I have no doubt now—considering what we have just witnessed!"

"Yes, he has found 'metal more attractive,'" said Charlie, rising. "I will now go and consult with him, after which I will depart without delay."

"You've been having a gallop, to judge from your heightened colour and flashing eyes," said Charlie to Dick when they met in the yard, half-an-hour later.

"N—no—not exactly," returned the seaman, with a slightly embarrassed air. "The fact is I've bin cruisin' about in the bush."

"What! lookin' for Redskins?"

"N—no; not exactly, but——"

"Oh! I see. Out huntin', I suppose. After deer—eh?"

"Well, now, that was a pretty fair guess, Charlie," said Dick, laughing. "To tell ye the plain truth, I have been out arter a dear—full sail—an'——"

"And you bagged it, of course. Fairly run it down, I suppose," said his friend, again interrupting.

"Well, there ain't no 'of course' about it, but as it happened, I did manage to overhaul her, and coming to close quarters, I——"

"Yes, yes, *I* know," interrupted Charlie a third time, with provoking coolness. "You ran her on to the rocks, Dick—which was unseamanlike in the extreme—at least you ran the dear aground on a fallen tree and, sitting down beside it, asked it to become Mrs. Darvall, and the amiable creature agreed, eh?"

"Why, how on earth did 'ee come for to know *that*?" asked Dick, in blazing astonishment.

"Well, you know, there's no great mystery about it. If a bold sailor *will* go huntin' close to the house, and run down his game right in front of Mr. Shank's windows, he must expect to have witnesses. However, give me your flipper, mess-mate, and let me congratulate you, for in my opinion there's not such another dear on all the slopes of the Rocky Mountains. But now that I've found you, I want to lay some of my future plans before you."

They had not been discussing these plans many minutes, when Mary was seen crossing the yard in company with Hunky Ben.

"If Hunky would only stop, we'd keep quite jolly till you return," observed Dick, in an undertone as the two approached.

"We were just talking of you, Ben," observed Charlie, as they came up.

"Are you goin' for a cruise, Miss Mary?" asked the seaman in a manner that drew the scout's attention.

"No," replied Mary with a little laugh, and anything but a little blush, that intensified the attention of the scout. He gave one of his quiet but quick glances at Dick and chuckled softly.

"So soon!" he murmured to himself; "sartinly your sea-dog is pretty slick at such matters."

Dick thought he heard the chuckle and turned a lightning glance on the scout, but that sturdy son of the forest had his leathern countenance turned towards the sky with profoundest gravity. It was characteristic of him, you see, to note the signs of the weather.

"Mr. Brooke," he said, with the slow deliberate air of the man who forms his opinions on solid grounds, "there's goin' to be a bu'st up o' the elements afore long, as sure as my name's Hunky."

"That's the very thing I want to talk about with you, Ben, for I meditate a long journey immediately. Come, walk with me."

Taking the scout's arm he paced with him slowly up and down the yard, while Dick and Mary went off on a cruise elsewhere.

CHAPTER XXX.

CHANGES THE SCENE SOMEWHAT VIOLENTLY, AND SHOWS OUR HERO IN A NEW LIGHT.

THE result of our hero's consultation with the scout was not quite as satisfactory as it might have been. Charlie had hoped that Hunky Ben would have been able to stay with Shank till he should return from the old country, but found, to his regret, that that worthy was engaged to conduct still further into the great western wilderness a party of emigrants who wished to escape the evils of civilisation, and to set up a community of their own which should be founded on righteousness, justice, and temperance.

"You see, sir," said the scout, "I've gi'n them my promise to guide them whenever they're ready to start, so, as they may git ready and call for my services at any moment, I must hold myself free o' other engagements. To say truth, even if they hadn't my promise I'd keep myself free to help 'em, for I've a likin' for the good man—half doctor, half parson as well as Jack-of-all-trades—as has set the thing agoin'—moreover, I've a strong belief that all this fightin', an' scalpin', an' flayin' alive, an' roastin', an' revenge, ain't the way to bring about good ends either among Red men or white."

"I agree with you heartily, Ben, though I don't very well see how we are to alter it. However, we must leave the discussion of that difficulty to another time. The question at present is, what hope is there of your staying here even for a short time after I leave? for in Dick Darvall's present condition of mind he is not much to be depended on, and Jackson is too busy. You see, I want Shank to go out on horseback as much as possible, but in this unsettled region and time he would not be safe except in the care of some one who knew the country and its habits, and who had some sort of sympathy with a broken-down man."

"All I can say, Mr. Brooke, is that I'll stay wi' your friend as long as I can," returned the scout, "an' when I'm obleeged to make tracks for the west, I'll try to git another man to take my place. Anyhow, I think that Mr. Reeves—that's the name o' the good man as wants me an' is boss o' the emigrants—won't be able to git them all ready to start for some weeks yet."

Charlie was obliged to content himself with this arrangement. Next day he was galloping eastward—convoyed part of the way by the scout on Black Polly and Dick Darvall on Wheelbarrow. Soon he got into the region of railways and steamboats, and, in a few weeks more was once again in Old England.

A post-card announced his arrival, for Charlie had learned wisdom from experience, and feared to take any one " by surprise "—especially his mother.

We need not describe this second meeting of our hero with his kindred and friends. In many respects it resembled the former, when the bad news about Shank came, and there was the same conclave in Mrs. Leather's parlour, for old Jacob Crossley happened to be spending a holiday in Sealford at the time.

Indeed he had latterly taken to spending much of his leisure time at that celebrated watering-place, owing, it was supposed, to the beneficial effect which the sea-air had on his rheumatism.

But May Leather knew better. With that discriminating penetration which would seem to be the natural accompaniment of youth and beauty, she discerned that the old gentleman's motive for going so frequently to Sealford was a compound motive.

First, Mr. Crossley was getting tired of old bachelorhood, and had at last begun to enjoy ladies' society, especially that of such ladies as Mrs. Leather and Mrs. Brooke, to say nothing of May herself and Miss Molloy—the worsted reservoir—who had come to reside permanently in the town and who had got the " Blackguard Boy " into blue tights and buttons, to the amazement and confusion of the little dog Scraggy, whose mind was weakened in consequence—so they said. Second, Mr. Crossley was remarkably fond of Captain Stride, whom he abused like a pick-pocket and stuck to like a brother, besides playing backgammon with him nightly, to the great satisfaction of the Captain's "missus" and their "little Mag." Third, Mr. Crossley had no occasion to attend to business, because business, somehow, attended to itself, and poured its profits perennially into the old gentleman's pocket — a pocket which was never full, because it had a charitable hole in it somewhere which let the cash run out as fast as it ran in. Fourth and last, but not least, Mr. Crossley found considerable relief in getting away occasionally from his worthy house-keeper Mrs. Bland. This relief, which he styled "letting off the steam" at one time, "brushing away the cobwebs" at another, was invariably followed by a fit of amiability, which resulted in a penitent spirit, and ultimately took him back to town where he remained till Mrs. Bland had again piled enough of eccentricity on the safety valve to render another letting off of steam on the sea-shore imperative.

What Charlie learned at the meeting held in reference to the disappearance of old Mr. Isaac Leather was not satisfactory. The wretched man had so muddled his brain by constant tippling that it had become a question at last whether he was quite responsible for his actions. In a fit of remorse, after an attack of delirium tremens, he had suddenly condemned himself as being a mean contemptible burden on his poor wife and daughter. Of course both wife and daughter asserted that his mere maintenance was no burden on them at all—as in truth it was not when compared with the intolerable weight of his intemperance—and they did their best to soothe him. But the idea seemed to have taken firm hold of him, and preyed upon his mind, until at last he left home one morning in a fit of despair, and had not since been heard of.

"Have you no idea, then, where he has gone?" asked Charlie.

"No, none," said Mrs. Leather, with a tear trembling in her eye.

"We know, mother," said May, "that he has gone to London. The booking clerk at the station, you know, told us that."

"Did the clerk say to what part of London he booked?"

"No, he could not remember."

"Besides, if he had remembered, that would be but a slight clew," said Mr. Crossley. "As well look for a needle in a bundle of hay as for a man in London."

"As well go to sea without rudder or compass," observed Captain Stride.

"Nevertheless," said Charlie, rising, "I will make the attempt."

"Hopeless," said Crossley. "Sheer madness," added Stride. Mrs. Leather shook her head and wept gently. Mrs. Brooke sighed and cast down her eyes. Miss Molloy—who was of the council, being by that time cognisant of all the family secrets—clasped her hands and looked miserable. Of all that conclave the only one who did not throw cold water on our hero was pretty little brown-eyed May. She cast on him a look of trusting gratitude which blew a long smouldering spark into such a flame that the waters of Niagara in winter would have failed to quench it.

"I can't tell you yet, friends, what I intend to do," said Charlie. "All I can say is that I'm off to London. I shall probably be away some time, but will write to mother occasionally. So good-bye."

He said a good deal more, of course, but that was the gist of it.

May accompanied him to the door.

"Oh! thank you—*thank* you!" she said, with trembling lip and tearful eyes as she held out her hand, "I feel *sure* that you will find father."

"I think I shall, May. Indeed I also feel sure that I shall—God helping me."

At the ticket office he found that the clerk remembered very little. He knew the old gentleman well by sight, indeed, but was in the habit of selling tickets to so many people that it was impossible for him to remember where they booked to. In fact the only thing that had fixed Mr. Leather at all in his memory was the fact that the old man had dropped his ticket, had no money to take another, and had pleaded earnestly to let him have one on trust, a request with which he dared not comply—but fortunately, a porter found and restored the ticket.

"Is the porter you refer to still here?" asked Charlie.

Yes, he was there; and Charlie soon found him. The porter recollected the incident perfectly, for the old gentleman, he said, had made a considerable fuss about the lost ticket.

"And you can't remember the station he went to?"

"No, sir, but I do remember something about his saying he wanted to go to Whitechapel—I think it was—or Whitehall, I forget which, but I'm sure it was white something."

With this very slender clew Charlie Brooke presented himself in due time at Scotland Yard, at which fountain-head of London policedom he gave a graphic account of the missing man and the circumstances attending his disappearance. Thence he went to the headquarters of the London City Mission; introduced himself to a sympathetic secretary there, and was soon put in communication with one of the most intelligent of those valuable

self-sacrificing and devoted men who may be styled
the salt of the London slums. This good man's
district embraced part of Whitechapel.

"I will help you to the extent of my power, Mr.
Brooke," he said, "but your quest will be a difficult
one, perhaps dangerous. How do you propose to
go about it?"

"By visiting all the low lodging-houses in Whitechapel first," said Charlie.

"That will take a long time," said the City
Missionary, smiling. "Low lodging-houses are somewhat numerous in these parts."

"I am aware of that, Mr. Stansfield, and mean to
take time," returned our hero promptly. "And
what I want of you is to take me into one or two of
them, so that I may see something of them while
under your guidance. After that I will get their
streets and numbers from you, or through you, and
will then visit them by myself."

"But, excuse me, my friend," returned the
missionary, "your appearance in such places will
attract more attention than you might wish, and
would interfere with your investigations, besides
exposing you to danger, for the very worst characters in London are sometimes to be found in such
places. Only men of the police force and we city
missionaries can go among them with impunity."

"I have counted the cost, Mr. Stansfield, and
intend to run the risk; but thank you, all the same,

for your well-meant warning. Can you go round one or two this afternoon ?"

"I can, with pleasure, and will provide you with as many lodging-house addresses as I can procure. Do you live far from this ?"

"No, quite close. A gentleman who was in your Secretary's office when I called recommended a small lodging-house kept by a Mrs. Butt in the neighbourhood of Flower and Dean Street. You know that region well, I suppose ?"

"Ay—intimately; and I know Mrs. Butt too—a very respectable woman. Come, then, let us start on our mission."

Accordingly Mr. Stansfield introduced his inexperienced friend into two of the principal lodging-houses in that neighbourhood. They merely passed through them, and the missionary, besides commenting on all that they saw, told his new friend where and what to pay for a night's lodging. He also explained the few rules that were connected with those sinks into which the dregs of the metropolitan human family ultimately settle. Then he accompanied Charlie to the door of his new lodging and bade him good-night.

It was a dingy little room in which our hero found himself, having an empty and rusty fire-grate on one side and a window on the other, from which there was visible a landscape of paved court. The foreground of the landscape was a pump, the middle distance a wash-tub, and the background a brick wall, about ten feet distant and fifteen feet high. There was no sky to the landscape, by reason of the next house. The furniture was in keeping with the view.

Observing a small sofa of the last century on its last legs in a corner, Charlie sat down on it and rose again instantly, owing apparently to rheumatic complaints from its legs.

"La! sir," said the landlady, who had followed him into the room, "you don't need to fear anythink. That sofar, sir, 'as bin in my family for three generations. The frame was renoo'd before I was born, an' the legs I 'ad taken off an' noo ones putt on about fifteen year ago last Easter as ever was. My last lodger ee went through the bottom of it, w'ich obliged me to 'ave that renoo'd, so it's stronger than ever it were. If you only keep it well shoved up agin the wall, sir, it'll stand a'most any weight—only it won't stand jumpin' on. You mustn't jump on it, sir, with your feet!"

Charlie promised solemnly that he would not jump on it either with his feet or head, and then asked if he could have tea and a fire. On being informed that he could have both, he drew out his purse and said—

"Now, Mrs. Butt, I expect to stay here for two or three weeks—perhaps longer. My name is Brooke. I was advised to come here by a gentleman in the

offices of the City Mission.   I shall have no visitors
—being utterly unknown in this neighbourhood—
except, perhaps, the missionary who parted from me
at the door——"

"Mr. Stansfield, sir?" said the landlady.

"Yes.   You know him?"

"I've knowed 'im for years, sir.   I shall only be
too pleased to 'ave any friend of 'is in my 'ouse, I
assure you."

"That's well.   Now, Mrs. Butt, my motive in
coming here is to discover a runaway relation——"

"La! sir—a little boy?"

"No, Mrs. Butt, a——"

"*Surely* not a little *gurl*, sir," said the landlady,
with a sympathetic expression.

"It is of no consequence what or who the runaway relation is, Mrs. Butt; I merely mention the
fact in order that you may understand the reason of
any little eccentricity you may notice in my conduct, and not perplex your mind about it.   For
instance, I shall have no regular hours—may be out
late or early—it may be even all night.   You will
give me a pass-key, and I will let myself in.
The only thing I will probably ask for will be a cup
of tea or coffee.   Pray let me have one about an
hour hence.   I'm going out at present.   Here is a
week's rent in advance."

"Shall I put on a fire, sir?" asked Mrs. Butt.

"Well, yes—you may."

"Toast, sir?"

"Yes, yes," said Charlie, opening the outer door.

"'Ot or cold, sir?"

"'Ot, and *buttered*," cried Charlie, with a laugh, as he shut the door after him and rendered further communication impossible.

Wending his way through the poor streets in the midst of which his lodging was situated, our hero at last found an old-clothes store, which he entered.

"I want a suit of old clothes," he said to the owner, a Jew, who came forward.

The Jew smiled, spread out his hands after the manner of a Frenchman, and said, "My shop, sir, is at your disposal."

After careful inspection Charlie selected a fustian coat of extremely ragged appearance, with trousers to match, also a sealskin vest of a mangy complexion, likewise a soiled and battered billycock hat, so shockingly bad that it was difficult to imagine it to have ever had better days at all.

"Are they clean?" he asked.

"Bin baked and fumigated, sir," answered the Jew solemnly.

As the look and smell of the garments gave some countenance to the truth of this statement, Charlie paid the price demanded, had them wrapped up in a green cotton handkerchief, and carried them off.

Arrived at his lodging he let himself in, entered

his room, and threw the bundle in a corner. Then he rang for tea.

It was growing dark by that time, but a yellow-cotton blind shut out the prospect, and a cheery fire in the grate lighted up the little room brightly, casting a rich glow on the yellow-white table-cloth, which had been already spread, and creating a feeling of coziness in powerful contrast to the sensation of dreariness which had assailed him on his first entrance. When Mrs. Butt had placed a paraffin lamp on the table, with a dark-brown teapot, a thick glass sugar-bowl, a cream-jug to match, and a plate of thick-buttered toast that scented the atmosphere deliciously, our hero thought —not for the first time in his life—that wealth was a delusion, besides being a snare.

"' One wants but little here below,'" he mused, as he glanced round the apartment; "but he wants it longer than *that*," thought he, as his eyes wandered to the ancient sofa, which was obviously eighteen inches too short for him.

"I 'ope you 've found 'im, sir," said Mrs. Butt anxiously, as she was about to retire.

"Found who ?"

"Your relation, sir; the little boy—I mean gurl."

"No, I have found neither the boy nor the girl," returned the lodger sharply. "Haven't even begun to look for them yet."

"Oh! beg parding, sir, I didn't know there was *two* of 'em."

"Neither are there. There's only one. Fetch me some hot water, Mrs. Butt, your tea is *too* good. I never take it strong."

The landlady retired, and, on returning with the water, found her lodger so deep in a newspaper that she did not venture to interrupt him.

Tea over, Charlie locked his door and clothed himself in his late purchase, which fitted him fairly well, considering that he had measured it only by eye. Putting on the billycock, and tying the green cotton kerchief loosely round his neck to hide his shirt, he stepped in front of the looking-glass above the mantelpiece.

At sight of himself he was prepared to be amused, but he had not expected to be shocked! Yet shocked he certainly was, for the transformation was so complete that it suddenly revealed to him something of the depth of degradation to which he *might* fall—to which many a man as good as himself, if not better, *had* fallen. Then amusement rose within him, for he was the very beau-ideal of a typical burglar, or a prize-fighter: big, square-shouldered, deep-chested, large-chinned. The only parts that did not quite correspond to the type were his straight, well-formed nose and his clear blue eyes, but these defects were put right by slightly drooping his eyelids, pushing his billycock a little back on his head, and drawing a lock of hair in a drunken fashion over his forehead.

Suddenly an idea occurred to him. Slipping his latchkey into his pocket he went out of the house and closed the door softly. Then he rang the bell.

"Is the gen'leman at 'ome?" he asked of Mrs. Butt, in a gruff, hoarse voice, as if still engaged in a struggle with a bad cold.

"What gentleman?" asked Mrs. Butt, eyeing him suspiciously.

"W'y, the gen'leman as sent for me to give 'im boxin' lessons—Buck or Book, or some sitch name."

"Brooke, you mean," said Mrs. Butt, still suspicious, and interposing her solid person in the doorway.

"Ay, that's the cove—the gen'leman I mean came here this arternoon to lodge wi' a Missis Butt or Brute, or suthin' o' that sort—*air* you Mrs. Brute?"

"*Certainly* not," answered the landlady, with indignation; "but I'm Mrs. Butt."

"Well, it's all the same. I ax yer parding for the mistake, but there's sitch a mixin' up o' Brutes an' Brookes, an' Butts an' Bucks, that it comes hard o' a man o' no edication to speak of to take it all in. This gen'leman, Mr. Brute, 'e said if 'e was hout w'en I called I was to wait, an' say you was to make tea for two, an' 'ave it laid in the bedroom as 'e'd require the parlour for the mill."

The man's evident knowledge of her lodger's affairs, and his gross stupidity, disarmed Mrs. Butt. She would have laughed at his last speech if it had not been for the astounding conclusion. Tea in the bedroom and a mill in the parlour the first night was a degree of eccentricity she had not even conceived of.

"Come in, then, young man," she said, making way. "You'll find Mr. Brooke in the parlour at his tea."

The prize-fighter stepped quickly along the dark passage into the parlour, and while the somewhat sluggish Mrs. Butt was closing the door she overheard her lodger exclaim—

"Ha! Jem Mace, this is good of you—very good of you—to come so promptly. Mrs. Butt," shouting at the parlour door, "another cup and plate for Mr. Mace, and—and bring the *ham !*"

"The 'am!" repeated Mrs. Butt softly to herself, as she gazed in perplexity round her little kitchen, "*did* 'e order a 'am?"

Unable to solve the riddle she gave it up and carried in the cup and saucer and plate.

"I beg your parding, sir, you mentioned a 'am," she began, but stopped abruptly on seeing no one there but the prize-fighter standing before the fire in a free-and-easy manner with his hands in his breeches pockets.

The light of the street-lamps had very imperfectly

revealed the person of Jem Mace. Now that Mrs. Butt saw him slouching in all his native hideousness against her mantelpiece in the full blaze of a paraffin lamp, she inwardly congratulated herself that Mr. Brooke was such a big strong man—almost a match, she thought, for Mace!

"I thought you said the gen'leman was in the parlour, Mrs. Brute?" said Mace inquiringly.

"So 'e—*was*," answered the perplexed lady, looking round the room ; "didn't I 'ear 'im a-shakin' 'ands wi' you, an' a-shoutin' for 'am ?"

"Well, Mrs. Brute, I dun know what you 'eard ; all I know is that I 've not seed 'im yet."

"'E must be in the bedroom," said Mrs. Butt, with a dazed look.

"No 'e ain't there," returned the prize-fighter; "I 've bin all over it—looked under the bed, into the cupboard, through the key'ole ;—p'r'aps," he added, turning quickly, "'e may be up the chimbly!"

The expression on poor Mrs. Butt's face now alarmed Charlie, who instantly doffed his billycock and resumed his natural voice and manner.

"Forgive me, Mrs. Butt, if I have been somewhat reckless," he said, "in testing my disguise on you. I really had no intention till a few minutes ago of playing such a practical——"

"Well, well, Mr. Brooke," broke in the amazed yet amiable creature at this point, "I do assure you as I 'd never 'ave know'd you from the worst character in W'itechapel. I wouldn't have trusted you—not with a sixpence. You was born to be a play-actor, sir! I declare that Jem Mace have given me a turn that—— But why disguise yourself in this way, Mr. Brooke?"

"Because I am going to haunt the low lodging-houses, Mrs. Butt, and I could not well do that, you know, in the character of a gentleman; and as you have taken it so amiably I'm glad I tried my hand here first, for it will make me feel much more at ease."

"And well it may, sir. I only 'ope it won't get you into trouble, for if the p'leece go lookin' for a burglar, or murderer, or desprit ruffian, where you 'appen to be, they're sure to run you in. The only think I would point out, sir, if I may be so free, is that your 'ands an' face is too clean."

"That is easily remedied," said Charlie, with a laugh, as he stooped and rubbed his hands among the ashes; then, taking a piece of cinder, he made sundry marks on his countenance therewith, which, when judiciously touched in with a little water and some ashes, converted our hero into as thorough a scoundrel as ever walked the streets of London at unseasonable hours of night.

CHAPTER XXXI.

FAILURE AND A NEW SCENT.

ALTHOUGH our hero's plan of search may seem to some rather Quixotic, there was nothing further from his thoughts than merely playing at the game of amateur detective. Being enthusiastic and sanguine, besides being spurred on by an intense desire to rescue the father of May Leather, Charlie Brooke was thoroughly in earnest in his plan. He knew that it would be useless to attempt such a search and rescue in any other capacity than that of a genuine pauper, at least in appearance and action. He therefore resolved to conduct the search in character, and to plunge at once into the deepest pools of the slums.

It is not our intention to carry the reader through the Arabian-night-like adventures which he experienced in his quest. Suffice it to say that he did not find the lost man in the pools in which he fished for him, but he ultimately, after many weeks, found one who led him to the goal he aimed at.

Meanwhile there were revealed to him numerous

phases of life—or, rather, of living death—in the slums of the great city which caused him many a heartache at the time, and led him ever afterwards to consider with anxious pity the condition of the poor, the so-called lost and lapsed, the depraved, degraded, and unfortunate. Of course he found— as so many had found before him—that the demon Drink was at the bottom of most of the misery he witnessed, but he also learned that whereas many weak and vicious natures dated the commencement of their final descent and fall from the time when they began to drink, many of the strong and ferocious spirits had begun a life of wickedness in early youth, and only added drink in after years as a little additional fuel to the already roaring flame of sin.

It is well known that men of all stamps and creeds and classes are to be found in the low lodging-houses of all great cities. At first Charlie did not take note of this, being too earnestly engaged in the search for his friend, and anxious to avoid drawing attention on himself; but as he grew familiar with these scenes of misery and destitution he gradually began to be interested in the affairs of other people, and, as he was eminently sympathetic, he became the confidant of several paupers, young and old. A few tried to draw him out, but he quietly checked their curiosity without giving offence.

It may be remarked here that he at once dropped

the style of talk which he had adopted when repre-
senting Jem Mace, because he found so many in
the lodging-houses who had fallen from a good
position in society that grammatical language was
by no means singular. His size and strength also
saved him from much annoyance, for the roughs,
who might otherwise have bullied him, felt that it
would be wise to leave him alone.

On one occasion, however, his pacific principles
were severely tested as well as his manhood, and
as this led to important results we must recount the
incident. .

There was a little lame, elderly man, who was a
habitual visitor at one of the houses which our hero
frequented. He was a humorous character, who
made light of his troubles, and was a general
favourite. Charlie had felt interested in the man,
and in ordinary circumstances would have inquired
into his history, but, as we have said, he laid some
restraint on his natural tendency to inquire and
sympathise. As it was, however, he showed his
goodwill by many little acts of kindness—such as
making way for Zook—so he was called—when he
wanted to get to the general fire to boil his tea or
coffee; giving him a portion of his own food on the
half pretence that he had eaten as much as he
wanted, etc.

There was another *habitué* of the same lodging,
named Stoker, whose temperament was the very

opposite to that of little Zook. He was a huge, burly dock labourer; an ex-prize-fighter and a disturber of the peace wherever he went. Between Stoker and Zook there was nothing in common save their poverty, and the former had taken a strong dislike to the latter, presumably on the ground of Zook's superiority in everything except bulk of frame. Charlie had come into slight collision with Stoker on Zook's account more than once, and had tried to make peace between them, but Stoker was essentially a bully; he would listen to no advice, and had more than once told the would-be peacemaker to mind his own business.

One evening, towards the close of our hero's search among the lodging-houses, little Zook entered the kitchen of the establishment, tea-pot and penny loaf in hand. He hastened towards the roaring fire that might have roasted a whole sheep, and which served to warm the entire basement story, or kitchen, of the tenement.

"Here, Zook," said Charlie, as the former passed the table at which he was seated taking his supper, "I've bought more than I can eat, as usual! I've got two red-herrings and can eat only one. Will you help me?"

"It's all fish that comes to my net, Charlie," said the little man, skipping towards his friend, and accepting the herring with a grateful but exaggerated bow.

We omitted to say that our hero passed among the paupers by his Christian name, which he had given as being, from its very universality, the best possible *alias*.

A few minutes later Stoker entered and went to the fire, where loud, angry voices soon told that the bully was at his old game of peace-disturber. Presently a cry of " shame " was heard, and poor Zook was seen lying on the floor with his nose bleeding.

" Who cried shame ?" demanded the bully, looking fiercely round.

" *I* did not," said Charlie Brooke, striding towards him, " for I did not know it was you who knocked him down, but I *do* cry shame on you now, for striking a man so much smaller than yourself, and without provocation, I warrant."

" An' pray who are *you* ? " returned Stoker, in a tone that was meant to be witheringly sarcastic.

" I am one who likes fair play," said Charlie, restraining his anger, for he was still anxious to throw oil on the troubled waters, " and if you call it fair play for a heavy-weight like you to attack such a light-weight as Zook, you must have forgotten somehow that you are an Englishman. Come, now, Stoker, say to Zook you are sorry and won't worry him any more, and I'm sure he'll forgive you ! "

" Hear ! hear ! " cried several of the on-lookers.

" Perhaps I *may* forgive 'im," said Zook, with a

humorous leer, as he wiped his bleeding nose—"I'd do a'most anything to please Charlie!"

This was received with a general laugh, but Stoker did not laugh; he turned on our hero with a look of mingled pity and contempt.

"No, Mister Charlie," he said, "I won't say I'm sorry, because I'd tell a big lie if I did, and I'll worry him just as much as I please. But I'll tell 'e what I'll do. If you show yourself as ready wi' your bunches o' fives as you are wi' yer tongue, and agree to fight me, I'll say to Zook that I'm sorry and won't worry 'im any more."

There was dead silence for a minute after the delivery of this challenge, and much curiosity was exhibited as to how it would be taken. Charlie cast down his eyes in perplexity. Like many big and strong men he was averse to use his superior physical powers in fighting. Besides this, he had been trained by his mother to regard it as more noble to suffer than to avenge insults, and there is no doubt that if the bully's insult had affected only himself he would have avoided him, if possible, rather than come into conflict. Having been trained, also, to let Scripture furnish him with rules for action, his mind irresistibly recalled the turning of the "other cheek" to the smiter, but the fact that he was at that moment acting in defence of another, not of himself, prevented that from relieving him. Suddenly —like the lightning flash—there arose to him the

words, "Smite a scorner and the simple will beware"!
Indeed, all that we have mentioned, and much more,
passed through his troubled brain with the speed of
light. Lifting his eyes calmly to the face of his
opponent he said—

"I accept your challenge."

"No, no, Charlie!" cried the alarmed Zook, in a
remonstrative tone, "you'll do nothing of the sort.
The man's a old prize-fighter! You haven't a
chance. Why, I'll fight him myself rather than
let you do it."

And with that the little man began to square up
and twirl his fists and skip about in front of the
bully in spite of his lameness—but took good care
to keep well out of his reach.

"It's a bargain, then," said Charlie, holding out
his hand.

"Done!" answered the bully, grasping it.

"Well, then, the sooner we settle this business
the better," continued Charlie. "Where shall it
come off?"

"Prize-fightin's agin the law," suggested an old
pauper, who seemed to fear they were about to set
to in the kitchen.

"So it is, old man," said Charlie, "and I would
be the last to engage in such a thing, but this is not
a prize-fight, for there's no prize. It's simply a
fight in defence of weakness against brute strength
and tyranny."

There were only a few of the usual inhabitants of the kitchen present at the time, for it was yet early in the evening. This was lucky, as it permitted of the fight being gone about quietly.

In the upper part of the building there was an empty room of considerable size which had been used as a furniture store, and happened at that time to have been cleared out with the view of adding it to the lodging. There, it was arranged, the event should come off, and to this apartment proceeded all the inhabitants of the kitchen who were interested in the matter. A good many, however, remained behind—some because they did not like fights, some because they did not believe that the parties were in earnest, others because they were too much taken up with and oppressed by their own sorrows, and a few because, being what is called fuddled, they did not understand or care anything about the matter at all. Thus it came to pass that all the proceedings were quiet and orderly, and there was no fear of interruption by the police.

Arrived at the scene of action, a ring was formed by the spectators standing round the walls, which they did in a single row, for there was plenty of room. Then Stoker strode into the middle of the room, pulled off his coat, vest, and shirt, which he flung into a corner, and stood up, stripped to the waist, like a genuine performer in the ring. Charlie also threw off coat and vest, but retained his shirt—

an old striped cotton one in harmony with his other garments.

"I'm not a professional," he said, as he stepped forward; "you've no objection, I suppose, to my keeping on my shirt?"

"None whatever," replied Stoker, with a patronising air; "p'r'aps it may be as well for fear you should kitch cold."

Charlie smiled, and held out his hand—"You see," he said, "that at least I understand the civilities of the ring."

There was an approving laugh at this as the champions shook hands and stood on guard.

"I am quite willing even yet," said Charlie, while in this attitude, "to settle this matter without fighting if you'll only agree to leave Zook alone in future."

This was a clear showing of the white feather in the opinion of Stoker, who replied with a thundering "No!" and at the same moment made a savage blow at Charlie's face.

Our hero was prepared for it. He put his head quickly to one side, let the blow pass, and with his left hand lightly tapped the bridge of his opponent's nose.

"Hah! a hammytoor!" exclaimed the ex-pugilist in some surprise.

Charlie said nothing, but replied with the grim smile with which in school-days he had been wont to indicate that he meant mischief. The smile passed quickly, however, for even at that moment he would gladly have hailed a truce, so deeply did he feel what he conceived to be the degradation of his position—a feeling which neither his disreputable appearance nor his miserable associates had yet been able to produce.

But nothing was further from the intention of Stoker than a truce. Savages usually attribute forbearance to cowardice. War to the knife was in his heart, and he rushed at Charlie with a shower of slogging blows, which were meant to end the fight at once. But they failed to do so. Our hero nimbly evaded the blows, acting entirely on the defensive, and when Stoker at length paused, panting, the hammytoor was standing before him quite cool, and with the grim look intensified.

"If you *will* have it—*take* it!" he exclaimed, and shot forth a blow which one of the juvenile bystanders described as a "stinger on the beak!"

The owner of the beak felt it so keenly, that he lost temper and made another savage assault, which was met in much the same way, with this difference, that his opponent delivered several more stingers on the unfortunate beak, which after that would have been more correctly described as a bulb.

Again the ex-pugilist paused for breath, and again the "hammytoor" stood up before him smiling more grimly than ever—panting a little, it is true, but quite unscathed about the face, for he had guarded it with great care although he had received some rather severe body blows.

Seeing this, Stoker descended to mean practices, and in his next assault attempted, and with partial success, to hit below the belt. This roused a spirit of indignation in Charlie, which gave strength to his arm and vigour to his action. The next time Stoker paused for breath, Charlie—as the juvenile bystander remarked—"went for him," planted a blow under each eye, a third on his forehead, and a fourth on his chest, with such astounding rapidity and force that the man was driven up against the wall with a crash that shook the whole edifice.

Stoker dropped and remained still. There were no seconds, no sponges or calling of time at that encounter. It was altogether an informal episode, and when Charlie saw his antagonist drop, he kneeled down beside him with a feeling of anxiety lest he had killed him.

"My poor man," he said, "are you much hurt?"

"Oh! you've no need to fear for me," said Stoker recovering himself a little, and sitting up—"but I throw up the sponge. Stoker's day is over w'en 'e's knocked out o' time by a hammytoor, and Zook is free to bile 'is pot unmorlested in futur'."

"Come, it was worth a fight to bring you to that state of mind, my man," said Charlie, laughing. "Here, two of you, help to take him down and wash the blood off him; and I say, youngster," he added, pulling out his purse and handing a sovereign to the juvenile bystander already mentioned, "go out and buy sausages for the whole company."

The boy stared at the coin in his hand in mute surprise, while the rest of the ring looked at each other with various expressions, for Charlie, in the rebound of feeling caused by his opponent's sudden recovery and submission, had totally forgotten his *rôle* and was ordering the people about like one accustomed to command.

As part of the orders were of such a satisfactory nature, the people did not object, and, to the ever-lasting honour of the juvenile bystander who resisted the temptation to bolt with the gold, a splendid supper of pork sausages was smoking on the various tables of the kitchen of that establishment in less than an hour thereafter.

When the late hours of night had arrived, and most of the paupers were asleep in their poor beds, dreaming, perchance, of "better days" when pork sausages were not so tremendous a treat, little Zook went to the table at which Charlie sat. He was staring at a newspaper, but in reality was thinking about his vain search, and beginning, if truth must be told, to feel discouraged.

"Charlie," said Zook, sitting down beside his champion, "or p'r'aps I should say *Mister* Charlie, the game 's up wi' you, whatever it was."

" What d' you mean, Zook ? "

" Well, I just mean that it 's o' no manner o' use your tryin' to sail any longer under false colours in this here establishment."

" I must still ask you to explain yourself," said Charlie, with a puzzled look.

" Well, you know," continued the little man, with a deprecatory glance, " w 'en a man in ragged clo'se orders people here about as if 'e was the commander-in-chief o' the British Army, an' flings yellow boys about as if 'e was chancellor o' the checkers, an' orders sassengers offhand for all 'ands, 'e *may* be a gentleman—wery likely 'e is,—but 'e ain't a redooced one, such as slopes into lodgin'-'ouse kitchens. W 'atever little game may 'ave brought you 'ere, sir, it ain't poverty—an' nobody will be fool enough in *this* 'ouse to believe it is."

" You are right, Zook. I 'm sorry I forgot myself," returned Charlie, with a sigh. " After all, it does not matter much, for I fear my little game— as you call it—was nearly played out, and it does not seem as if I were going to win."

Charlie clasped his hands on the table before him, and looked at the newspaper somewhat disconsolately.

" It 's bin all along o' takin' up my cause," said the little man, with something like a whimper in his voice. " You 've bin wery kind to me, sir, an' I 'd give a lot, if I 'ad it, an' would go a long way if I warn't lame, to 'elp you."

Charlie looked steadily in the honest, pale, care-worn face of his companion for a few seconds without speaking. Poverty, it is said, brings together strange bed-fellows. Not less, perhaps, does it lead to unlikely confidants. Under a sudden impulse our hero revealed to poor Zook the cause of his being there—concealing nothing except names.

"You 'll 'scuse me, sir," said the little man, after the narrative was finished, "but I think you 've gone on summat of a wild-goose chase, for your man may never have come so low as to seek shelter in sitch places."

"Possibly, Zook; but he was penniless, and this, or the work-house, seemed to me the natural place to look for him in."

"'Ave you bin to the work-'ouses, sir?"

"Yes—at least to all in this neighbourhood."

"What! in that toggery?" asked the little man, with a grin.

"Not exactly, Zook, I can change my shell like the hermit crabs."

"Well, sir, it 's my opinion that you may go on till doomsday on this scent an' find nuthin'; but there 's a old 'ooman as I knows on that might be able to 'elp you. Mind I don't say she could, but she *might*. Moreover, if she can she will."

"How?" asked Charlie, somewhat amused by the earnestness of his little friend.

"Why, this way. She 's a good old soul who lost

'er 'usband an' 'er son—if I ain't mistaken—through
drink, an' ever since, she 'as devoted 'erself body
an' soul to save men an' women from drink. She
attends temperance meetin's an' takes people there
—a'most drags 'em in by the scruff o' the neck.
She keeps 'er eyes open, like a weasel, an' w'enever
she sees a chance o' what she calls pluckin' a brand
out o' the fire, she plucks it, without much regard
to burnin' 'er fingers. Sometimes she gits one an'
another to submit to her treatment, an' then she
locks 'em up in 'er 'ouse—though it ain't a big un
—an' treats 'em, as she calls it. She's got one
there now, it's my belief, though w'ether it's a he
or a she I can't tell. Now, she may 'ave seen your
friend goin' about—if 'e stayed long in Whitechapel."

"It may be so," returned our hero wearily, for
he was beginning to lose heart, and the prospect
opened up to him by Zook did not on the first blush
of it seem very brilliant. "When could I see this
old woman?"

"First thing to-morror arter breakfast, sir."

"Very well; then you'll come and breakfast with
me at eight?"

"I will, sir, with all the pleasure in life. In this
'ere 'ouse, sir, or in a resterang?"

"Neither. In my lodgings, Zook."

Having given his address to the little man, Charlie
bade him good-night and retired to his pauper-bed
for the last time.

CHAPTER XXXII.

SUCCESS AND FUTURE PLANS.

PUNCTUAL to the minute Zook presented himself to Mrs. Butt next morning and demanded audience.

Mrs. Butt had been forewarned of the impending visit, and, although she confessed to some uncomfortable feelings in respect of infection and dirt, received him with a gracious air.

"You've come to breakfast, I understand?"

"Well, I believe I 'ave," answered the little man, with an involuntary glance at his dilapidated clothes; "'avin' been inwited—unless," he added, somewhat doubtfully, "the inwite came in a dream."

"You may go in and clear up that point for yourself," said the landlady, as she ushered the poor man into the parlour, where he was almost startled to find an amiable gentleman waiting to receive him.

"Come along, Zook, I like punctuality. Are you hungry?"

"'Ungry as a 'awk, sir," replied Zook, glancing at

that's 'ow I come to know old Missis Mag, an' it's down 'ere she lives."

They turned into a narrow passage which led to a small court at the back of a mass of miserable buildings, and here they found the residence of the old woman.

"By the way, Zook, what's her name?" asked Charlie.

"Mrs. Mag Samson."

"Somehow the name sounds familiar to me," said Charlie, as he knocked at the door.

A very small girl opened it and admitted that her missis was at 'ome; whereupon our hero turned to his companion.

"I'll manage her best without company, Zook," he said; "so you be off; and see that you come to my lodging to-night at six to hear the result of my interview and have tea."

"I will, sir."

"And here, Zook, put that in your pocket, and take a good dinner."

"I will, sir."

"And—hallo! Zook, come here. Not a word about all this in the lodging-house;—stay, now I think of it, don't go to the lodging-house at all. Go to a casual ward where they'll make you take a good bath. Be sure you give yourself a good scrub. D'ye hear?"

"Yes, sir."

He walked away murmuring, "More 'am and hegg an' buttered toast to-night! Zook, you're in luck to-day—in clover, my boy! in clover!"

Meanwhile, Charlie Brooke found himself in the presence of a bright-eyed little old woman, who bade him welcome with the native grace of one who is a born though not a social lady, and beautified by Christianity. Her visitor went at once straight to the point.

"Forgive my intrusion, Mrs. Samson," he said, taking the chair to which the old woman pointed, "but, indeed, I feel assured that you will, when I state that the object of my visit is to ask you to aid in the rescue of a friend from drink."

"No man intrudes on me who comes on such an errand; but how does it happen, sir, that you think *I* am able to aid you?"

To this Charlie replied by giving her an account of his meeting and conversation with Zook, and followed that up with a full explanation of his recent efforts and a graphic description of Isaac Leather.

The old woman listened attentively, and, as her visitor proceeded, with increasing interest not un-mingled with surprise and amusement.

When he had concluded, Mrs. Samson rose, and, opening a door leading to another room, held up her finger to impose silence, and softly bade him look in.

He did so. The room was a very small one, scantily furnished, with a low truckle-bed in one corner, and there, on the bed, lay the object of his quest—Isaac Leather! Charlie had just time to see that the thin pale face was not that of a dead but of a sleeping man when the old woman gently pulled him back and re-closed the door.

"That's your man, I think."

"Yes, that's the man—I thank God for this most astonishing and unlooked-for success."

"Ah! sir," returned the woman, sitting down again, "most of our successes are unlooked for, and when they do come we are not too ready to recognise the hand of the Giver."

"Nevertheless you must admit that some incidents do seem almost miraculous," said Charlie. "To have found *you* out in this great city, the very person who had Mr. Leather in her keeping, does seem unaccountable, does it not?"

"Not so unaccountable as it seems to you," replied the old woman, "and certainly not so much of a miracle as it would have been if you had found him by searching the lodging-houses. Here is the way that God seems to have brought it about. I have for many years been a pensioner of the house of Withers and Co., by whom I was employed until the senior partner made me a sort of female city-missionary amongst the poor. I devoted myself particularly to the reclaiming of drunkards—having special sympathy with them. A friend of mine, Miss Molloy, also employed by the senior partner in works of charity, happened to be acquainted with Mr. Leather and his family. She knew of his failing, and she found out—for she has a strange power that I never could understand of inducing people to make a confidant of her,—she found out (what no one else knew, it seems) that poor Mr. Leather wished to put himself under some sort of restraint, for he could not resist temptation when it came in his way. Knowing about me, she naturally advised him to put himself in my hands. He objected at first, but agreed at last, on condition that none of his people should be told anything about it. I did not like to receive him on such conditions, but gave in because he would come on no other. Well, sir, you came down here because you had information which led you to think Mr. Leather had come to this part of the city. You met with a runaway servant of Withers and Co.—not very wonderful that. He naturally knows about me and fetches you here. Don't you see?"

"Yes, I see," replied Charlie, with an amused expression; "still I cannot help looking on the whole affair as very wonderful, and I hope that that does not disqualify me from recognising God's leading in the matter."

"Nay, young sir," returned the old woman, "that ought rather to qualify you for such recognition, for are not His ways said to be wonderful—ay, sometimes 'past finding out'? But what we know not now we shall know hereafter.   I thought that when my poor boy went to sea——"

"Mrs. Samson!" exclaimed Charlie, with a sudden start, "I see it now!   Was your boy's name Fred?"

"It was."

"And he went to sea in the *Walrus*, that was wrecked in the Southern Ocean ?"

"Yes," exclaimed the old woman eagerly.

"Then," said Charlie, drawing a packet from the breast-pocket of his coat, "Fred gave me this for you. I have carried it about me ever since, in the hope that I might find you.   I came to London, but found you had left the address written on the packet, and it never occurred to me that the owners of the *Walrus* would know anything about the mother of one of the men who sailed in her.   I have a message also from your son."

The message was delivered, and Charlie was still commenting on it, when the door of the inner room opened and Isaac Leather stood before them.

"Charlie Brooke!" he exclaimed, in open-eyed amazement, not unmingled with confusion.

"Ay, and a most unexpected meeting on both sides," said Charlie, advancing and holding out his hand.   "I bring you good news, Mr. Leather, of your son Shank."

"Do you indeed ?" said the broken-down man, eagerly grasping his young friend's hand.   "What have you to tell me ?   Oh Charlie, you have no idea what terrible thoughts I've had about that dear boy since he went off to America! My sin has found me out, Charlie. I've often heard that said before, but have never fully believed it till now."

"God sends you a message of mercy, then," said our hero, who thereupon began to relieve the poor man's mind by telling him of his son's welfare and reformation.

But we need not linger over this part of the story, for the reader can easily guess a good deal of what was said to Leather, while old Mrs. Samson was perusing the letter of her dead son, and tears of mingled sorrow and joy coursed down her withered cheeks.

That night, however, Charlie Brooke conceived a vast idea, and partially revealed it at the tea-table to Zook—whose real name, by the way, was Jim Smith.

"'Ave you found 'er, sir ?" said Mrs. Butt, putting the invariable, and by that time annoying, question as Charlie entered his lodging.

"No, Mrs. Butt, I haven't found 'er, and I don't expect to find 'er at all."

"Lawk ! sir, I'm *so* sorry."

"Has Mr. Zook come ?"

"Yes, sir 'e's inside and looks impatient. The smell o' the toast seems a'most too strong a temptation for 'im; I'm glad you've come."

"Look here, Zook," said Charlie, entering his parlour, "go into that bedroom. You'll find a bundle of new clothes there. Put them on. Wrap your old clothes in a handkerchief, and bring them to me. Tea will be ready when you are."

The surprised pauper did as he was bid, without remark, and re-entered the parlour a new man!

"My own mother, if I 'ad one, wouldn't know me, sir," he said, glancing admiringly at his vest.

"Jim Smith, Esquire," returned Charlie, laughing. "I really don't think she would."

"Zook, sir," said the little man, with a grave shake of the head; "couldn't think of changin' my name at my time of life; let it be Zook, if you please, sir, though in course I've no objection to esquire, w'en I 'ave the means to maintain my rank."

"Well, Zook, you have at all events the means to make a good supper, so sit down and go to work, and I'll talk to you while you eat,—but, stay, hand me the bundle of old clothes."

Charlie opened the window as he spoke, took hold of the bundle, and discharged it into the back yard.

"There," he said, sitting down at the table, "that will prove an object of interest to the cats all night, and a subject of surprise to good Mrs. Butt in the morning. Now, Zook," he added, when his guest was fairly at work taking in cargo, "I want to ask you— have you any objection to emigrate to America?"

"Not the smallest," he said—as well as was possible through a full mouth. "Bein' a orphling, so to speak, owin' to my never 'avin' 'ad a father or mother—as I knows on—there's nothin' that chains me to old England 'cept poverty."

"Could you do without drink?"

"Sca'sely, sir, seein' the doctors say that man is about three parts—or four, is it?—made up o' water; I would be apt to grow mummified without drink, wouldn't I, sir?"

"Come, Zook—you know that I mean *strong* drink—alcohol in all its forms."

"Oh, I see. Well, sir, as to that, I've bin in the 'abit of doin' without it so much of late from need-cessity that I don't think I'd find much difficulty in knocking it off altogether if I was to bring prin-ciple to bear."

"Well, then," continued Charlie, "(have some more ham?) I have just conceived a plan. I have a friend in America who is a reformed drunkard. His father in this country is also, I hope, a reformed drunkard. There is a good man out there, I understand, who has had a great deal to do with reformed drunkards, and he has got up a large body of friends and sym-pathisers who have determined to go away into the far west and there organise a total abstinence com-munity, and found a village or town where nothing in the shape of alcohol shall be admitted except as physic.

"Now, I have a lot of friends in England who, I think, would go in for such an expedition if——"

. "Are *they* all reformed drunkards, sir?" asked Zook in surprise, arresting a mass of sausage in its course as he asked the question.

"By no means," returned Charlie with a laugh, "but they are earnest souls, and I'm sure will go if I try to persuade them."

"You're *sure* to succeed, sir," said Zook, "if your persuasions is accompanied wi' sassengers, 'am, an' buttered toast," remarked the little man softly, as he came to a pause for a few seconds.

"I'll bring to bear on them all the arguments that are available, you may be sure. Meanwhile I shall count you my first recruit."

"No. 1 it is, sir, w'ich is more than I can say of this here slice," said Zook, helping himself to more toast.

While the poor but happy man was thus pleasantly engaged, his entertainer opened his writing portfolio and began to scribble off note after note, with such rapidity that the amazed pauper at his elbow fairly lost his appetite, and, after a vain attempt to recover it, suggested that it might be as well for him to retire to one of the palatial fourpence-a-night residences in Dean and Flower Street.

"Not to-night. You've done me a good turn that I shall never forget," said Charlie, rising and ringing the bell with needless vigour.

"Be kind enough, Mrs. Butt, to show Mr. Zook to his bedroom."

"My heye!" murmured the pauper, marching off with two full inches added to his stature. "Not in there, I suppose, missis," he said facetiously, as he passed the coal-hole.

"Oh, lawks! no—this way," replied the good woman, who was becoming almost imbecile under the eccentricities of her lodger. "This is your bedroom, and I only 'ope it won't turn into a band-box before morning, for of all the transformations an' pantimimes as 'as took place in this 'ouse since Mr. Brooke entered it, I——"

She hesitated, and, not seeing her way quite clearly to the fitting end of the sentence, asked if Mr. Zook would 'ave 'ot water in the morning.

"No, thank you, Missis," replied the little man with dignity, while he felt the stubble on his chin; "'avin left my razors at 'ome I prefers the water cold."

Leaving Zook to his meditations, Mrs. Butt retired to bed, remarking, as she extinguished the candle, that Mr. Brooke was still "a-writin' like a 'ouse a fire!"

CHAPTER XXXIII.

SWEETWATER BLUFF.

WE must now leap over a considerable space, not only of distance, but of time, in order to appreciate fully the result of Charlie Brooke's furious letter-writing and amazing powers of persuasion.

Let the reader try to imagine a wide plateau, dotted with trees and bushes, on one of the eastern slopes of the Rocky Mountains, where that mighty range begins to slide into union with the great prairies. It commands a view of mingled wood-land and rolling plain, diversified by river and lake, extending to a horizon so faint and far away as to suggest the idea of illimitable space.

Early one morning in spring five horsemen emerging from a belt of woodland, galloped to the slope that led to the summit of this plateau. Drawing rein, they began slowly to ascend. Two of the cavaliers were young, tall, and strong; two were portly and old, though still hearty and vigor-ous; one, who led them, on a coal-black steed, was a magnificent specimen of the backwoods-man, and one, who brought up the rear, was a thin little man,

who made up for what he wanted in size by the
energy and vigour of his action, as, with hand and
heel, he urged an unwilling horse to keep up with
the rest of the party.

Arrived at the summit of the plateau, the leading
horseman trotted to its eastern edge, and halted as
if for the purpose of surveying the position.

"Here we are at last," he said, to the tallest of
his comrades; "Sweetwater Bluff—and the end of
our journey!"

"And a most noble end it is!" exclaimed the tall
comrade. "Why, Hunky Ben, it far surpasses my
expectations and all you have said about it."

"Most o' the people I've had to guide over this
trail have said pretty much the same thing in
different words, Mr. Brooke," returned the scout,
dismounting. "Your wife will find plenty o' subjects
here for the paintin' she's so fond of."

"Ay, May will find work here to keep her brushes
busy for many a day to come," replied Charlie,
"though I suspect that other matters will claim
most of her time at first, for there is nothing but
a wilderness here yet."

"You've yet to larn, sir, that we don't take as
long to fix up a town hereaway as you do in the
old country," remarked Hunky Ben, as old Jacob
Crossley ambled up on the staid creature which we
have already introduced as *Wheelbarrow*.

Waving his hand with enthusiasm the old gentle-

man exclaimed, "Glorious!"   Indeed, for a few
minutes he sat with glistening eyes and heaving
chest, quite unable to give vent to any other sentiment than "glorious!"   This he did at intervals.
His interest in the scene, however, was distracted
by the sudden advent of Captain Stride, whose
horse—a long-legged roan—had an awkward
tendency, among other eccentricities, to advance
sideways with a waltzing gait, that greatly discon-
certed the mariner.

"Woa! you brute.   Back your tops'ls, won't you?
I *never* did see sitch a craft for heavin' about like
a Dutch lugger in a cross sea.   She sails side on,
no matter where she's bound for.   Forges ahead
a'most entirely by means of leeway, so to speak.
Hallo! woa!   Ketch a grip o' the painter, Dick,
an' hold on till I git off the hurricane deck o' this
walrus—else I'll be overboard in a——.   There——"

The captain came to the ground suddenly as he
spoke, without the use of stirrup, and, luckily, without injury.

"Not hurt, I hope?" asked Dick Darvall, assisting
his brother-salt to rise.

"Not a bit of it, Dick.   You see I'm a'most
as active as yourself, though double your age, if
not more.   I say, Charlie, this *is* a pretty look-out.
Don't 'ee think so, Mr. Crossley?   I was sure that
Hunky Ben would find us a pleasant anchorage and
safe holding-ground at last, though it did seem

as if we was pretty long o' comin' to it. Just as we was leavin' the waggins to ride on in advance I said to my missus—says I—Maggie, you may depend——"

"Hallo! Zook," cried Charlie, as the little man of the slums came limping up, "what have you done with your horse?"

"Cast 'im loose, sir, an' gi'n 'im leave of absence as long as 'e pleases. It's my opinion that some o' the 'osses o' the western prairies ain't quite eekal to some o' the 'osses I've bin used to in Rotten Row. Is this the place, Hunky? Well, now," continued the little man, with flashing eyes, as he looked round on the magnificent scene, "it'll do. Beats W'ite-chapel an' the Parks any'ow. An' there's lots o' poultry about, too!" he added, as a flock of wild ducks went by on whistling wings. "I say, Hunky Ben, w'at's yon brown things over there by the shores o' the lake?"

"Buffalo," answered the scout.

"What! wild uns?"

"There's no tame ones in them diggin's as I knows on. If there was, they'd soon become wild, you bet."

"An' w'at's yon monster crawlin' over the farthest plain, like the great sea-serpent?"

"Why, man," returned the scout, "them's the waggins. Come, now, let's to work an' git the fire lit. The cart wi' the chuck an' tents'll be here in

a few minutes, an' the waggins won't be long arter
'em——''

" Ay, wi' the women an' kids shoutin' for grub,"
added Zook, as he limped after the scout, while the
rest of the little band dispersed—some to cut firewood, others to select the best positions for the tents.
The waggons, with a supply of food, arrived soon
after under the care of Roaring Bull himself, with
two of his cowboys. They were followed by Buttercup, who bestrode, man-fashion, a mustang nearly
as black as herself and even more frisky.

In a wonderfully short time a number of white
tents arose on the plateau and several fires blazed,
and at all the fires Buttercup laboured with super-
human effect, assisted by the cowboys, to the
unbounded admiration of Zook, who willingly super-
intended everything, but did little or nothing. A
flat rock on the highest point was chosen for the
site of a future block-house or citadel, and upon this
was ere long spread a breakfast on a magnificent
scale. It was barely ready when the first waggons
arrived and commenced to lumber up the ascent,
preceded by two girls on horseback, who waved
their hands, and gave vent to vigorous little
feminine cheers as they cantered up the slope.

These two were our old friends whom we knew
as May Leather and Mary Jackson, but who must
now be re-introduced to the reader as Mrs. Charlie
Brooke and Mrs. Dick Darvall. On the same day

they had changed their names at the Ranch of Roaring Bull, and had come to essay wedded life in the far west.

We need hardly say that this was the great experimental emigrant party, led by the Rev. William Reeves, who had resolved to found a colony on total abstinence principles, and with as many as possible of the sins of civilisation left behind. They found, alas! that sin is not so easily got rid of; nevertheless, the effort was not altogether fruitless, and Mr. Reeves carried with him a sovereign antidote for sin in the shape of a godly spirit.

The party was a large one, for there were many men and women of the frontier whose experiences had taught them that life was happier and better in every way without the prevalent vices of gambling and drinking.

Of course the emigrants formed rather a motley band. Among them, besides those of our friends already mentioned, there were our hero's mother and all the Leather family. Captain Stride's daughter as well as his "Missus," and Mr. Crossley's housekeeper, Mrs. Bland. That good woman, however, had been much subdued and rendered harmless by the terrors of the wilderness, to which she had been recently exposed. Miss Molloy was also there, with an enormous supply of knitting needles and several bales of worsted.

Poor Shank Leather was still so much of an invalid as to be obliged to travel in a spring cart with his father, but both men were rapidly regaining physical strength under the influence of temperance, and spiritual strength under a higher power.

Soon the hammer, axe, and saw began to resound in that lovely western wilderness; the net to sweep its lakes; the hook to invade its rivers; the rifle to crack in the forests, and the plough to open up its virgin soil. In less time, almost, than a European would take to wink, the town of Sweetwater Bluff sprang into being; stores and workshops, a school and a church, grew up like mushrooms; seed was sown, and everything, in short, was done that is characteristic of the advent of a thriving community. But not a gambling or drinking saloon, or a drop of firewater, was to be found in all the town.

In spite of this, Indians brought their furs to it; trappers came to it for supplies; emigrants turned aside to see and rest in it; and the place soon became noted as a flourishing and pre-eminently peaceful spot.

CHAPTER XXXIV.

THE LAST.

BUT a little cloud arose ere long on the horizon of Sweetwater Bluff. Insignificant at first, it suddenly spread over the sky and burst in a wild storm.

The first intimation of its approach came from Charlie Brooke one quiet autumn evening, in that brief but delightful season known as the Indian Summer.

Charlie entered his garden that evening with a fowling-piece on his shoulder, and two brace of prairie hens at his girdle. May was seated at her cottage door, basking in sunshine, chatting with her mother—who was knitting of course—and Shank was conversing with Hunky Ben, who rested after a day of labour.

"There, May, is to-morrow's dinner," said Charlie, throwing the birds at his wife's feet, and sitting down beside her. "Who d'you think I passed when I was out on the plains to-day, Hunky? Your old friend Crux the Cowboy."

"He's no friend o' mine," said the scout, while

something like a frown flitted across his usually placid brow. "I'm not over pleased to hear that he's comin', for it's said that some old uncle or aunt o' his—I forget which—has left him a lot o' dollars. I hope he ain't comin' to spend 'em here, for he'd never git along without gamblin' an' drinkin'."

"Then, I can tell you that he *is* just coming to stay here," returned Charlie, "for he has several waggons with him, and a dozen men. I asked him where he was going to, and he said, to locate himself as a store-keeper at Sweetwater Bluff; but he did not seem inclined to be communicative, so I left him and galloped on to report the news. What d' you think about it?"

"I think it'll be a bad day for Sweetwater Bluff when Crux comes to settle in it. Howsoever, this is a free country, an' we've no right to interfere with him so long as he don't break the laws. But I doubt him. I'm afeard he'll try to sell drink, an' there's some o' our people who are longin' to git back to that."

The other members of the party, and indeed those heads of the town generally who knew Crux, were of much the same opinion, but some of them thought that, being in a free country, no one had a right to interfere. The consequence was that Crux and his men were permitted to go to work. They hired a shed in which to stow their goods, while they were engaged in building a store, and in course of time this was finished; but there was a degree of mystery about the ex-cowboy's proceedings which baffled investigation, and people did not like to press inquiry too far; for it was observed that all the men who had accompanied Crux were young and powerful fellows, well armed with rifle and revolver.

At last, however, the work was finished, and the mystery was cleared up, for, one fine morning, the new store was opened as a drinking and gambling saloon; and that same evening the place was in full swing—sending forth the shouts, songs, cursing and demoniac laughter for which such places are celebrated.

Consternation filled the hearts of the community, for it was not only the men brought there by Crux who kept up their revels in the new saloon, but a sprinkling of the spirited young fellows of the town also, who had never been very enthusiastic in the temperance cause, and were therefore prepared to fall before the first temptation.

At a conference of the chief men of the town it was resolved to try to induce Crux to quit quietly, and for this end to offer to buy up his stock-in-trade. Hunky Ben, being an old acquaintance, was requested to go to the store as a deputation.

But the ex-cowboy was inexorable. Neither the offer of money nor argument had any effect on him.

" Well, Crux," said the scout, at the conclusion of

his visit, "you know your own affairs best, but, rememberin' as I do what you used to be, I thought there was more of fair-play about you."

"Fair-play! What d'ye mean?"

"I mean that when folk let *you* alone, you used to be willin' to let *them* alone. Here has a crowd o' people come back all this way into the Rockies to escape from the curse o' strong drink and gamblin', an' here has Crux—a lover o' fair-play—come all this way to shove that curse right under their noses. I'd thowt better of ye, Crux, lad."

"It don't matter much what you thowt o' me, old man," returned the cowboy, somewhat sharply; "an', as to fair-play, there's a lot of men here who don't agree wi' your humbuggin' notions about temperance an' tee-totalism—more of 'em, maybe, than you think. These want to have the drink, an' I've come to give it 'em. I see nothin' unfair in that."

Hunky Ben carried his report back to the council, which for some time discussed the situation. As in the case of most councils, there was some difference of opinion: a few of the members being inclined to carry things with a high hand—being urged thereto by Captain Stride—while others, influenced chiefly by Mr. Reeves, were anxious to try peaceable means.

At last a sub-committee was appointed, at Hunky Ben's suggestion, to consider the whole matter, and take what steps seemed advisable. Hunky was an adroit and modest man—he could not have been a first-rate scout otherwise! He managed not only to become convener of the committee, but succeeded in getting men chiefly of his own opinion placed on it. At supper that night in Charlie's cottage, while enjoying May's cookery and presence, and waited on by the amused and interested Buttercup, the sub-committee discussed and settled the plan of operations.

"It's all nonsense," said Hunky Ben, "to talk of tryin' to persuade Crux. He's as obstinate as a Texas mule wi' the toothache."

"Rubbish!" exclaimed Captain Stride, smiting the table with his fist. "We mustn't parley with him, but heave him overboard at once! I said so to my missus this very day. 'Maggie,' says I——"

"And what do *you* think, Charlie?" asked Mr. Crossley.

"I think with Hunky Ben, of course. He knows Crux, and what is best to be done in the circumstances. The only thing that perplexes me is what shall we do with the liquor when we've paid for it? A lot of it is good wine and champagne, and although useless as a beverage it is useful as a medicine, and might be given to hospitals."

"Pour it out!" exclaimed Shank, almost fiercely.

"Ay, the hospitals can look out for themselves," added Shank's father warmly.

"Some hospitals, I've bin told, git on well enough without it altogether," said Dick Darvall. "However, it's a subject that deserves consideration.——

2 D

Hallo ! Buttercup, what is it that tickles your fancy an' makes your mouth stretch out like that ? "

Buttercup became preternaturally grave on the instant, but declined to tell what it was that tickled her fancy.

Shortly after the party rose and left the house, Hunky Ben remarking, with a quiet laugh, that deeds of darkness were best hatched at night.

What the conspirators hatched became pretty evident next day, for, during the breakfast hour, a band of forty horsemen rode slowly down the sloping road which led to the plains, and on the side of which Crux had built his saloon.

Crux and his men turned out in some surprise to watch the cavalcade as it passed. The band was led by Charlie Brooke, and the scout rode in advance on Black Polly as guide.

" Is it the Reds or the Buffalo you're after to-day, Hunky, with such a big crowd ? " asked Crux.

" Halt ! " cried Charlie, at that moment.

The forty men obeyed, and, turning suddenly to the left, faced the saloon.

" Hands up ! " said Charlie, whose men at the same moment pointed their rifles at Crux and his men. These were all too familiar with the order to dare to disobey it.

Our hero then ordered a small detachment of his men to enter the saloon and fetch out all rifles and pistols, and those of Crux's people who chanced to have their weapons about them were disarmed.

Another detachment went off to the stables behind ·
the saloon.

While they were thus engaged Charlie addressed
Crux.

"We have decided to expel you, Crux, from this
town," he said, as he drew an envelope from his
pocket. "We have tried to convince you that,
as the majority of the people here don't want you,
it is your duty to go. As you don't seem to see
this we now take the law into our own hands. We
love fair-play, however, so you will find in this
envelope a cheque which we have reason to believe
is fully equal to the value of your saloon and all its
contents. Your lost time and trouble is your own
affair. As you came without invitation, you must
go without compensation. Here are your rifles, and
revolvers, emptied of cartridges, and there are your
horses saddled."

As he spoke, one detachment of his men handed
rifles and revolvers to the party, who were stricken
dumb with amazement. At the same time, their
horses, saddled and bridled, were led to the front
and delivered to them.

"We have no provisions," said Crux, at last
recovering the use of his tongue; "and without
ammunition we cannot procure any."

"That has been provided for," said our hero,
turning to Hunky Ben.

"Ay, Crux," said the scout, "we don't want to
starve you, though the 'arth wouldn't lose much if

we did. At the other end o' the lake, about five mile from here, you'll find a red rag flyin' at the branch of a tree. In the hole of a rock close beside it you'll find three days' provisions for you and your men, an' a lot of ammunition."

"Now, mount and go," said Charlie, "and if you ever show face here again, except as friends, your blood be on your own heads!"

Crux did not hesitate. He and his men saw that "the game was up"; without another word they mounted their horses and galloped away.

While this scene was being enacted a dark creature, with darker designs, entered the drinking saloon and descended to the cellar. Finding a spirit-cask with a tap in it, Buttercup turned it on, then, pulling a match-box out of her pocket she muttered, "I t'ink de hospitals won't git much ob it!" and applied a light. The effect was more powerful than she had expected. The spirit blazed up with sudden fury, singeing off the girl's eyebrows and lashes, and almost blinding her. In her alarm Buttercup dashed up to the saloon, missed her way, and found herself on the stair leading to the upper floor. A cloud of smoke and fire forced her to rush up. She went to the window and yelled, on observing that it was far too high to leap. She rushed to another window and howled in horror, for escape was apparently impossible.

Charlie heard the howl. He and his men had retired to a safe distance when the fire was first observed—thinking the place empty—but the howl touched a chord in our hero's sympathetic breast, which was ever ready to vibrate. From whom the howl proceeded mattered little or nothing to Charlie Brooke. Sufficient that it was the cry of a living being in distress. He sprang at once through the open doorway of the saloon, through which was issuing a volume of thick smoke mingled with flame.

"God help him! the place 'll blow up in a few minutes," cried Hunky Ben, losing, for once, his imperturbable coolness, and rushing wildly after his friend. But at that moment the thick smoke burst into fierce flame and drove him back.

Charlie sprang up the staircase three steps at a time, holding his breath to avoid suffocation. He reached the landing, where Buttercup ran, or, rather, fell, almost fainting, into his arms. At the moment an explosion in the cellar shook the building to its foundation, and, shattering one of the windows, caused a draught of air to drive aside the smoke. Charlie gasped a mouthful of air and looked round. Flames were by that time roaring up the only staircase. A glance from the nearest window showed that a leap thence meant broken limbs, if not death, to both. A ladder up to a trap-door suggested an exit by the roof. It might only lead to a more terrible leap, but meanwhile it offered relief from imminent suffocation. Charlie bore the half-dead girl to the top rung, and found the trap-door padlocked, but a thrust from his powerful shoulder wrenched hasp and padlock from their hold, and next moment a wild cheer greeted him as he stood on a corner of the gable. But a depth of forty or fifty feet was below him with nothing to break his fall to the hard earth.

"Jump!" yelled one of the onlookers. "No, don't!" cried another, "you'll be killed."

"Hold your noise," roared Hunky Ben, "and lend a hand here—sharp!—the house'll blow up in a minute."

He ran as he spoke towards a cart which was partly filled with hay. Seizing the trams he raised them. Willing hands helped, and the cart was run violently up against the gable—Hunky shouting to some of the men to fetch more hay.

But there was no time for that. Another explosion took place inside the building, which Charlie knew must have driven in the sides of more casks and let loose fresh fuel. A terrible roar, followed by ominous cracking of the roof, warned him that there was no time to lose. He looked steadily at the cart for a moment and leaped. His friends held their breath as the pair descended. The hay would not have sufficed to break the fall sufficiently, but happily the cart was an old one. When they came down on it like a thunderbolt the bottom gave way. Crashing through it the pair came to the ground, heavily indeed, but uninjured!

The fall, which almost stunned our hero, had the

curious effect of reviving Buttercup, for she muttered something to the effect that " dat was a mos' drefful smash " as they conveyed her and her rescuer from the vicinity of danger.

This had scarcely been done when the house blew up—its walls were driven outwards, its roof was blown off, its bottles were shattered, all its baleful contents were scattered around, and, amid an appropriate hurricane of blue fire, that drinking and gambling saloon was blown to atoms.

Would that a like fate might overtake every similar establishment in the world !

This was the first and last attempt to disturb the peace of Sweetwater Bluff. It is said, indeed, that Crux and some of his men did, long afterwards, make their appearance in that happy and flourishing town, but they came as reformed men, not as foes—men who had found out that in very truth sobriety tends to felicity, that honesty is the best policy, and that the fear of the Lord is the beginning of wisdom.

THE END.

Printed by T. and A. Constable, Printers to Her Majesty,
at the Edinburgh University Press.